CITY of ILLUSION

Victoria Ying

colorist Lynette Wong

VIKING

VIKING
An imprint of Penguin Random House LLC New York

First published in the United States of America by Viking,
an imprint of Penguin Random House LLC, 2021.

Visit us online at penguinrandomhouse.com.

Library of Congress Cataloging-in-Publication Data is available.

Manufactured in China

ISBN 9780593114520 (PB) / 9780593114513 (HC)

10 9 8 7 6 5 4 3 2 1

The art for this book was created with Comic Draw App, Procreate, and Photoshop.

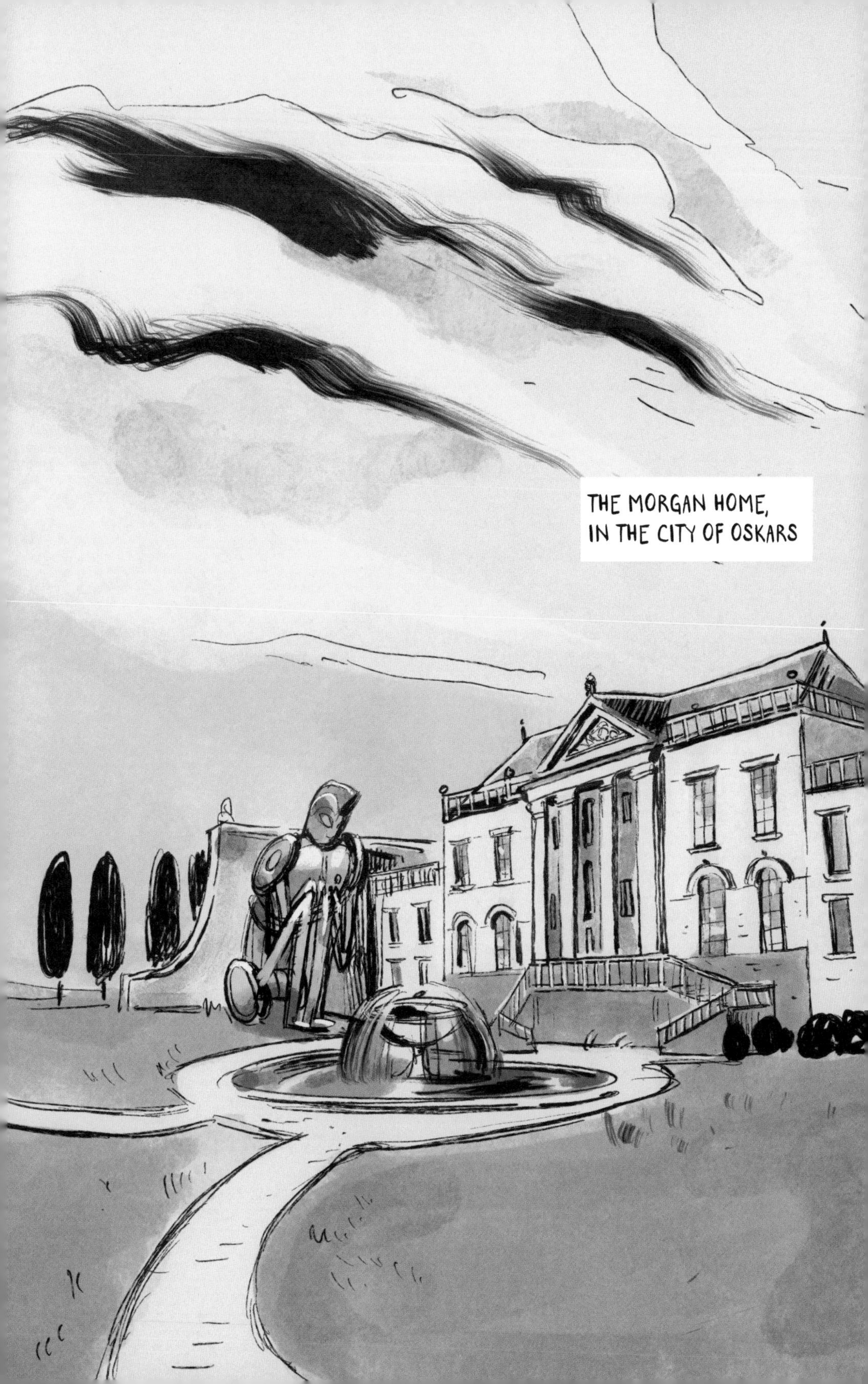
THE MORGAN HOME,
IN THE CITY OF OSKARS

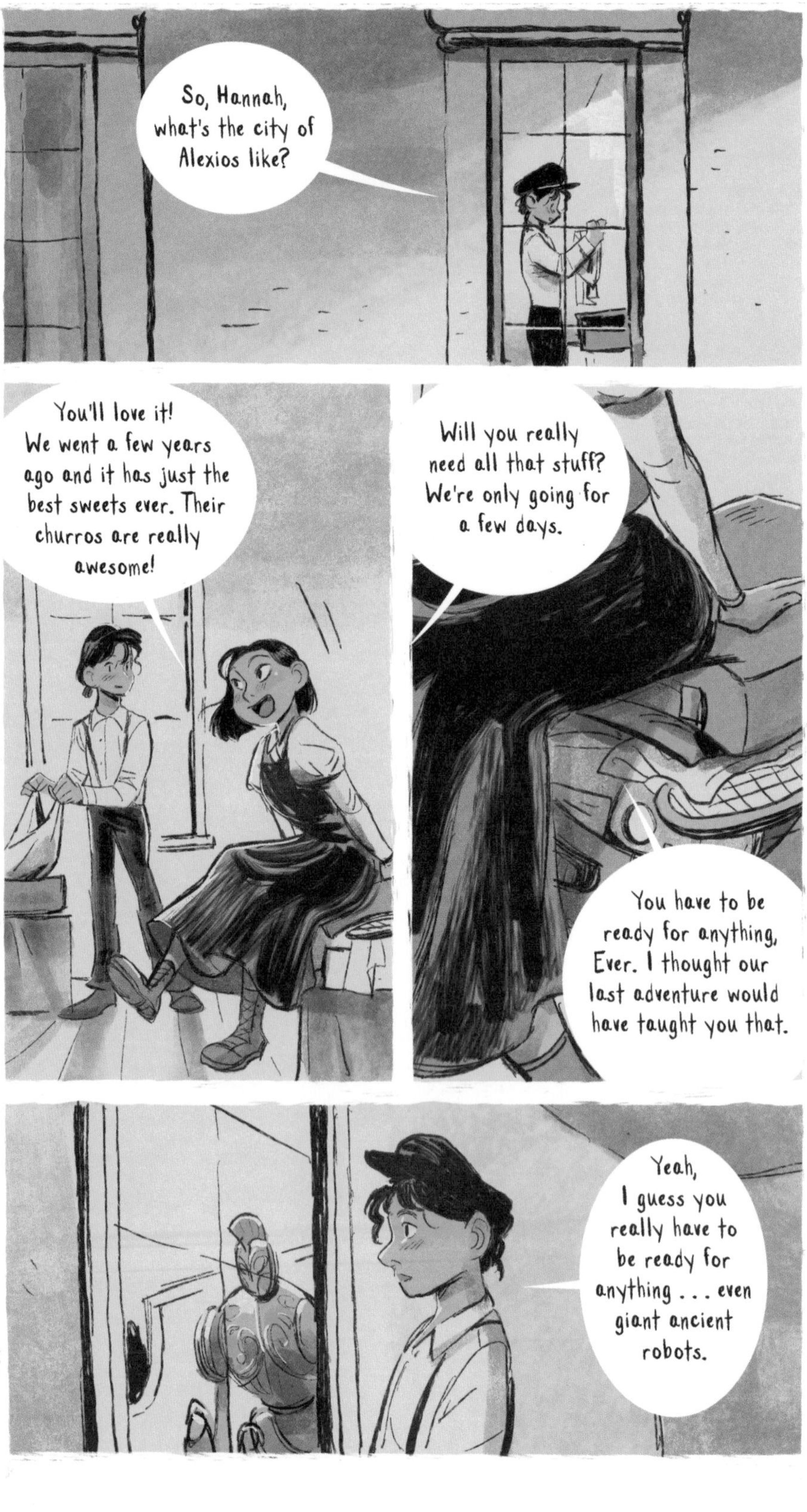
So, Hannah, what's the city of Alexios like?
You'll love it! We went a few years ago and it has just the best sweets ever. Their churros are really awesome!
Will you really need all that stuff? We're only going for a few days.
You have to be ready for anything, Ever. I thought our last adventure would have taught you that.
Yeah, I guess you really have to be ready for anything . . . even giant ancient robots.

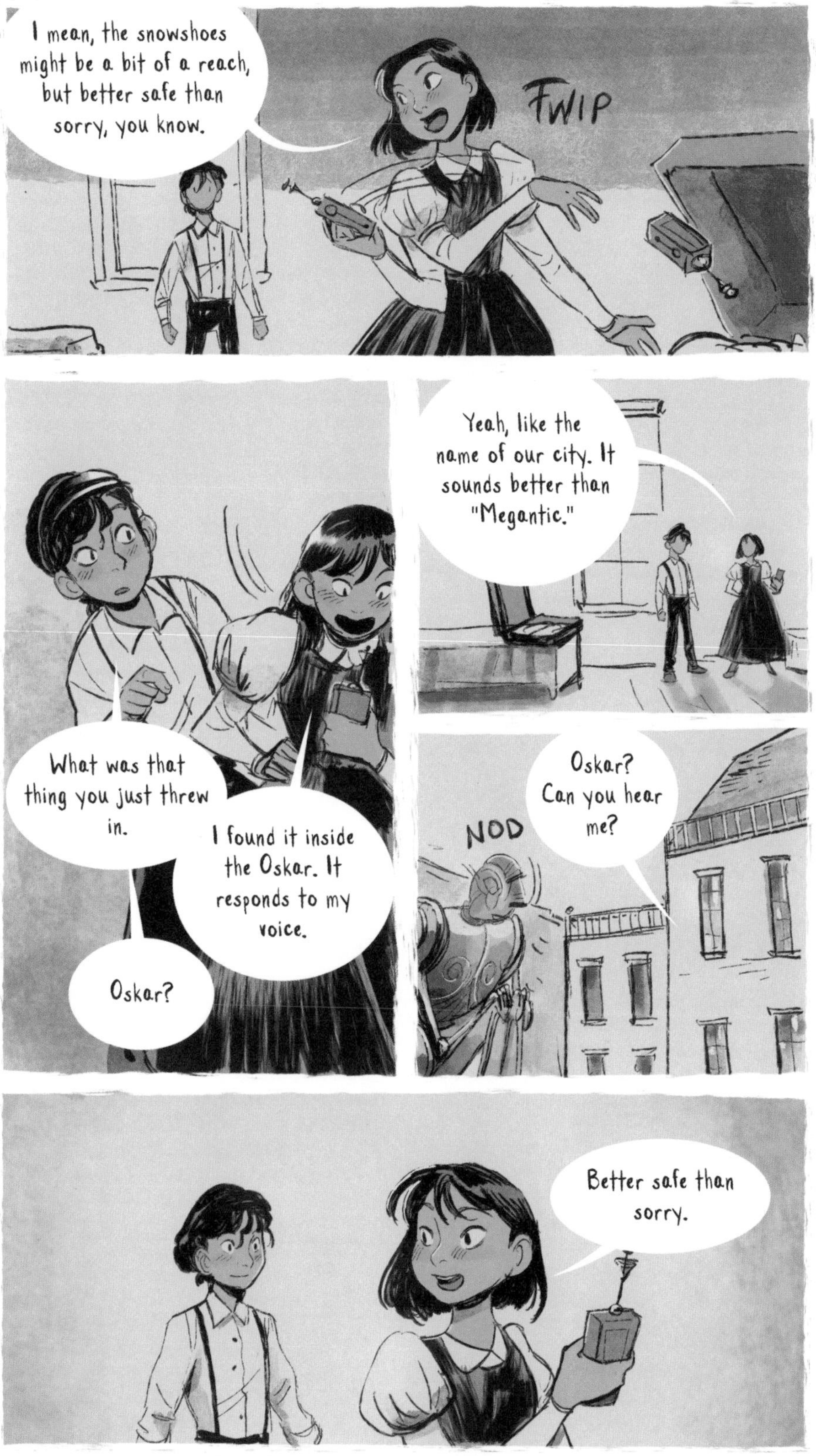
I mean, the snowshoes might be a bit of a reach, but better safe than sorry, you know.
FWIP
What was that thing you just threw in.
I found it inside the Oskar. It responds to my voice.
Oskar?
Yeah, like the name of our city. It sounds better than "Megantic."
NOD
Oskar? Can you hear me?
Better safe than sorry.

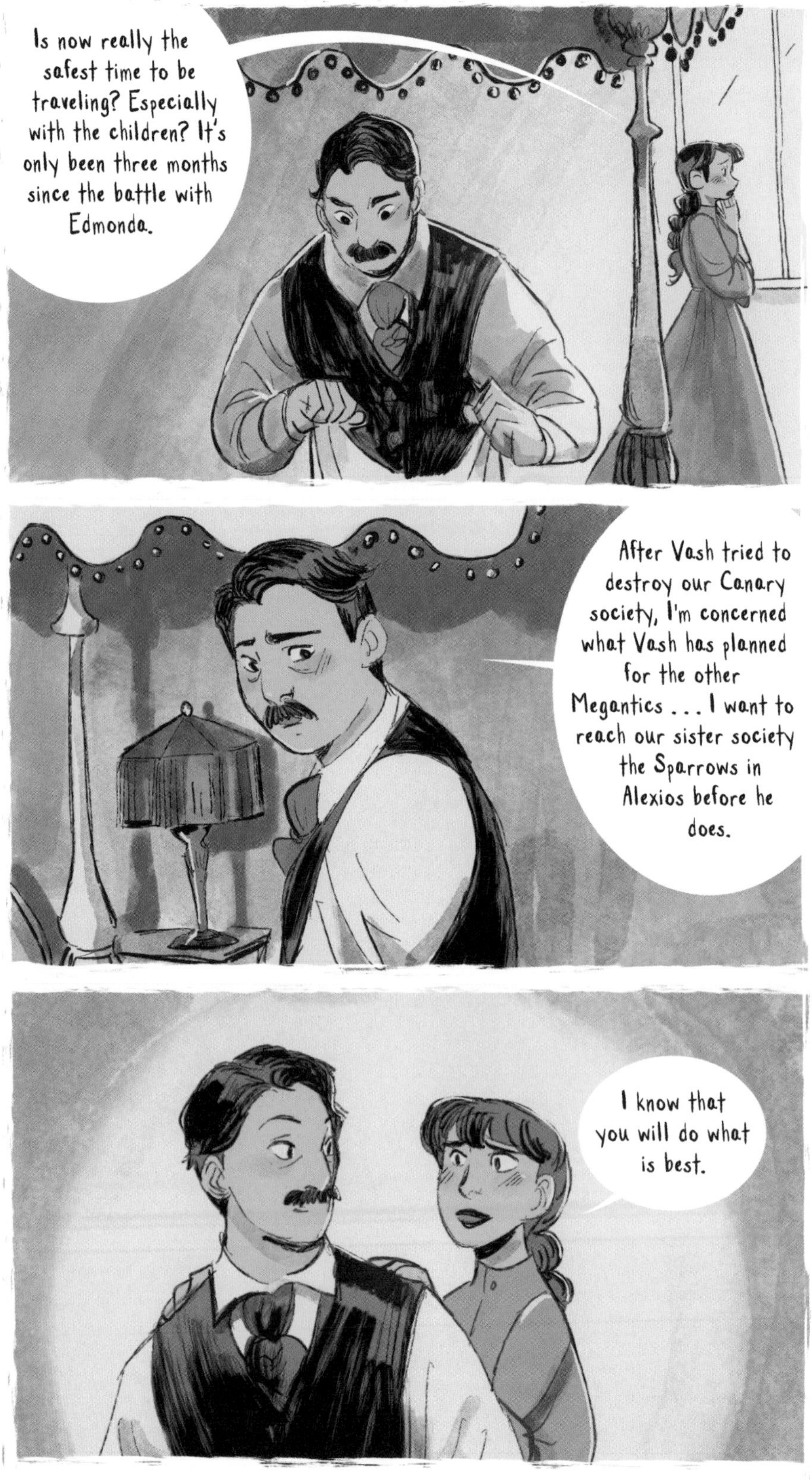
Is now really the safest time to be traveling? Especially with the children? It's only been three months since the battle with Edmonda.
After Vash tried to destroy our Canary society, I'm concerned what Vash has planned for the other Megantics . . . I want to reach our sister society the Sparrows in Alexios before he does.
I know that you will do what is best.

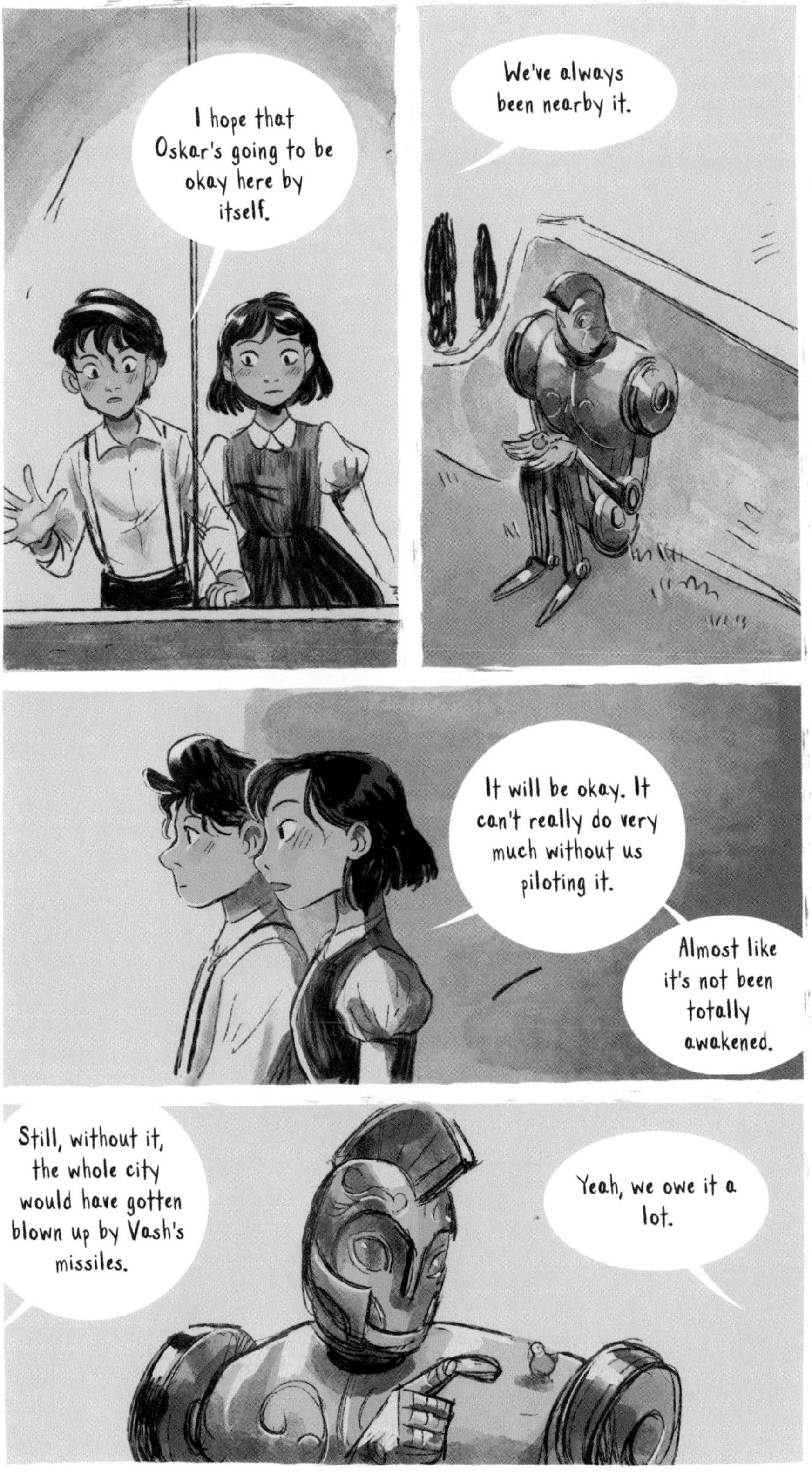
I hope that Oskar's going to be okay here by itself.
We've always been nearby it.
It will be okay. It can't really do very much without us piloting it.
Almost like it's not been totally awakened.
Still, without it, the whole city would have gotten blown up by Vash's missiles.
Yeah, we owe it a lot.

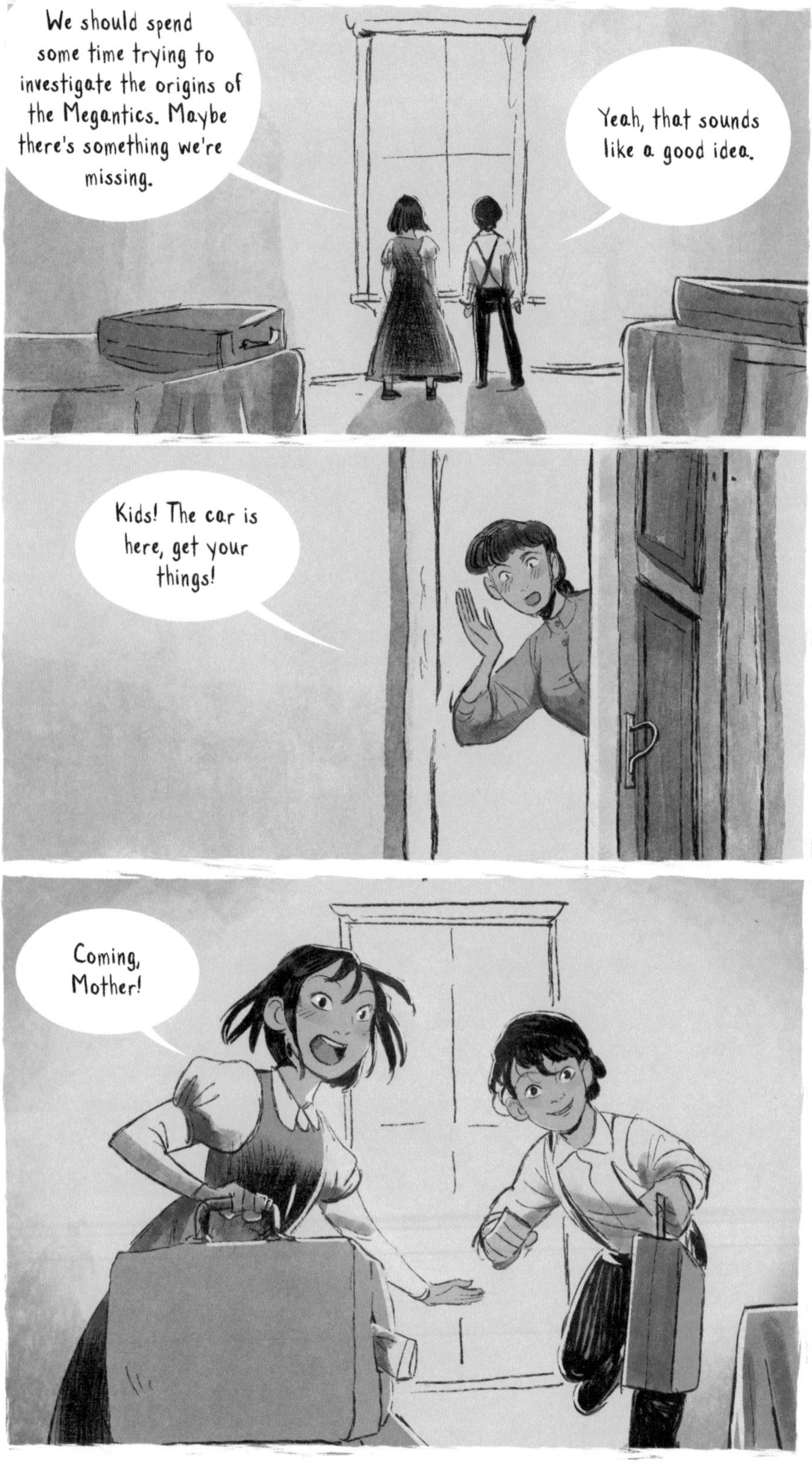
We should spend some time trying to investigate the origins of the Megantics. Maybe there's something we're missing.
Yeah, that sounds like a good idea.
Kids! The car is here, get your things!
Coming, Mother!

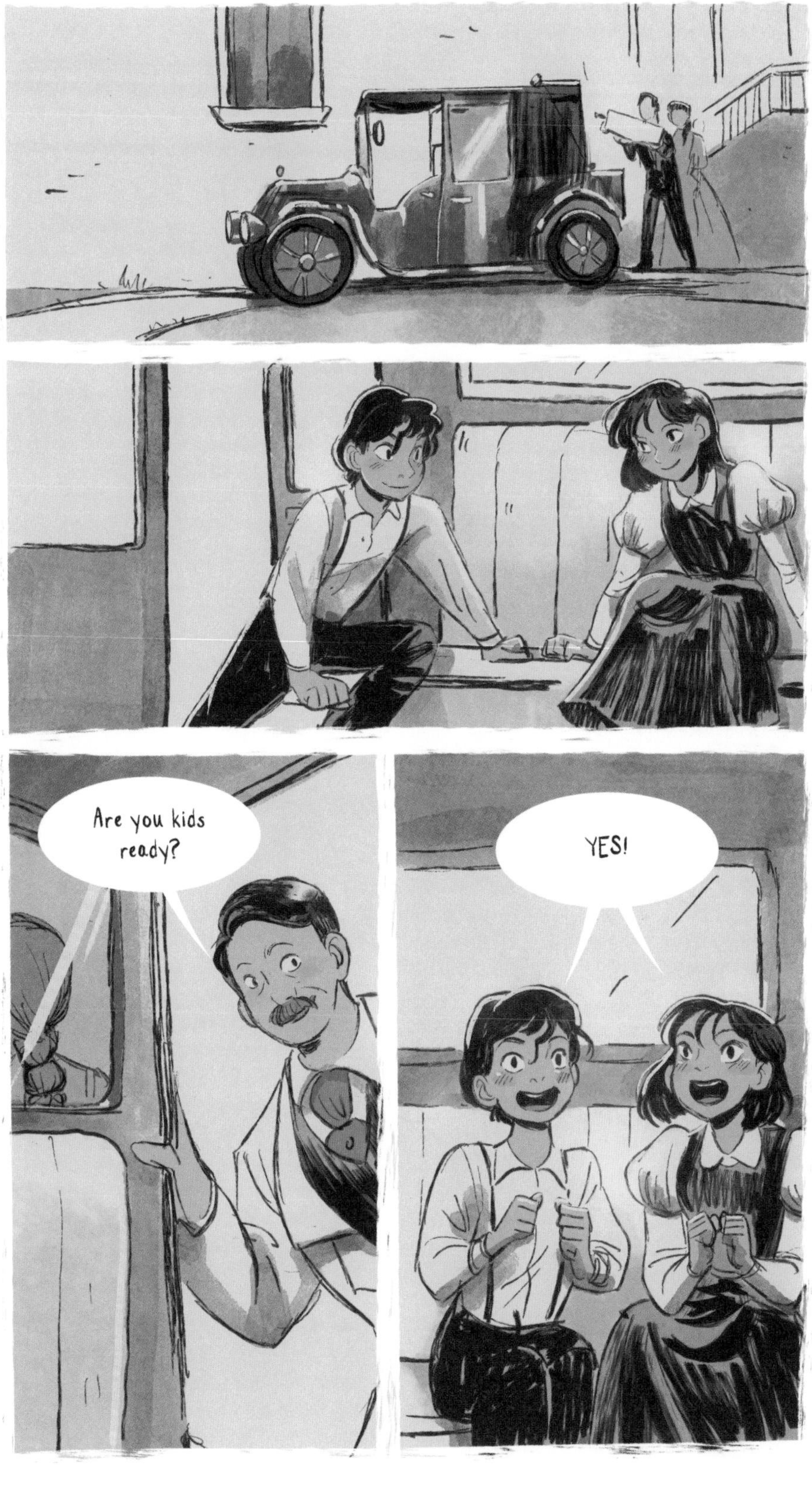

Are you kids ready?
YES!

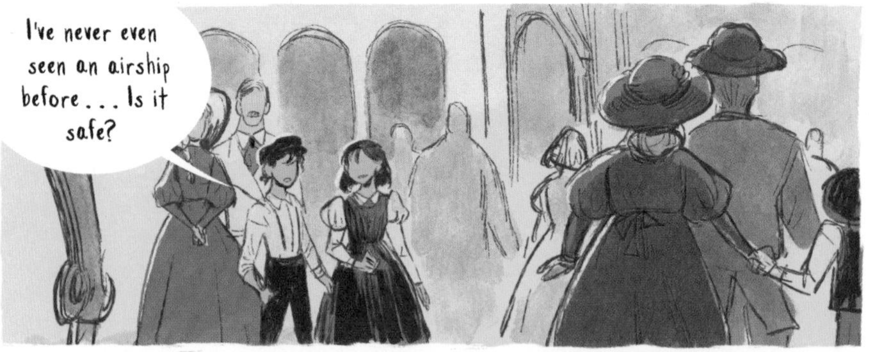
I've never even seen an airship before . . . Is it safe?

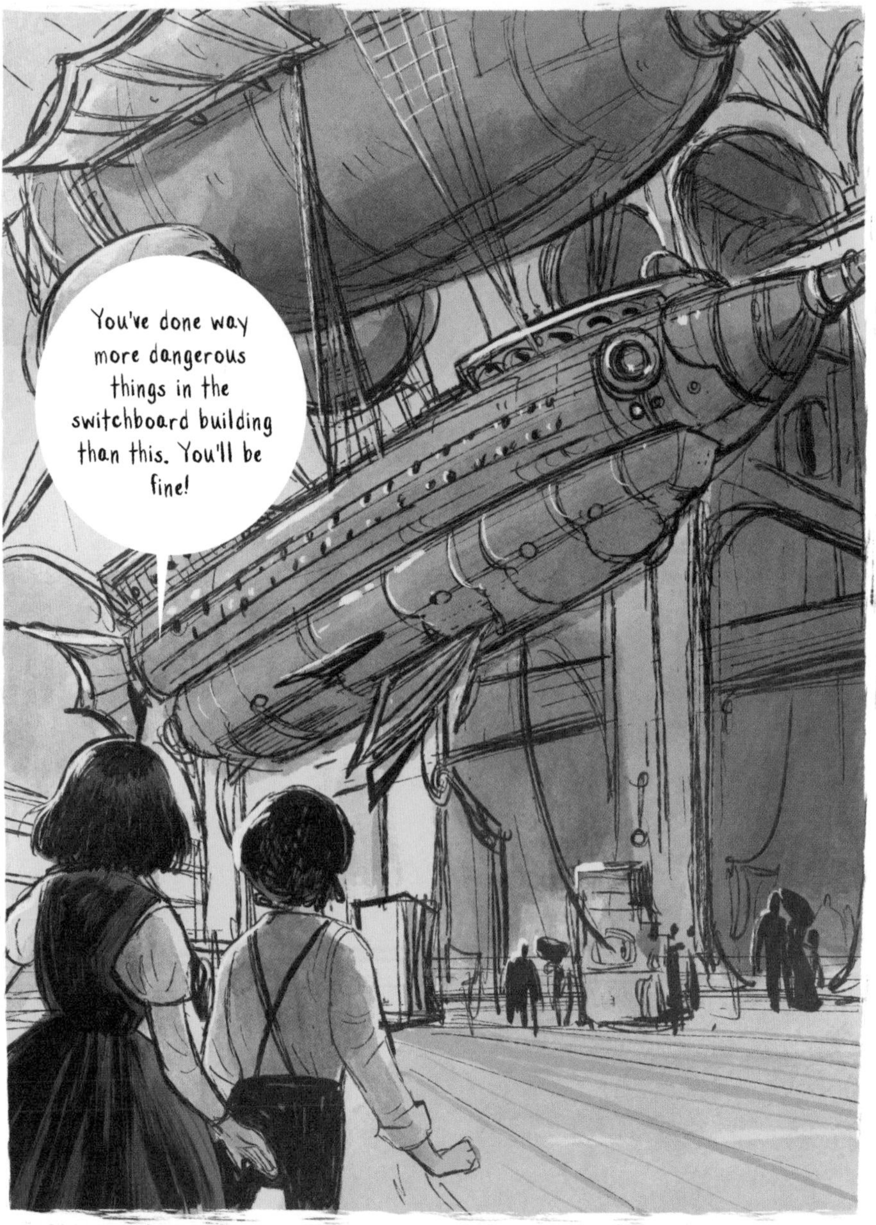
You've done way more dangerous things in the switchboard building than this. You'll be fine!

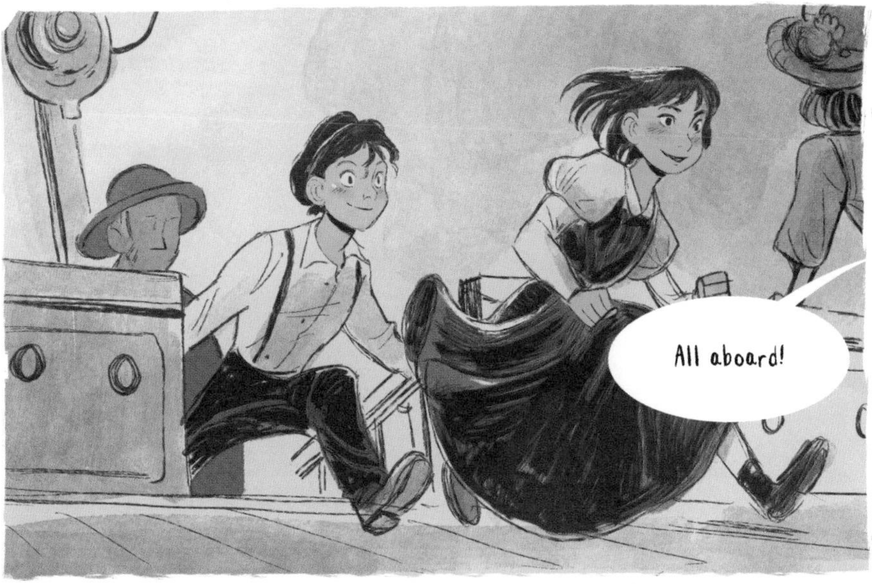
All aboard!

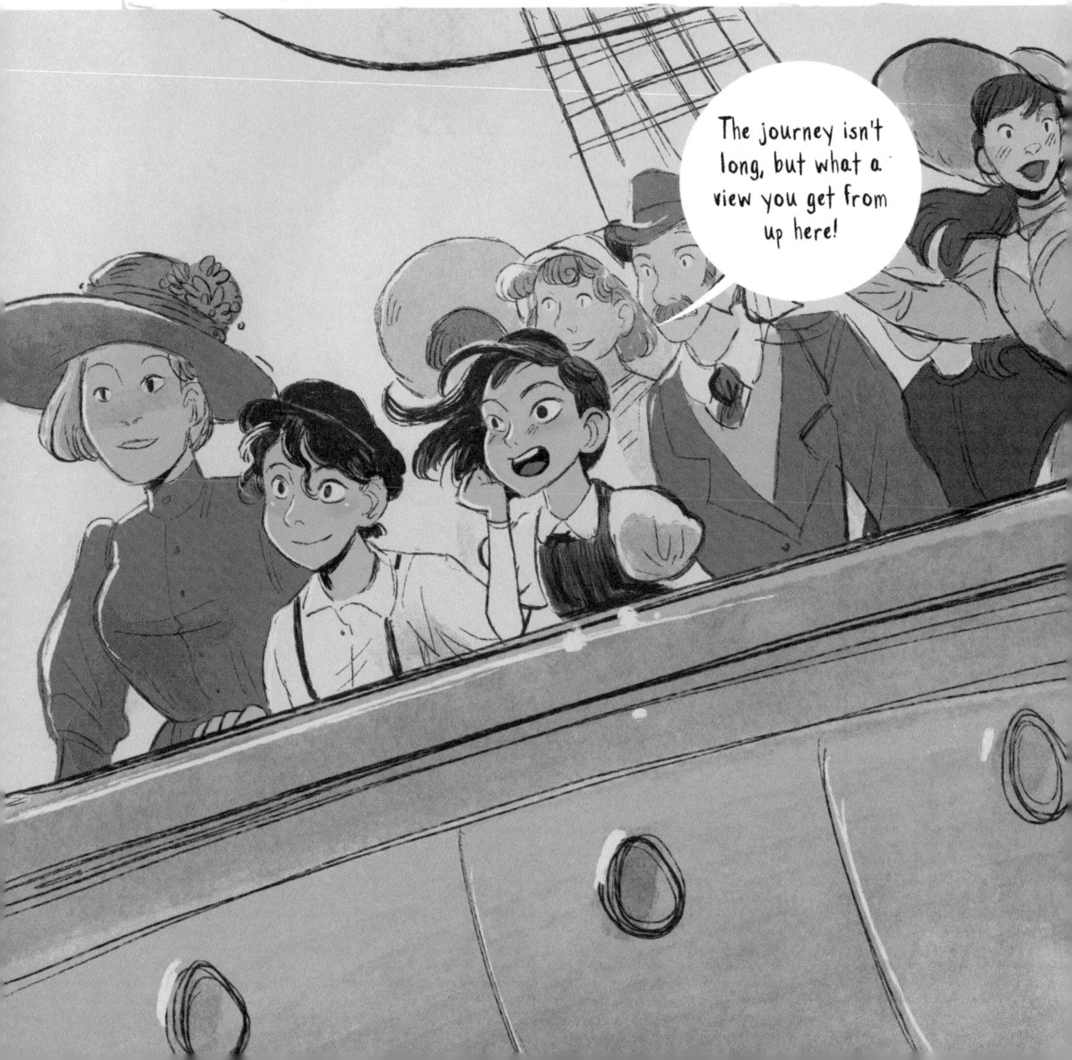
The journey isn't long, but what a view you get from up here!

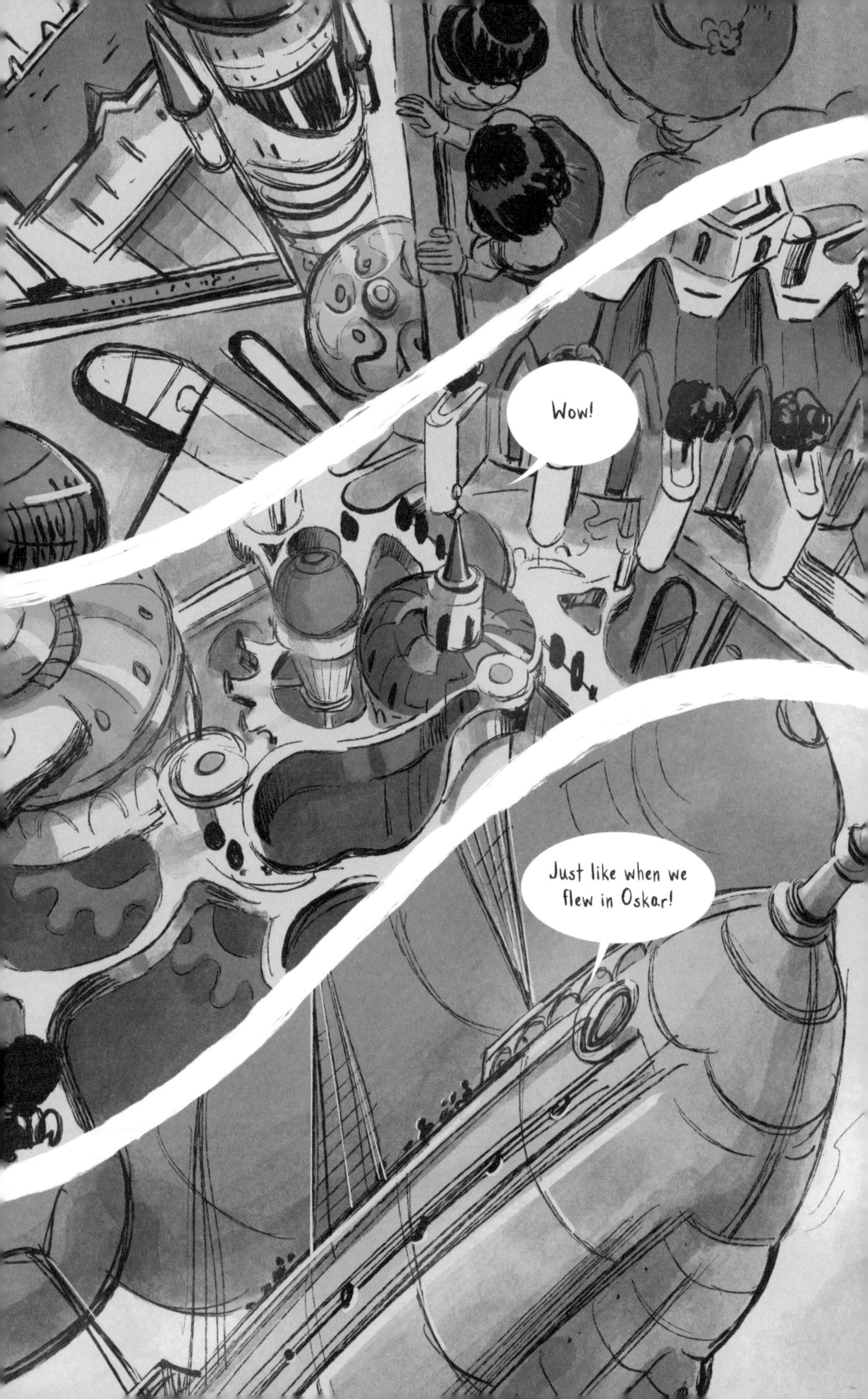
Wow!
Just like when we flew in Oskar!

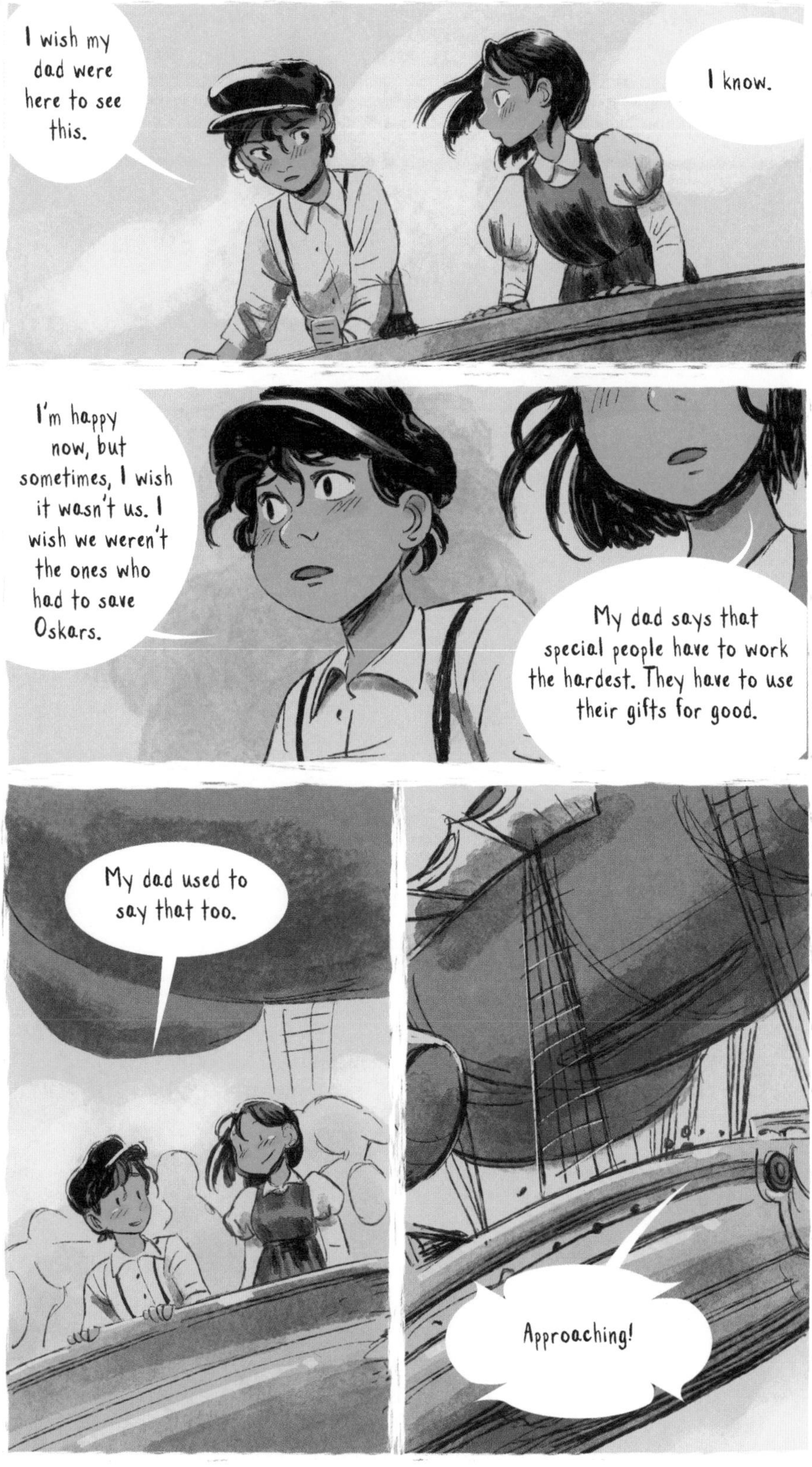
I wish my dad were here to see this.
I know.
I'm happy now, but sometimes, I wish it wasn't us. I wish we weren't the ones who had to save Oskars.
My dad says that special people have to work the hardest. They have to use their gifts for good.
My dad used to say that too.
Approaching!

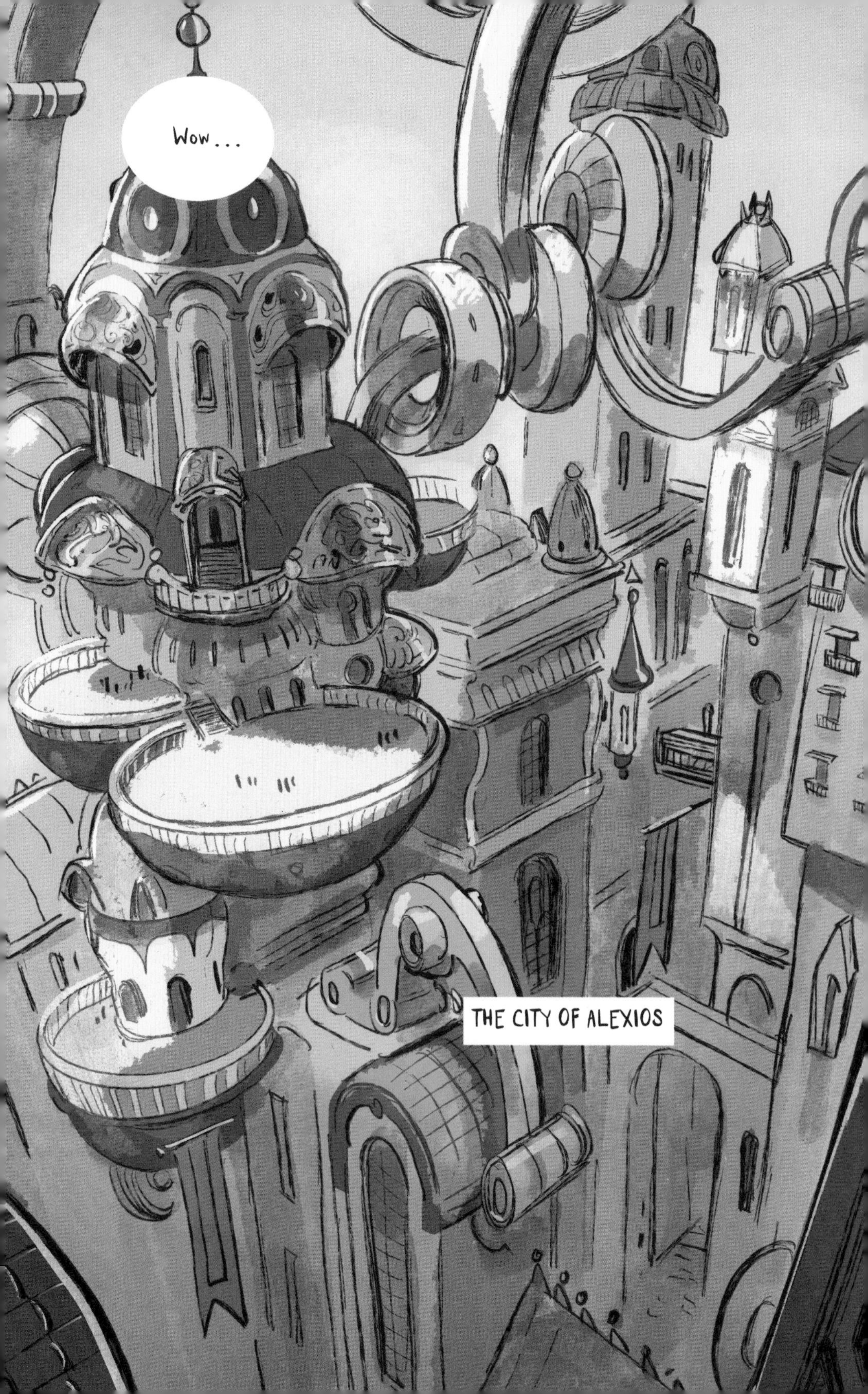
Wow...
THE CITY OF ALEXIOS

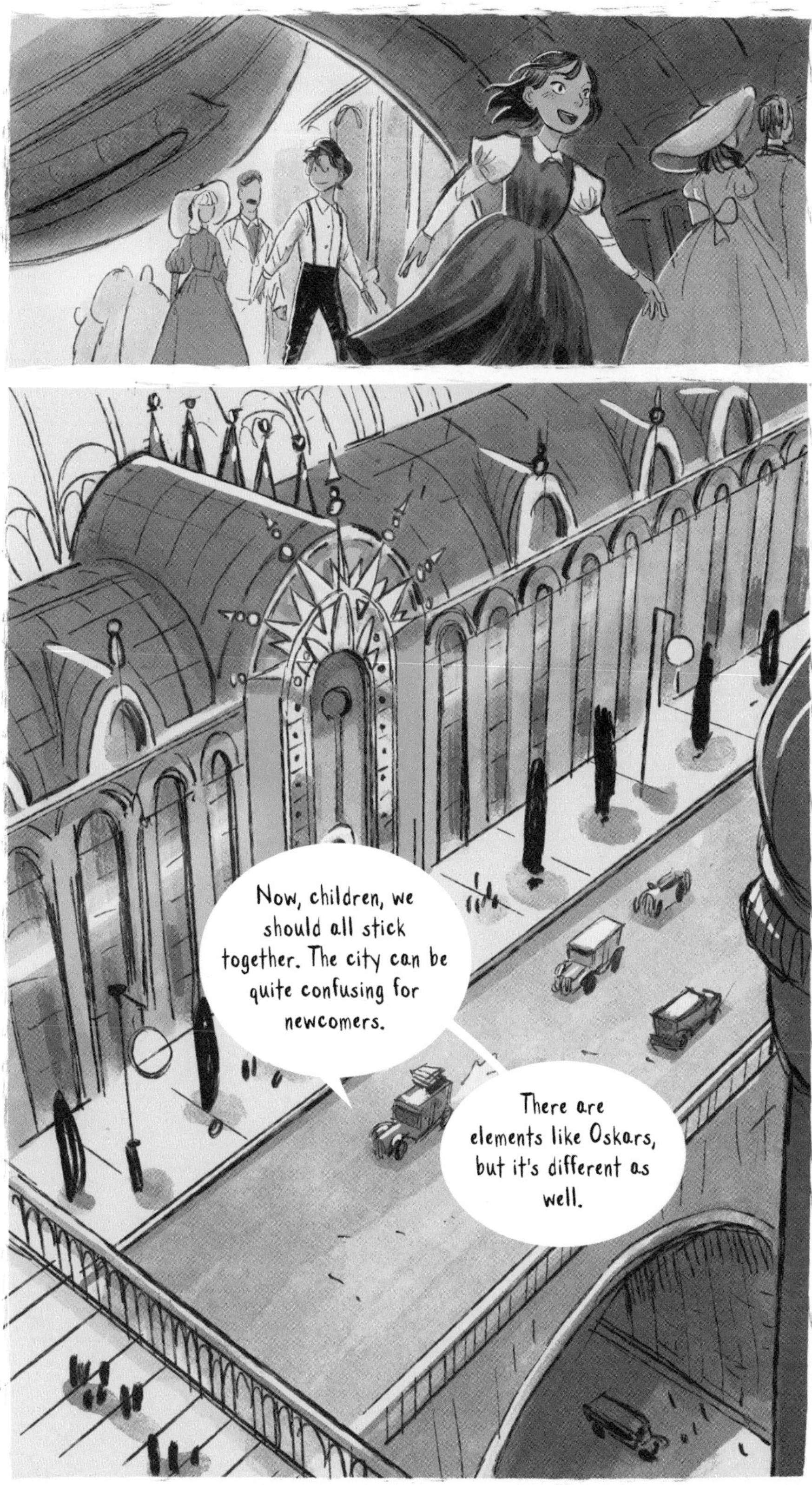
Now, children, we should all stick together. The city can be quite confusing for newcomers.
There are elements like Oskars, but it's different as well.

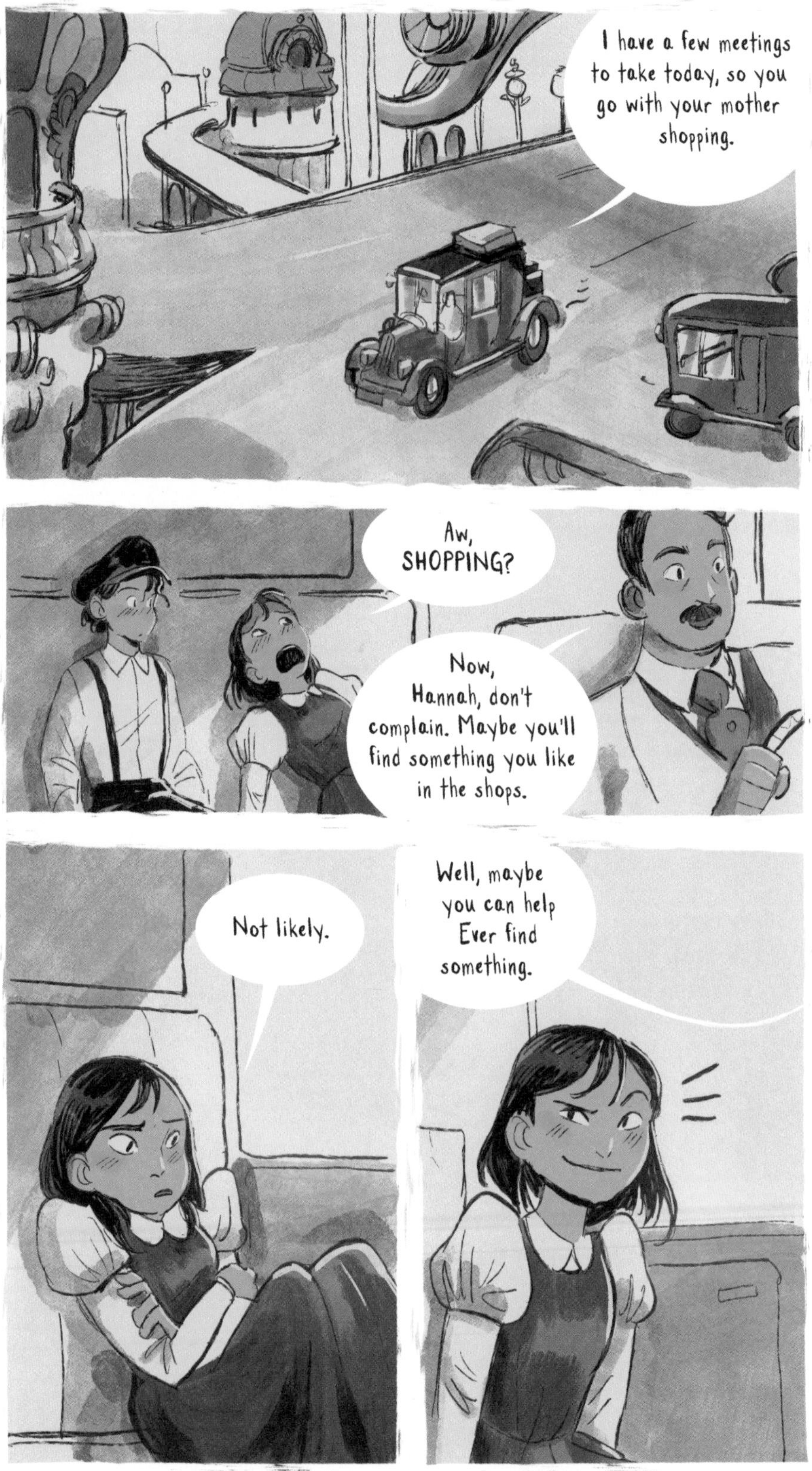
I have a few meetings to take today, so you go with your mother shopping.
Aw, SHOPPING?
Now, Hannah, don't complain. Maybe you'll find something you like in the shops.
Not likely.
Well, maybe you can help Ever find something.

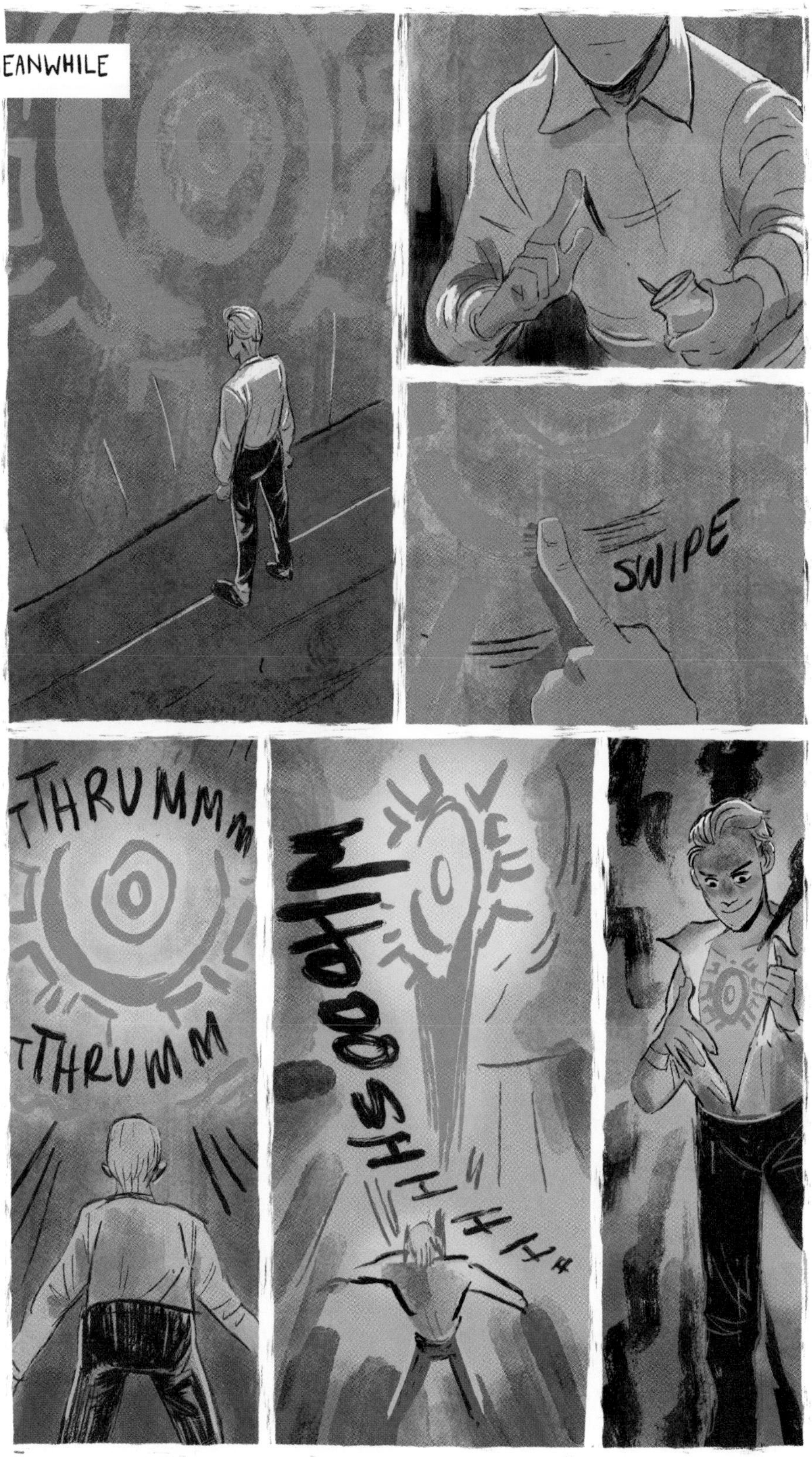
MEANWHILE
SWIPE
TTHRUMMM
TTHRUMM
WHOOOSHHHHH

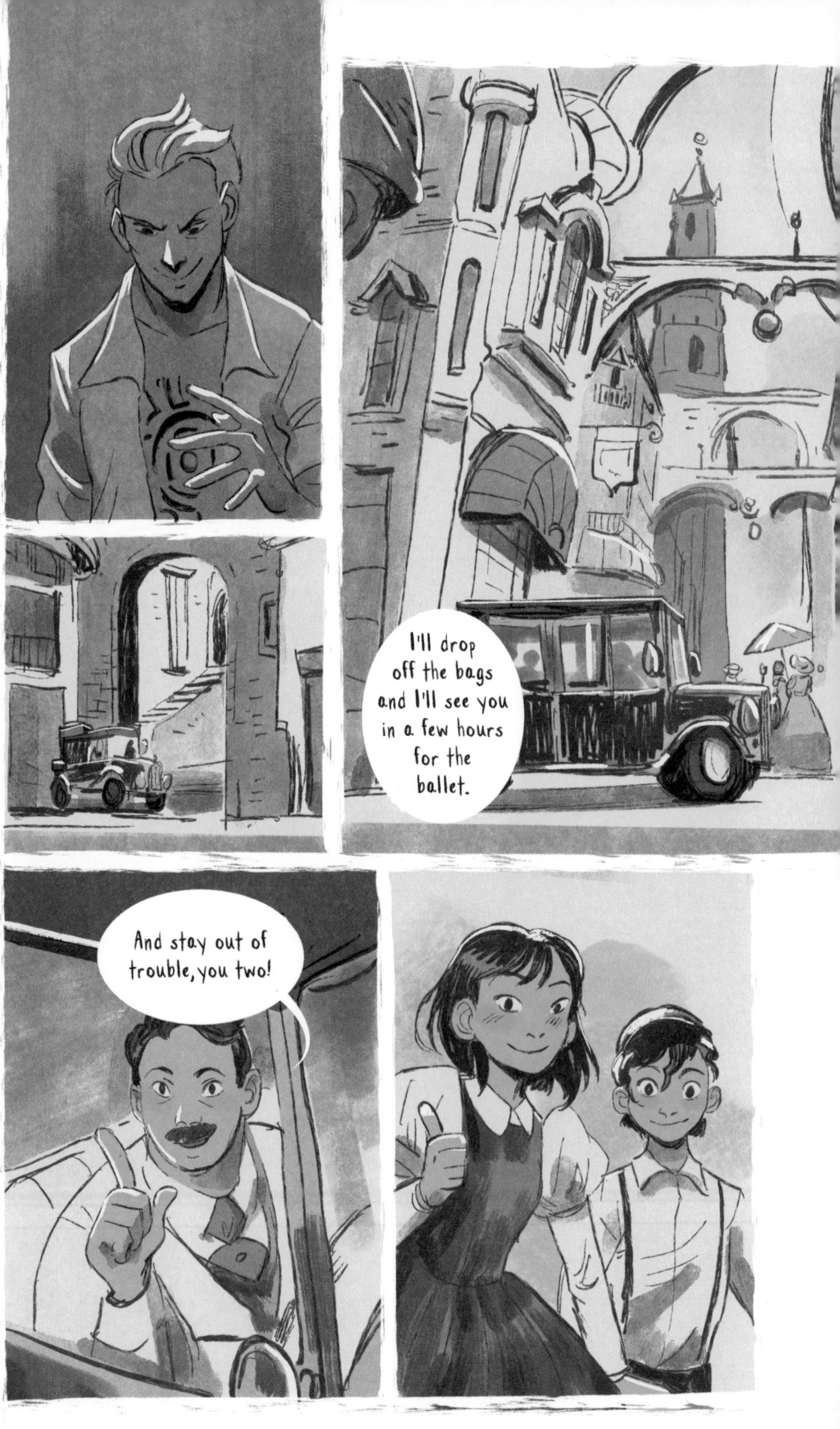
I'll drop off the bags and I'll see you in a few hours for the ballet.
And stay out of trouble, you two!

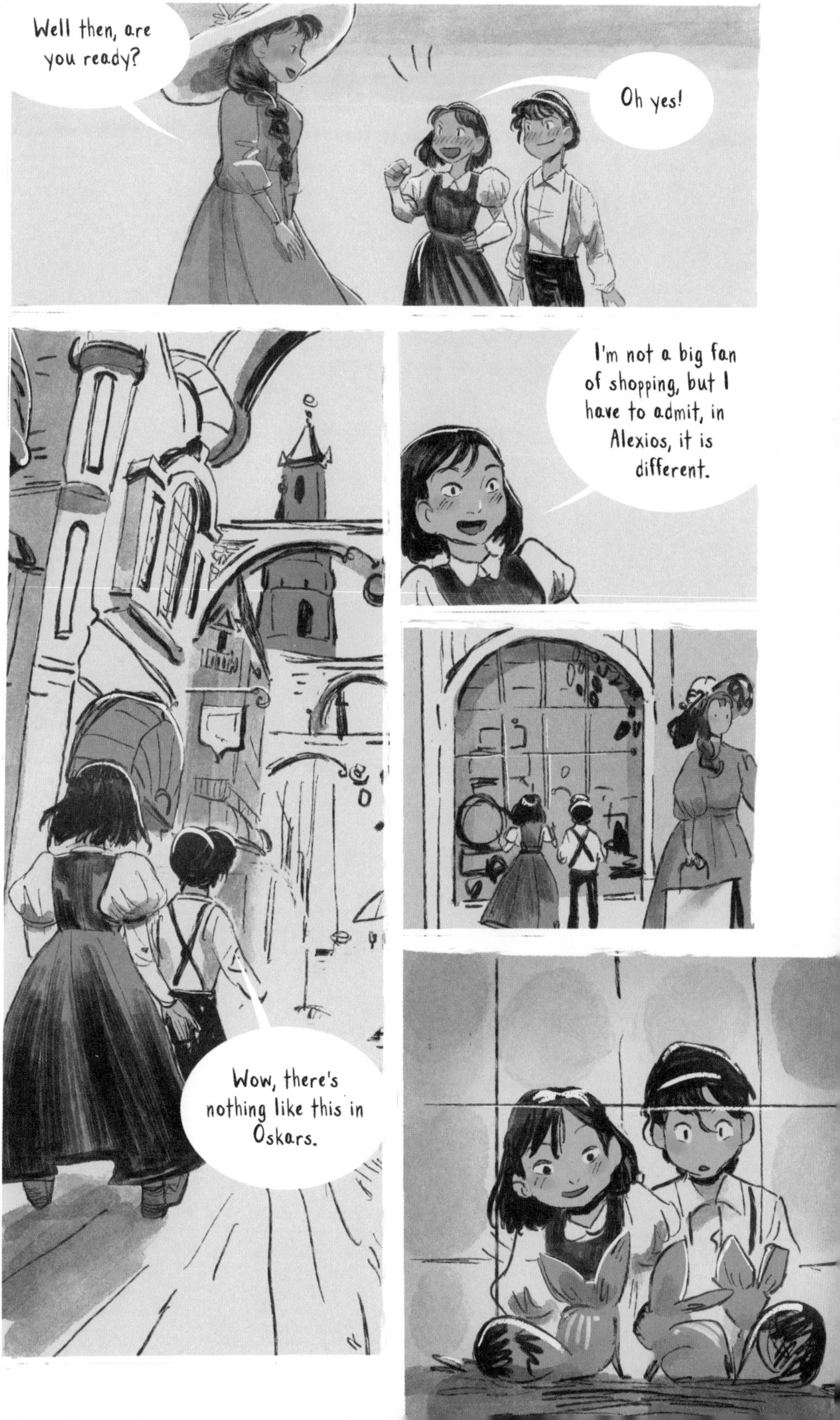
Well then, are you ready?
Oh yes!
Wow, there's nothing like this in Oskars.
I'm not a big fan of shopping, but I have to admit, in Alexios, it is different.

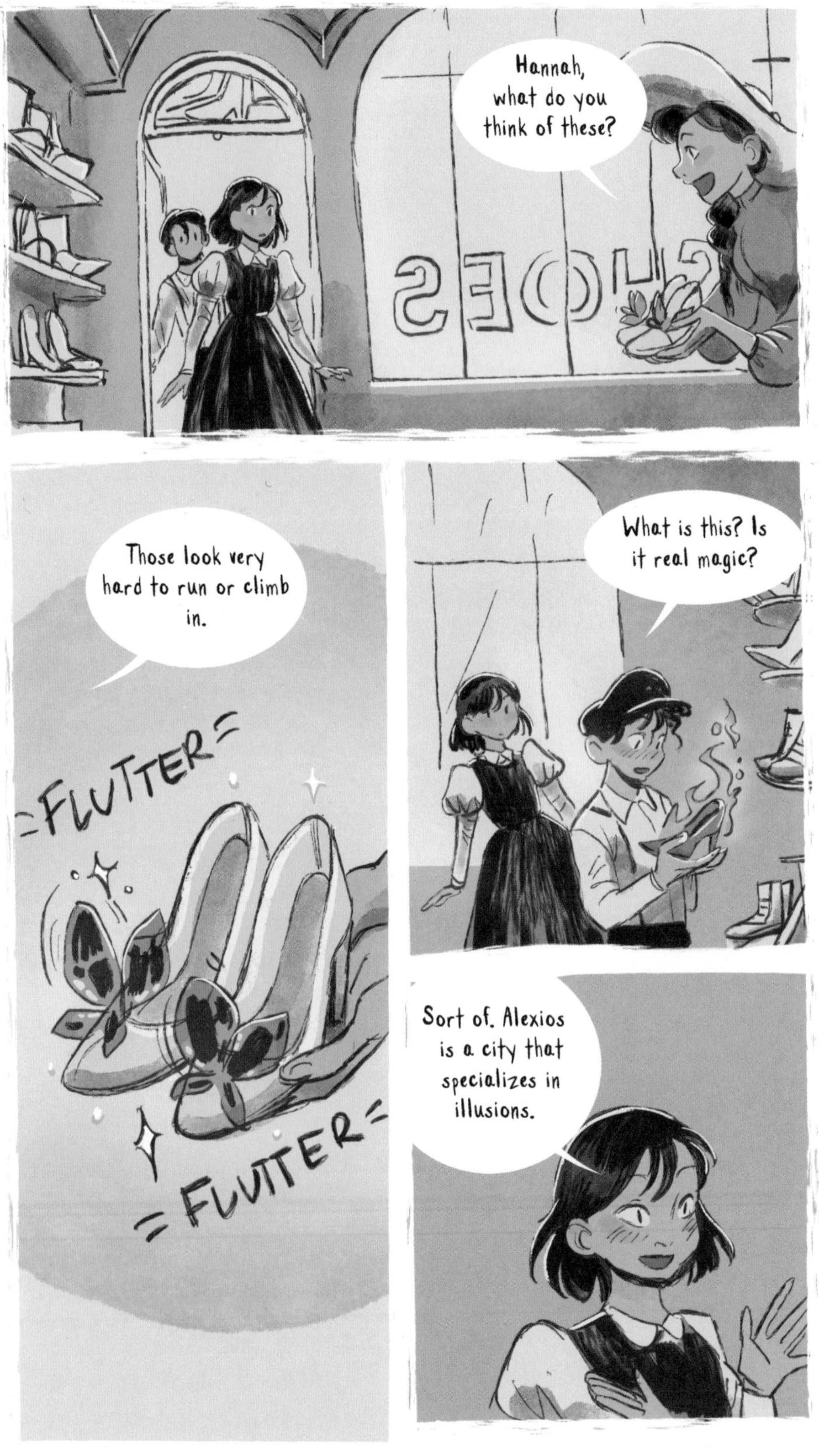
Hannah, what do you think of these?
Those look very hard to run or climb in.
FLUTTER
FLUTTER
What is this? Is it real magic?
Sort of. Alexios is a city that specializes in illusions.

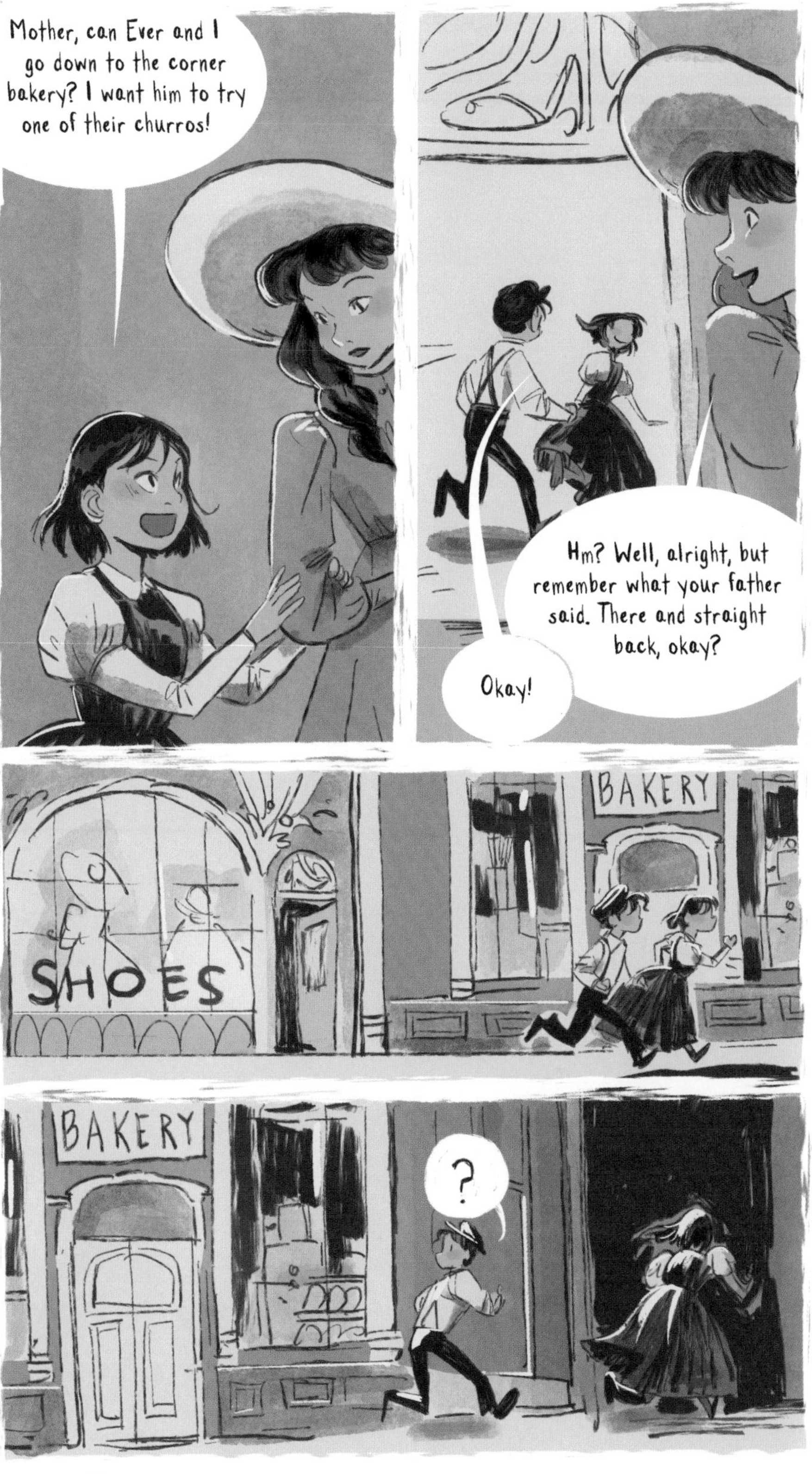
Mother, can Ever and I go down to the corner bakery? I want him to try one of their churros!
Hm? Well, alright, but remember what your father said. There and straight back, okay?
Okay!
SHOES
BAKERY
BAKERY
?

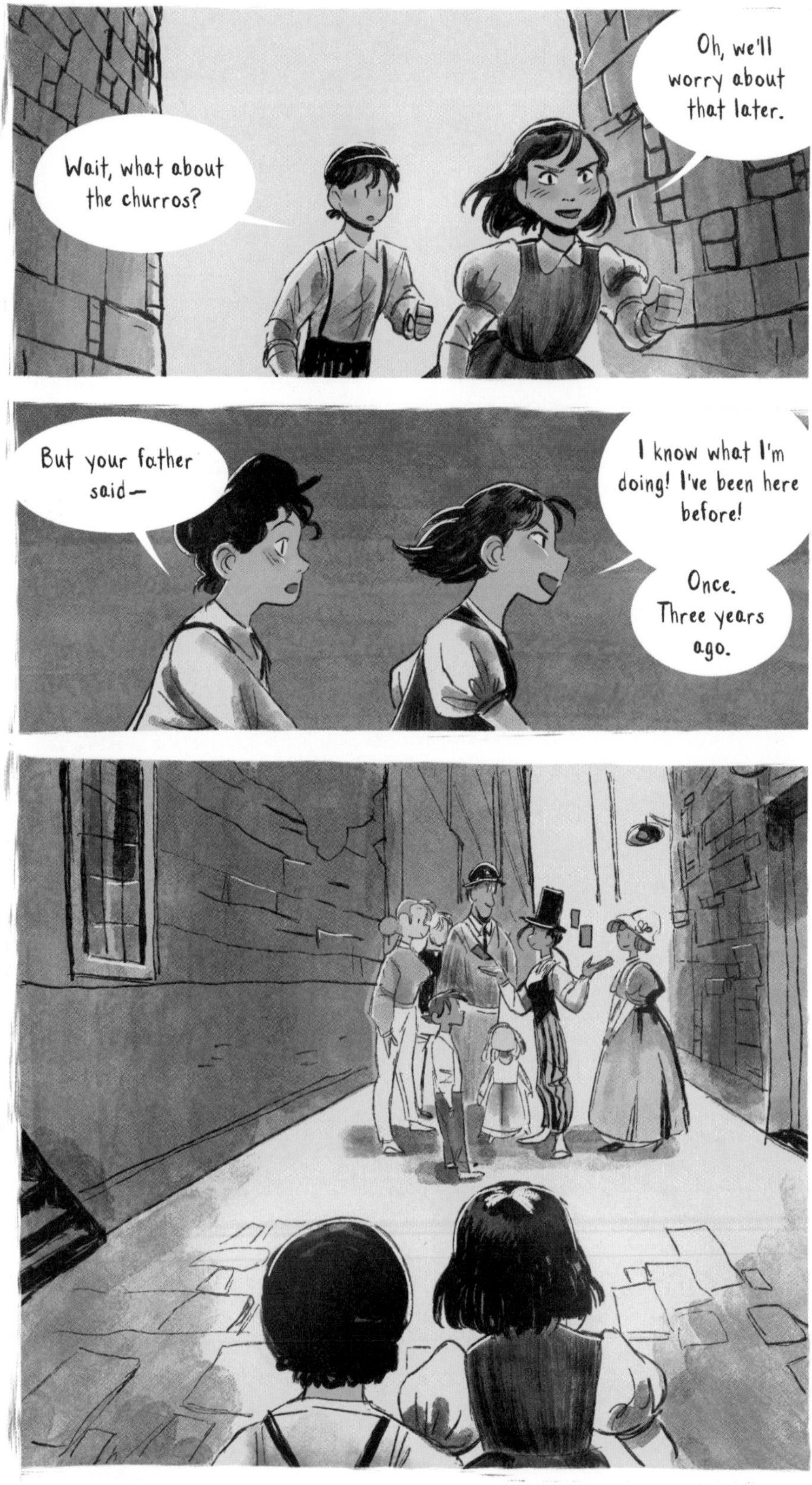
Wait, what about the churros?
Oh, we'll worry about that later.
But your father said—
I know what I'm doing! I've been here before!
Once. Three years ago.

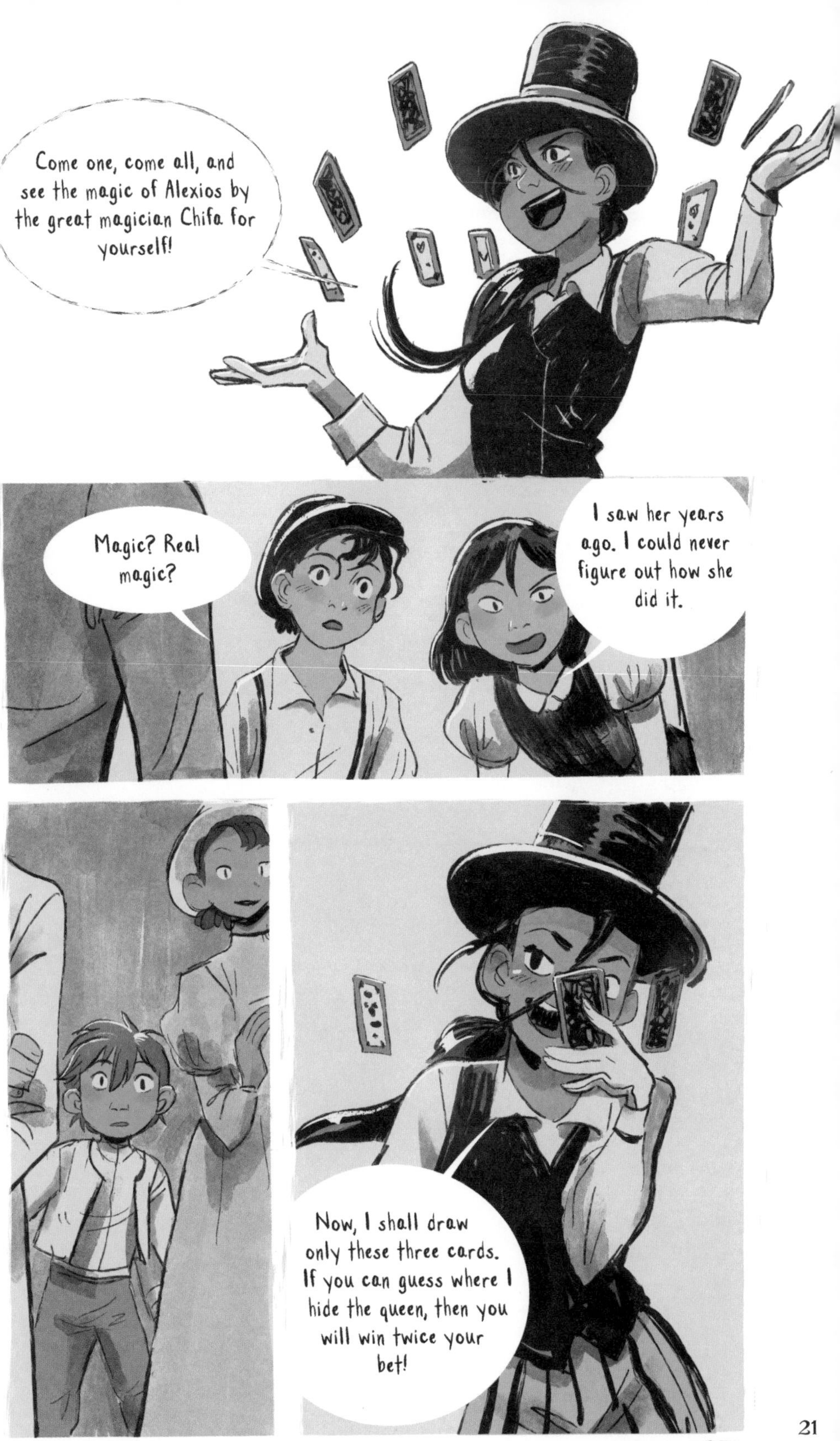
Come one, come all, and see the magic of Alexios by the great magician Chifa for yourself!
Magic? Real magic?
I saw her years ago. I could never figure out how she did it.
Now, I shall draw only these three cards. If you can guess where I hide the queen, then you will win twice your bet!

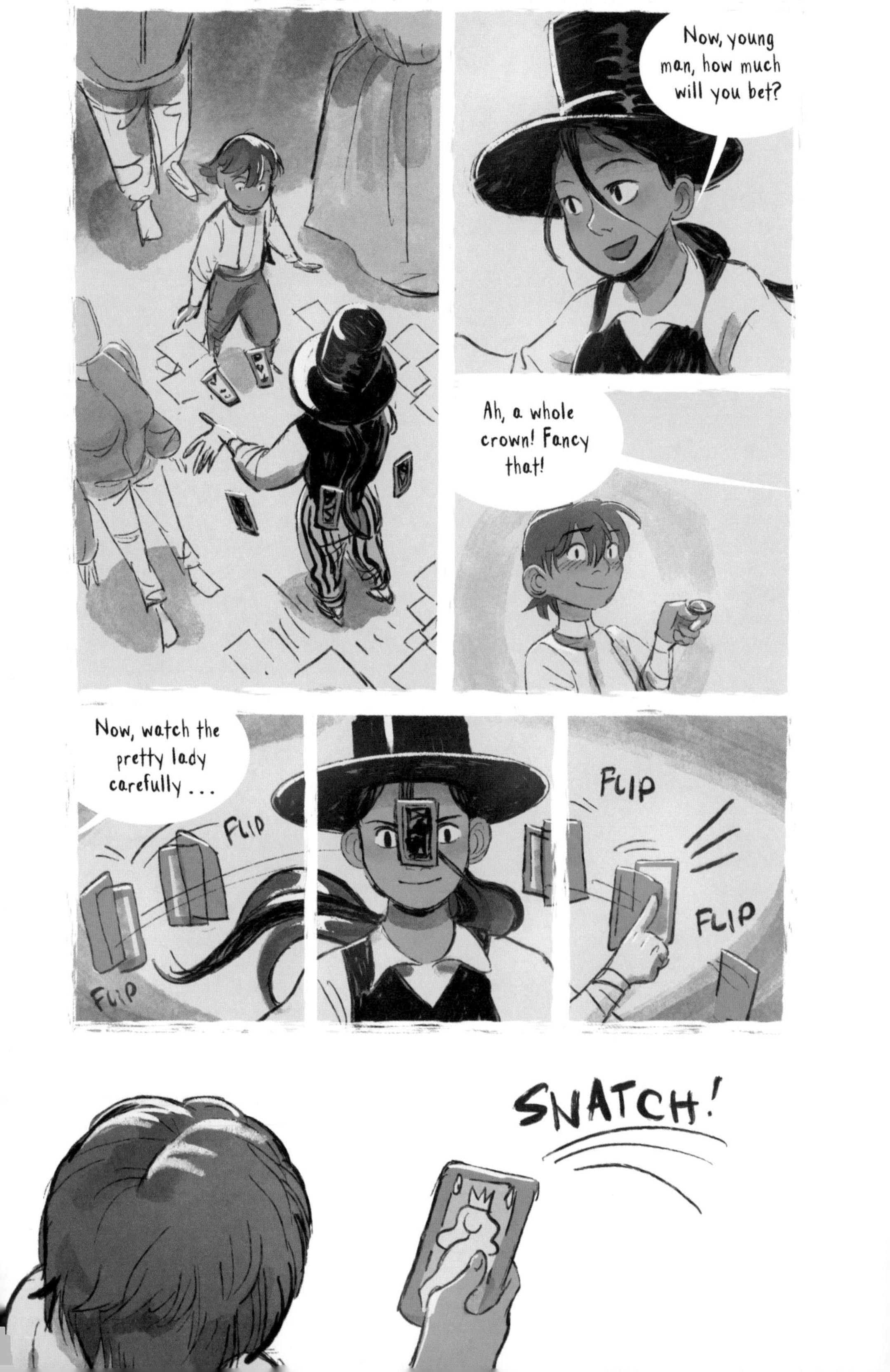
Now, young man, how much will you bet?
Ah, a whole crown! Fancy that!
Now, watch the pretty lady carefully . . .
FLIP
FLIP
FLIP
FLIP
SNATCH!

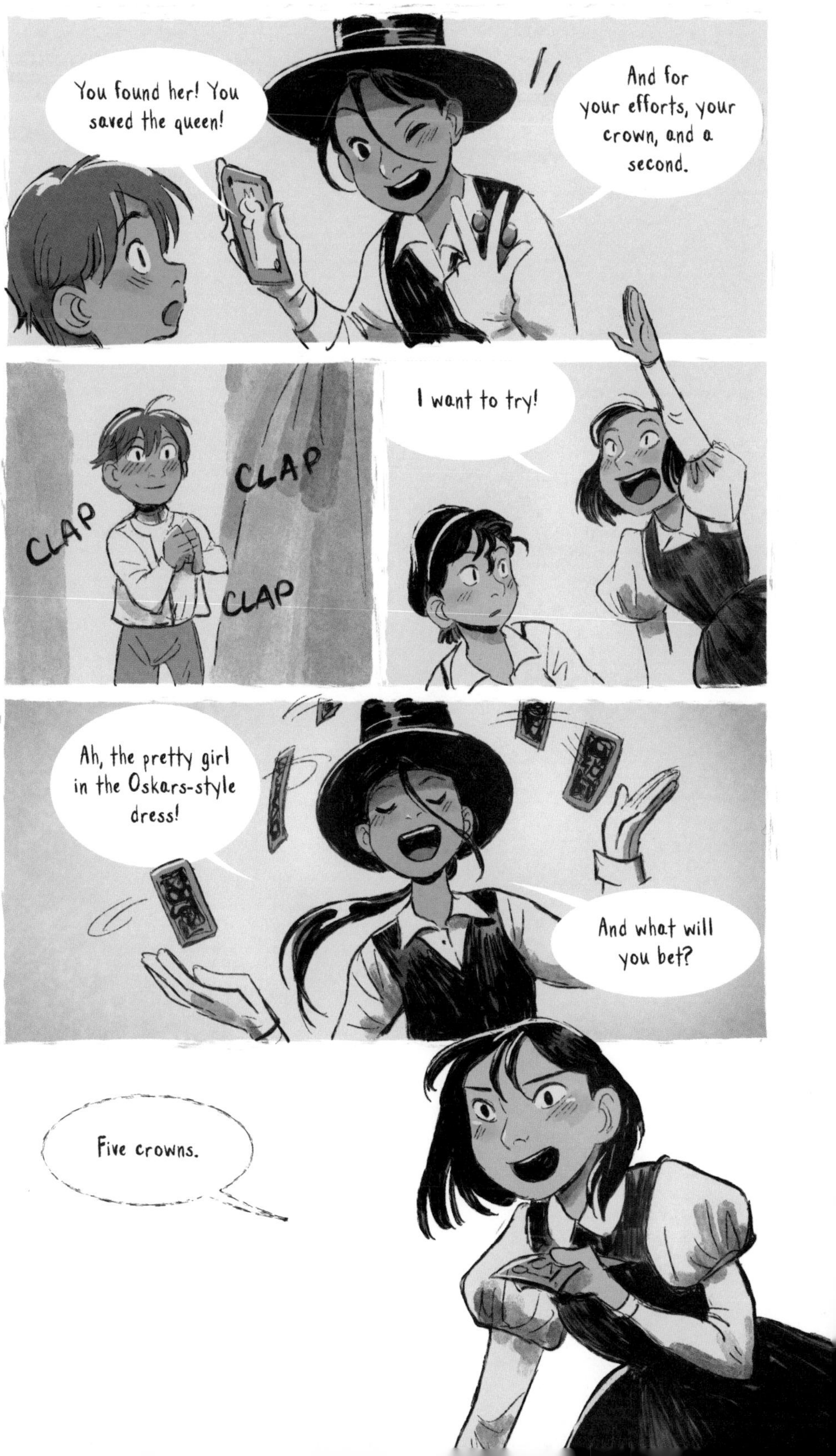
You found her! You saved the queen!
And for your efforts, your crown, and a second.
CLAP
CLAP
CLAP
I want to try!
Ah, the pretty girl in the Oskars-style dress!
And what will you bet?
Five crowns.

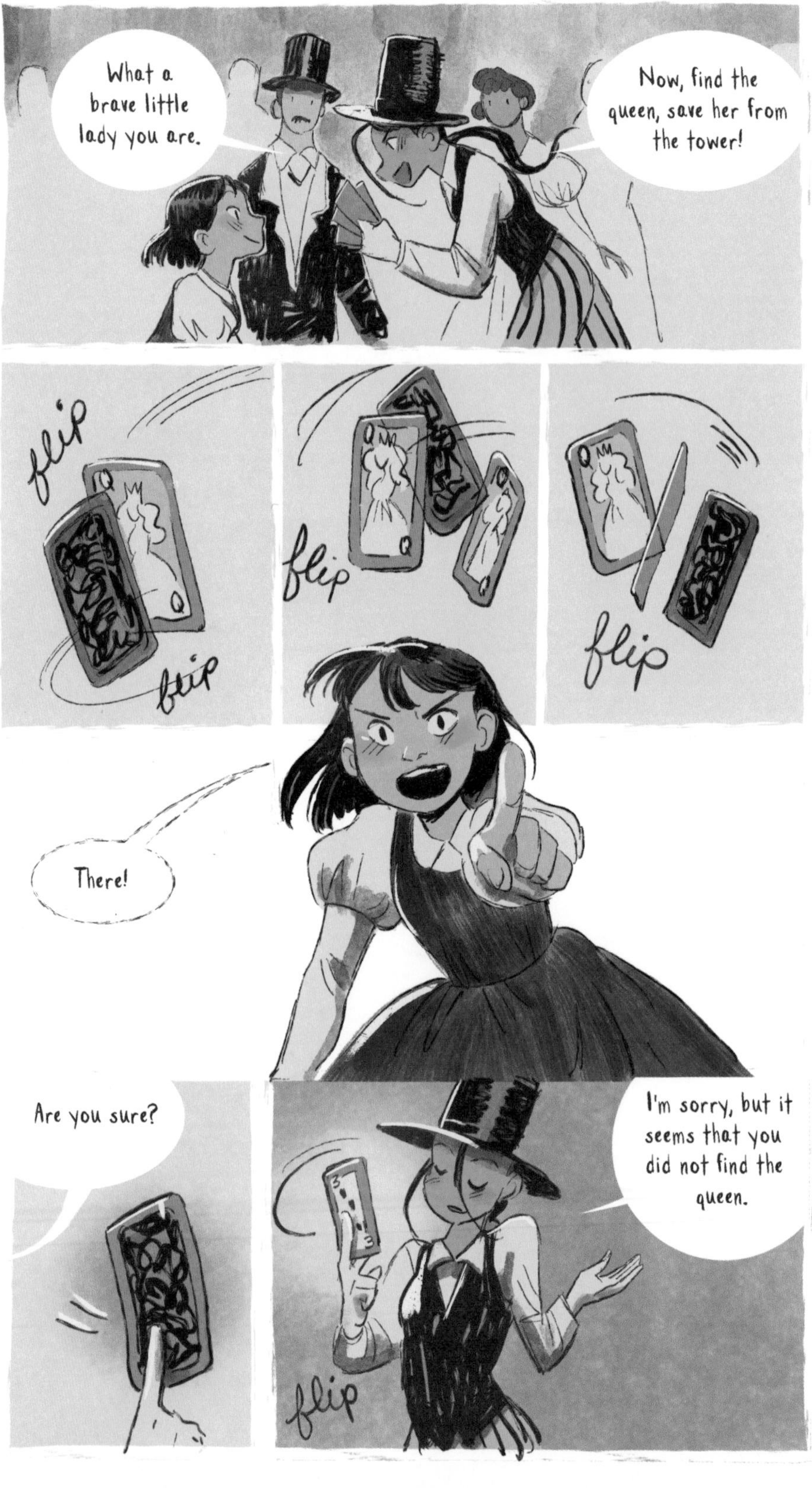
What a brave little lady you are.
Now, find the queen, save her from the tower!
flip
flip
flip
flip
There!
Are you sure?
I'm sorry, but it seems that you did not find the queen.
flip

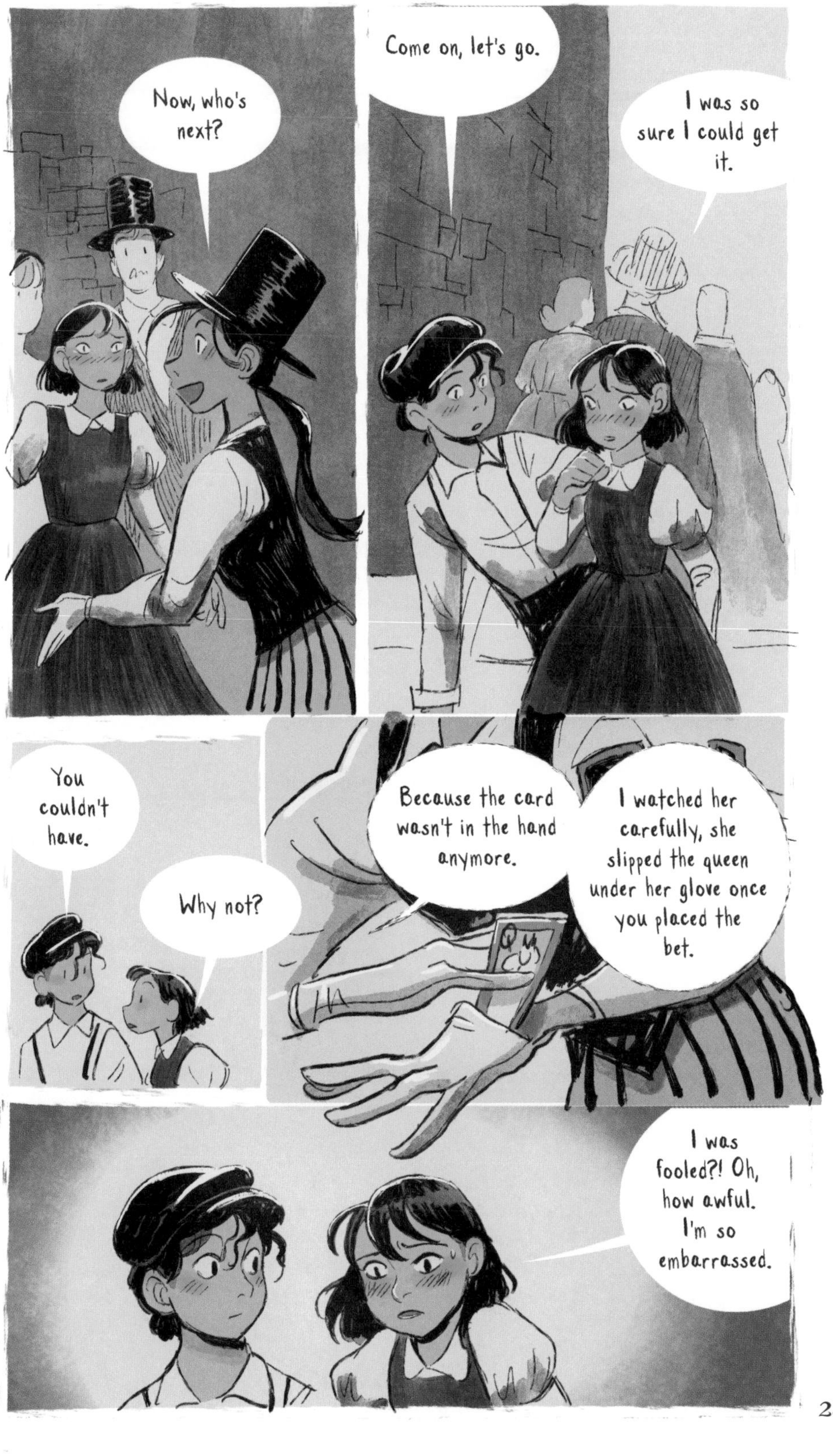
Now, who's next?
Come on, let's go.
I was so sure I could get it.
You couldn't have.
Why not?
Because the card wasn't in the hand anymore.
I watched her carefully, she slipped the queen under her glove once you placed the bet.
I was fooled?! Oh, how awful. I'm so embarrassed.

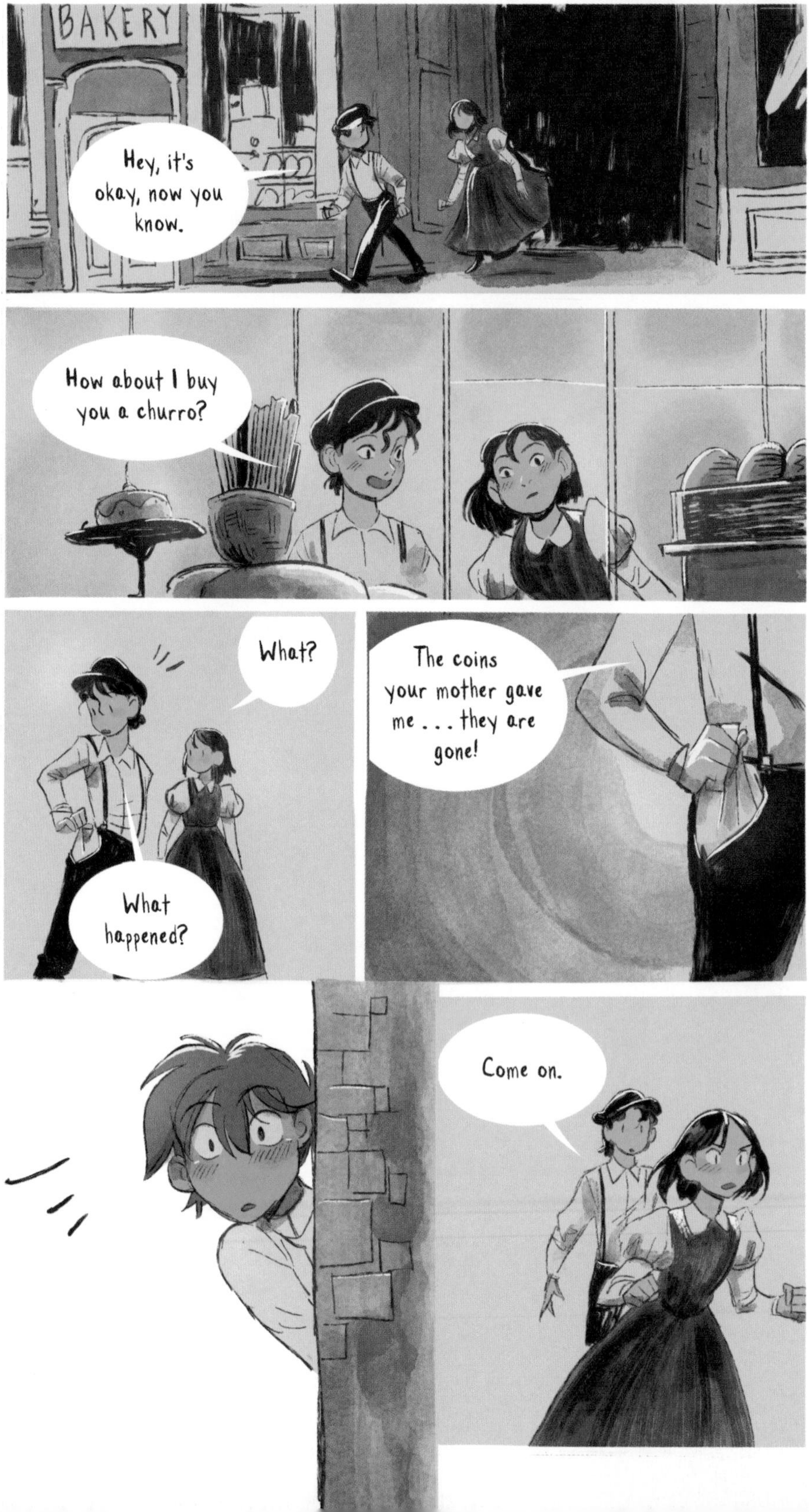
BAKERY
Hey, it's okay, now you know.
How about I buy you a churro?
What?
What happened?
The coins your mother gave me . . . they are gone!
Come on.

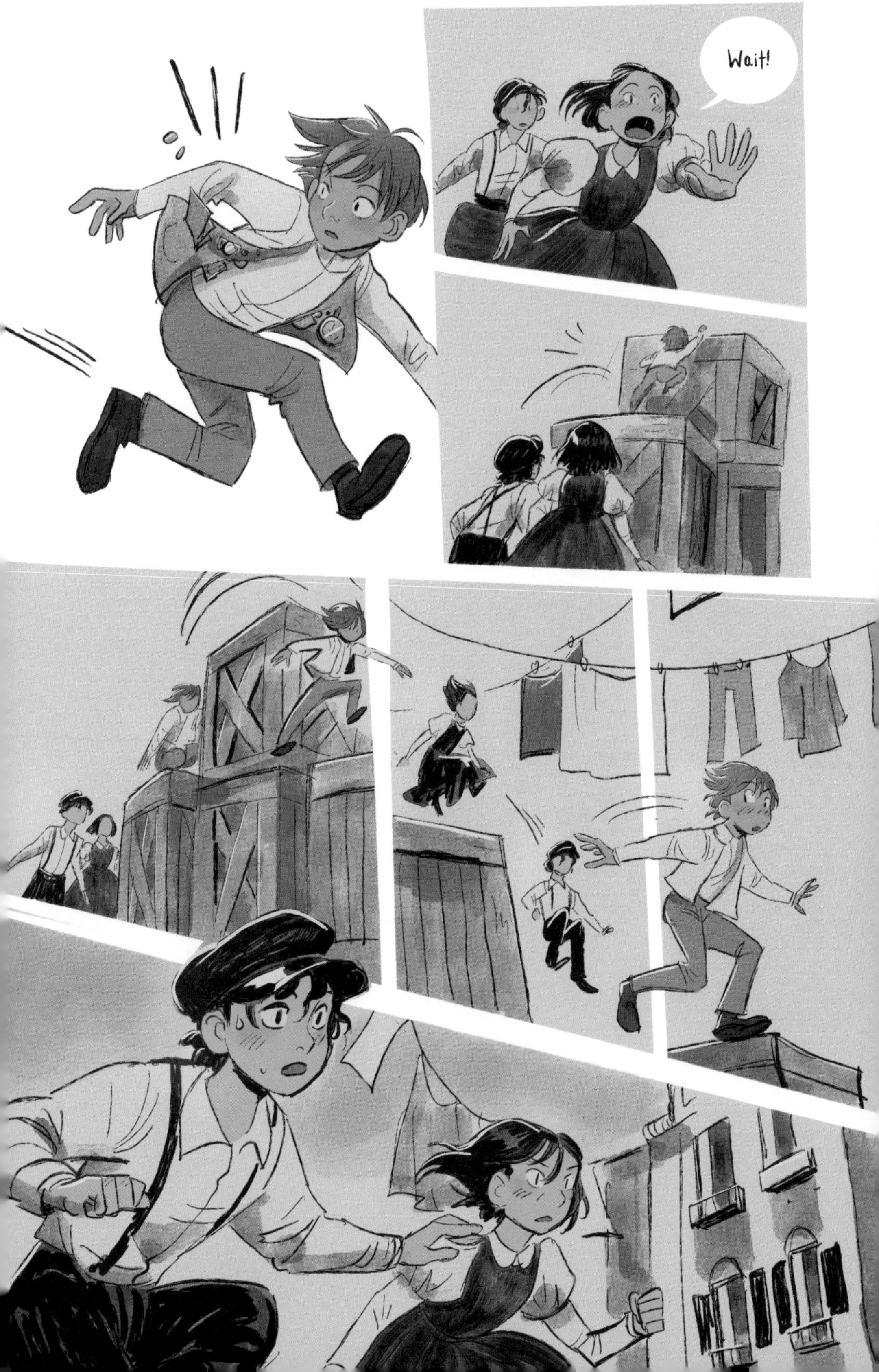
Wait!

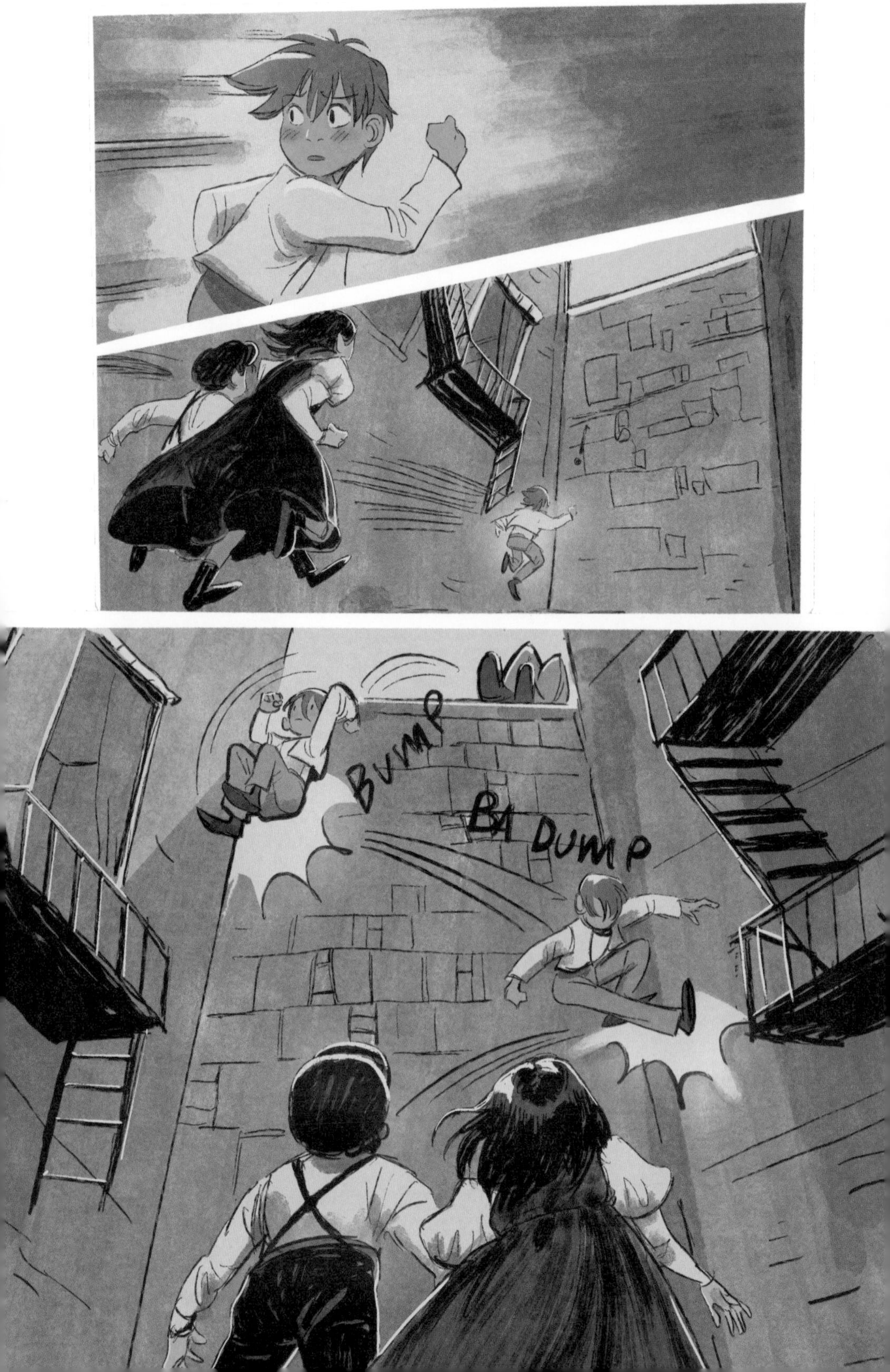
BUMP
BA DUMP

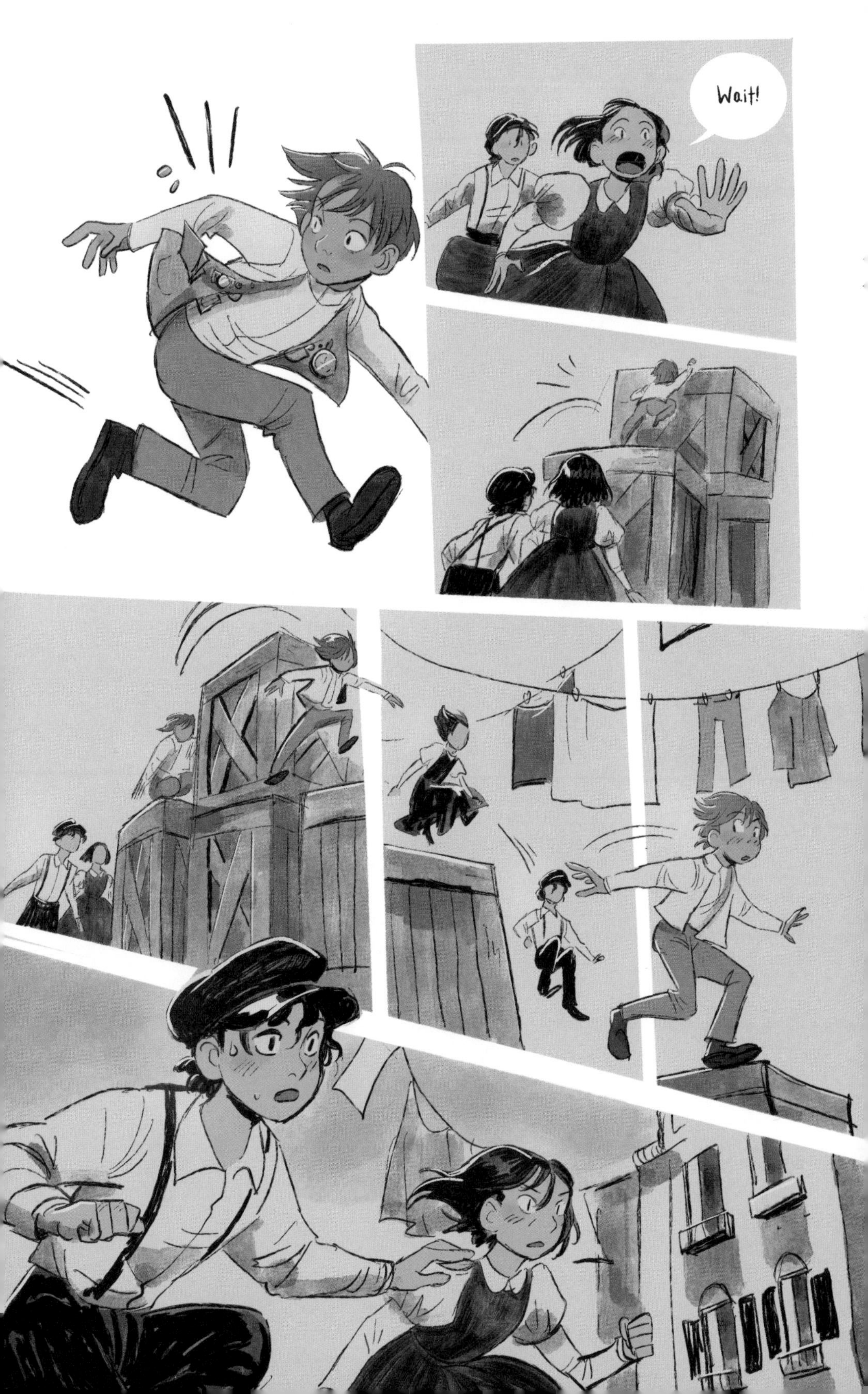
Wait!

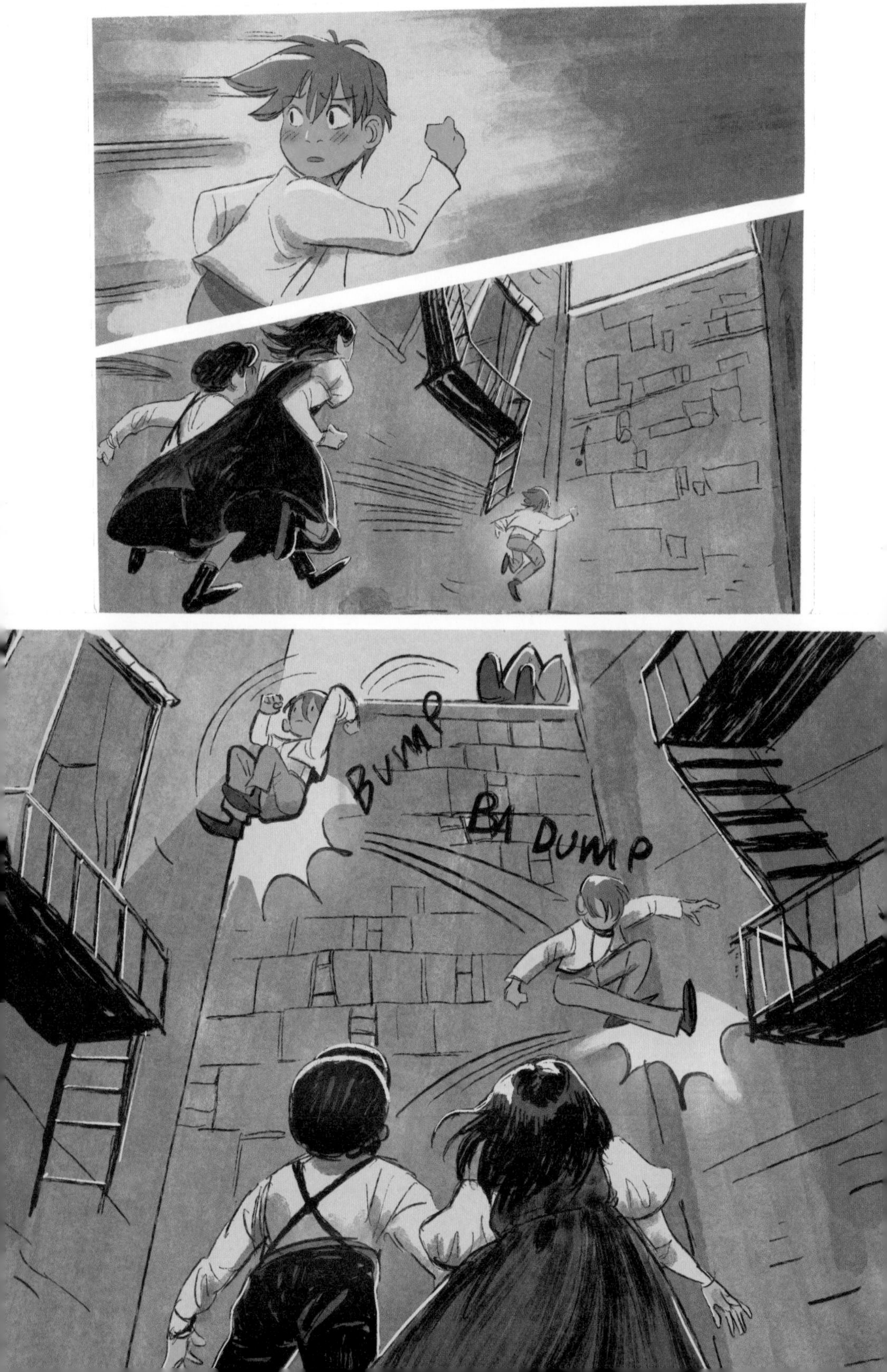
BUMP
BA DUMP

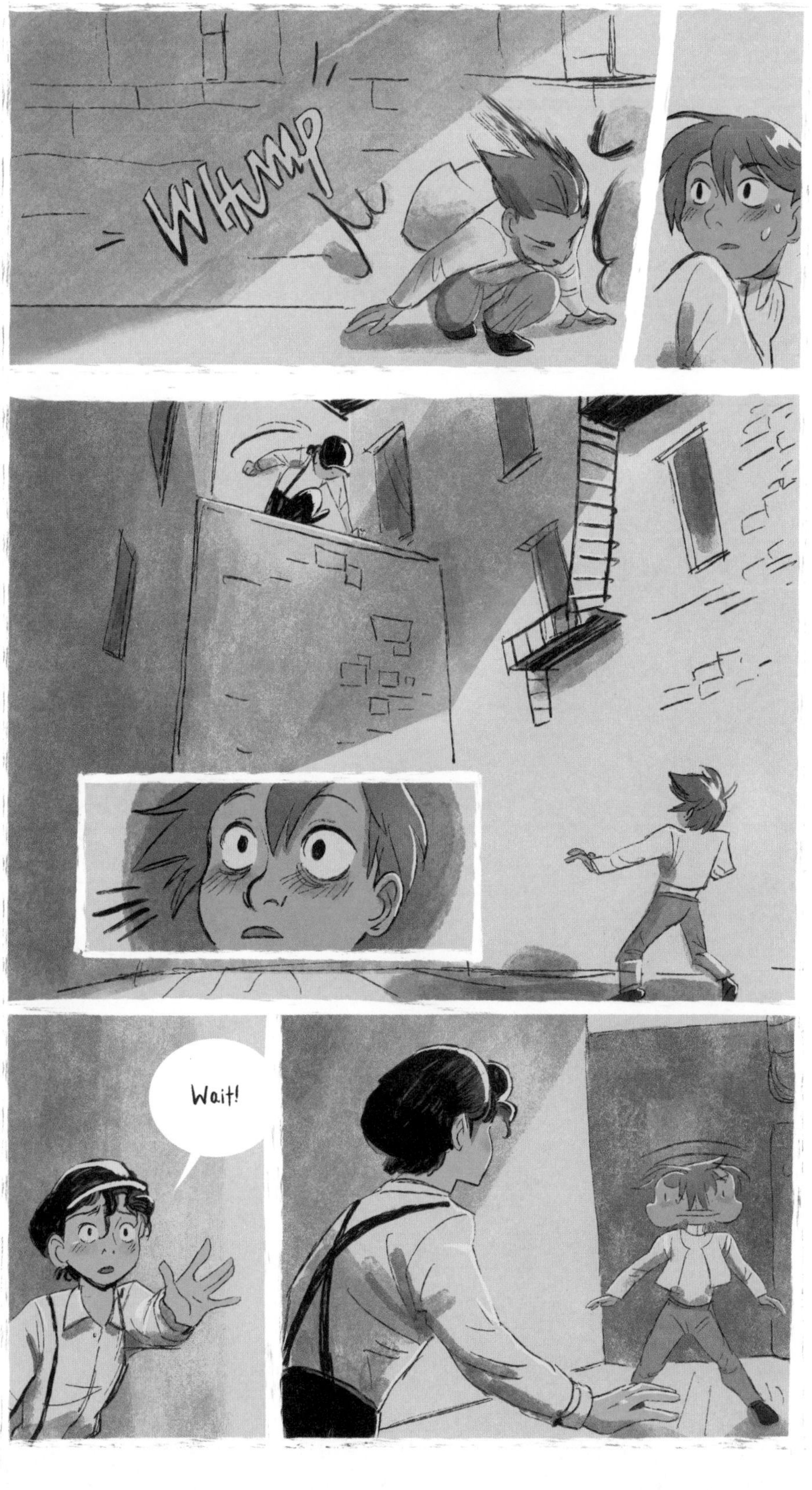
WHUMP
Wait!

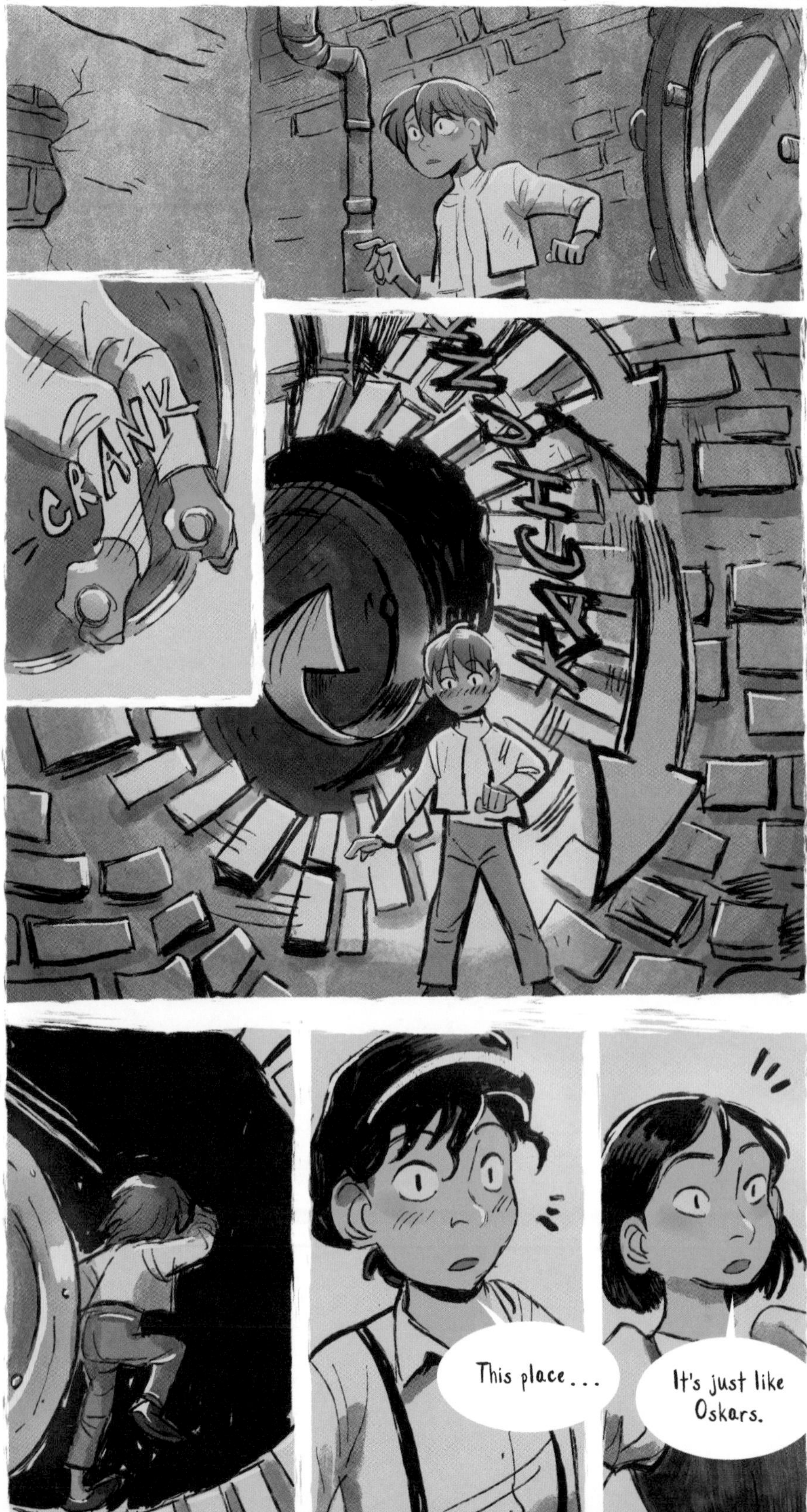
CRANK
KACHUNK
This place...
It's just like Oskars.

31

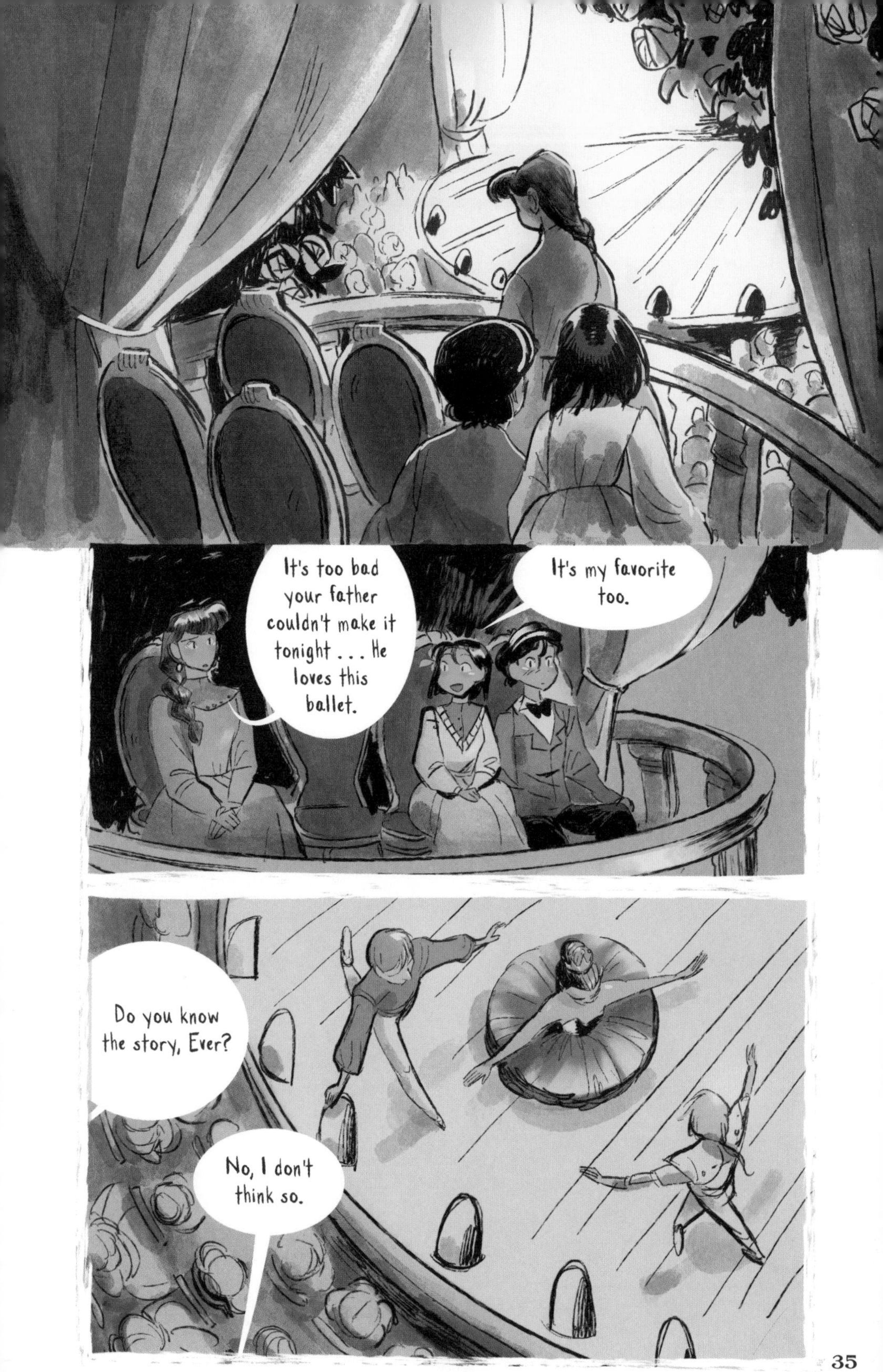
It's too bad your father couldn't make it tonight . . . He loves this ballet.
It's my favorite too.
Do you know the story, Ever?
No, I don't think so.

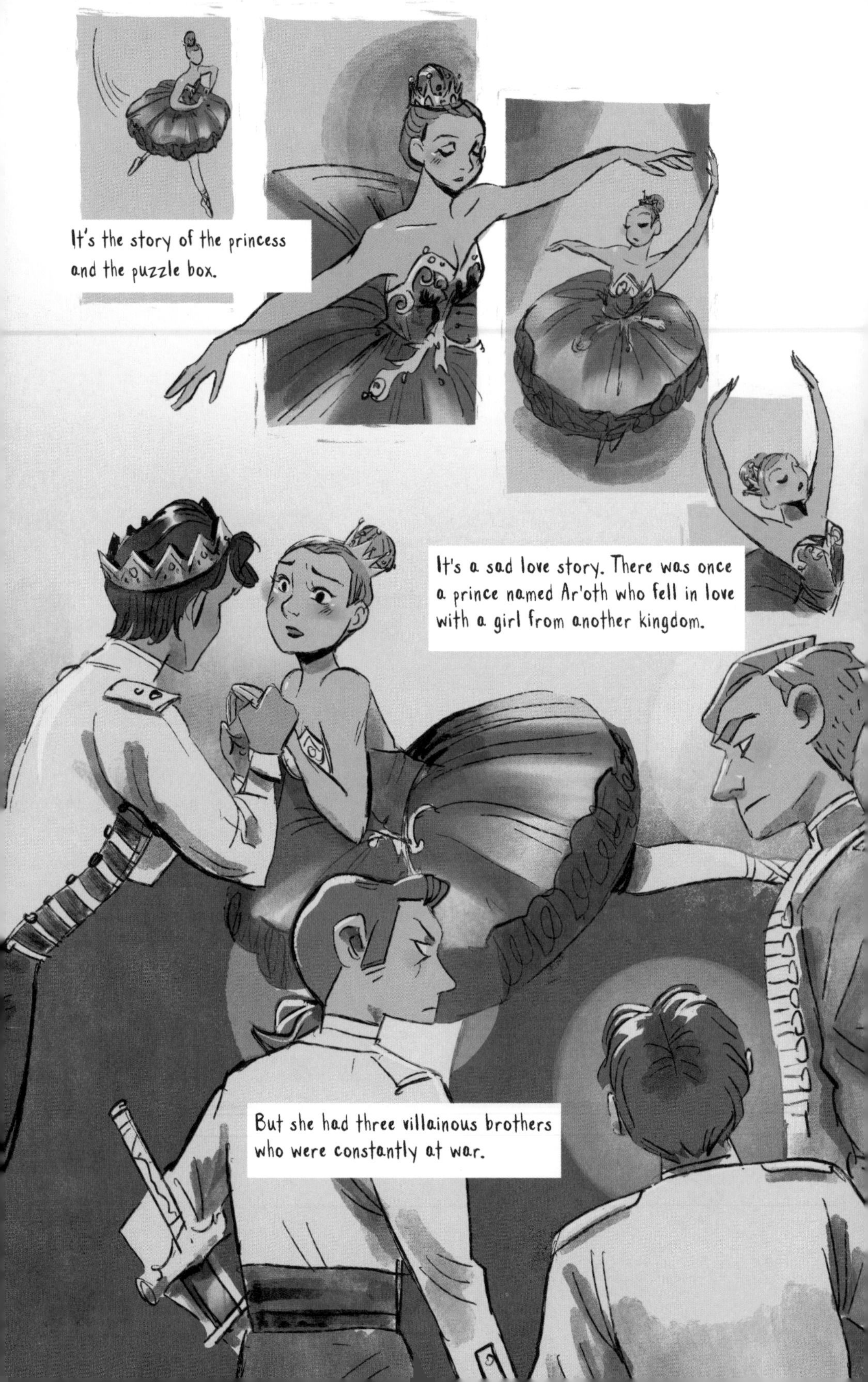
It's the story of the princess and the puzzle box.
It's a sad love story. There was once a prince named Ar'oth who fell in love with a girl from another kingdom.
But she had three villainous brothers who were constantly at war.

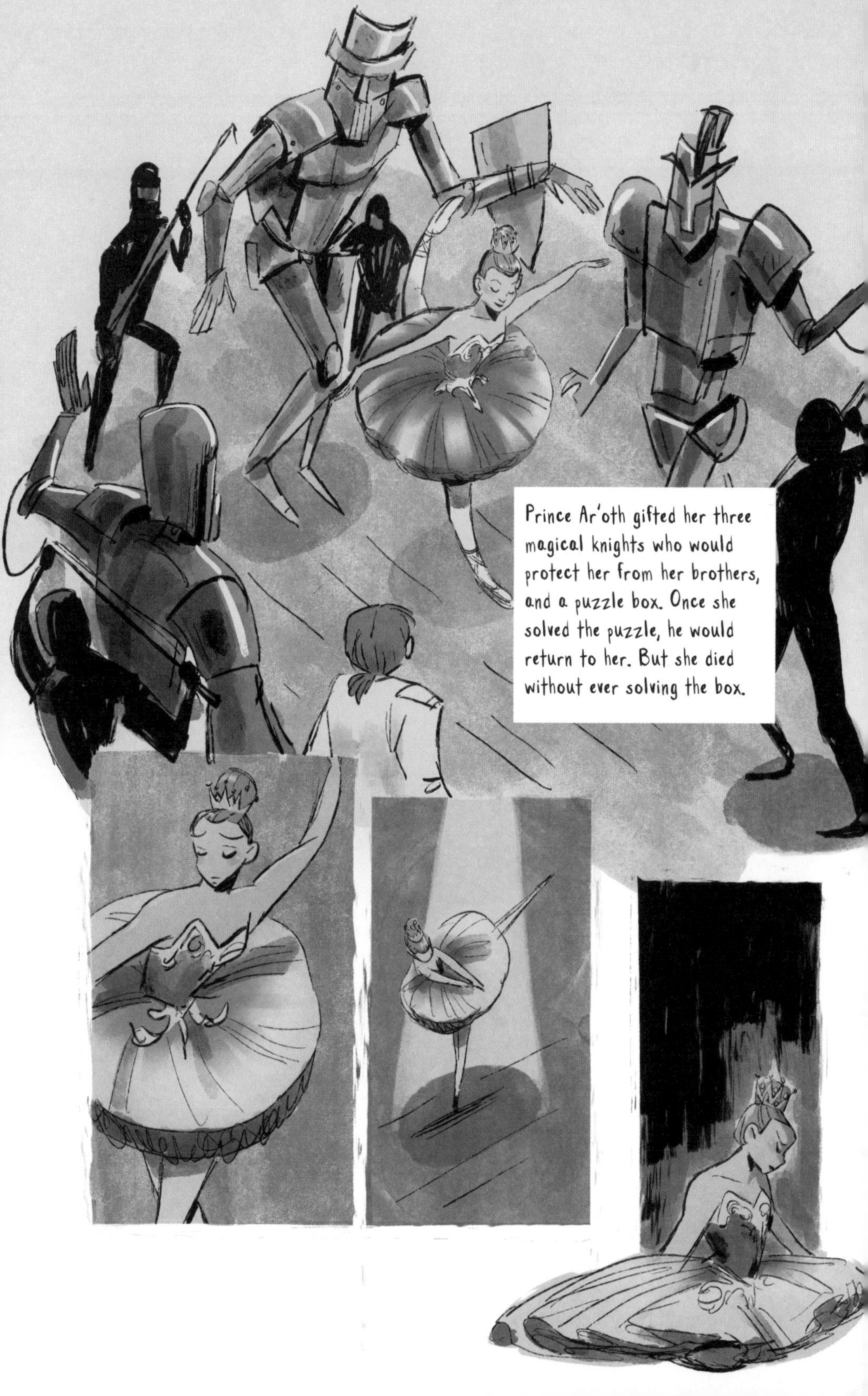
Prince Ar'oth gifted her three magical knights who would protect her from her brothers, and a puzzle box. Once she solved the puzzle, he would return to her. But she died without ever solving the box.

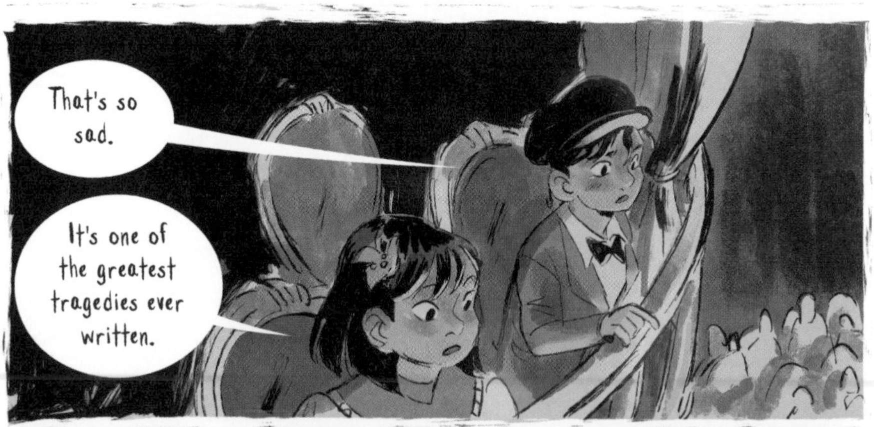
That's so sad.
It's one of the greatest tragedies ever written.
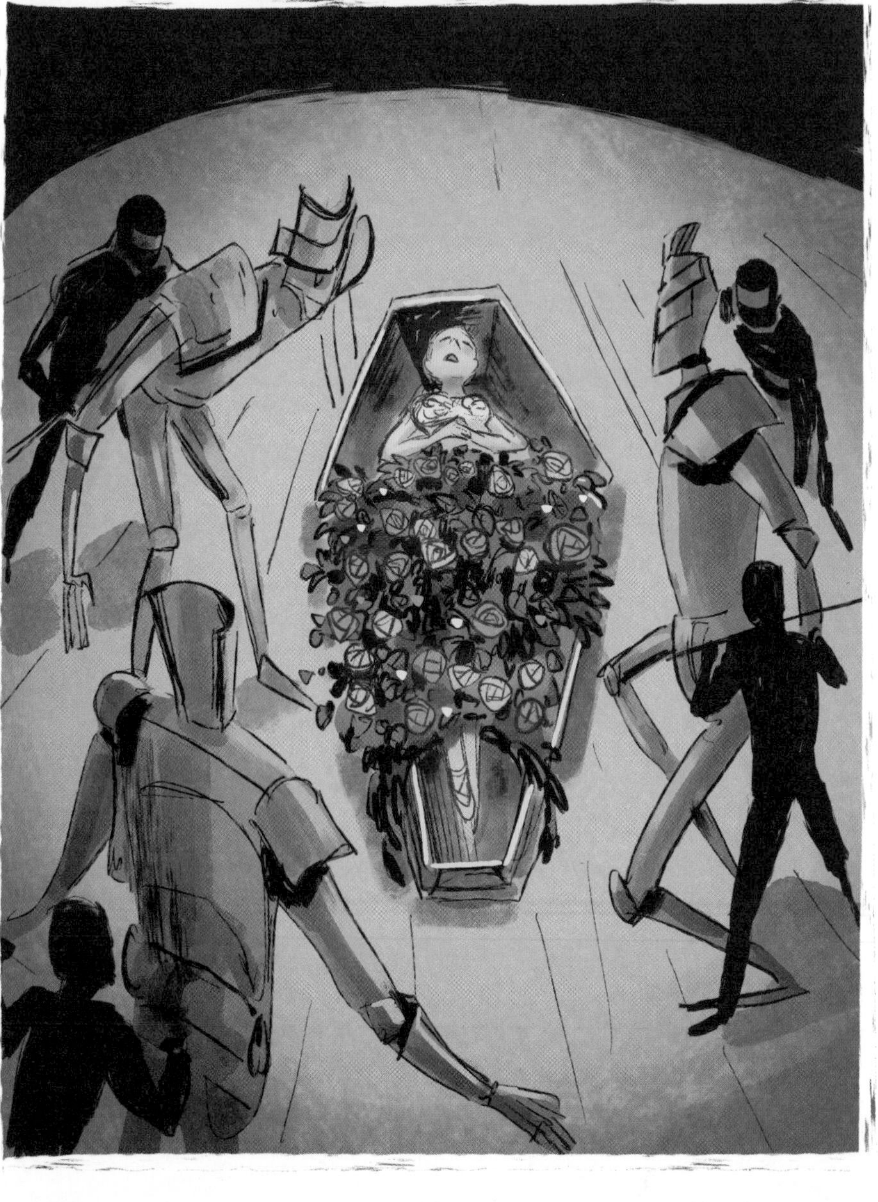

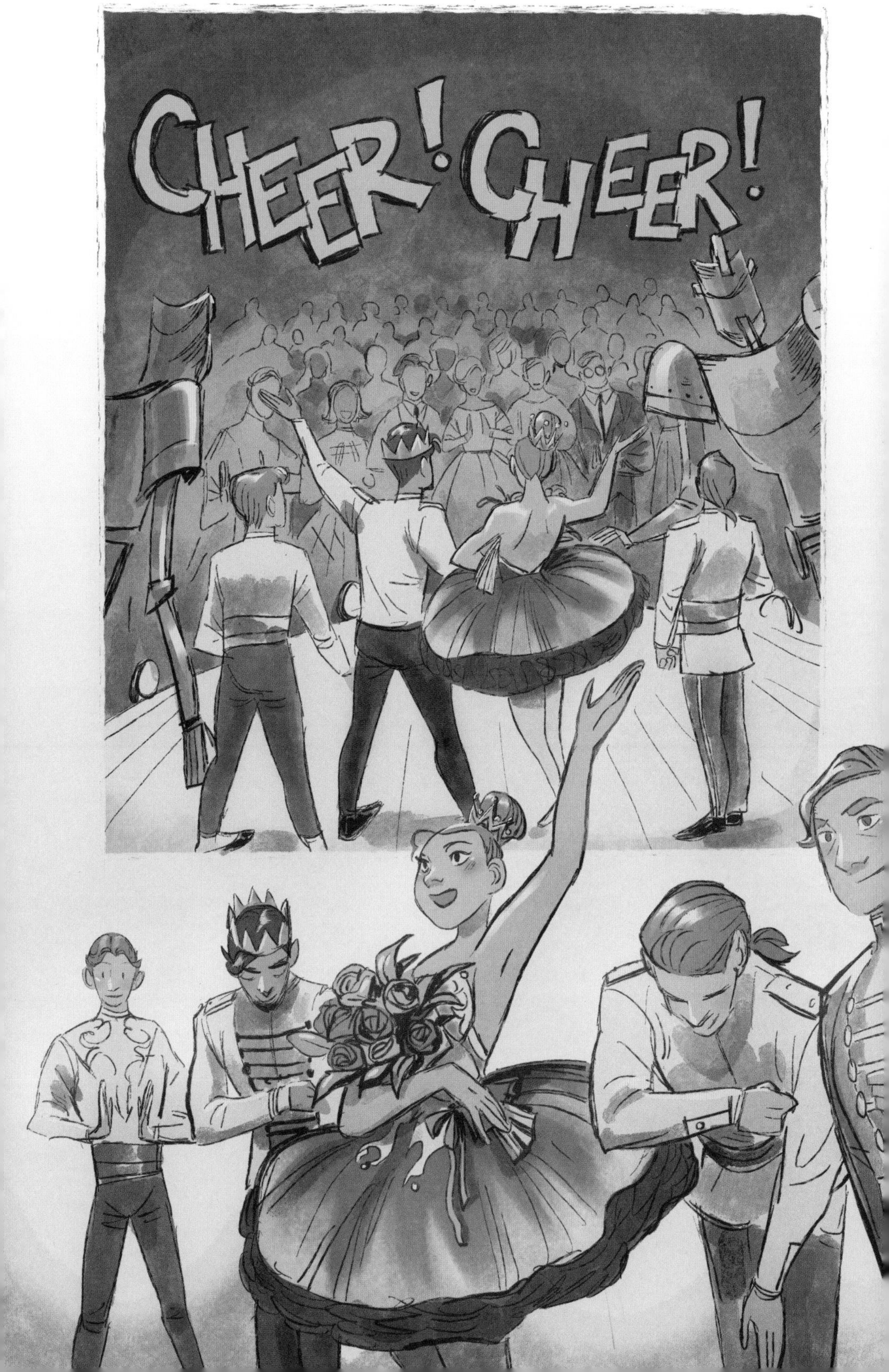
CHEER! CHEER!

41

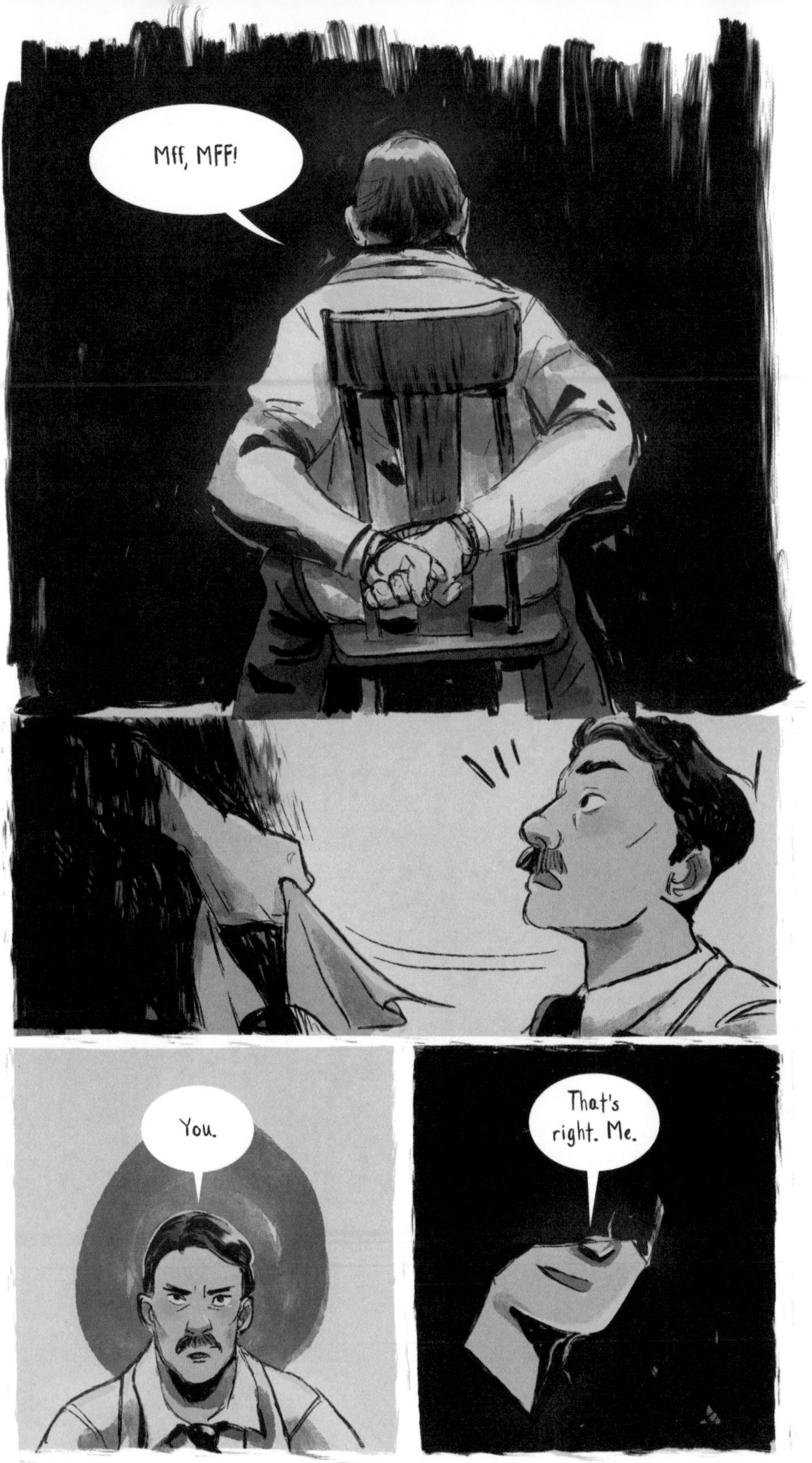
Mff, MFF!
You.
That's right. Me.

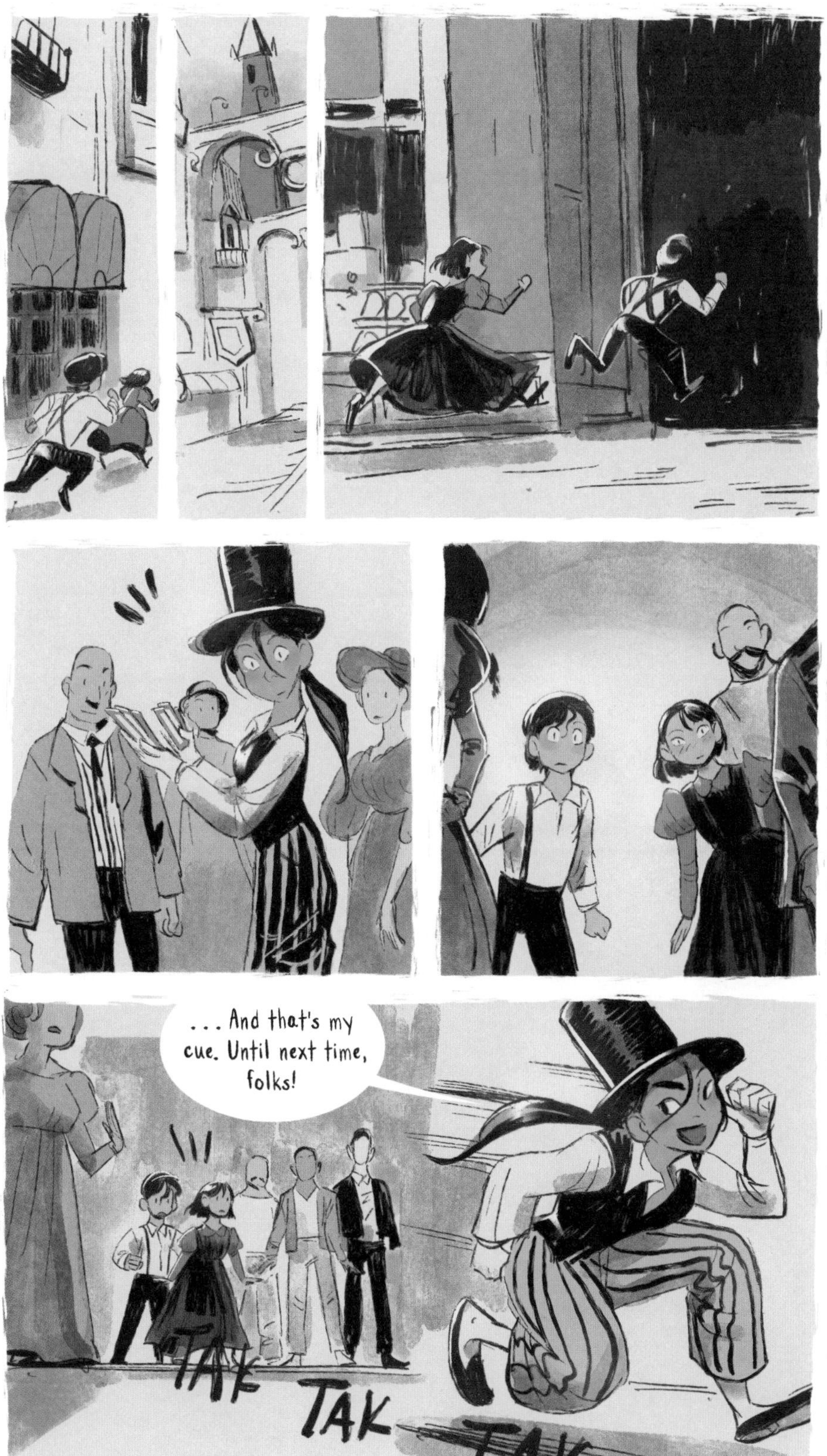
... And that's my cue. Until next time, folks!
TAK
TAK

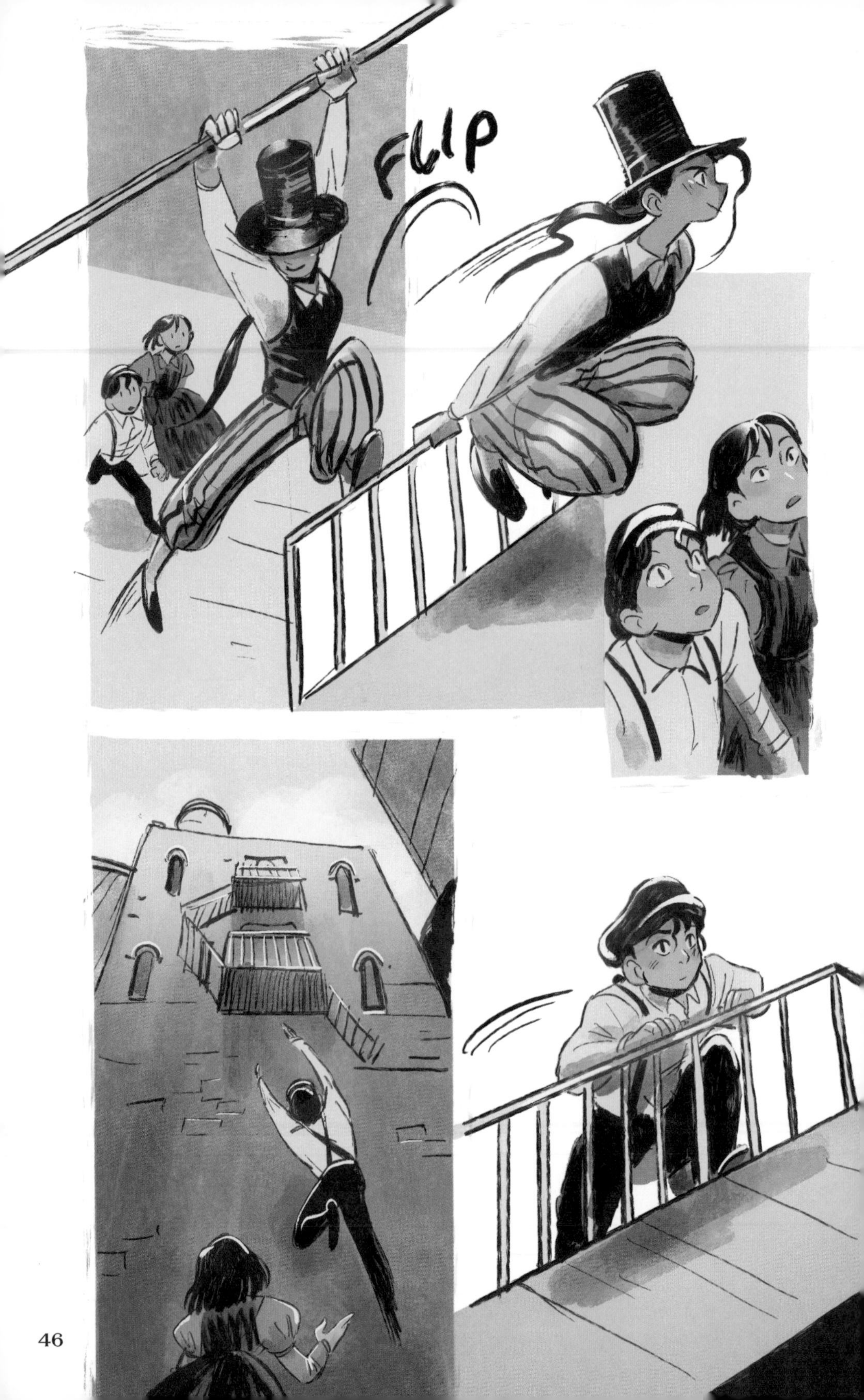
FLIP

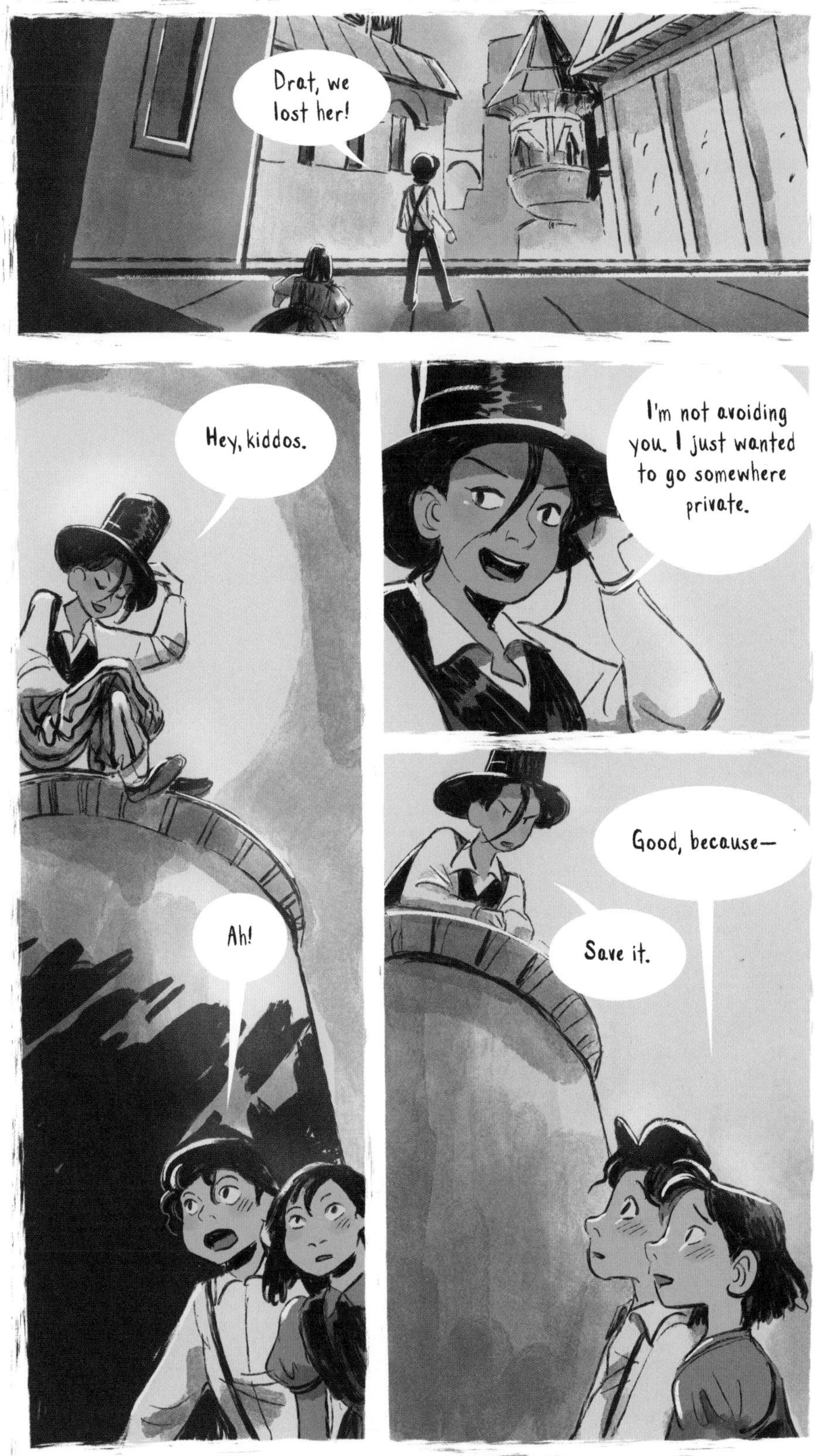
Drat, we lost her!
Hey, kiddos.
I'm not avoiding you. I just wanted to go somewhere private.
Ah!
Good, because—
Save it.

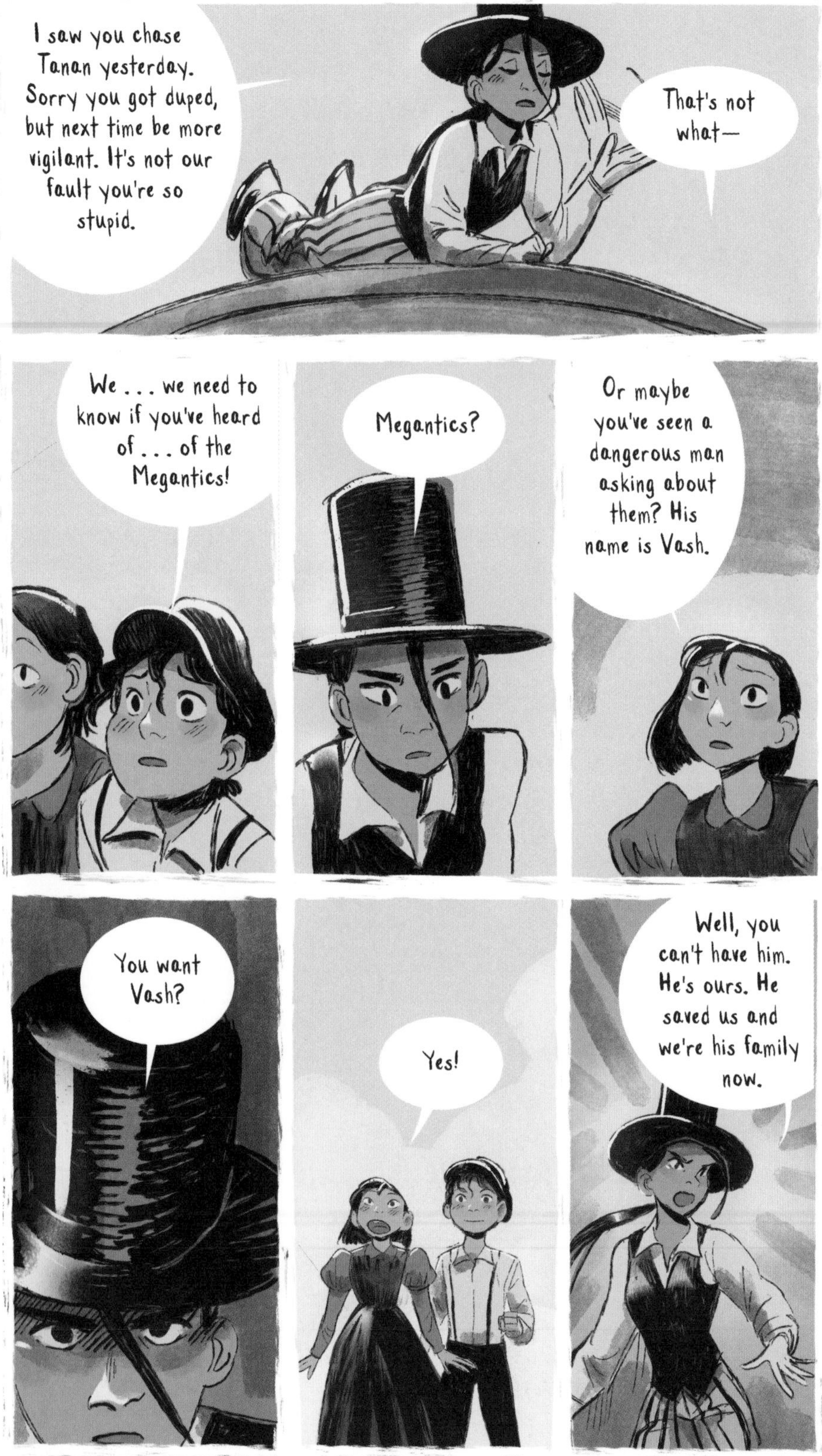
I saw you chase Tanan yesterday. Sorry you got duped, but next time be more vigilant. It's not our fault you're so stupid.
That's not what—
We . . . we need to know if you've heard of . . . of the Megantics!
Megantics?
Or maybe you've seen a dangerous man asking about them? His name is Vash.
You want Vash?
Yes!
Well, you can't have him. He's ours. He saved us and we're his family now.

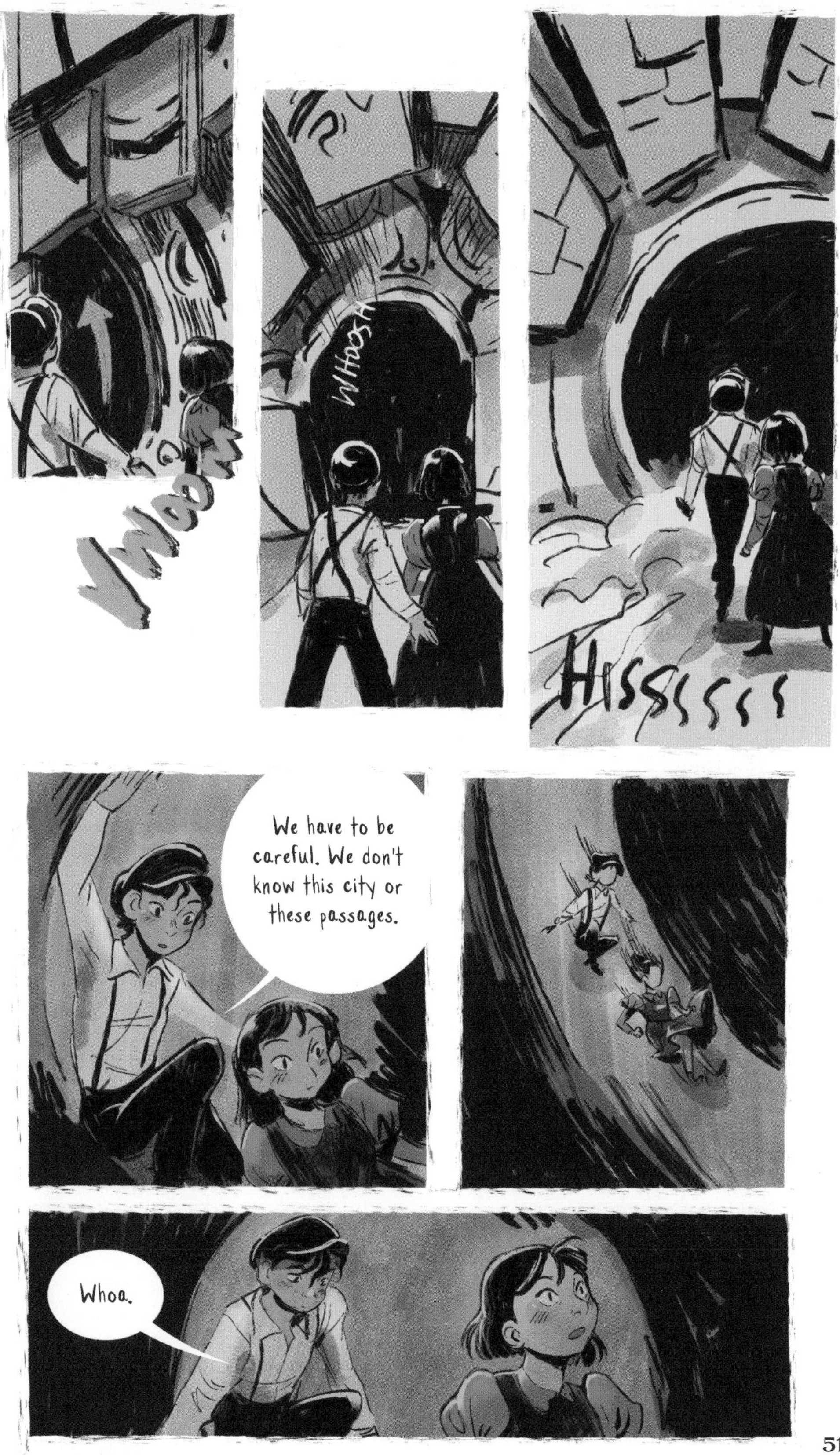
VWOO
WHOOSH
HISSSSSS
We have to be careful. We don't know this city or these passages.
Whoa.

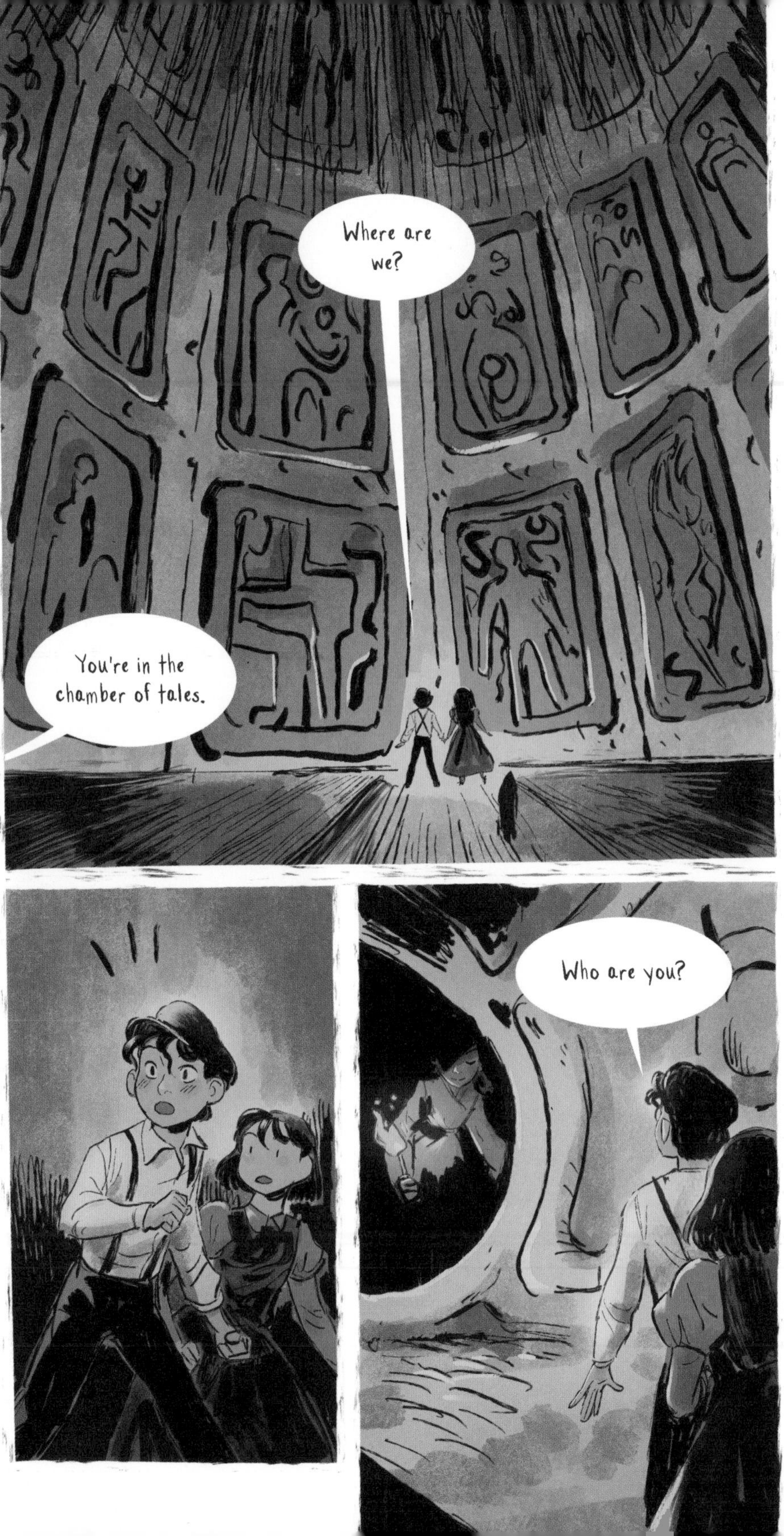
Where are we?
You're in the chamber of tales.
Who are you?

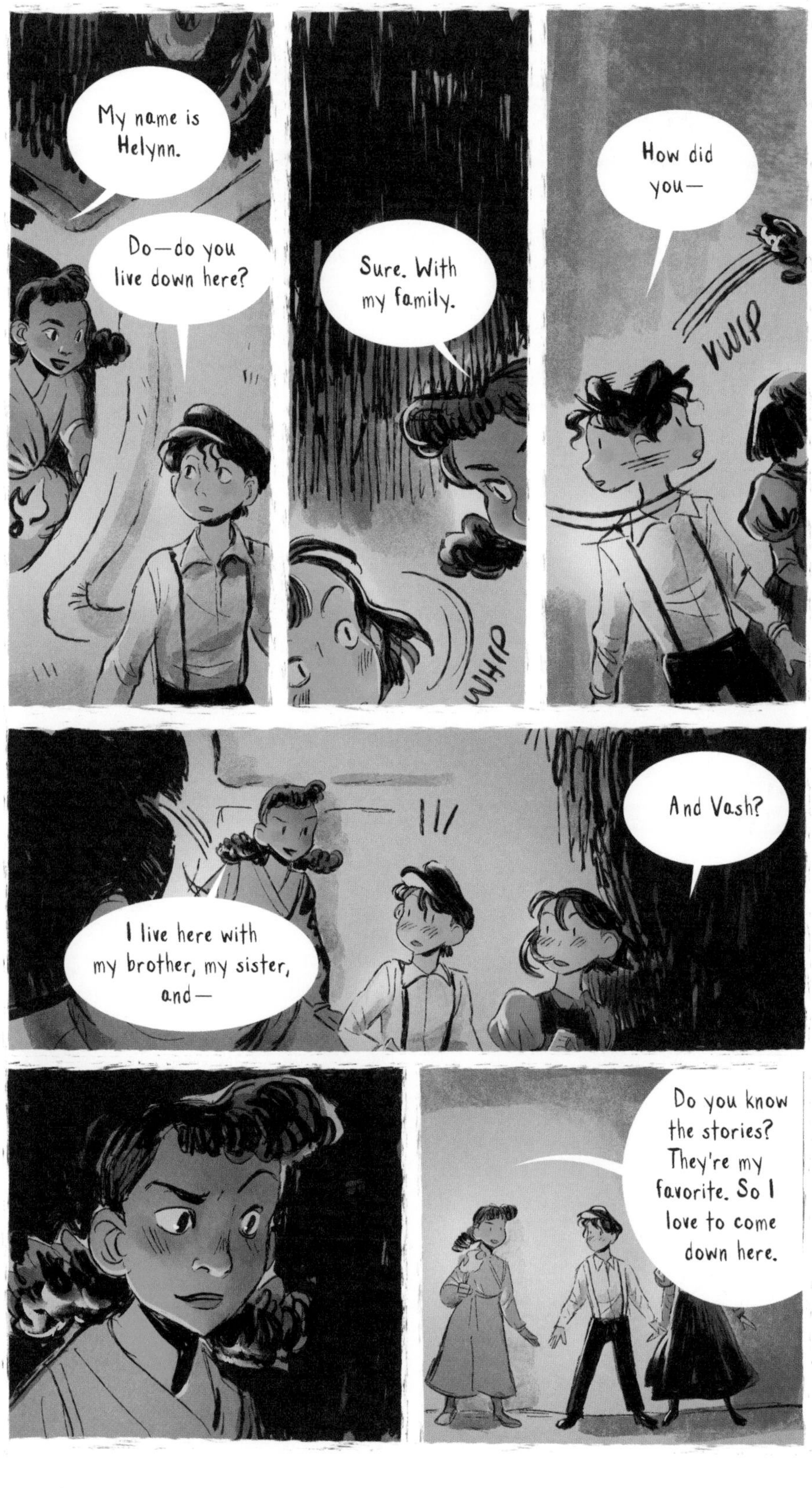

My name is Helynn.
Do—do you live down here?
Sure. With my family.
WHIP
How did you—
VWIP
I live here with my brother, my sister, and—
And Vash?
Do you know the stories? They're my favorite. So I love to come down here.

55

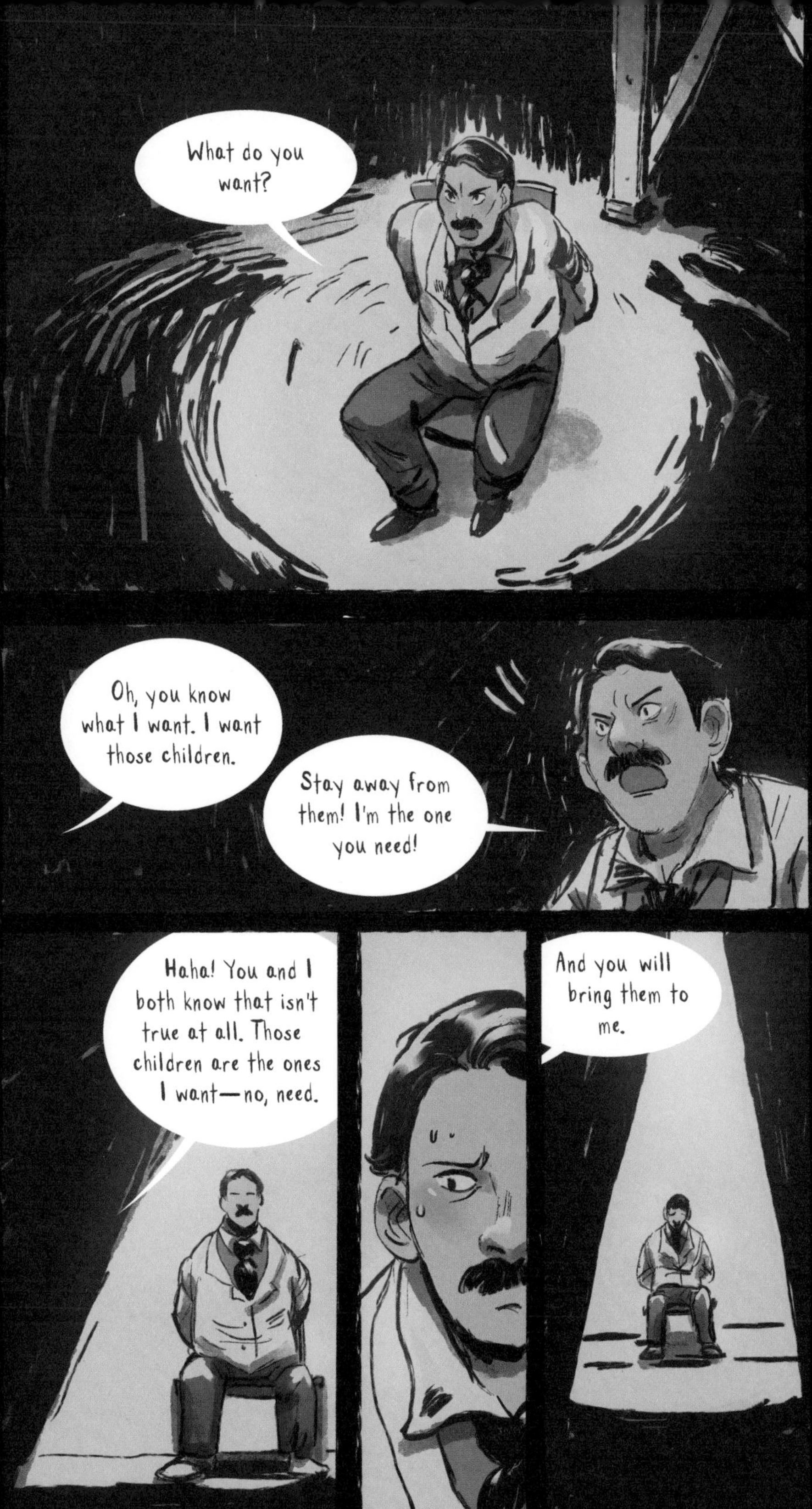
What do you want?
Oh, you know what I want. I want those children.
Stay away from them! I'm the one you need!
Haha! You and I both know that isn't true at all. Those children are the ones I want—no, need.
And you will bring them to me.

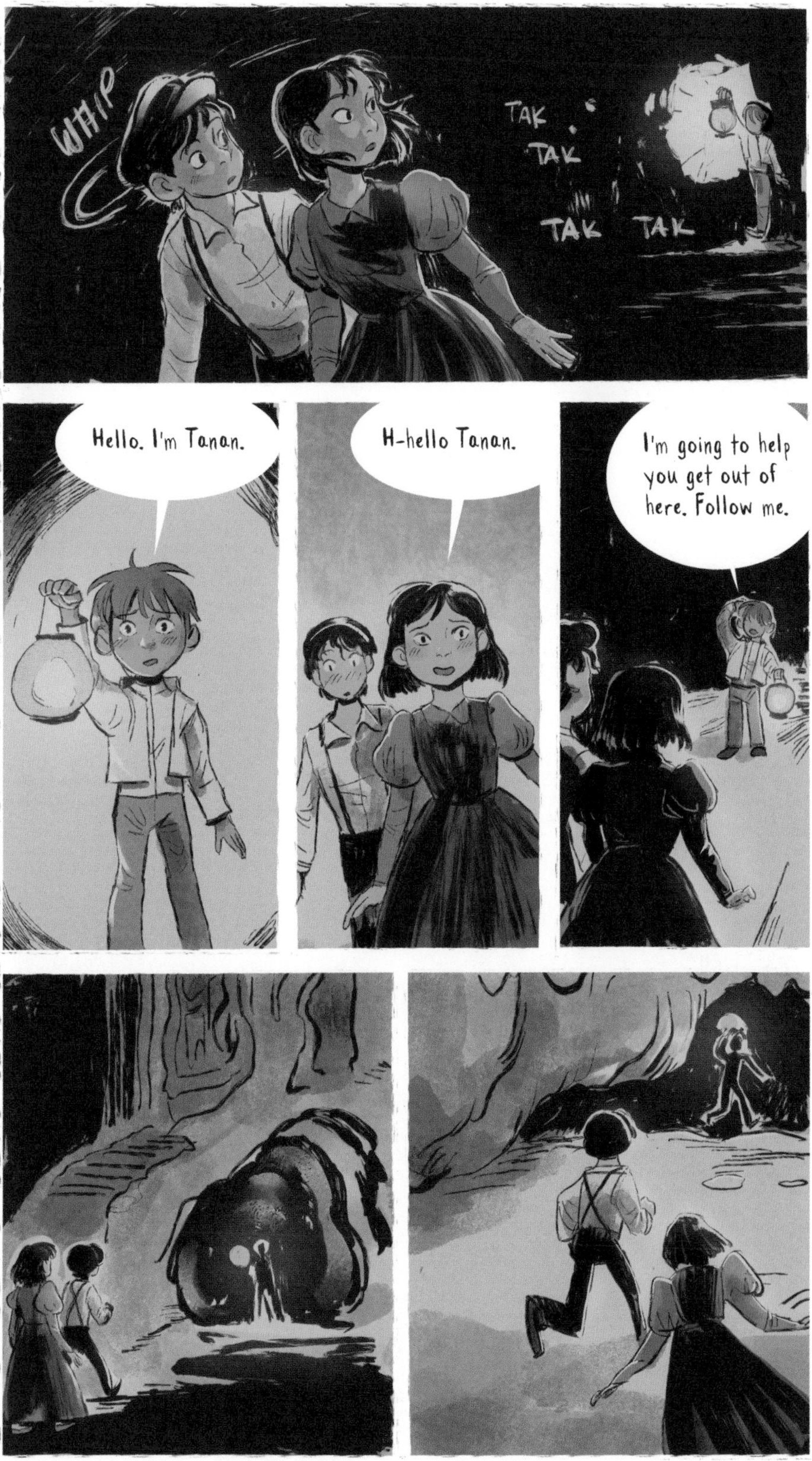
WHIP
TAK
TAK
TAK TAK
Hello. I'm Tanan.
H-hello Tanan.
I'm going to help you get out of here. Follow me.

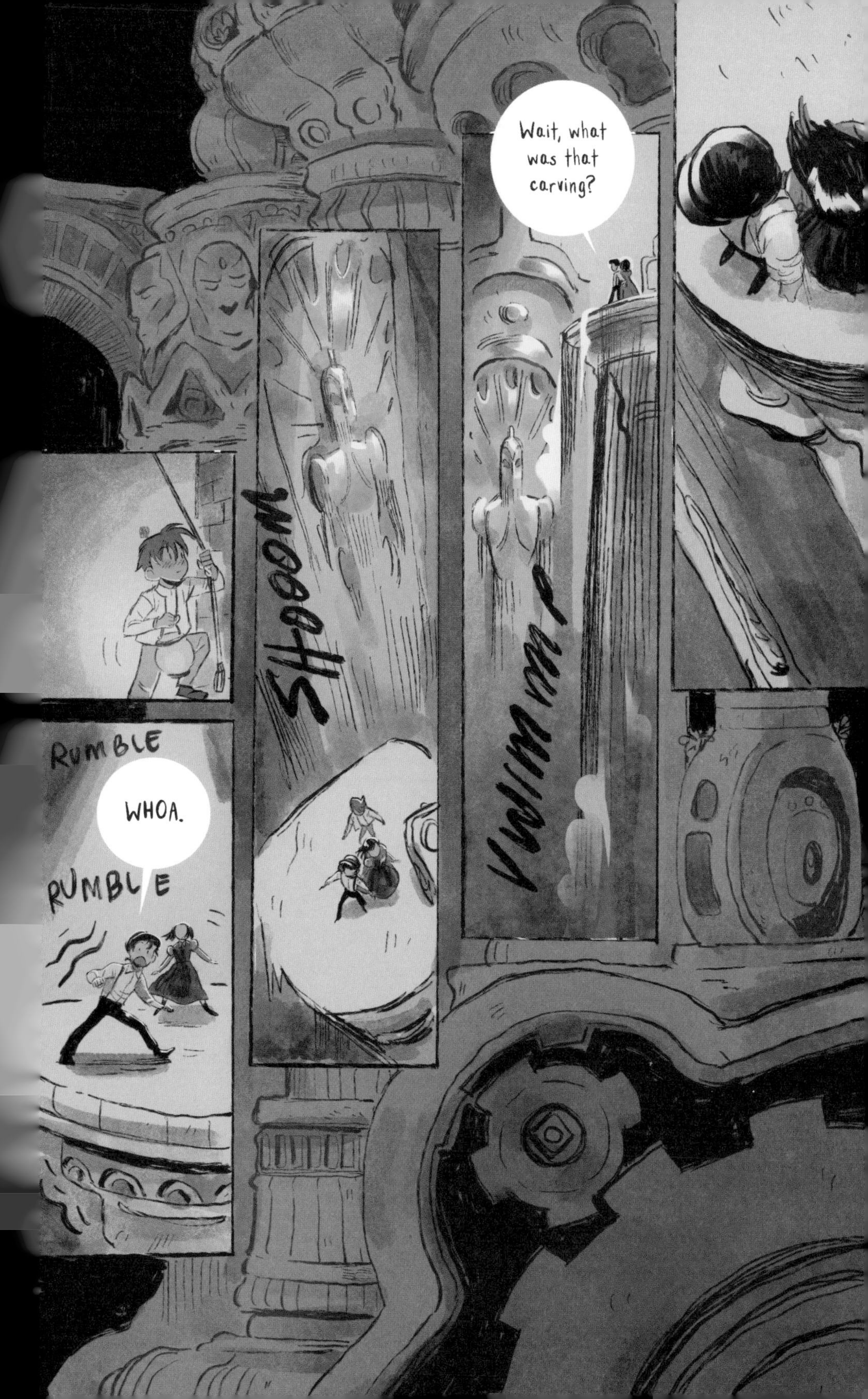
RUMBLE
WHOA.
RUMBLE
Wait, what was that carving?

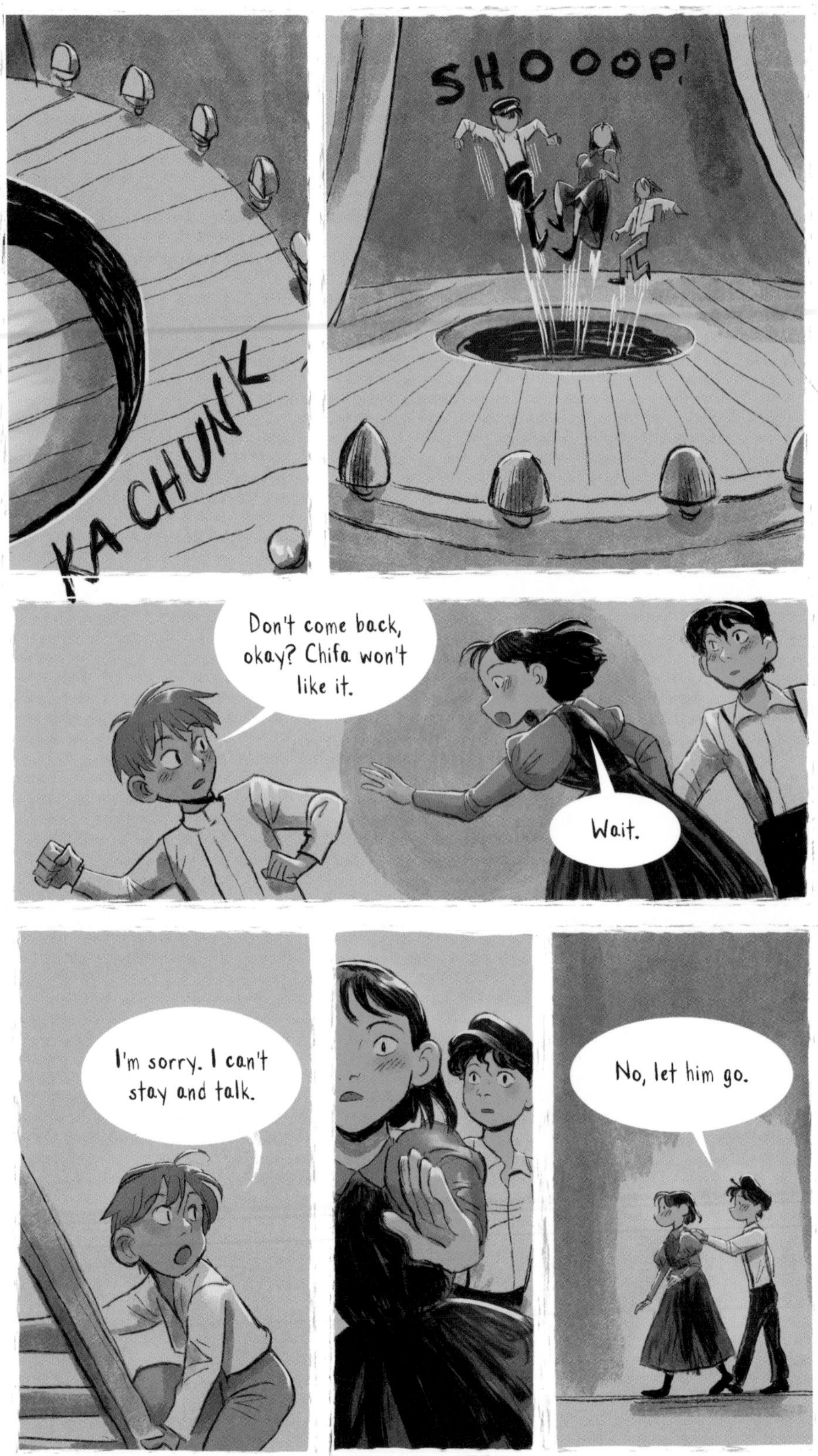
KA CHUNK
SHOOOP!
Don't come back, okay? Chifa won't like it.
Wait.
I'm sorry. I can't stay and talk.
No, let him go.

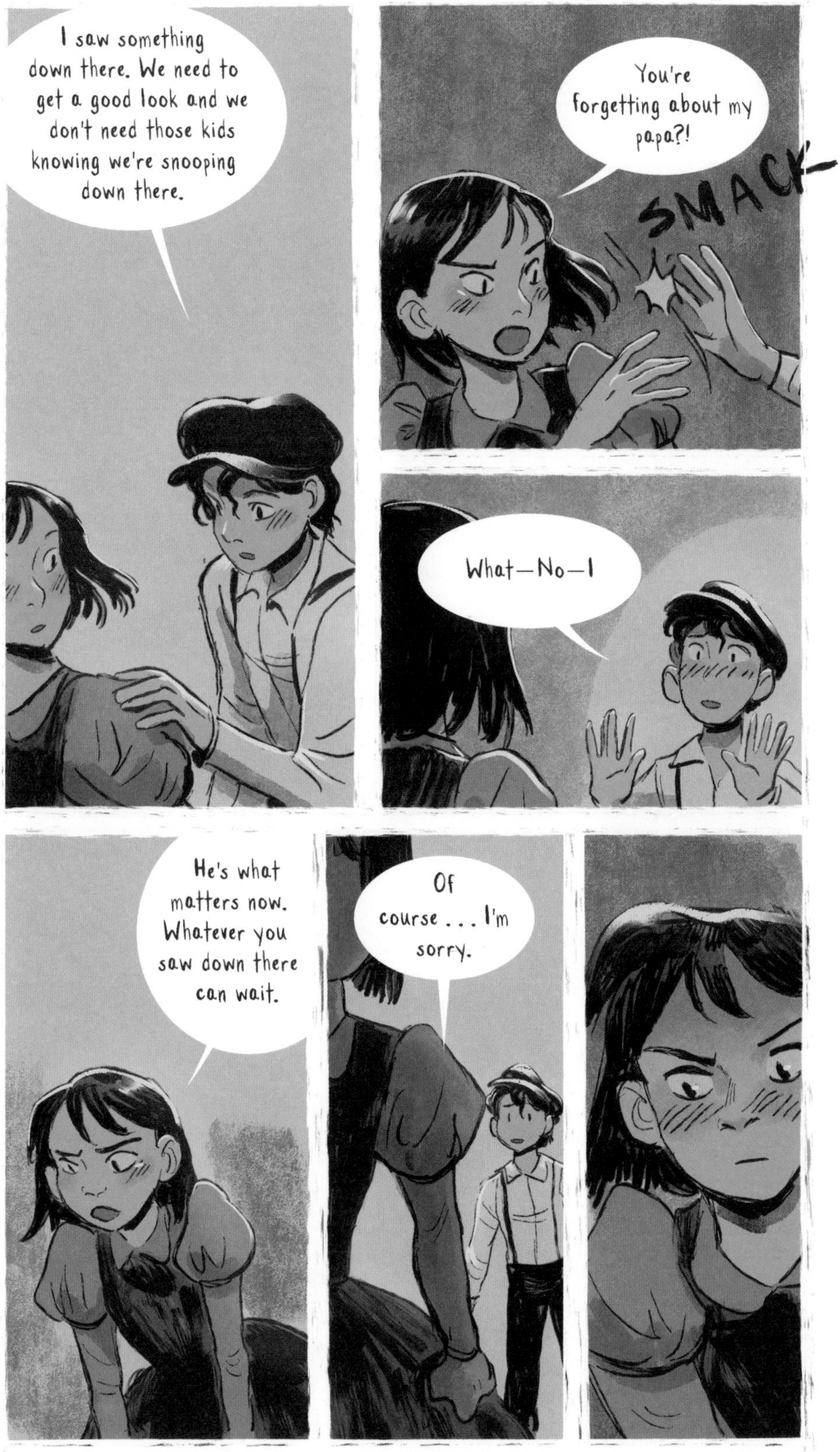
I saw something down there. We need to get a good look and we don't need those kids knowing we're snooping down there.
You're forgetting about my papa?!
SMACK
What—No—I
He's what matters now. Whatever you saw down there can wait.
Of course . . . I'm sorry.

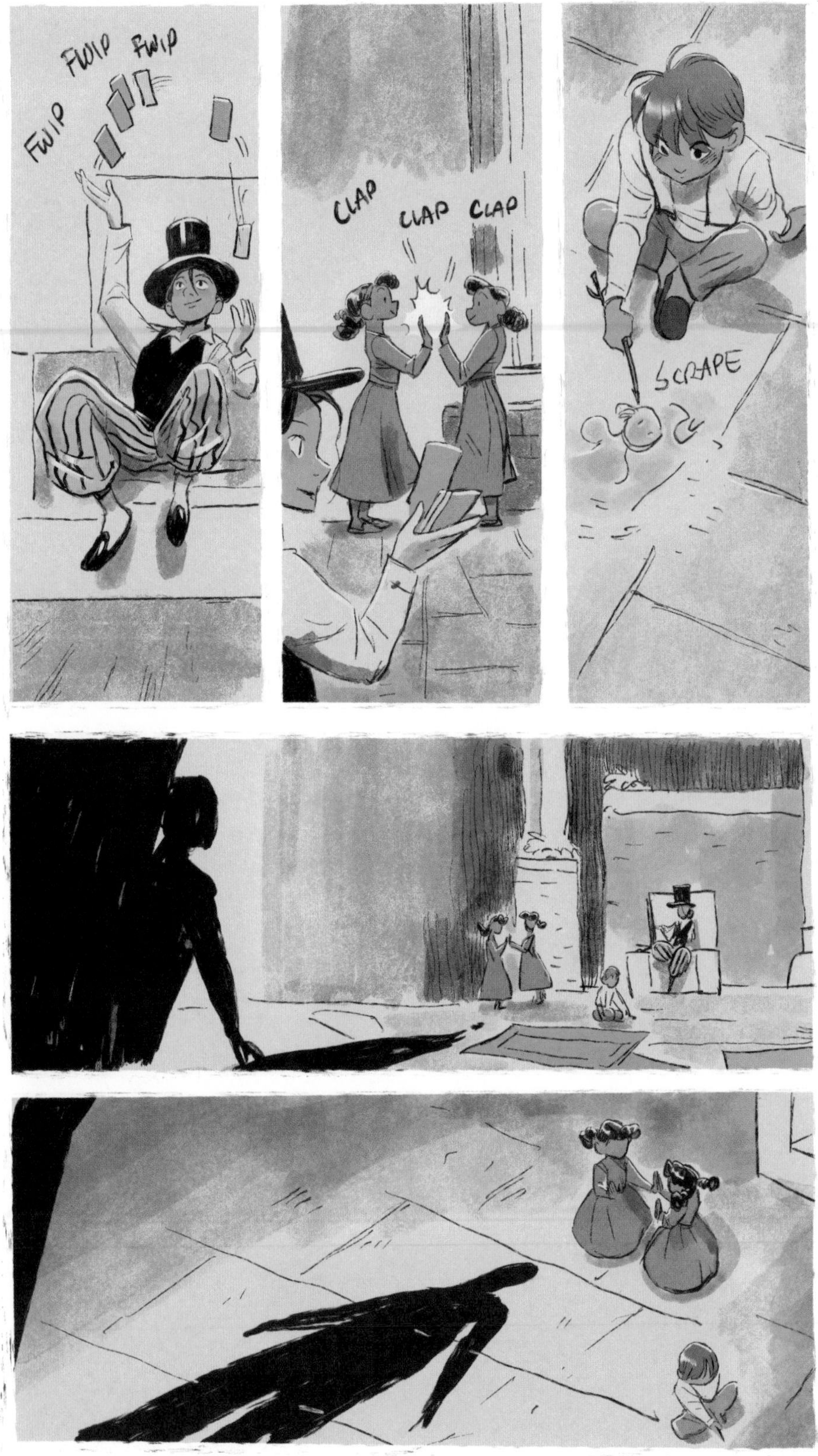
FWIP
FWIP FWIP
CLAP
CLAP CLAP
SCRAPE

Vash!

Look what I've been practicing!

Well, well. Look at you! I've brought something for you, my little sparrows, too.

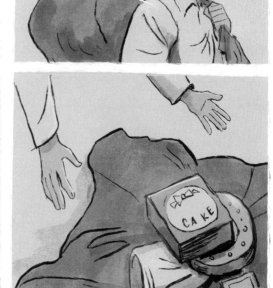

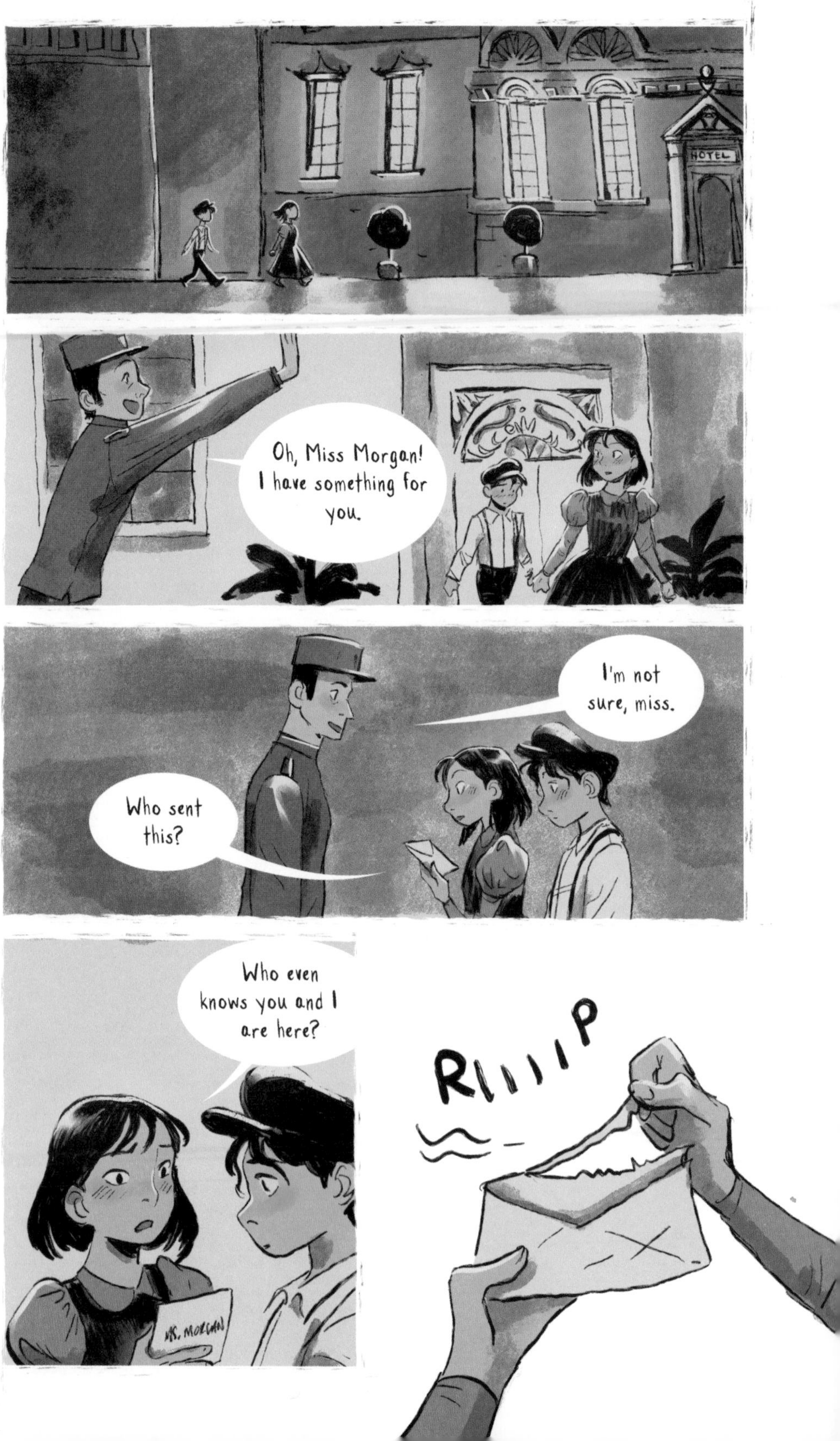
HOTEL
Oh, Miss Morgan! I have something for you.
Who sent this?
I'm not sure, miss.
Who even knows you and I are here?
MS. MORGAN
RIIIIP

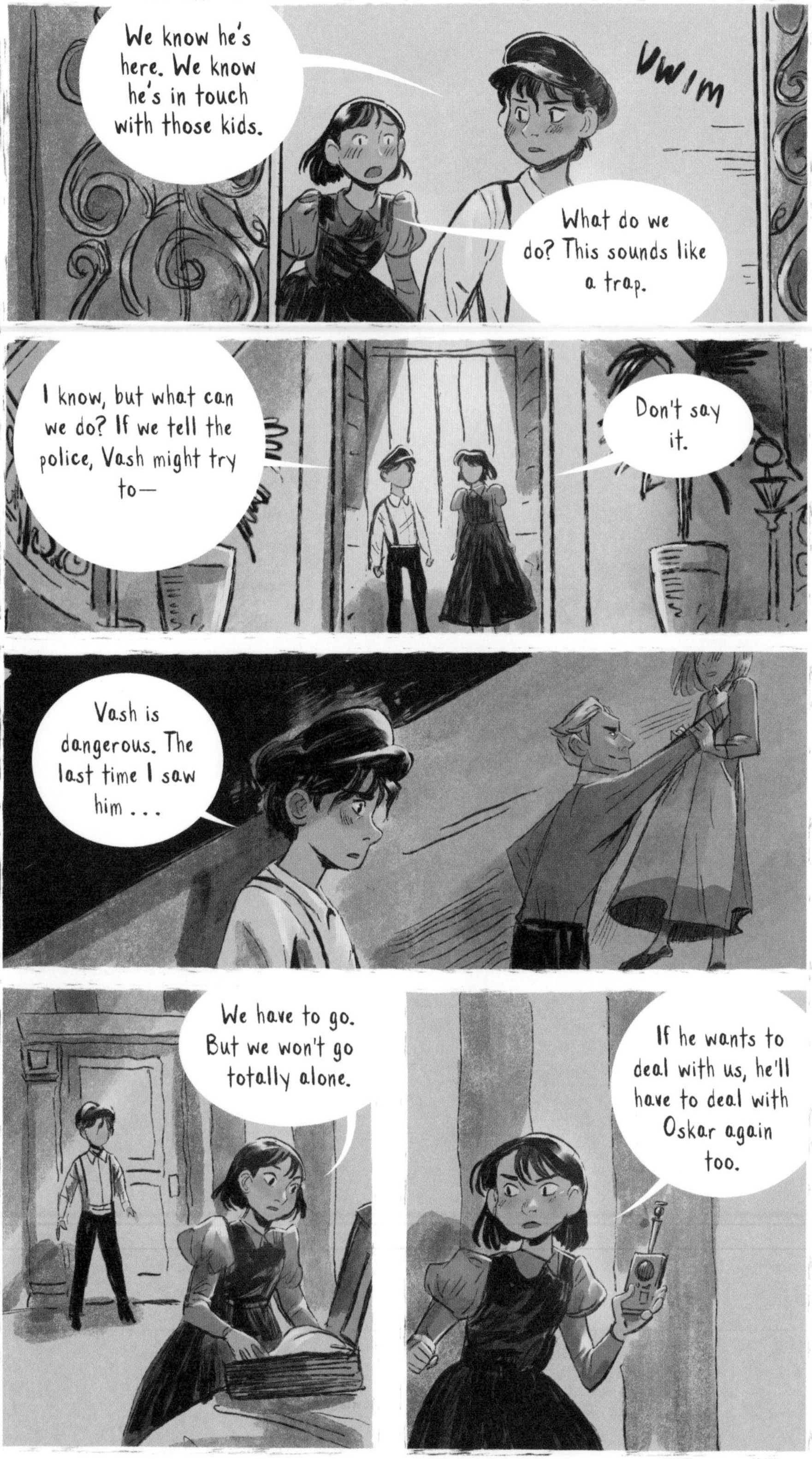
We know he's here. We know he's in touch with those kids.
UWIM
What do we do? This sounds like a trap.
I know, but what can we do? If we tell the police, Vash might try to—
Don't say it.
Vash is dangerous. The last time I saw him . . .
We have to go. But we won't go totally alone.
If he wants to deal with us, he'll have to deal with Oskar again too.

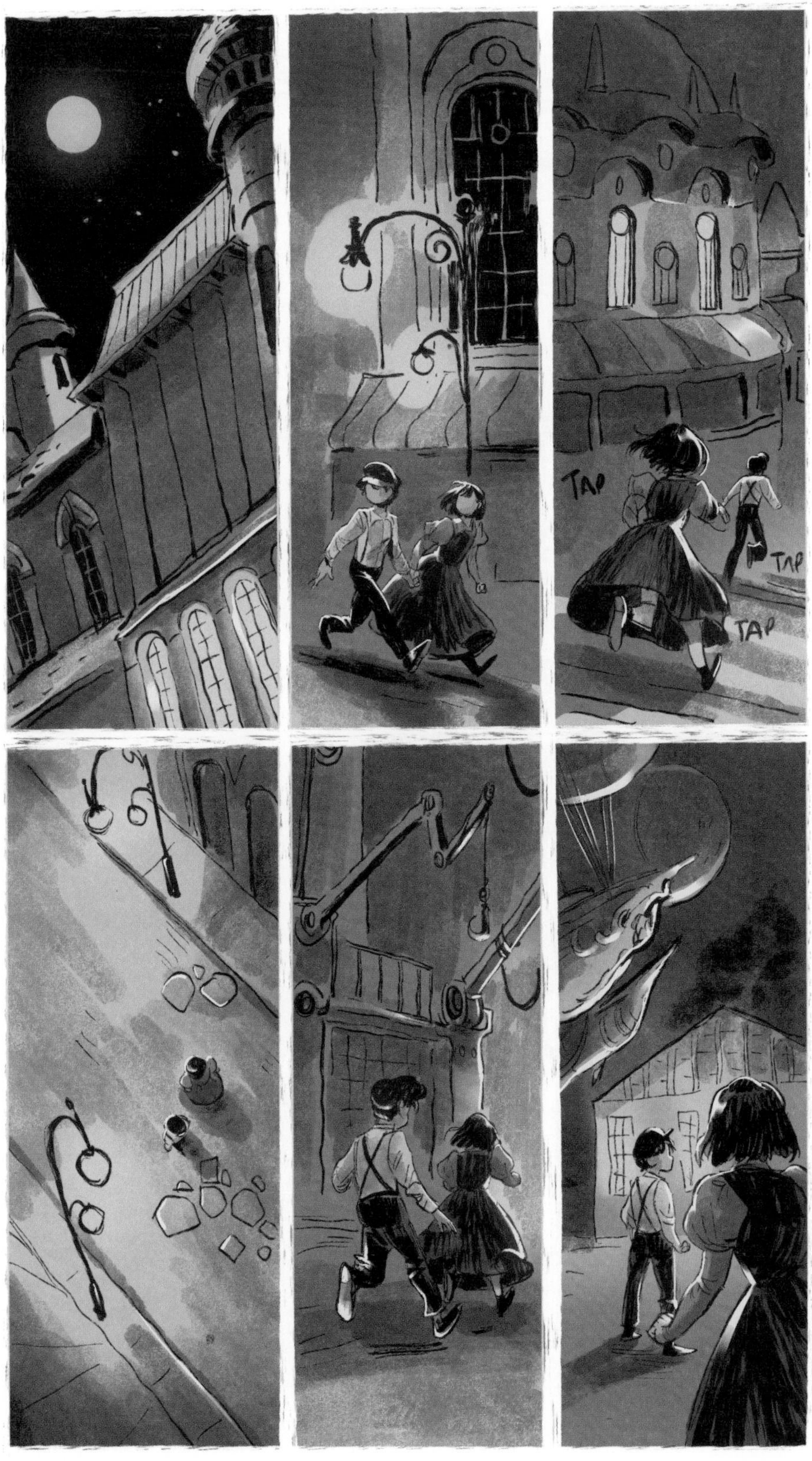
TAP
TAP
TAP

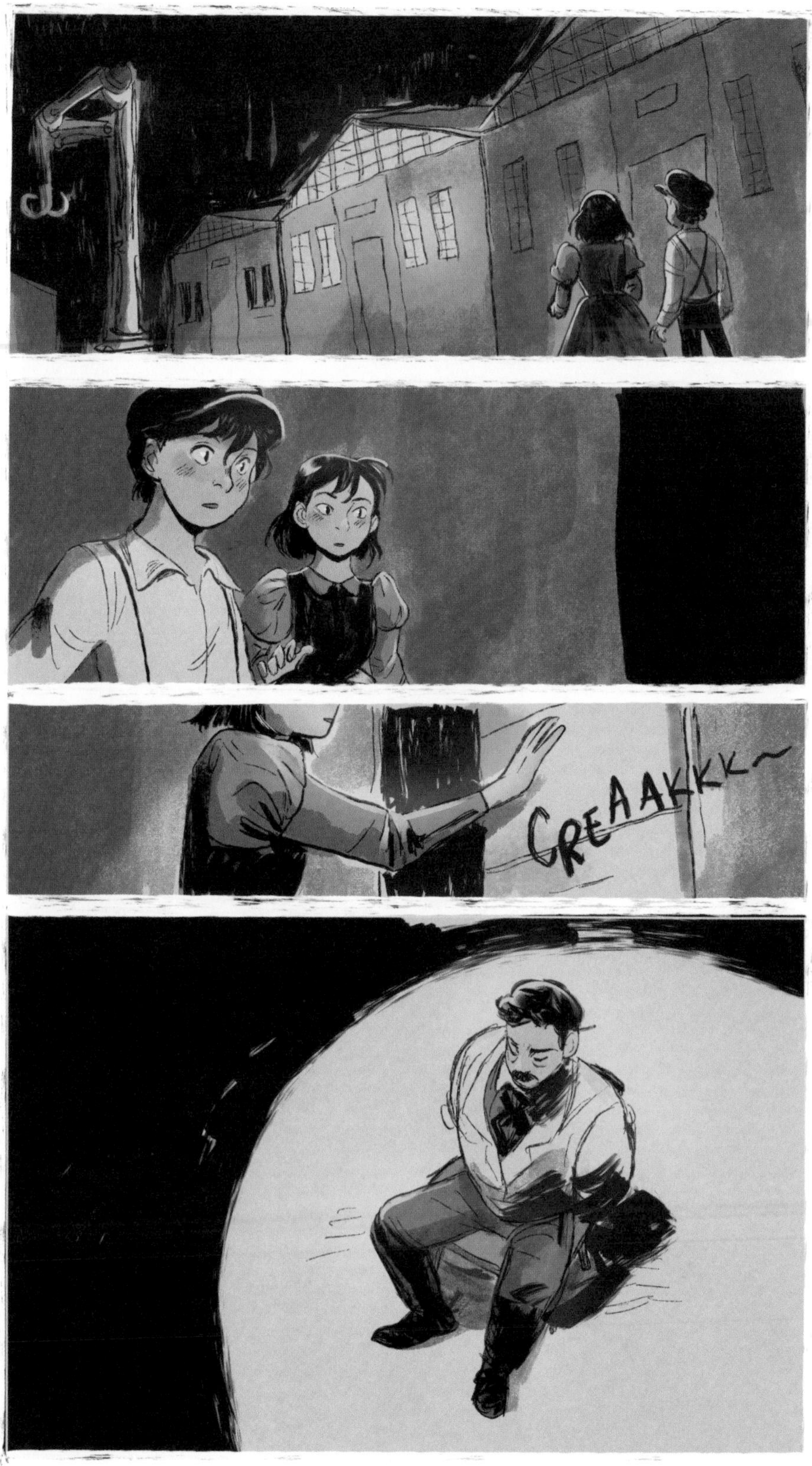
CREAAKKK~

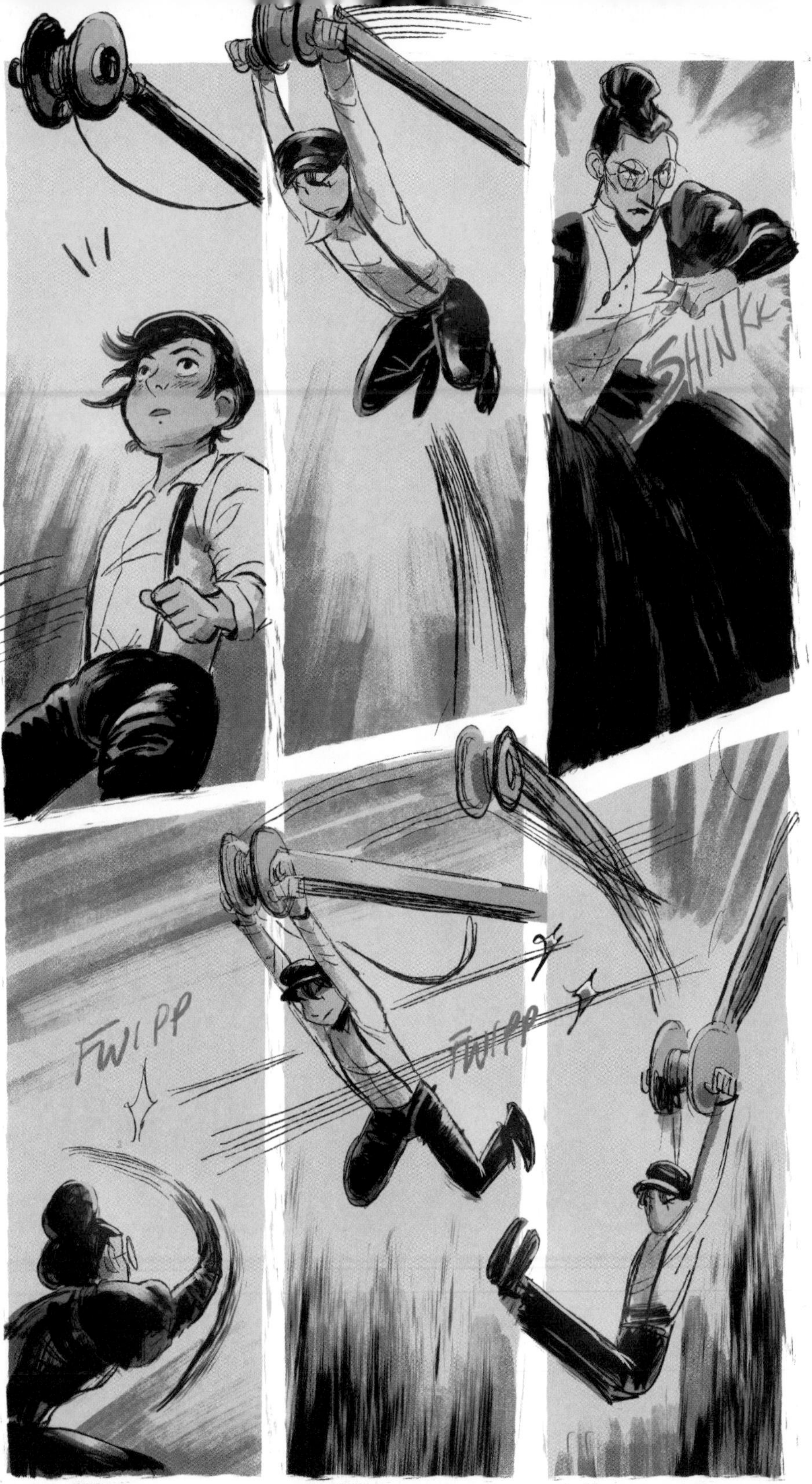
SHINKK
FWIPP
FWIPP

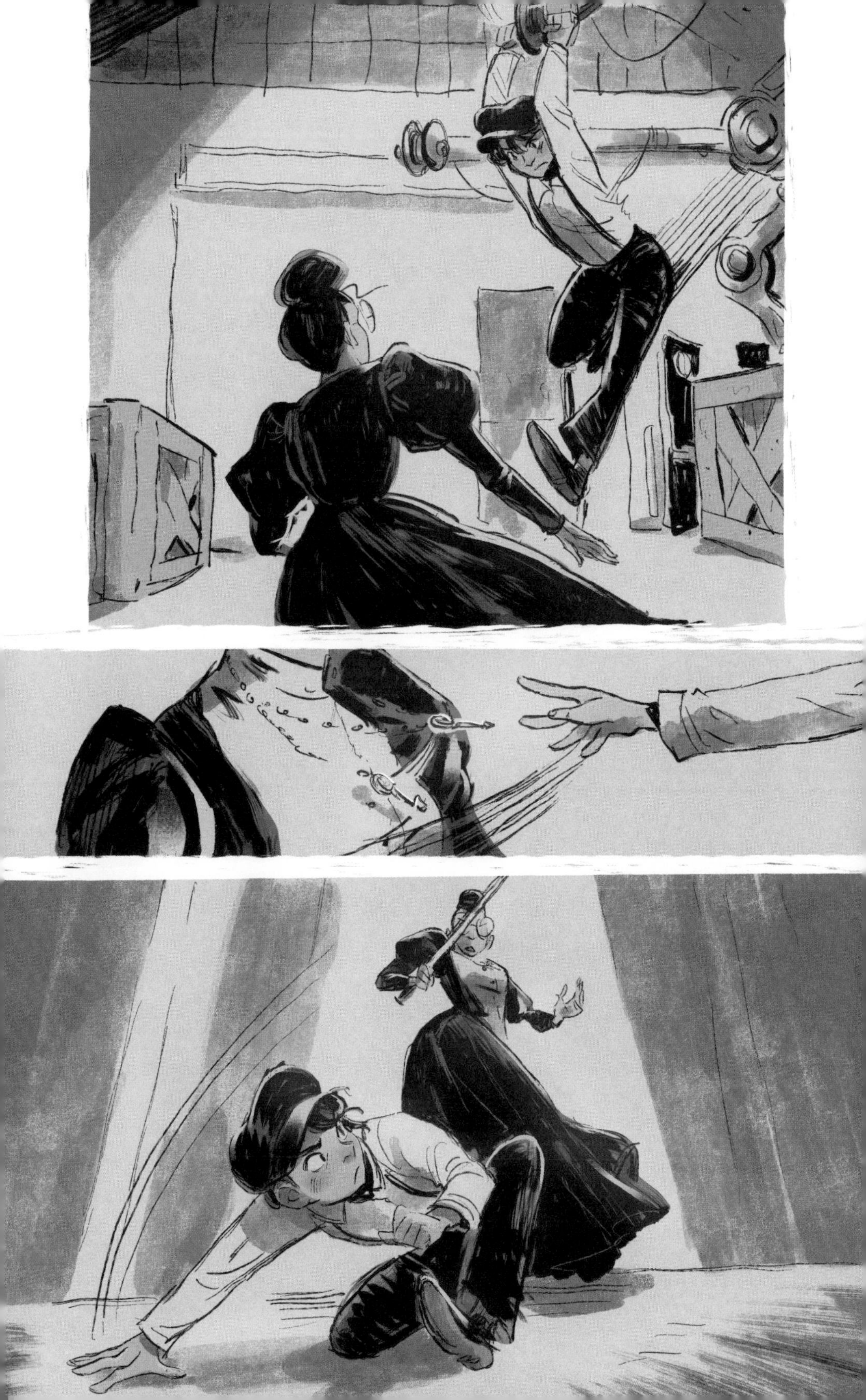

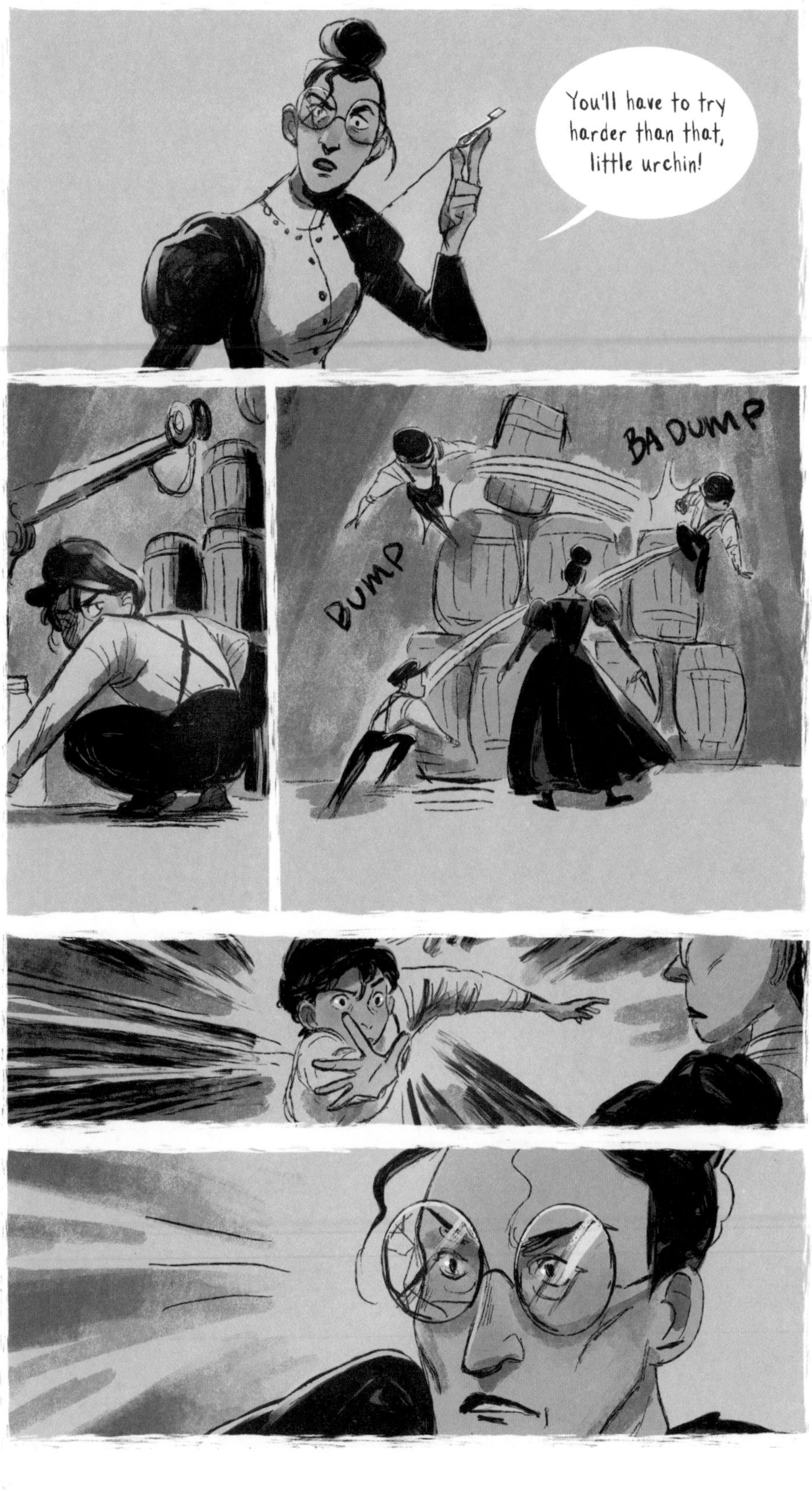
You'll have to try harder than that, little urchin!
BA DUMP
BUMP

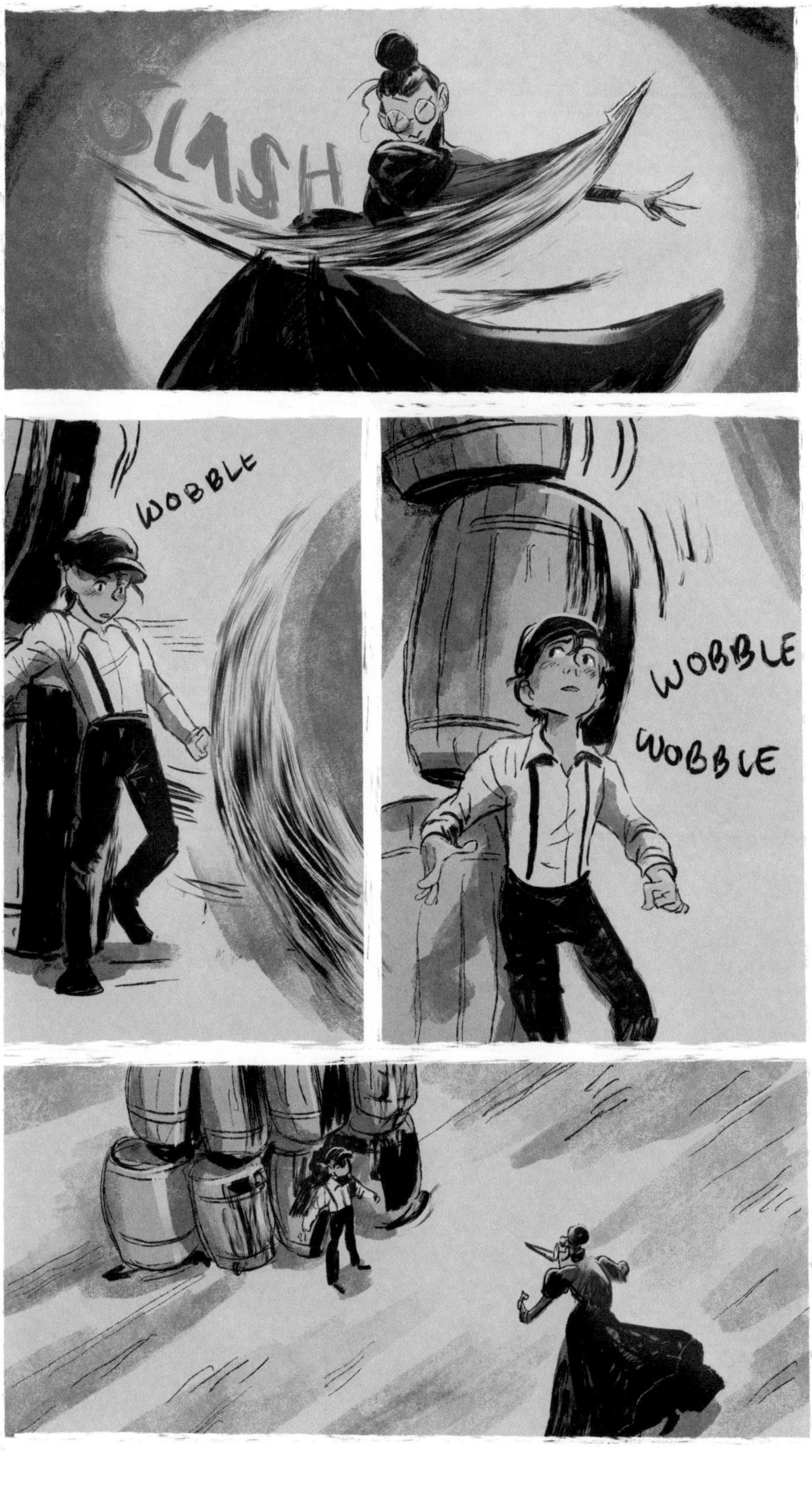
SLASH
WOBBLE
WOBBLE
WOBBLE

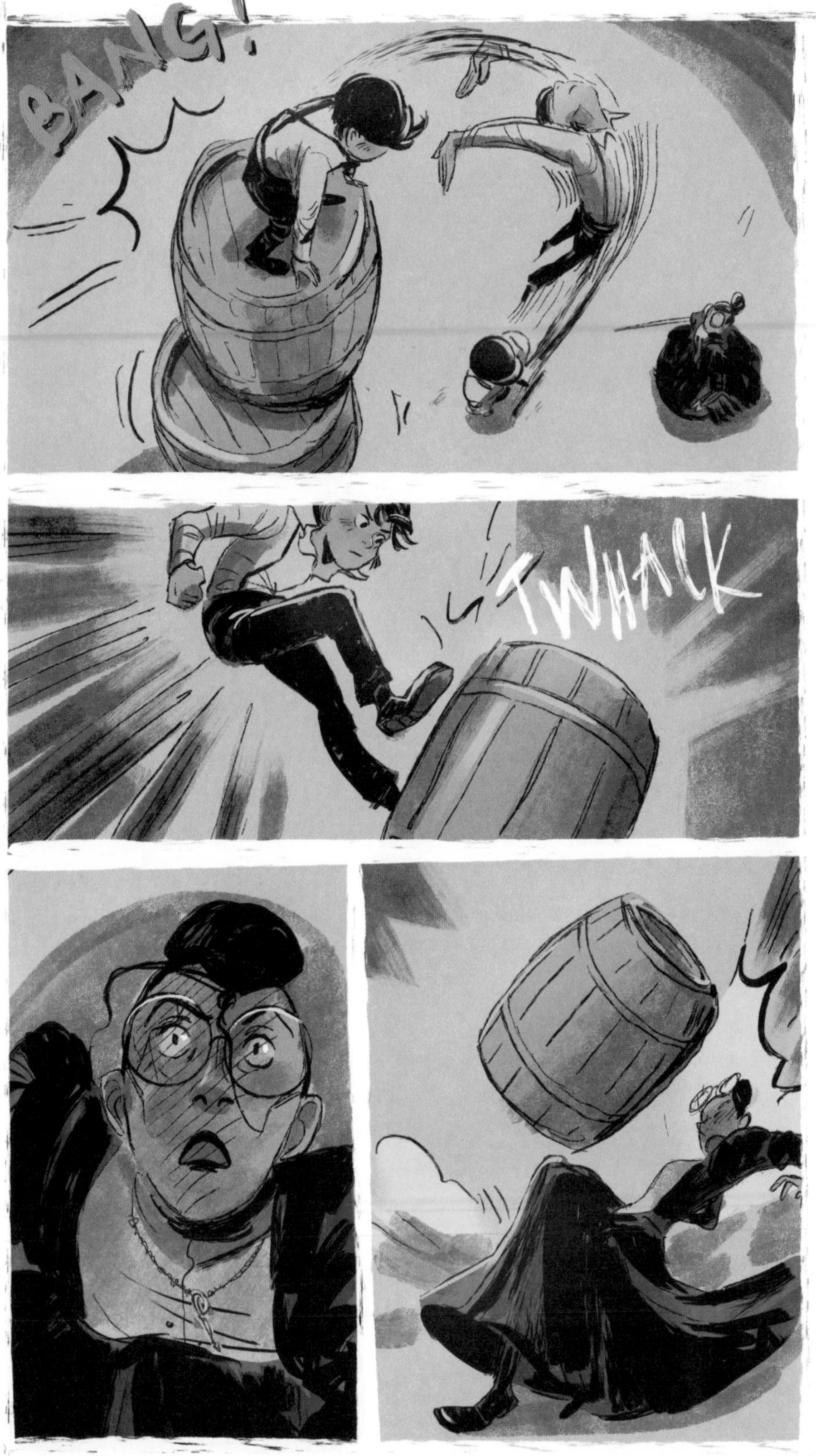
BANG!
TWHACK

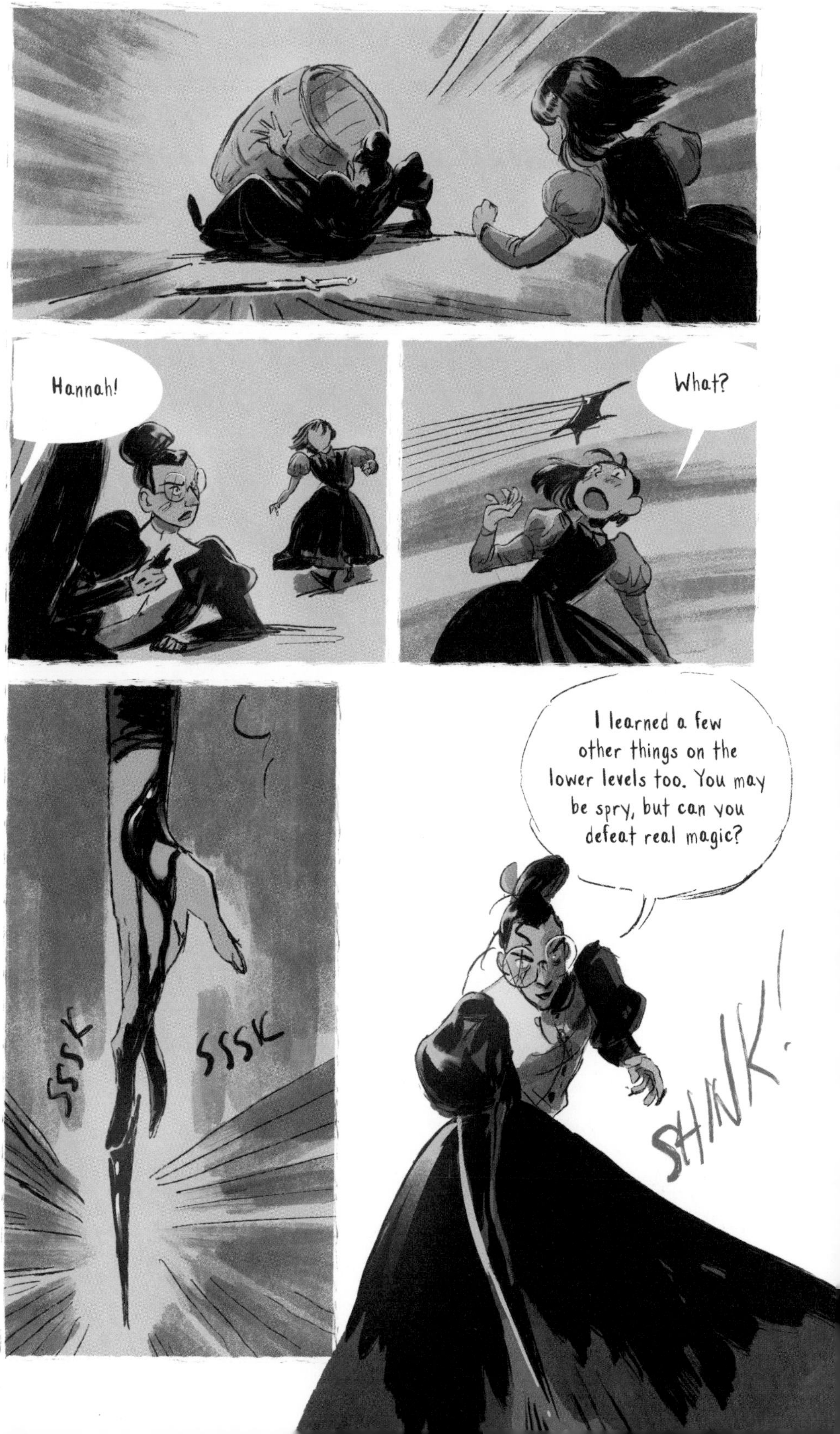
Hannah!
What?
I learned a few other things on the lower levels too. You may be spry, but can you defeat real magic?
SSSK
SSSK
SHINK!

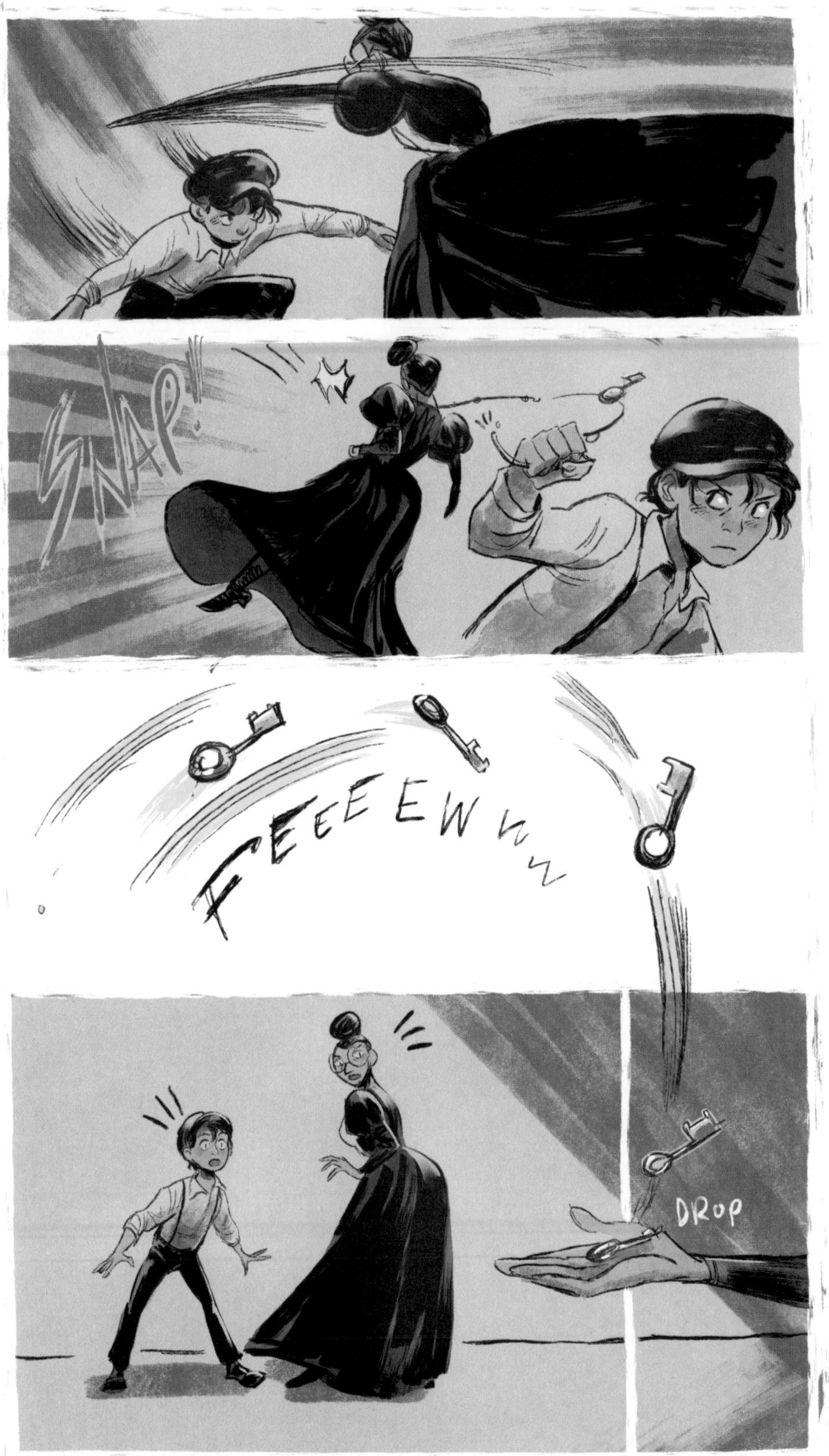
SNAP!!
FEEEEEWWW
DROP

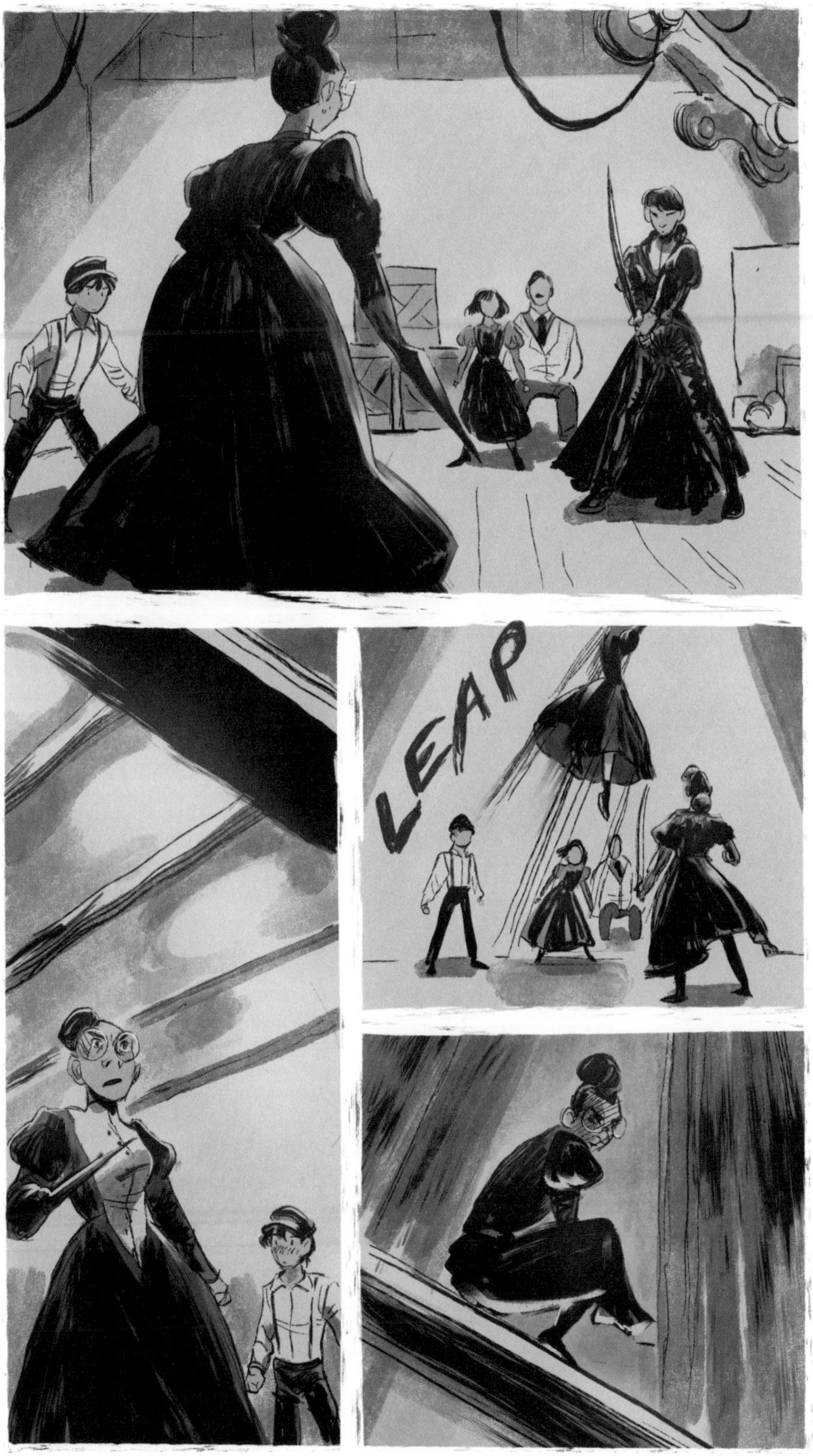
LEAP

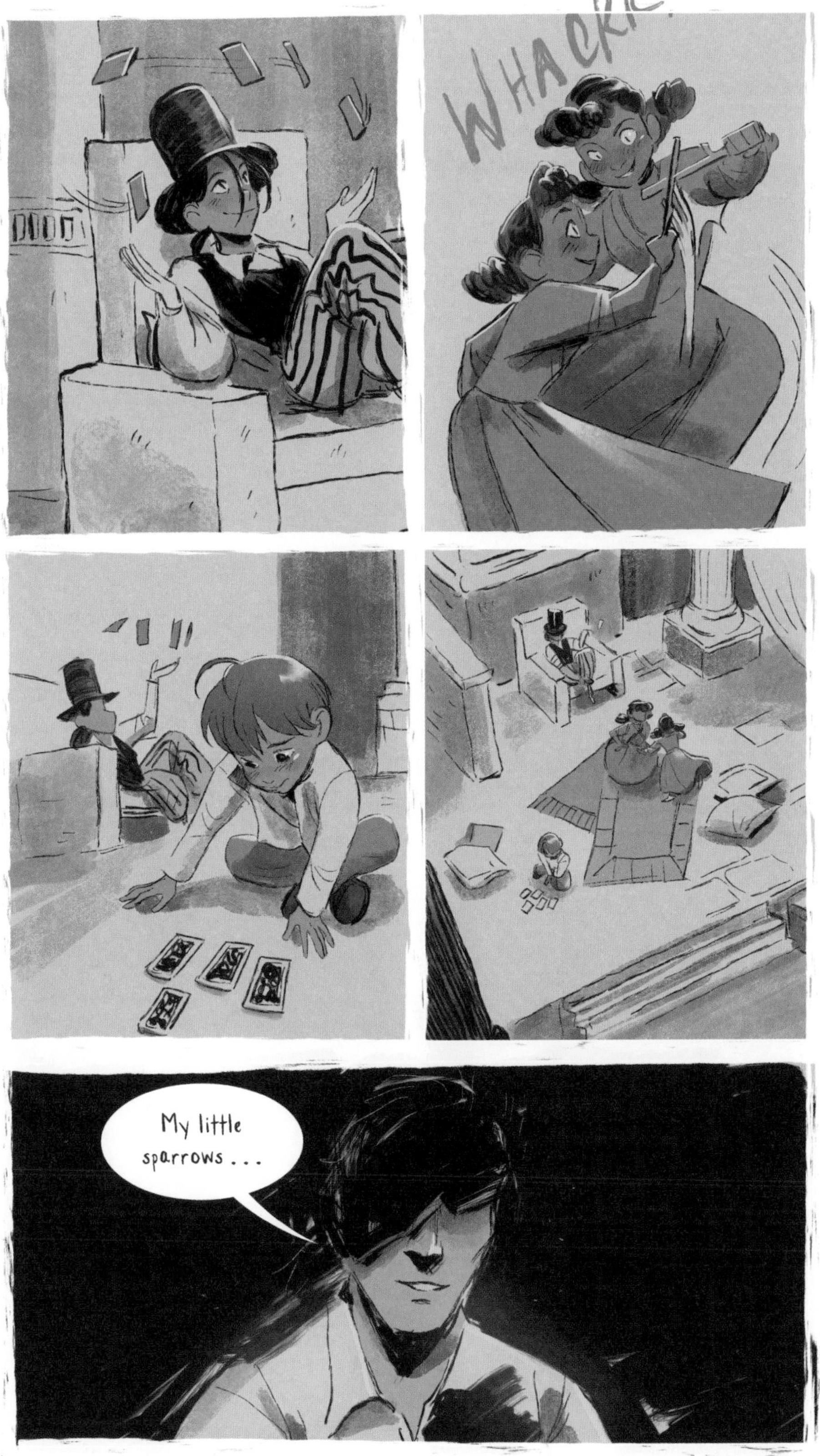
WHACK!
My little sparrows . . .

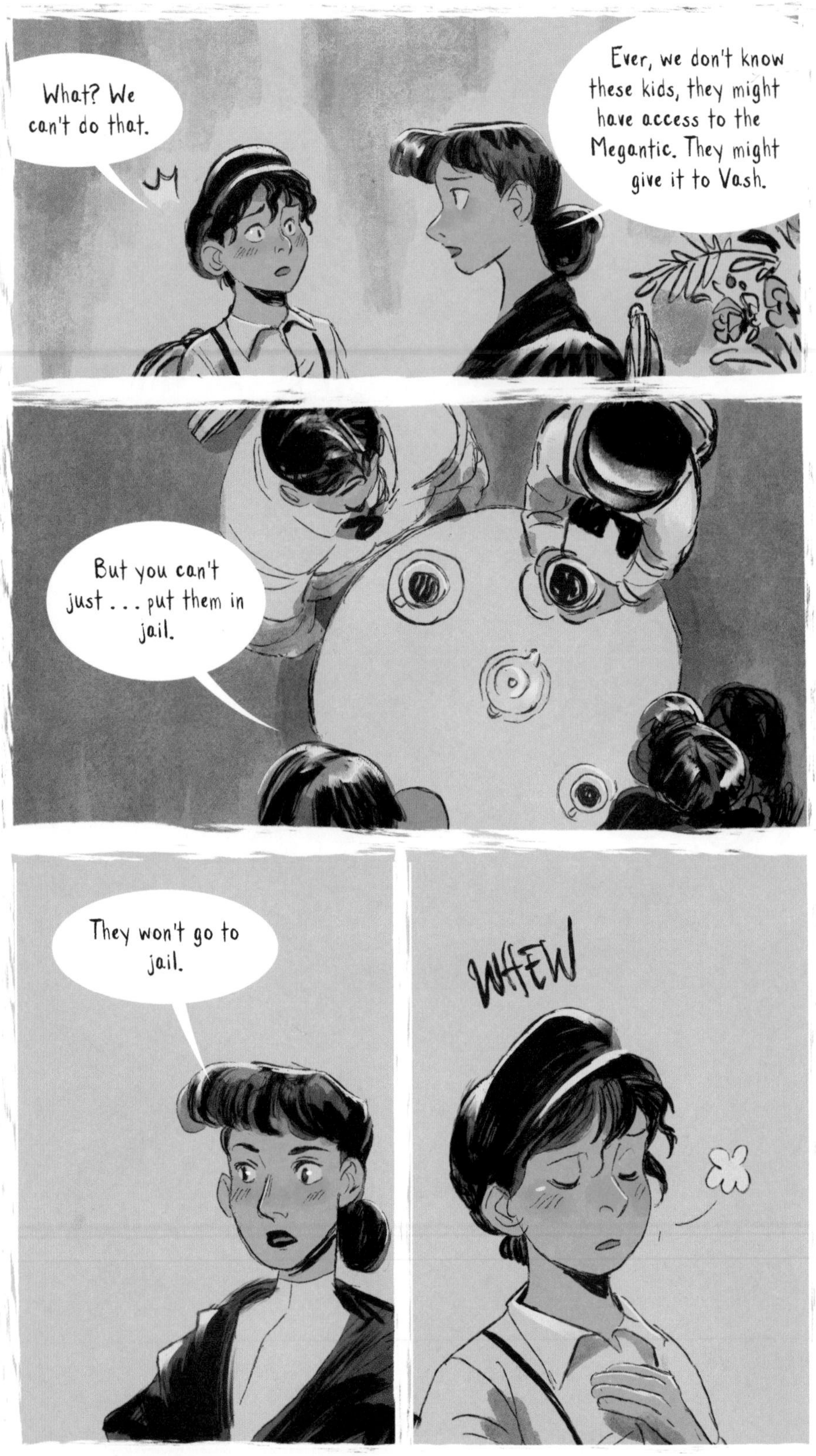
What? We can't do that.
Ever, we don't know these kids, they might have access to the Megantic. They might give it to Vash.
But you can't just . . . put them in jail.
They won't go to jail.
WHEW

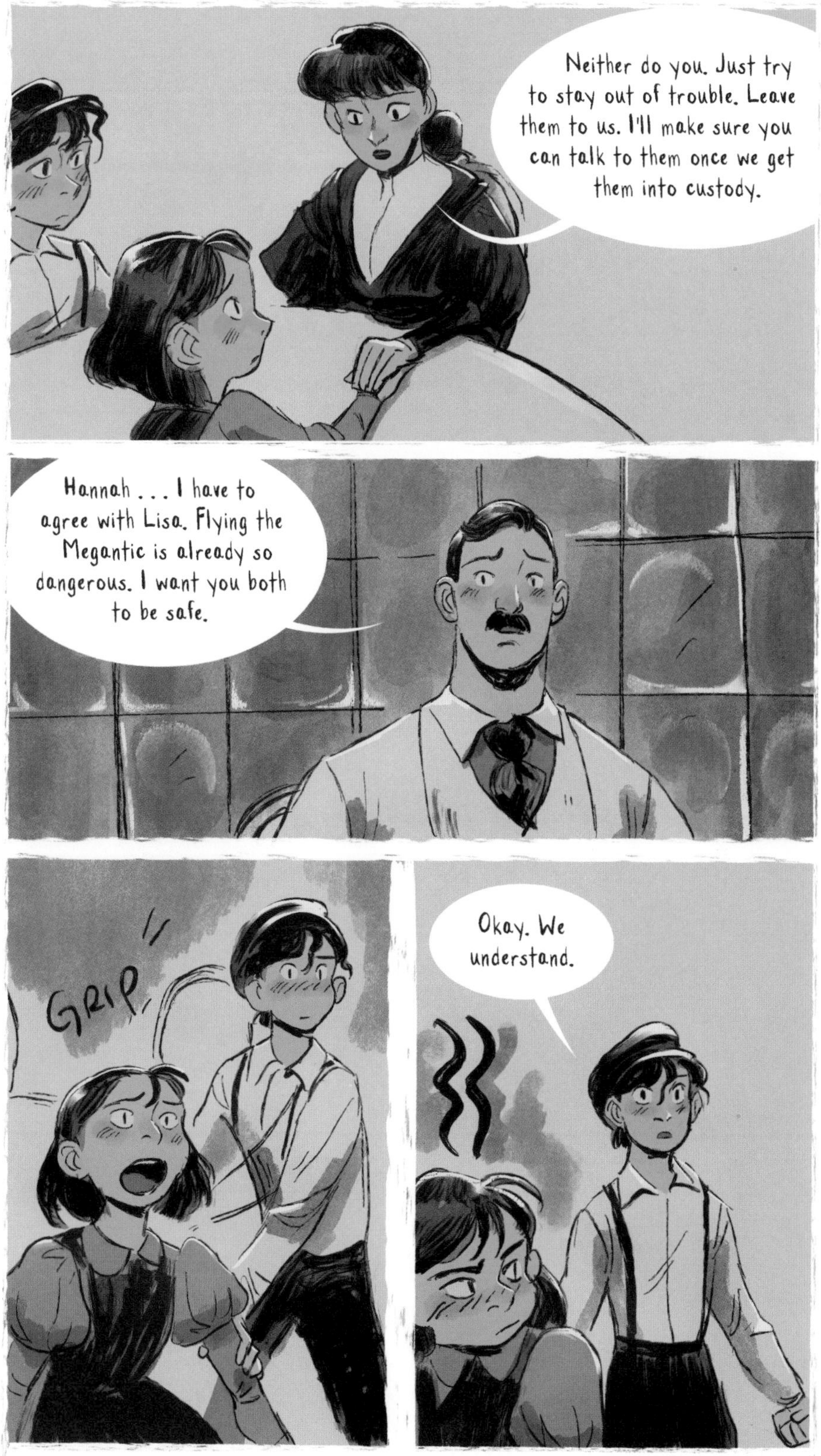
Neither do you. Just try to stay out of trouble. Leave them to us. I'll make sure you can talk to them once we get them into custody.
Hannah . . . I have to agree with Lisa. Flying the Megantic is already so dangerous. I want you both to be safe.
GRIP
Okay. We understand.

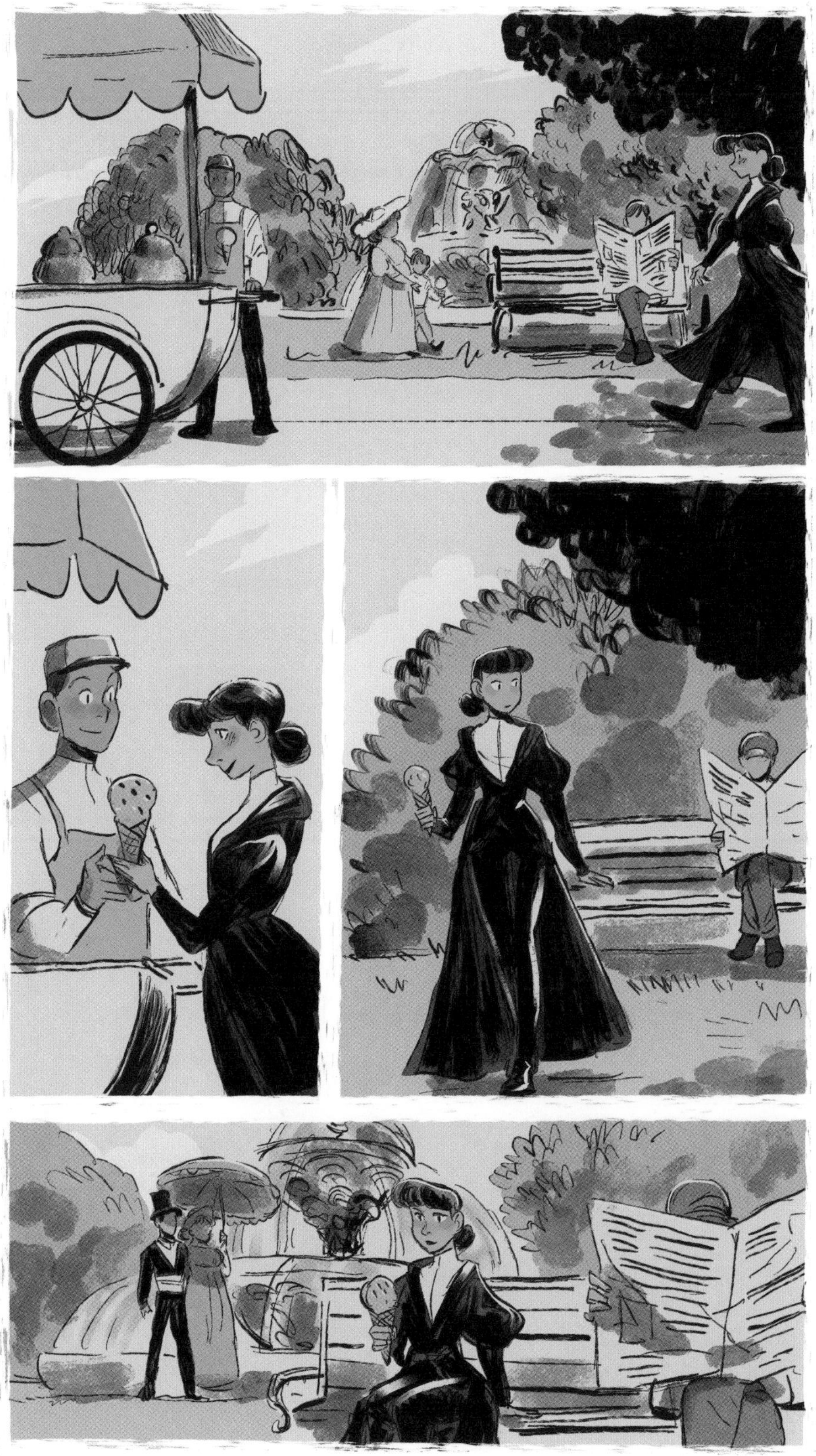

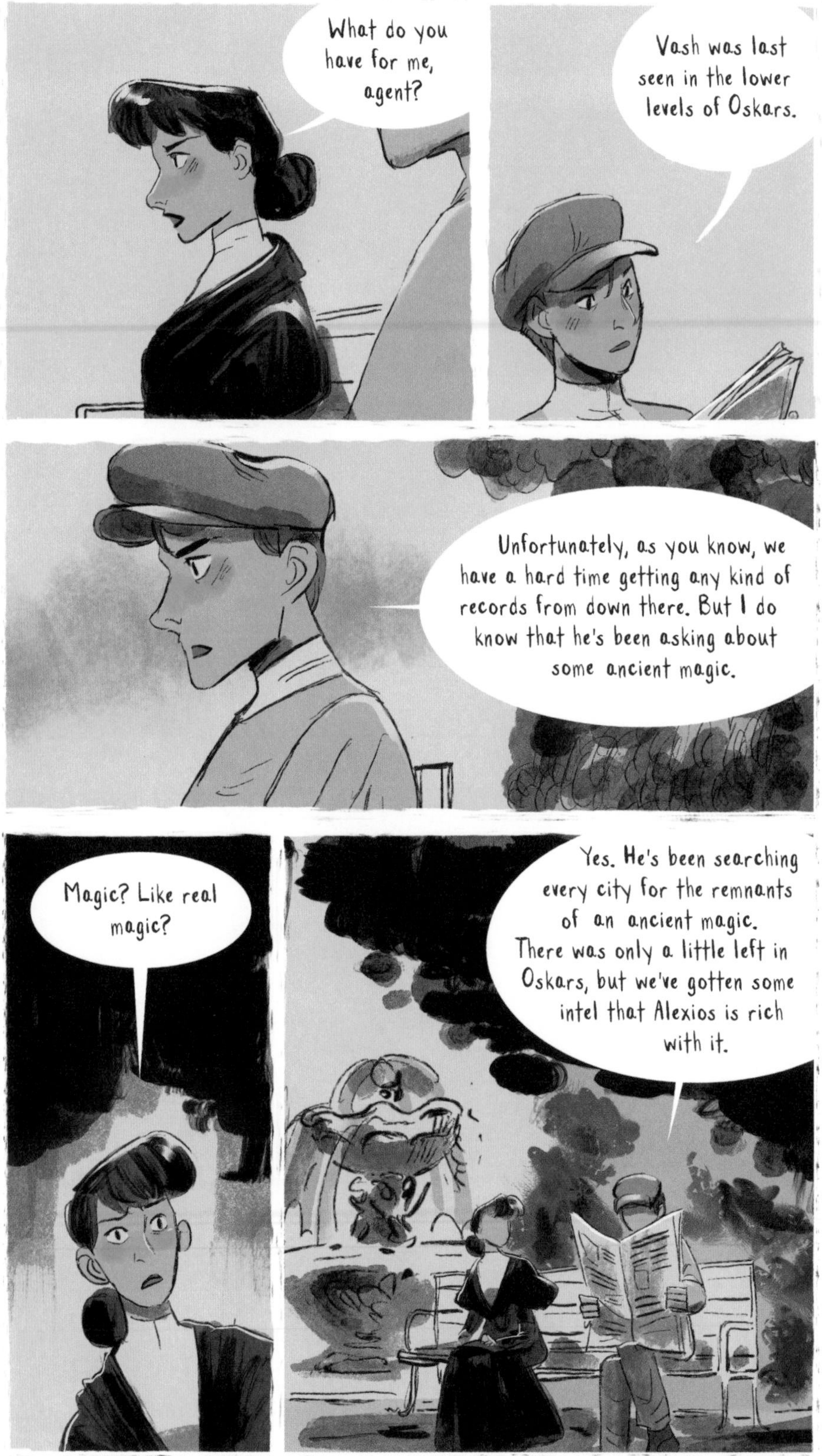
What do you have for me, agent?
Vash was last seen in the lower levels of Oskars.
Unfortunately, as you know, we have a hard time getting any kind of records from down there. But I do know that he's been asking about some ancient magic.
Magic? Like real magic?
Yes. He's been searching every city for the remnants of an ancient magic. There was only a little left in Oskars, but we've gotten some intel that Alexios is rich with it.

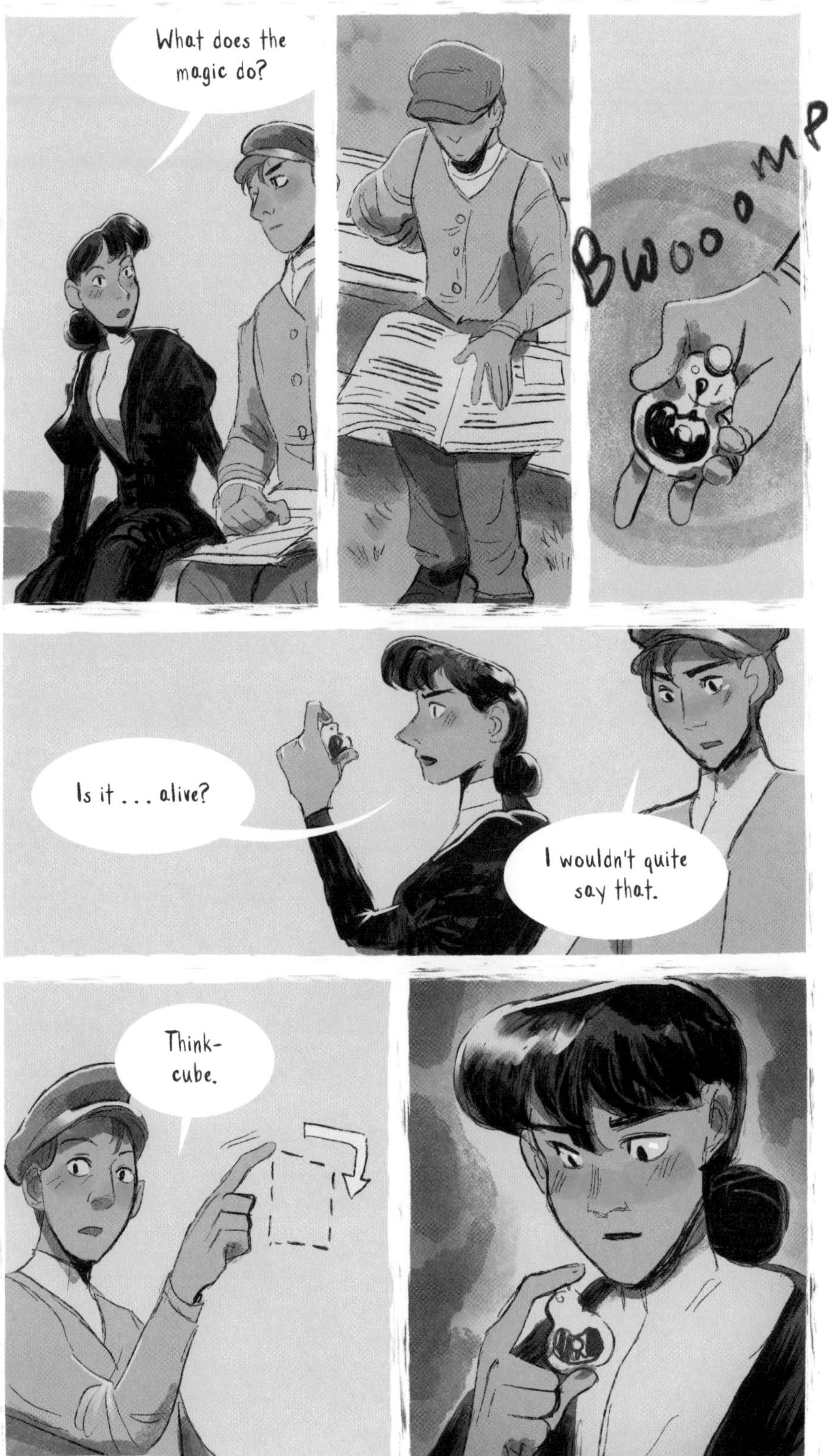
What does the magic do?
BWOOOOMP
Is it . . . alive?
I wouldn't quite say that.
Think-cube.

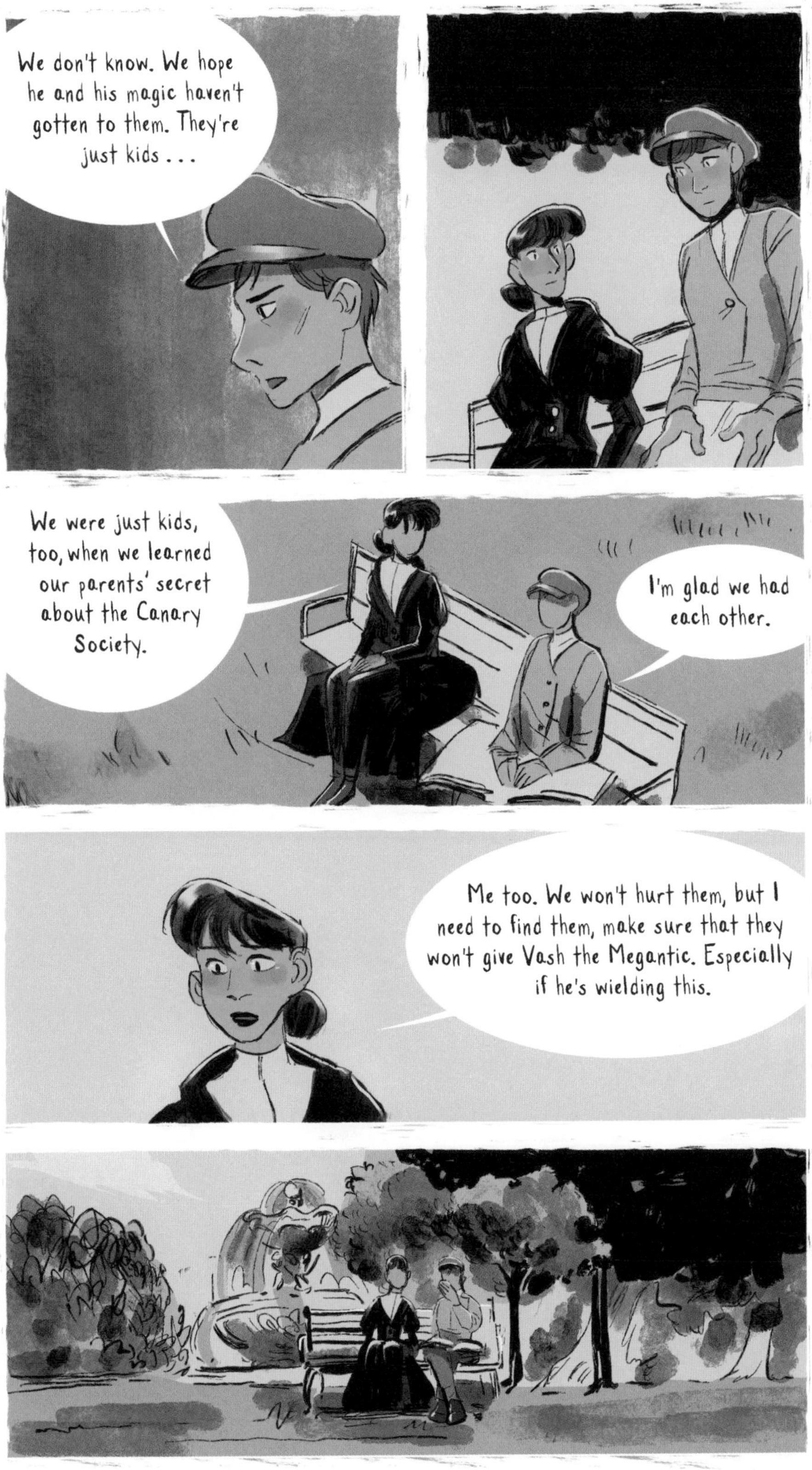
We don't know. We hope he and his magic haven't gotten to them. They're just kids . . .
We were just kids, too, when we learned our parents' secret about the Canary Society.
I'm glad we had each other.
Me too. We won't hurt them, but I need to find them, make sure that they won't give Vash the Megantic. Especially if he's wielding this.

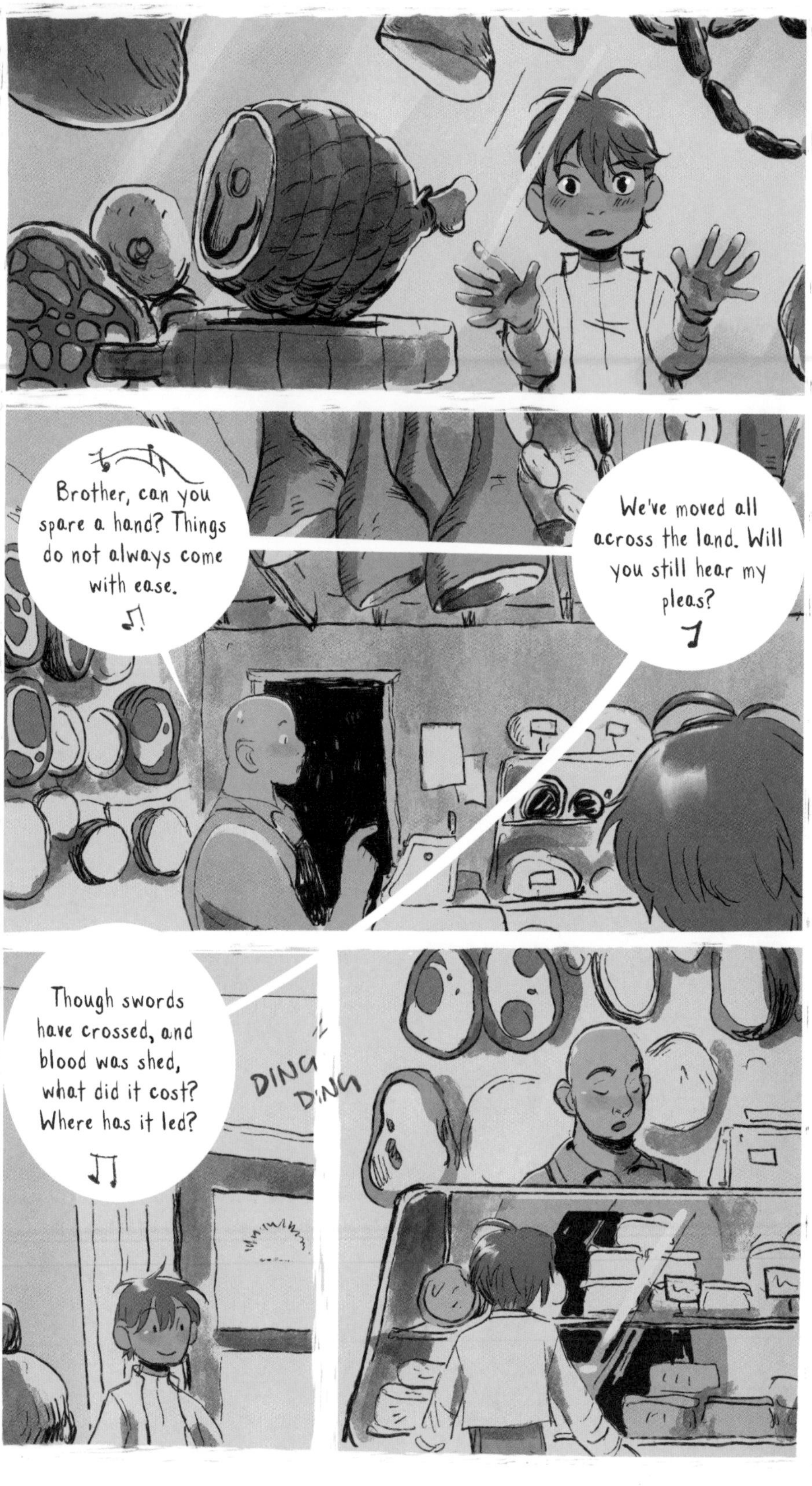
Brother, can you spare a hand? Things do not always come with ease.
We've moved all across the land. Will you still hear my pleas?
Though swords have crossed, and blood was shed, what did it cost? Where has it led?
DING DING

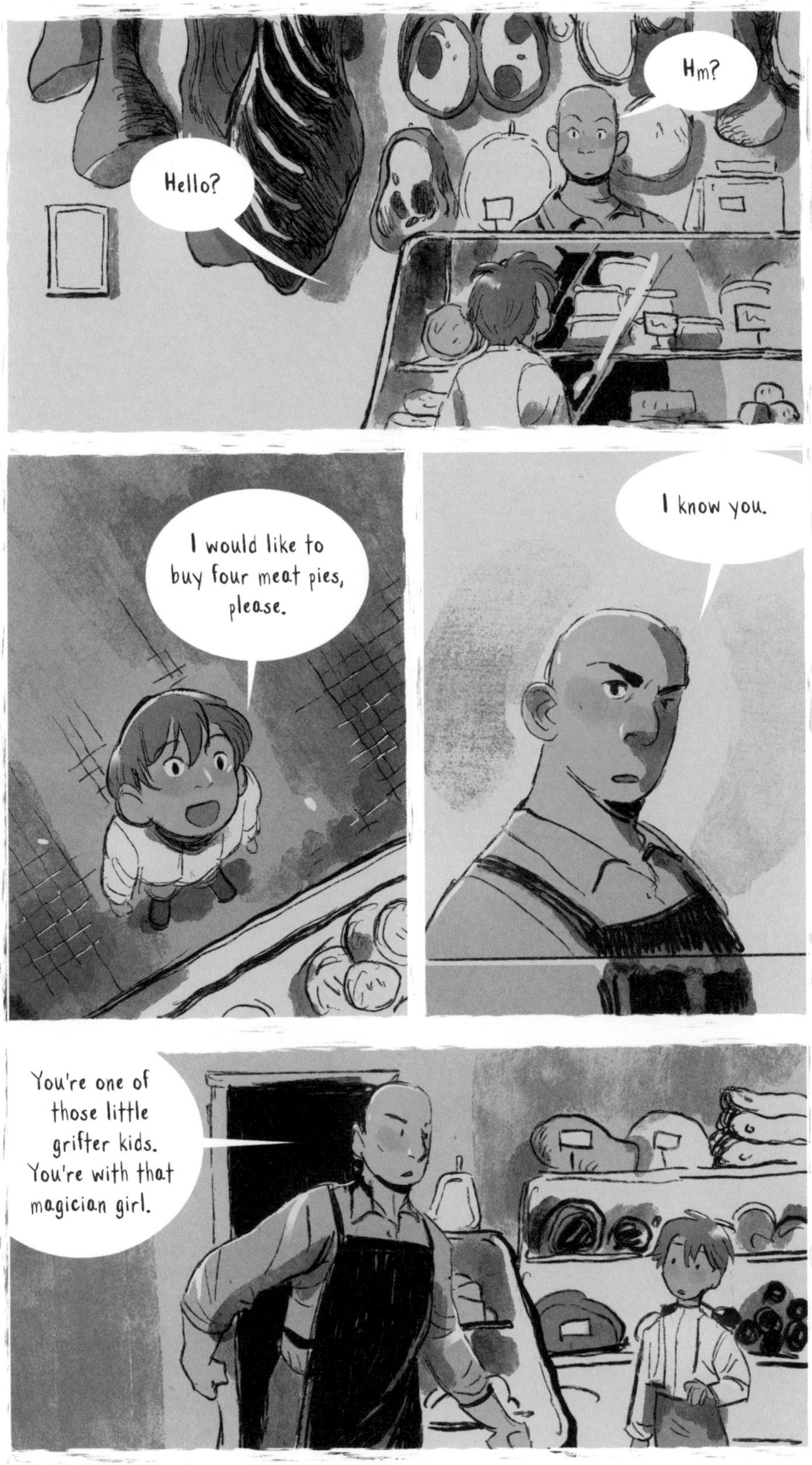
Hm?
Hello?
I would like to buy four meat pies, please.
I know you.
You're one of those little grifter kids. You're with that magician girl.

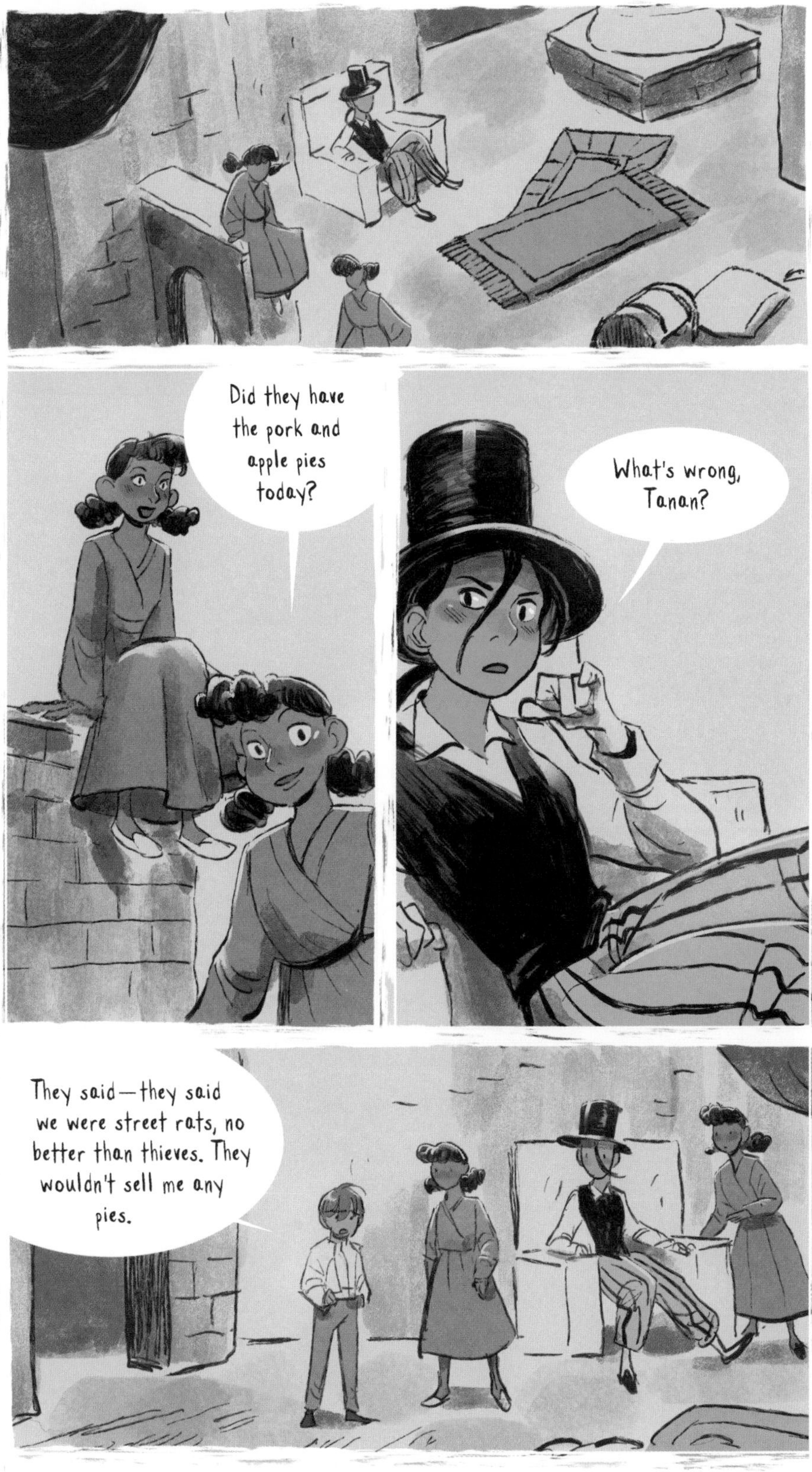
Did they have the pork and apple pies today?
What's wrong, Tanan?
They said—they said we were street rats, no better than thieves. They wouldn't sell me any pies.

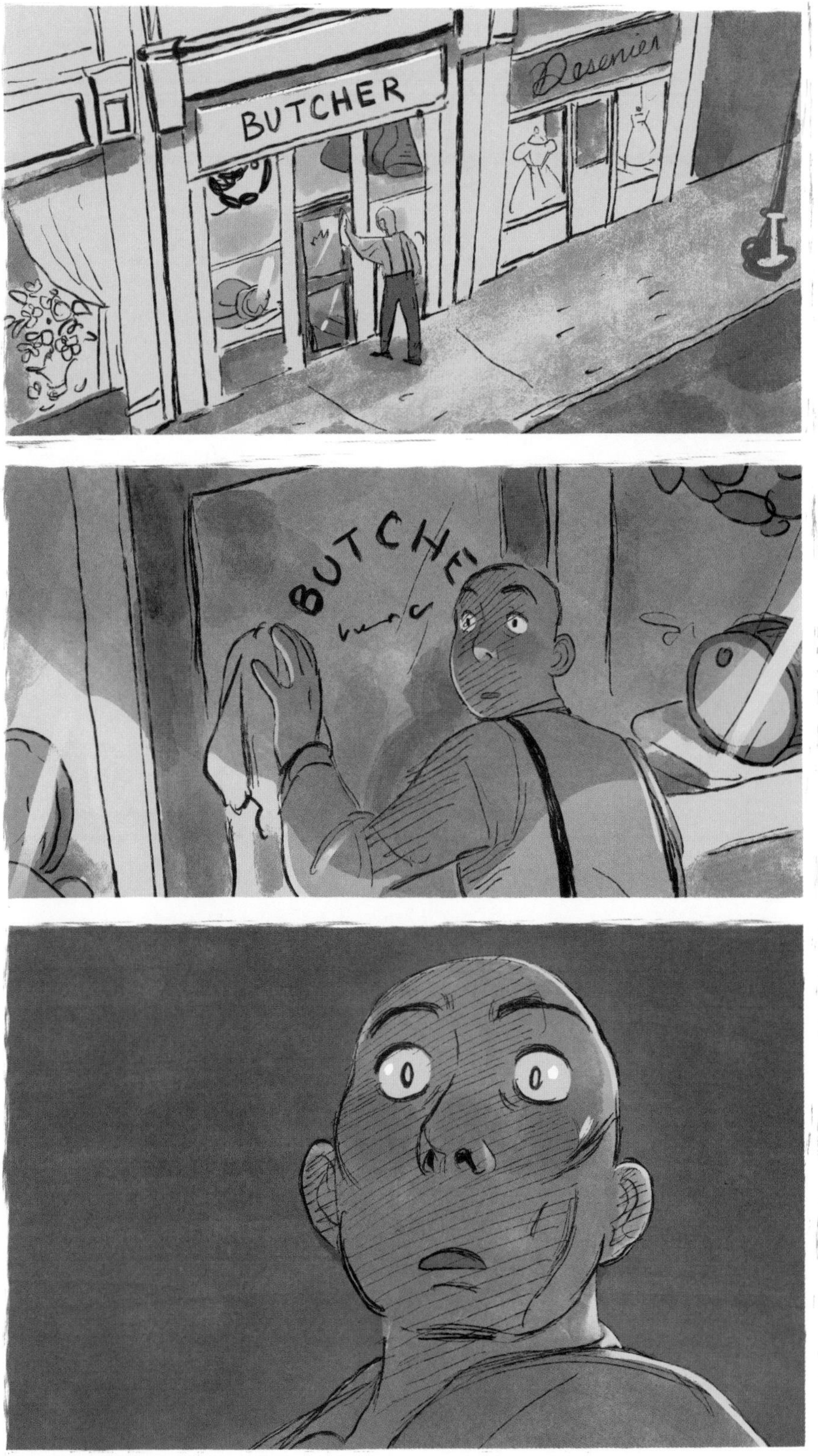
BUTCHER
Desenier
BUTCHE

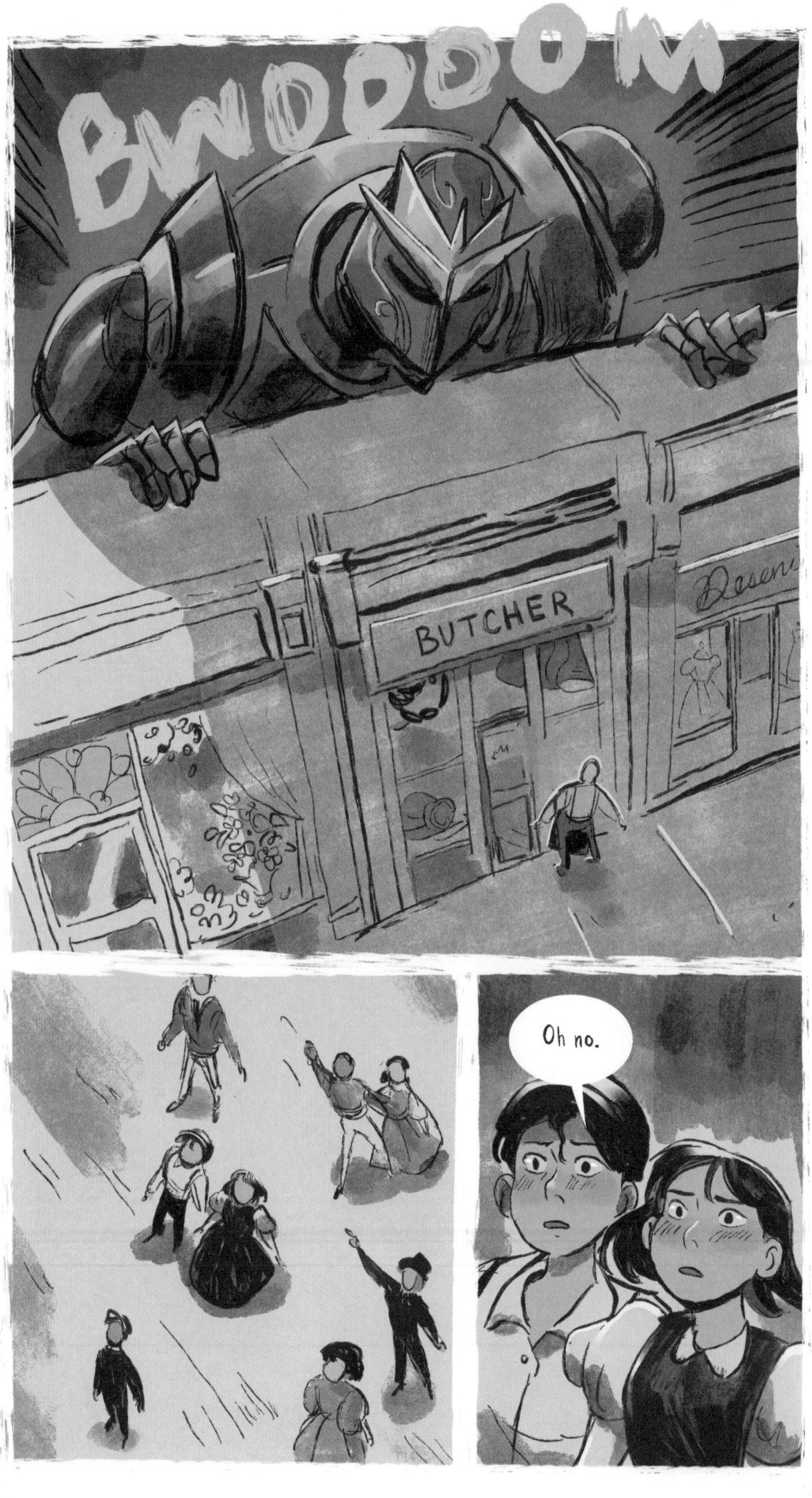
BWOOOOM
BUTCHER
Oh no.

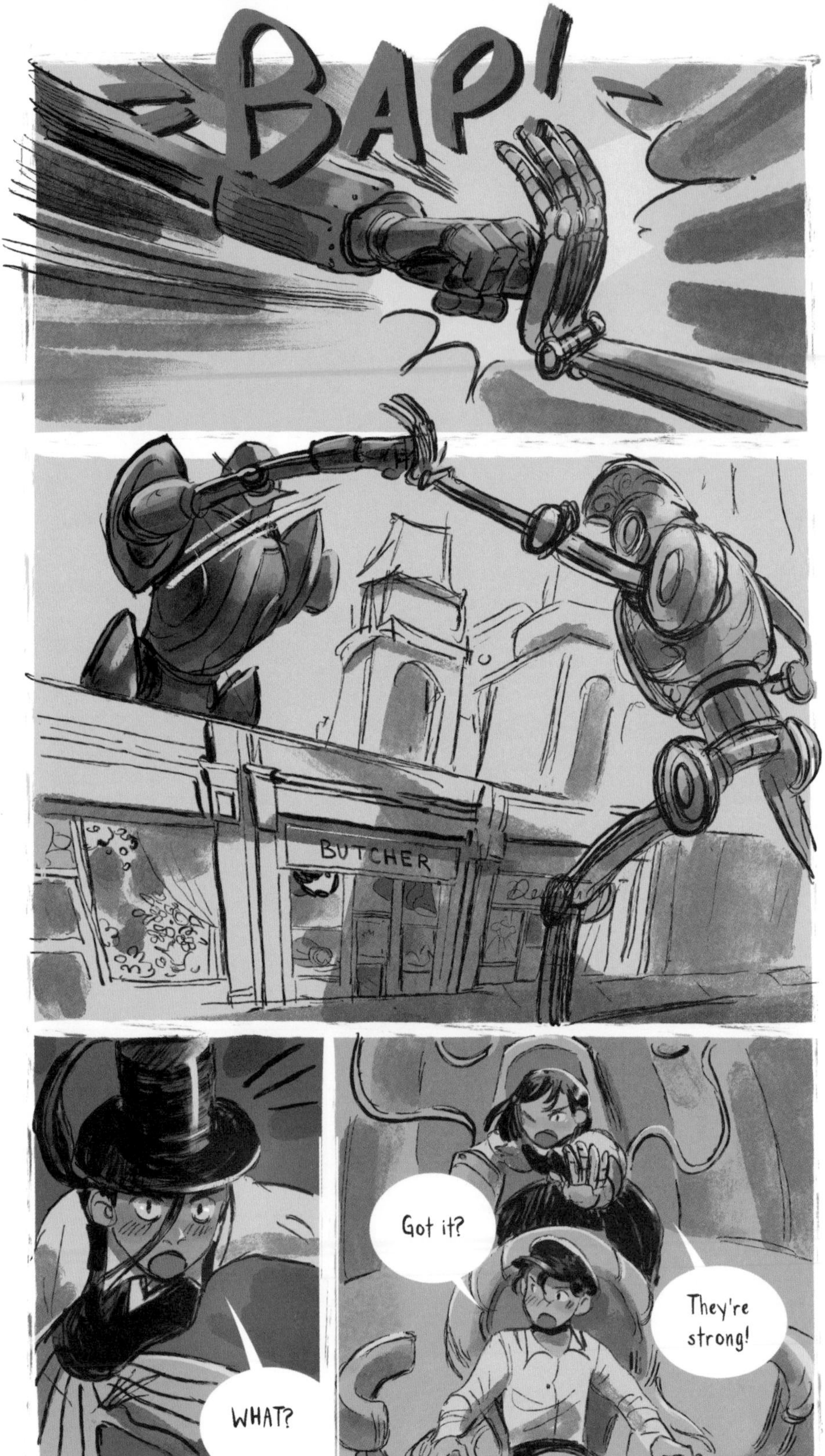
BAP!
BUTCHER
WHAT?
Got it?
They're strong!

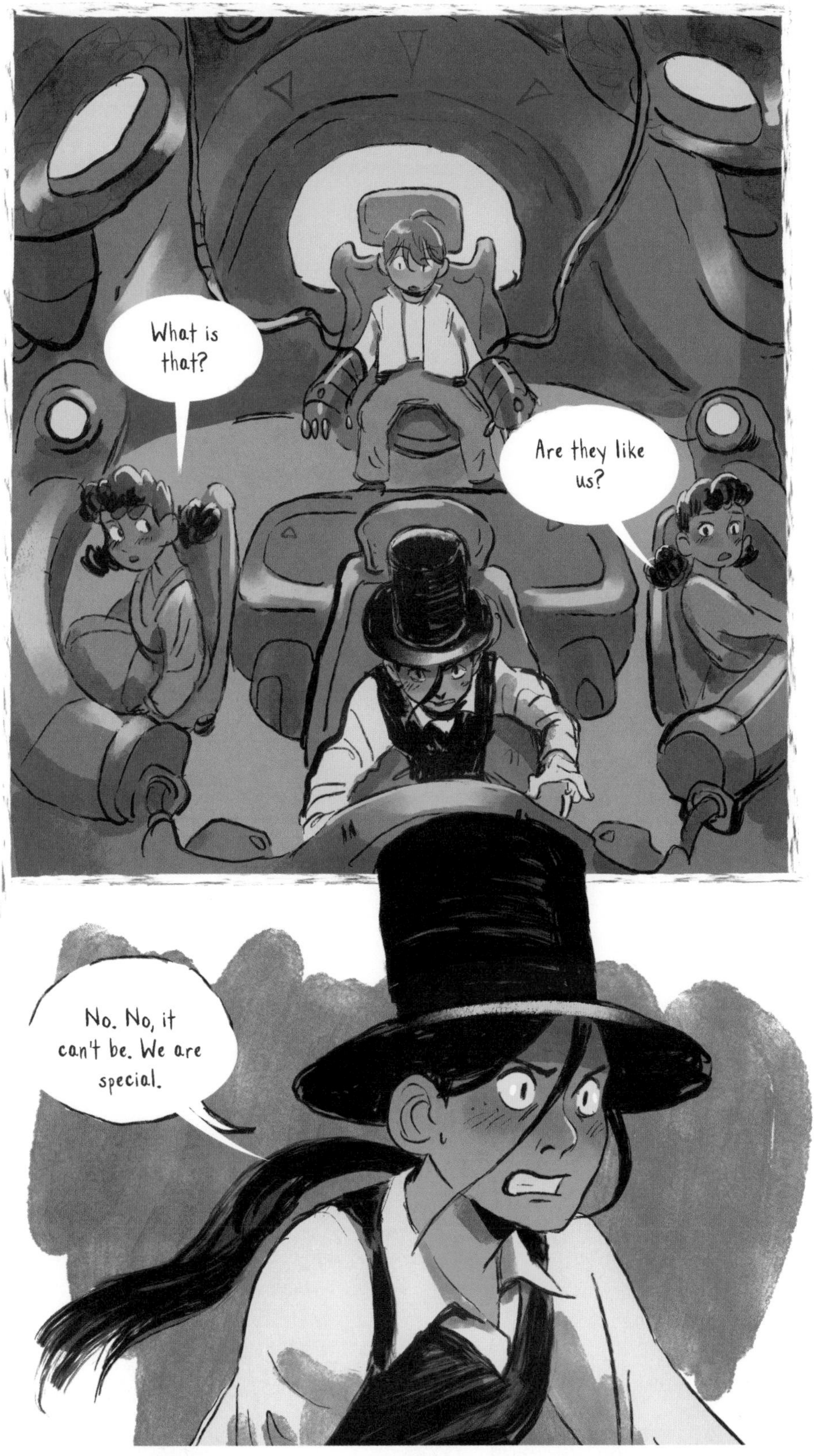
What is that?
Are they like us?
No. No, it can't be. We are special.

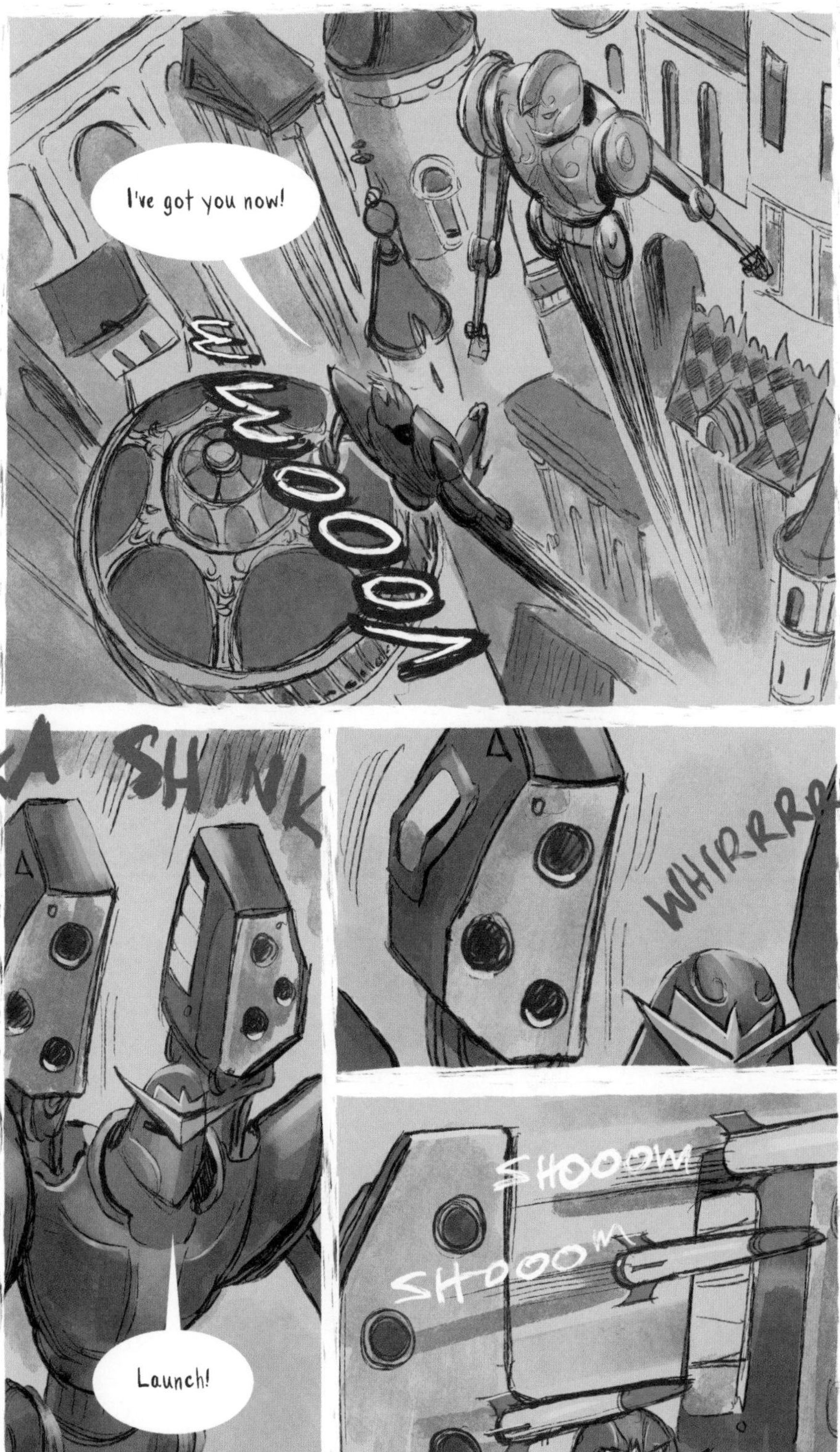
I've got you now!
EWOOOOOM
KA SHINK
WHIRRRRR
Launch!
SHOOOM
SHOOOM

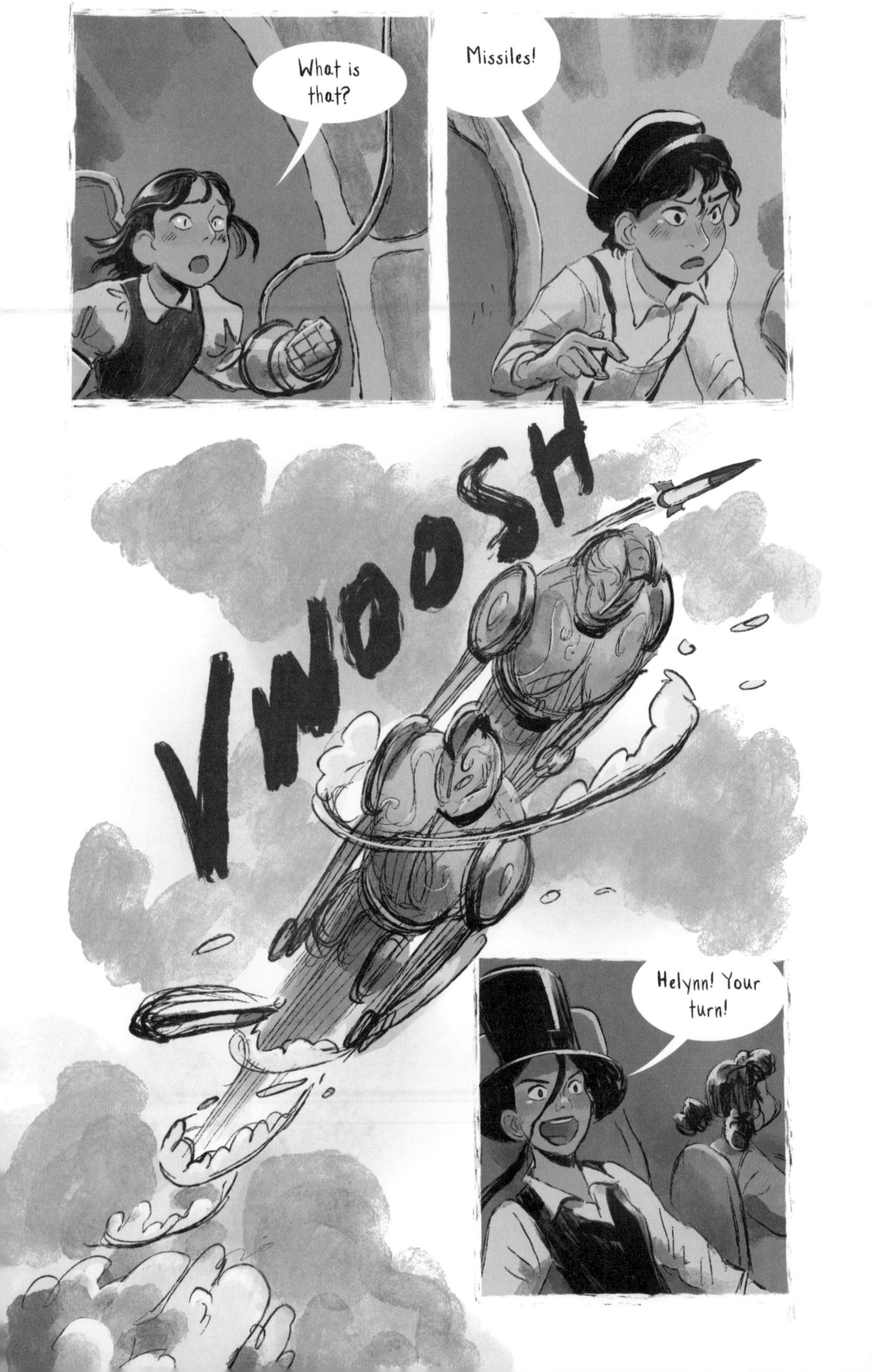
What is that?
Missiles!
VWOOSH
Helynn! Your turn!

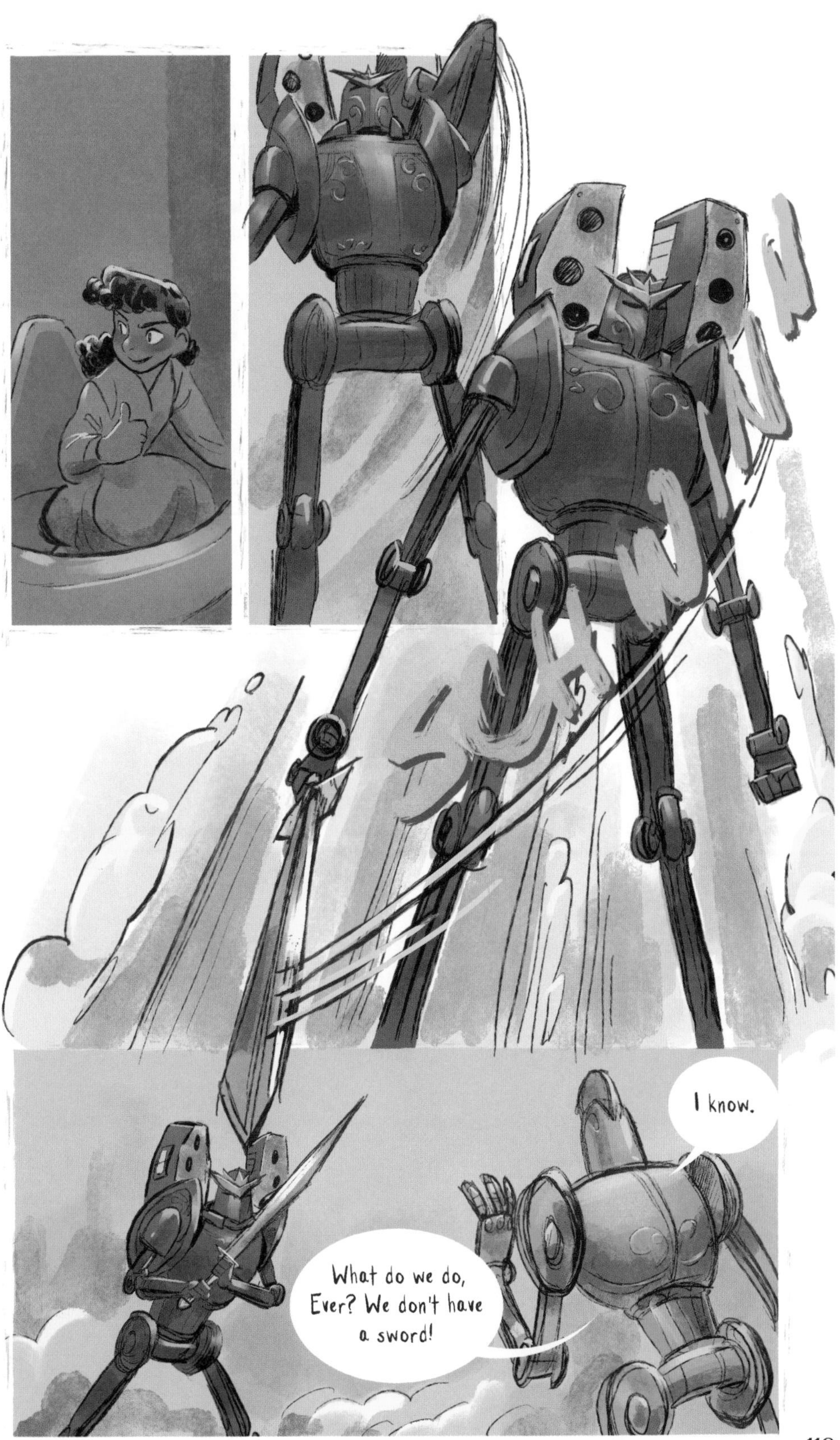
What do we do, Ever? We don't have a sword!
I know.

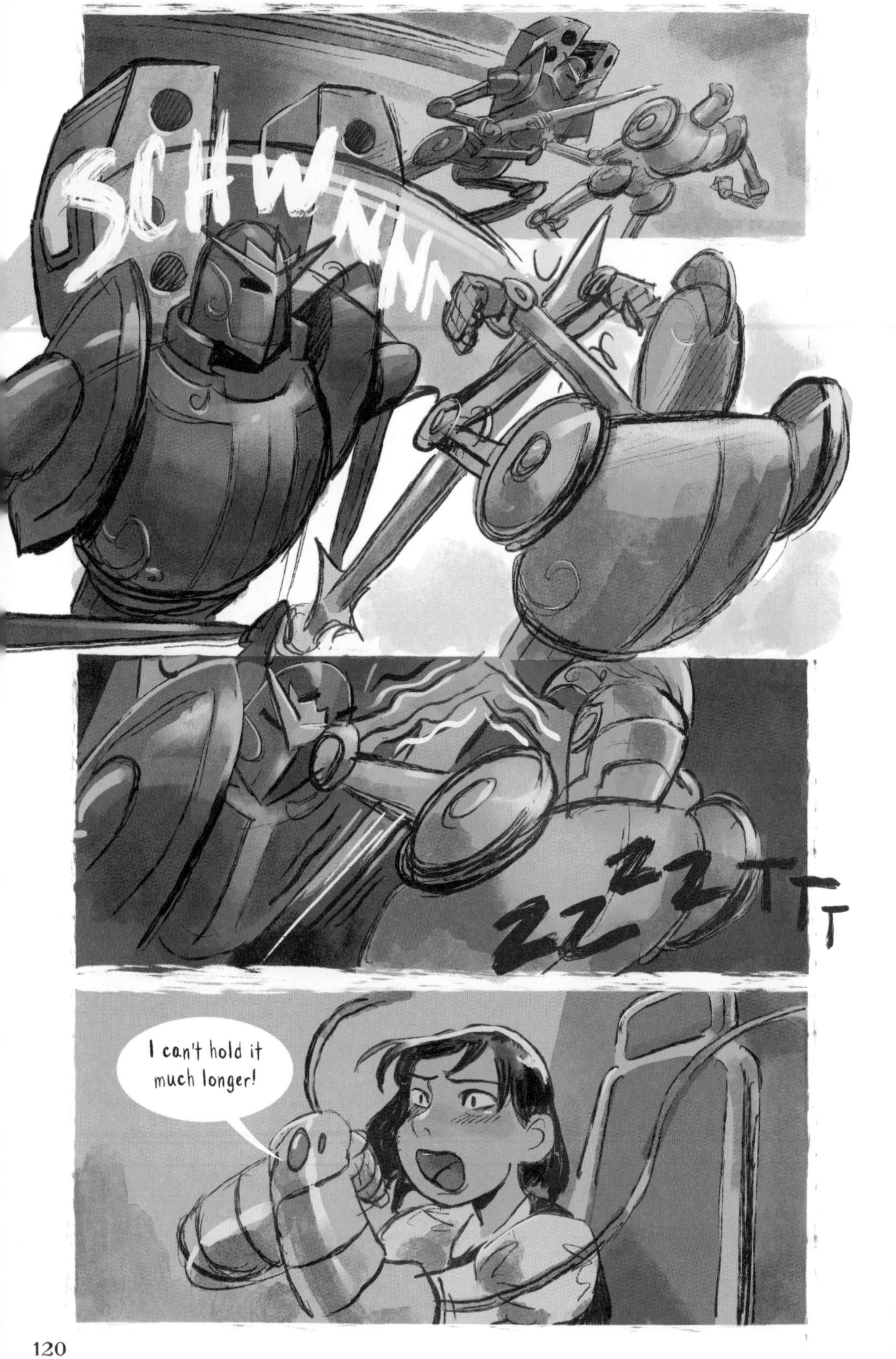
SCHWNNN
ZZZZZTTT
I can't hold it much longer!

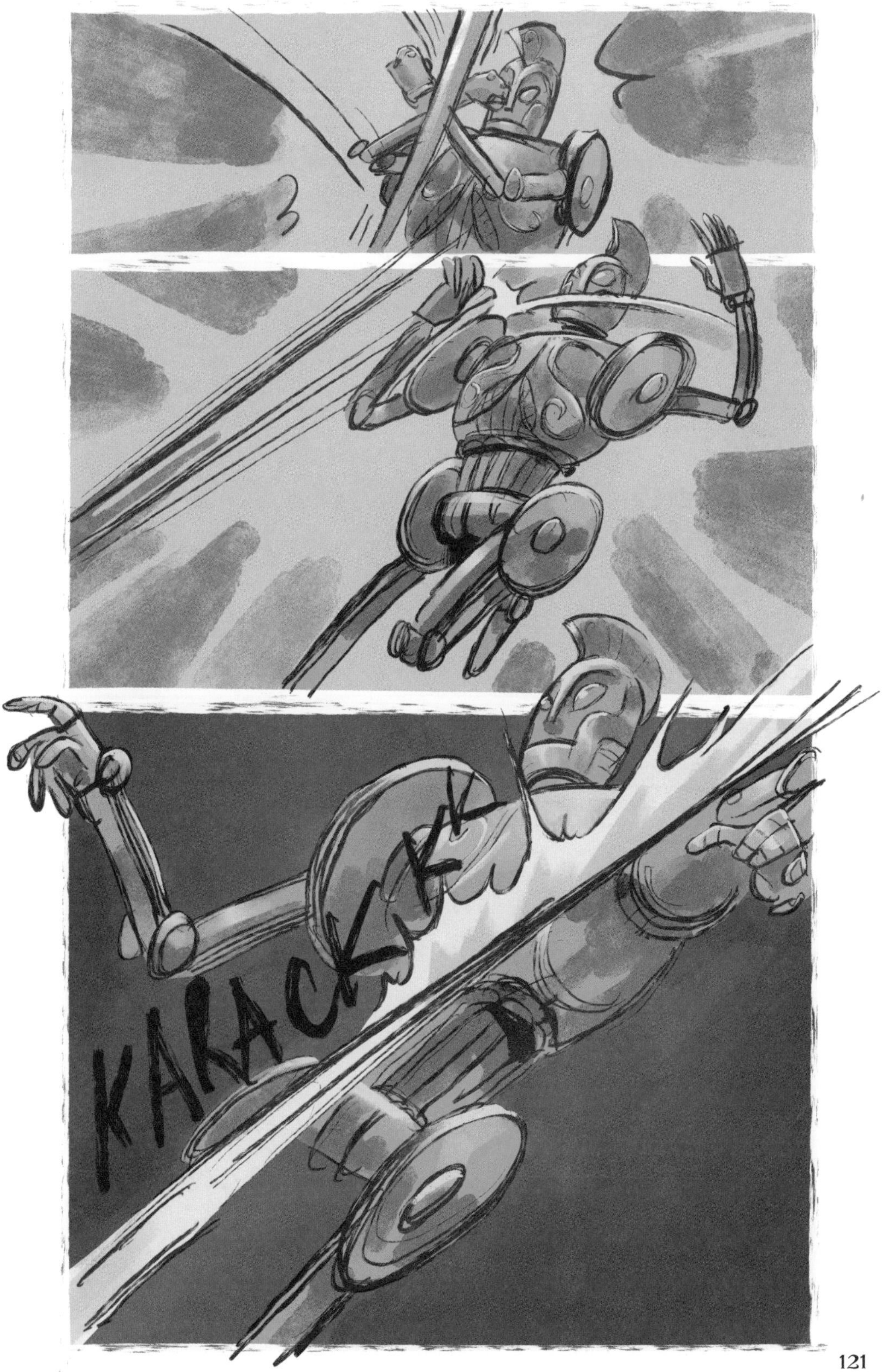
KARACKKK

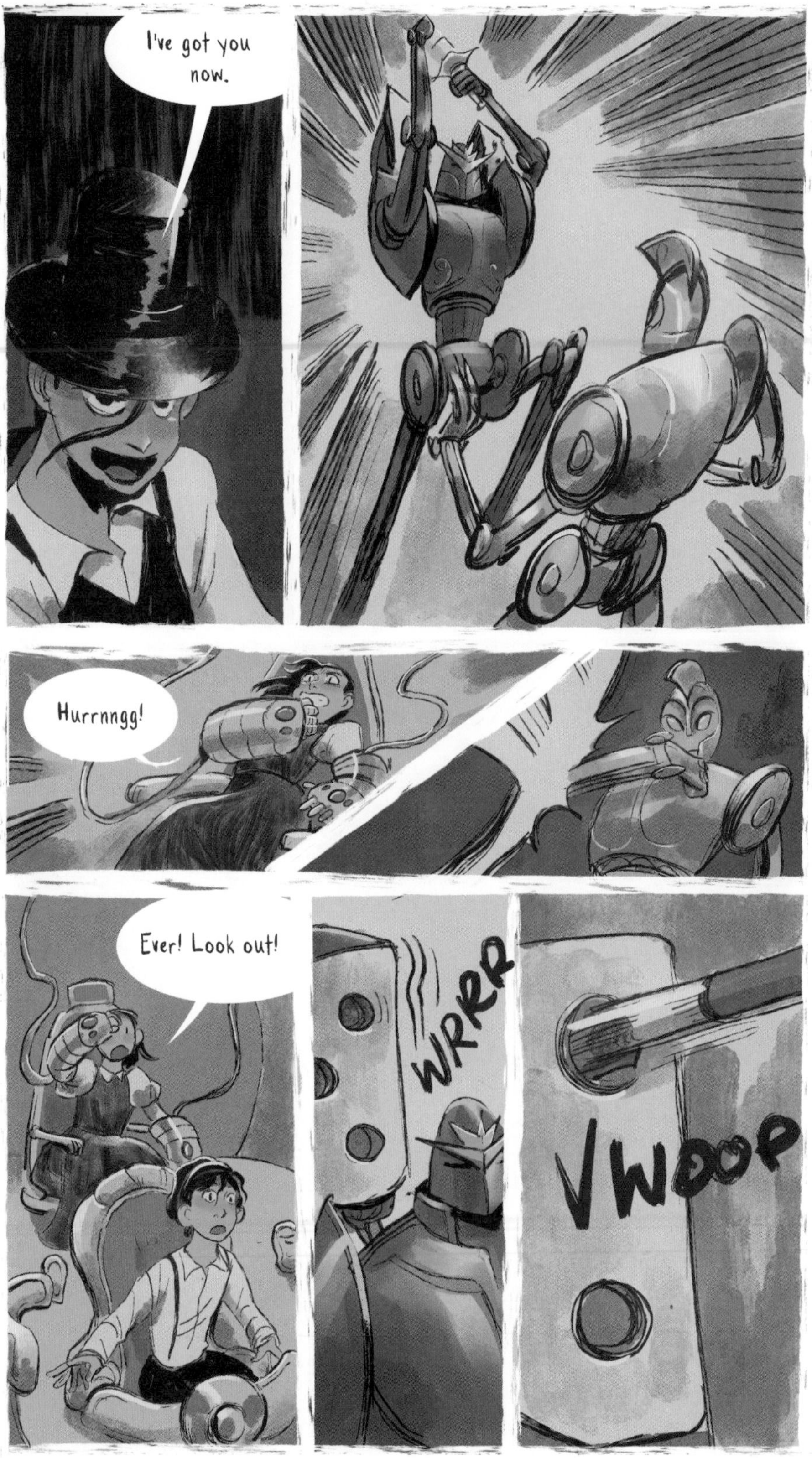
I've got you now.
Hurrnngg!
Ever! Look out!
WRRR
VWOOP

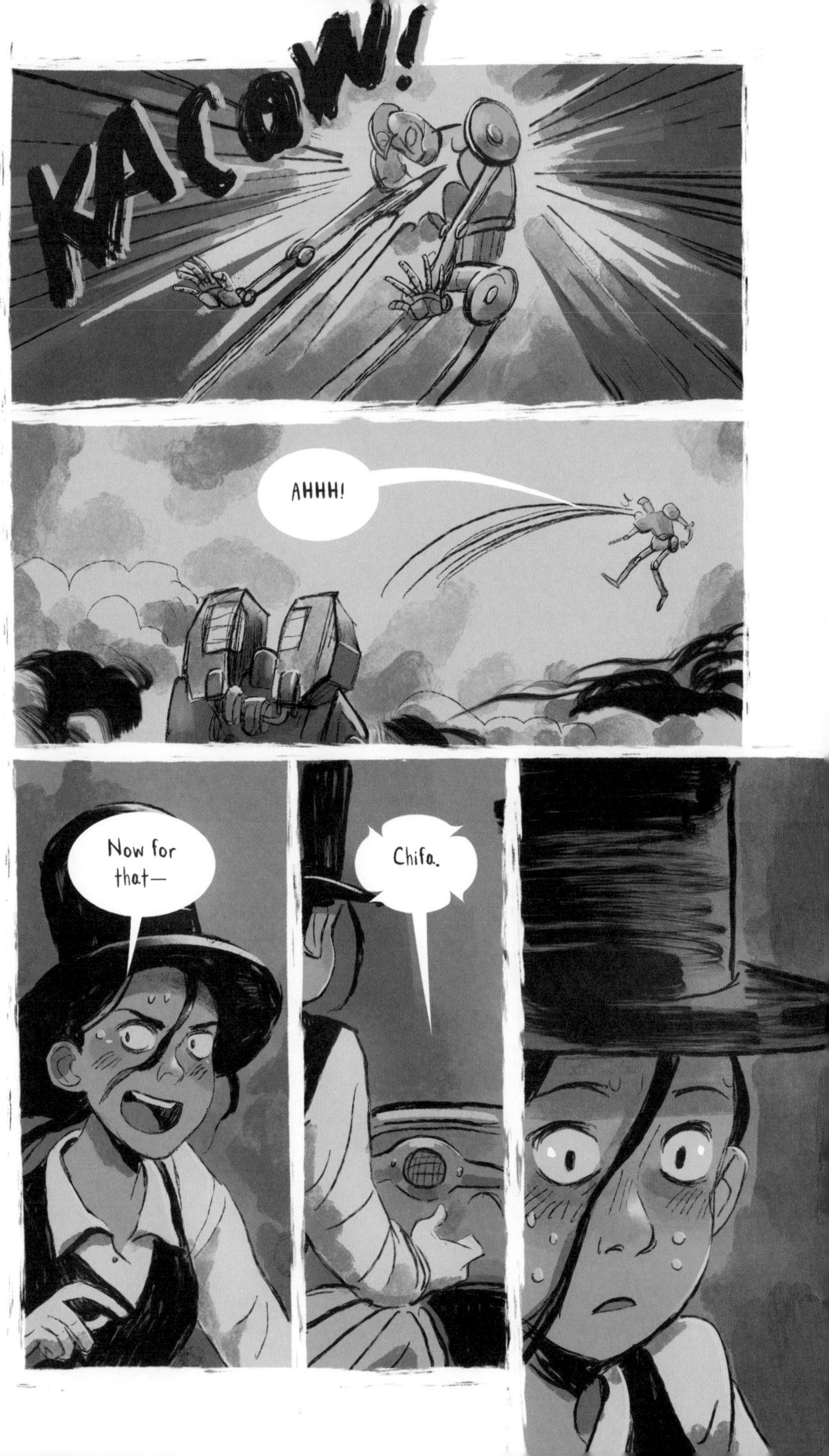
KACOW!
AHHH!
Now for that—
Chifa.

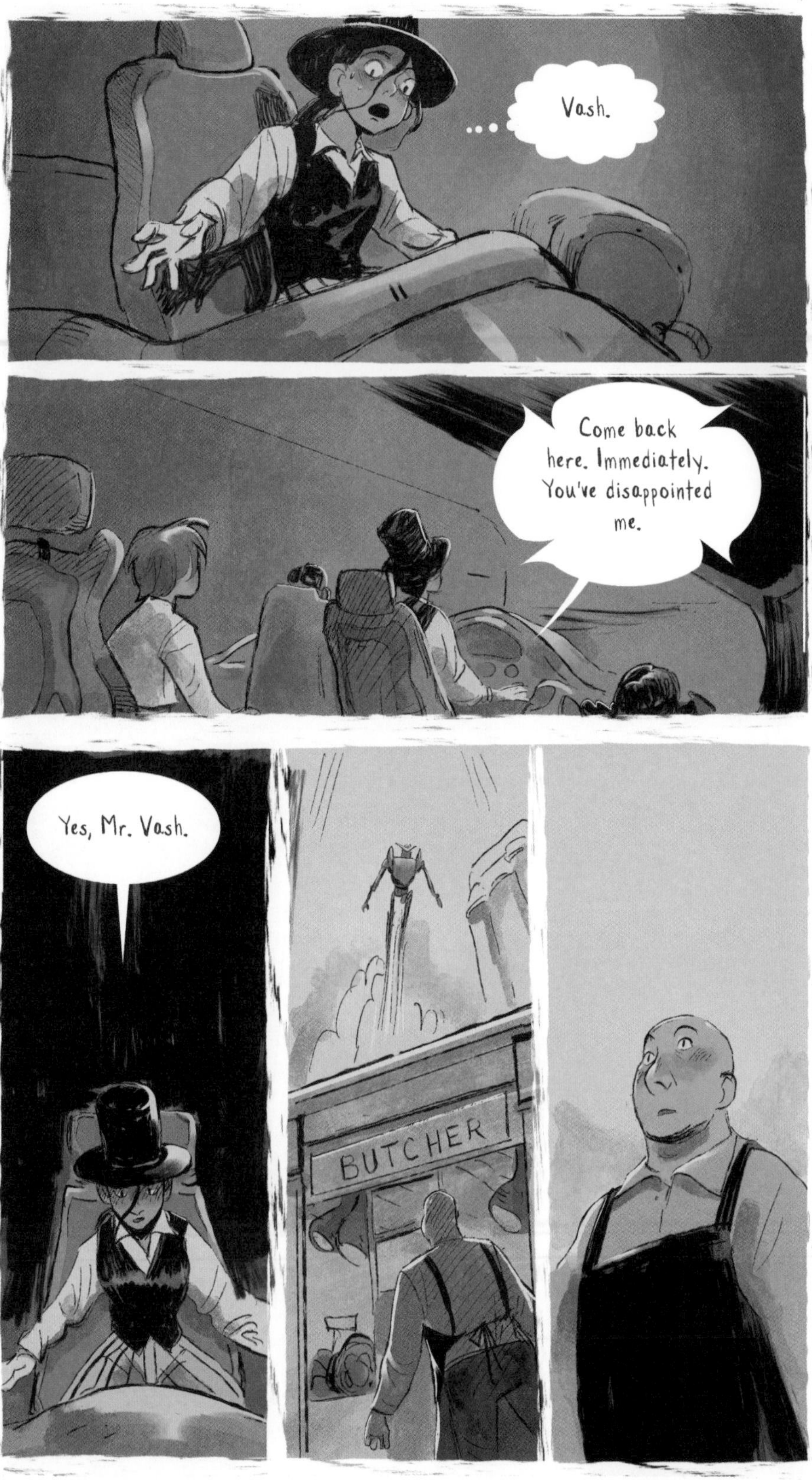
...
Vash.
Come back here. Immediately. You've disappointed me.
Yes, Mr. Vash.
BUTCHER

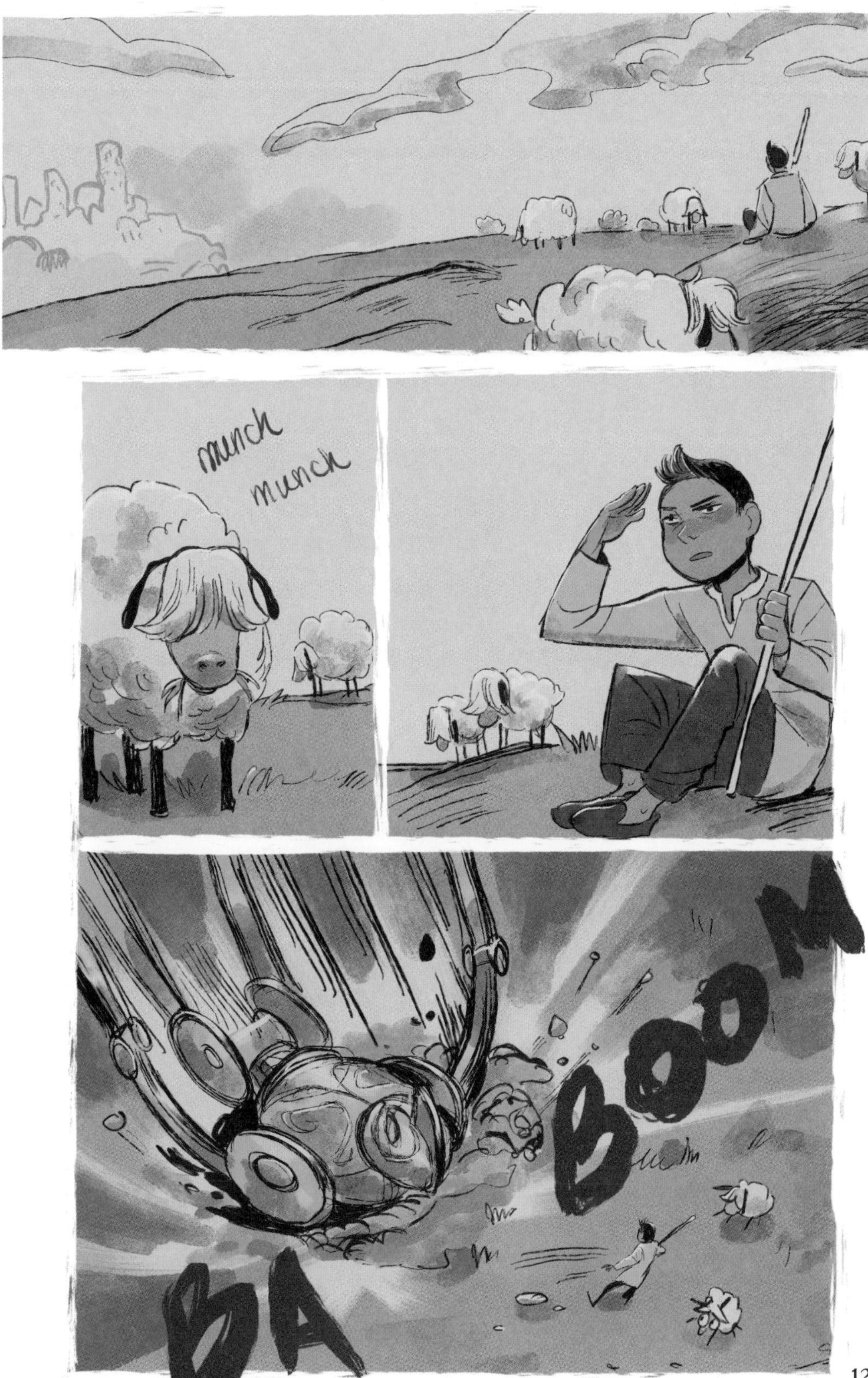
munch munch
BA
BOOM

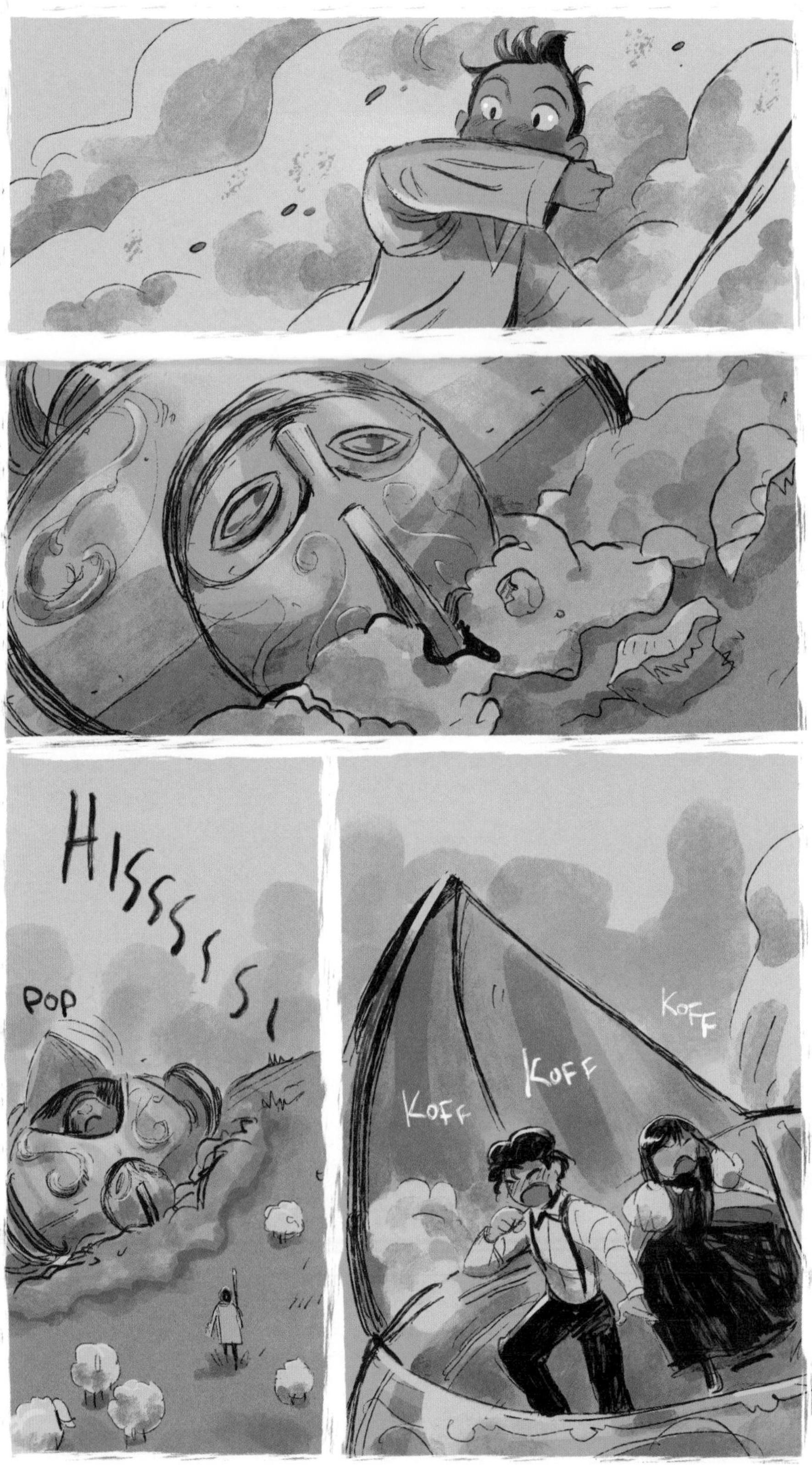
HISSSSSI
POP
KOFF
KOFF
KOFF

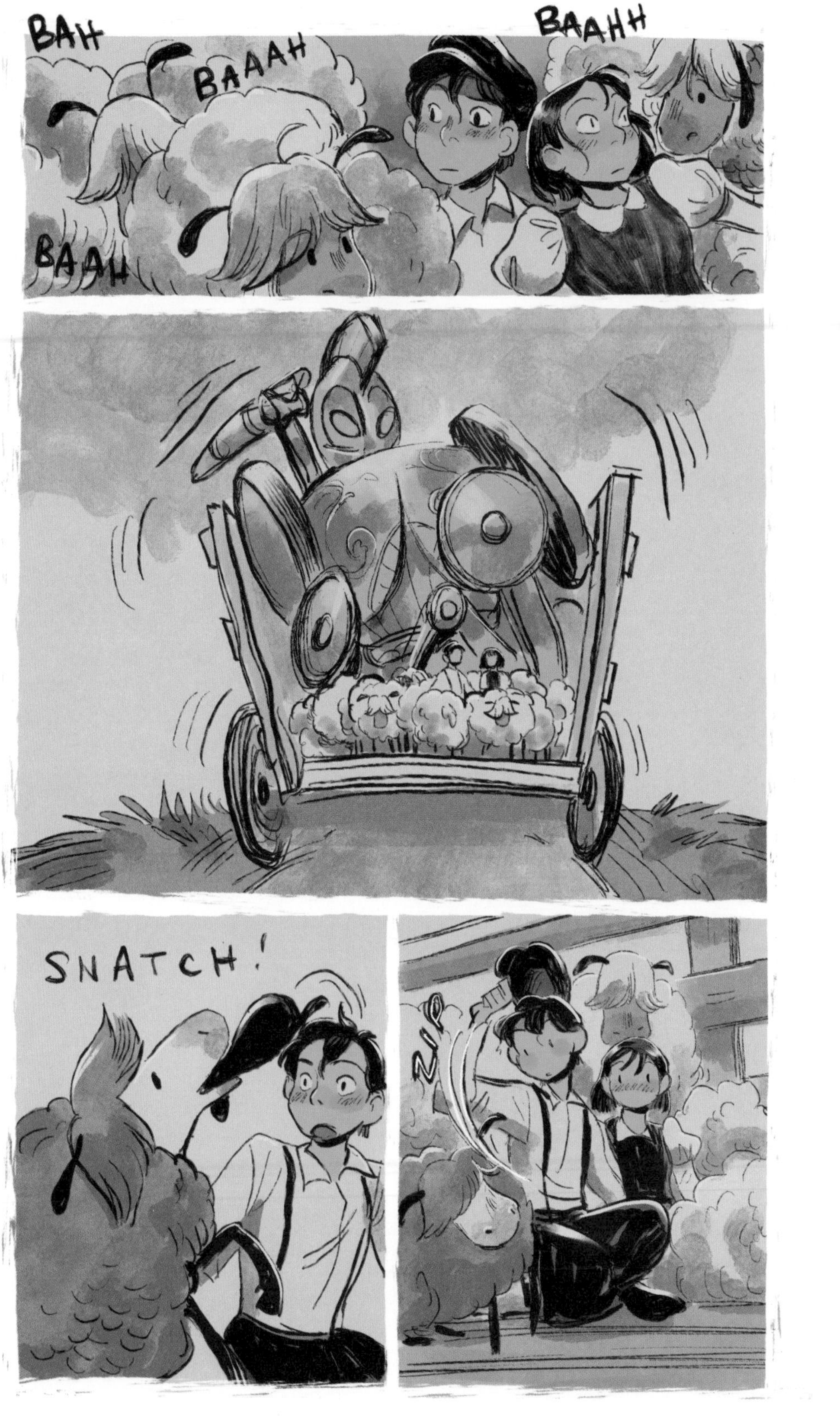
BAH
BAAAH
BAAHH
BAAH
SNATCH!
ZIP

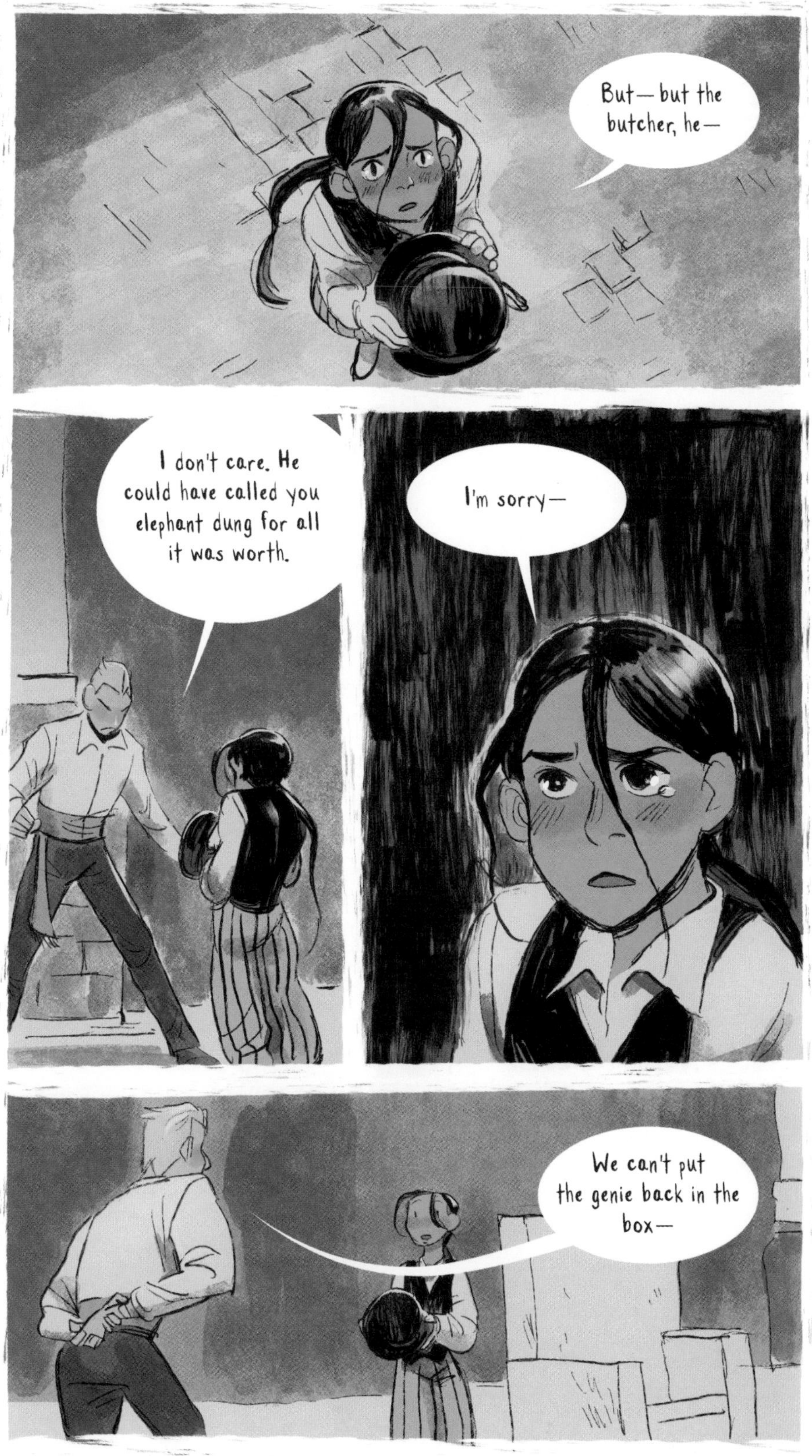
But— but the butcher, he—
I don't care. He could have called you elephant dung for all it was worth.
I'm sorry—
We can't put the genie back in the box—

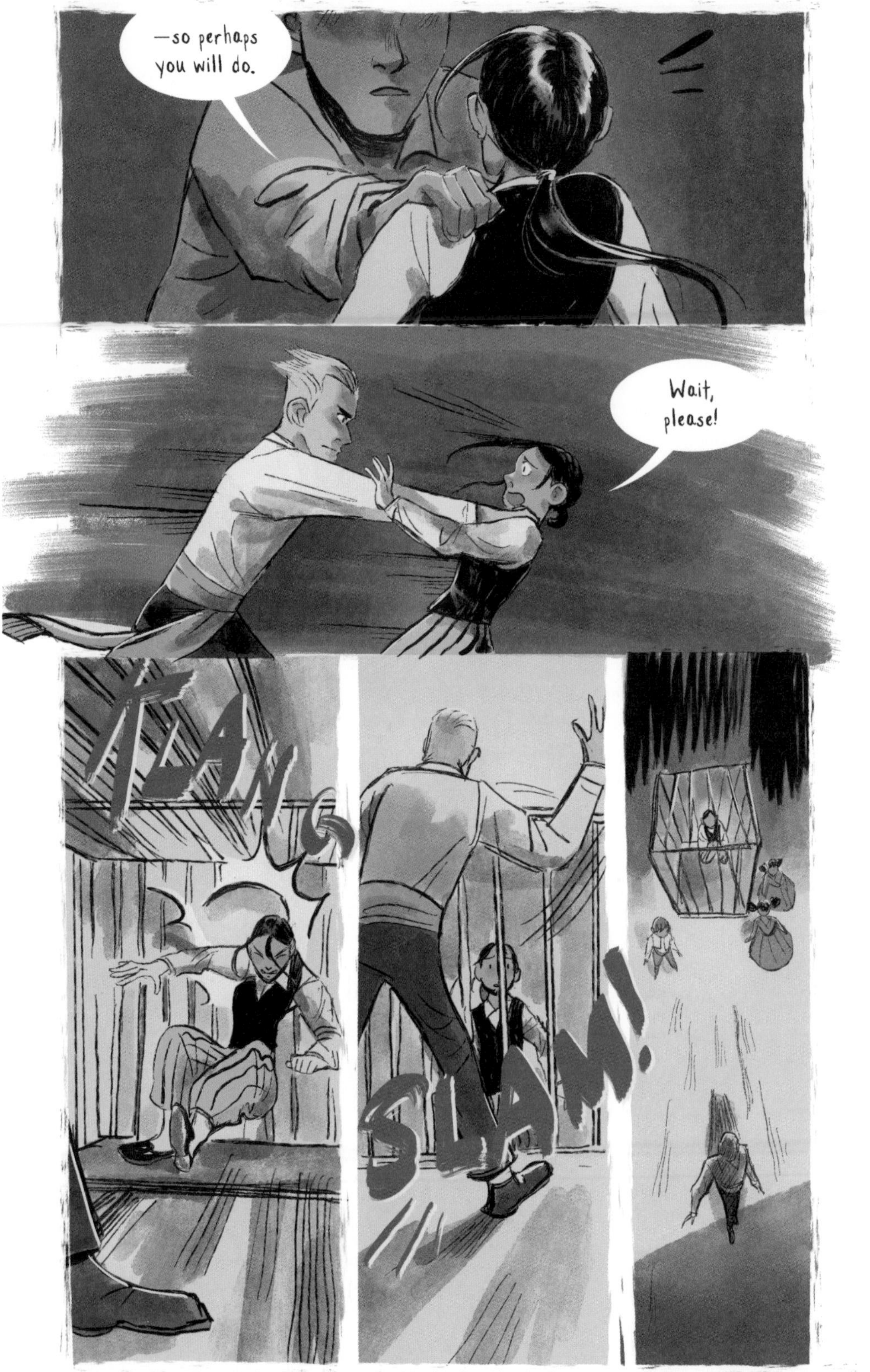
—so perhaps you will do.
Wait, please!
KLANG
SLAM!

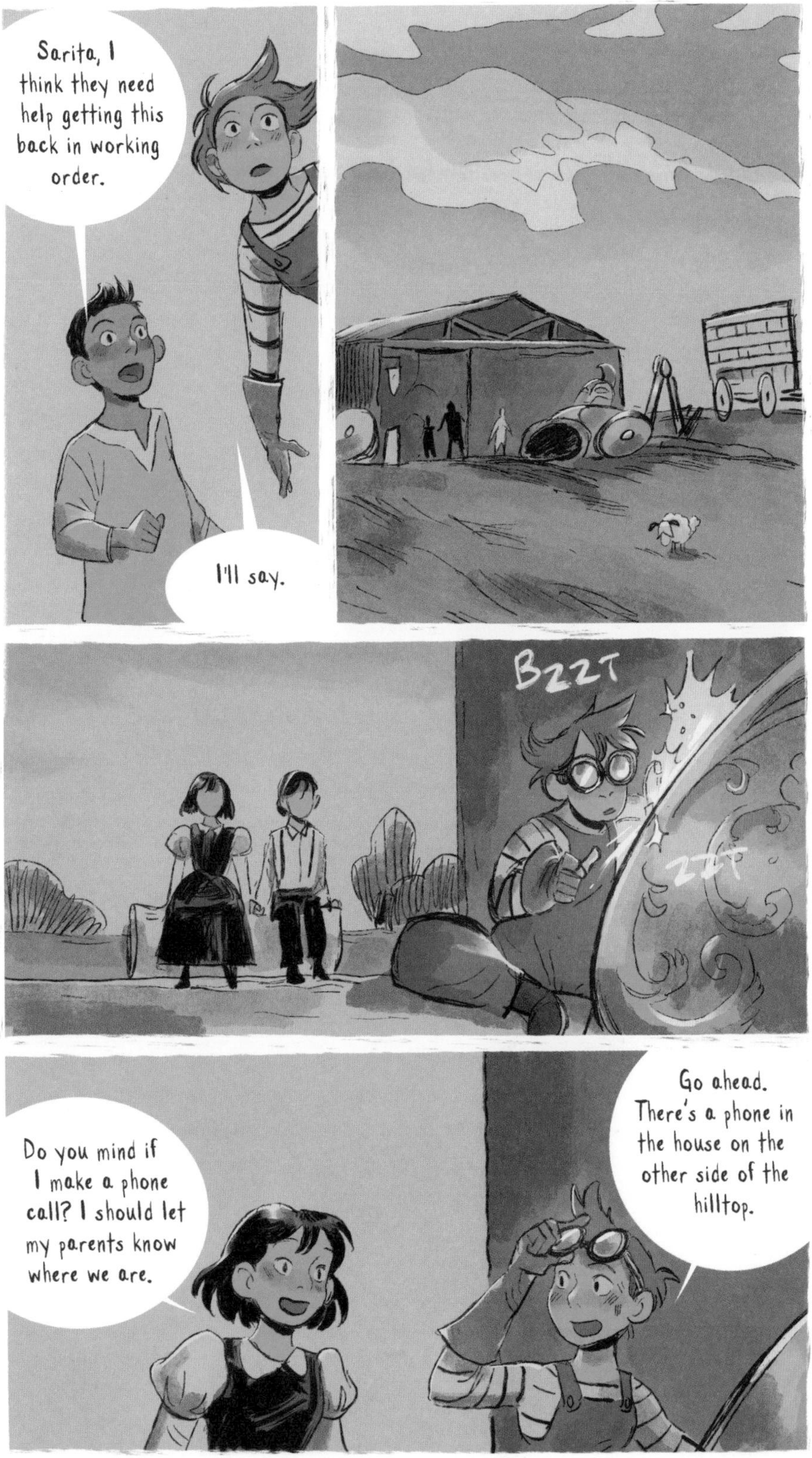
Sarita, I think they need help getting this back in working order.
I'll say.
BZZT
ZZT
Do you mind if I make a phone call? I should let my parents know where we are.
Go ahead. There's a phone in the house on the other side of the hilltop.

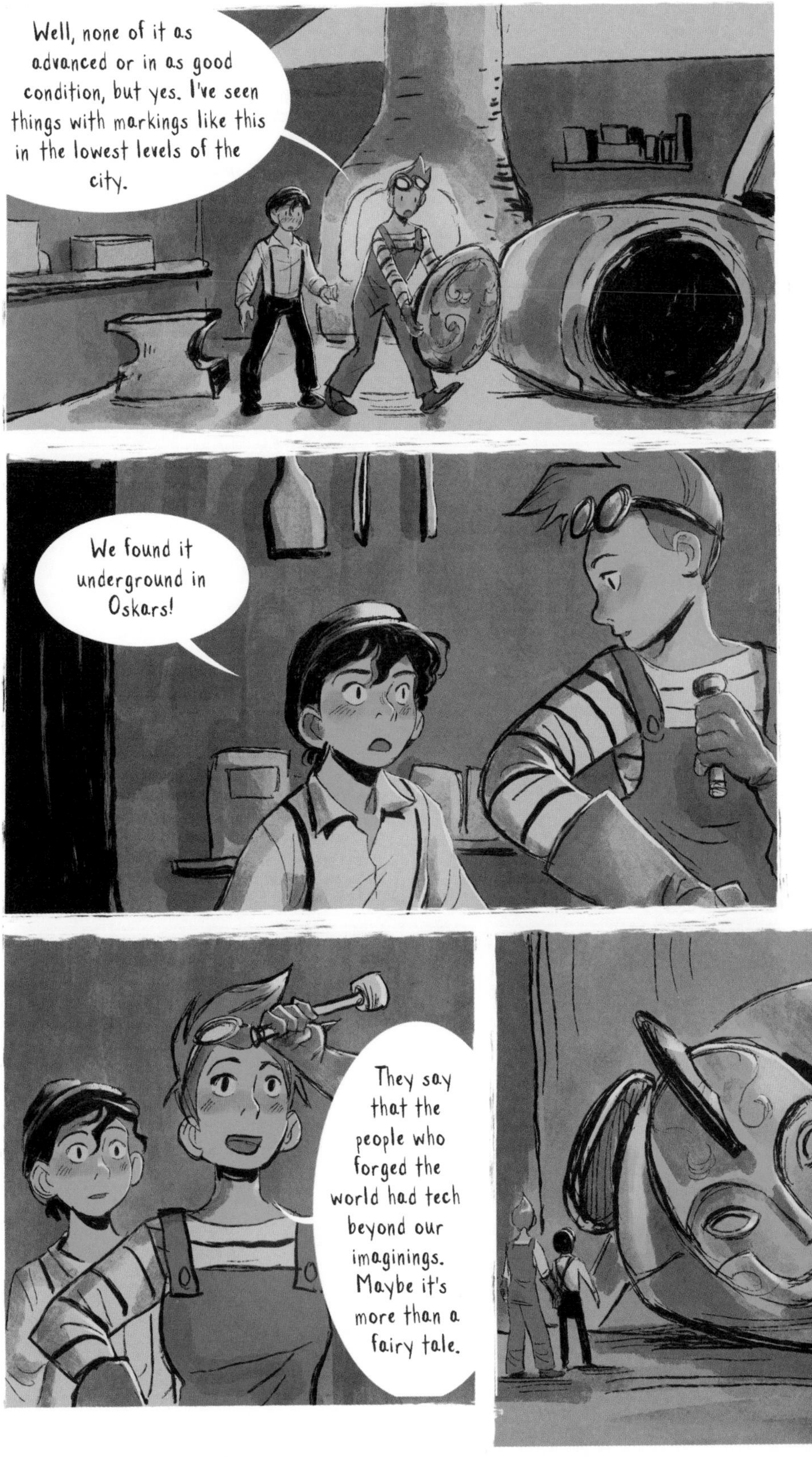
Well, none of it as advanced or in as good condition, but yes. I've seen things with markings like this in the lowest levels of the city.
We found it underground in Oskars!
They say that the people who forged the world had tech beyond our imaginings. Maybe it's more than a fairy tale.

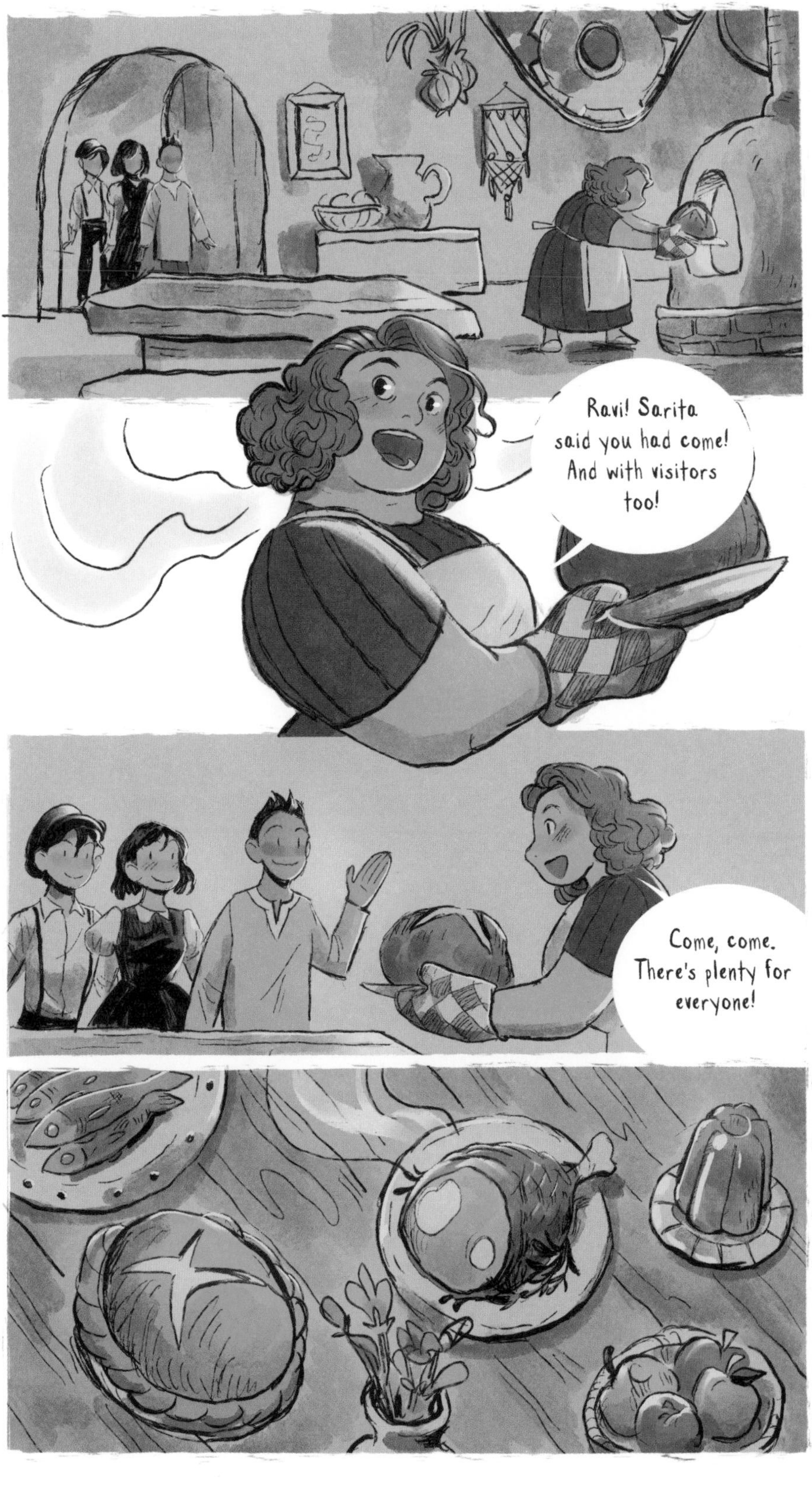
Ravi! Sarita said you had come! And with visitors too!
Come, come. There's plenty for everyone!

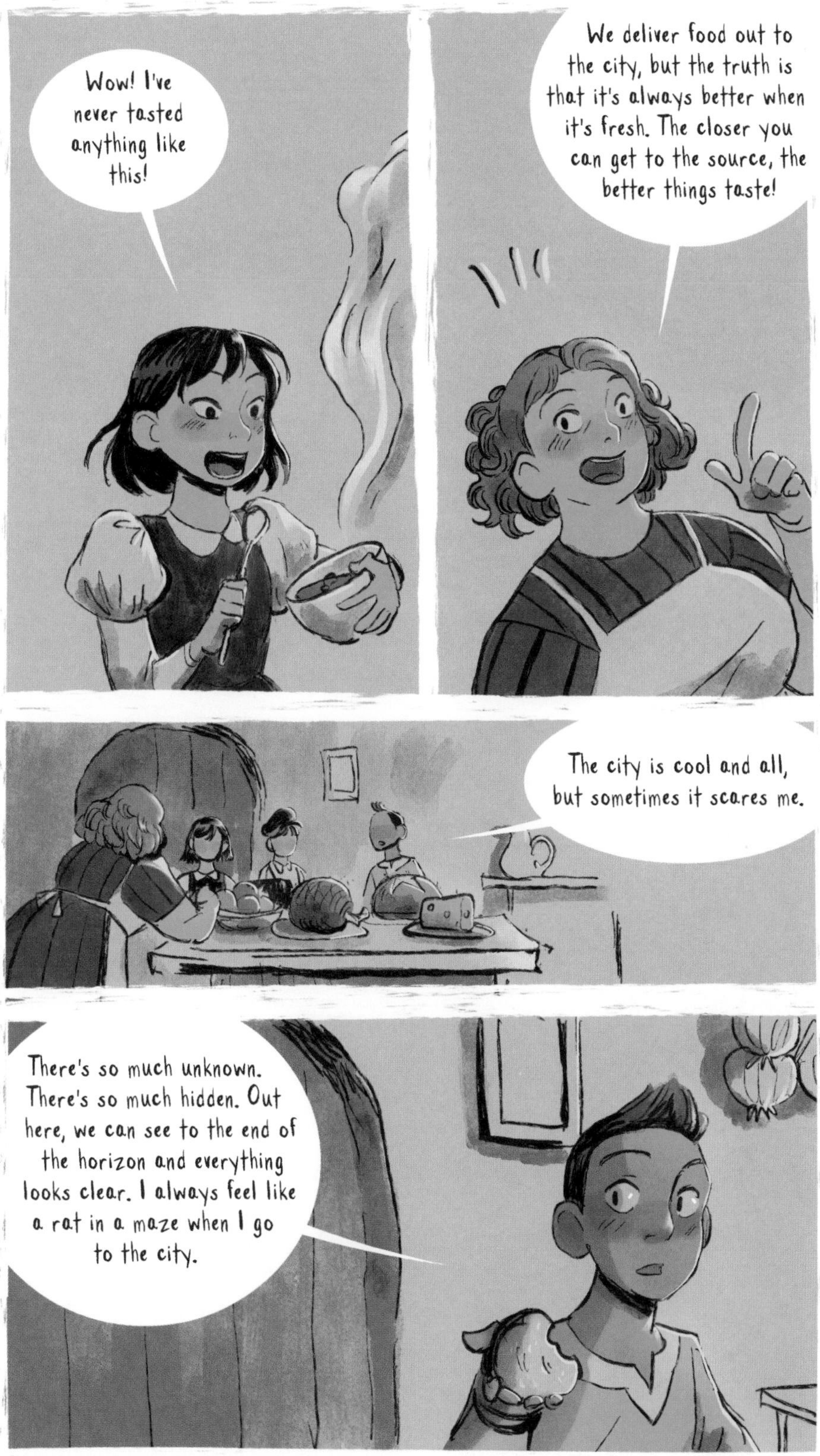
Wow! I've never tasted anything like this!
We deliver food out to the city, but the truth is that it's always better when it's fresh. The closer you can get to the source, the better things taste!
The city is cool and all, but sometimes it scares me.
There's so much unknown. There's so much hidden. Out here, we can see to the end of the horizon and everything looks clear. I always feel like a rat in a maze when I go to the city.

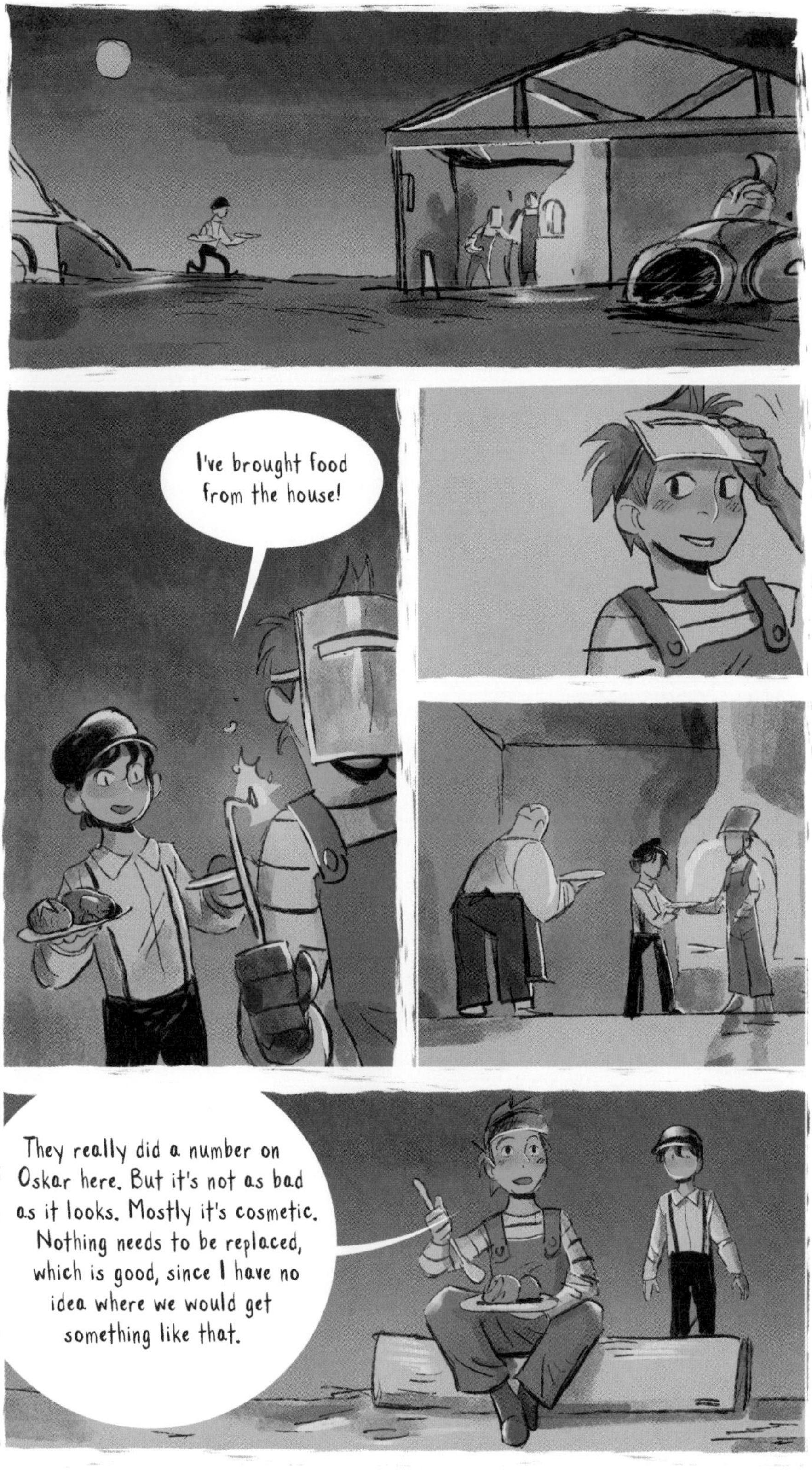
I've brought food from the house!
They really did a number on Oskar here. But it's not as bad as it looks. Mostly it's cosmetic. Nothing needs to be replaced, which is good, since I have no idea where we would get something like that.

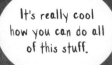

It's really cool how you can do all of this stuff.

Not that impressive, really. What's impressive is how you and Hannah can fly it. How did that happen, by the way?

It's a long story . . .

Well, why don't you tell it to me while I weld? It will make the time go faster.

Have you heard the tale of the princess and the puzzle box?
I have.
It's not just a fairy tale. Some say it's the origins of our world.
What?
In the story, there's a princess with three brothers who are always at war. They say that humans, we are that princess. The brothers are the three cities of Oskars, Edmonda, and Alexios.
ALEXIOS
The kingdoms were always at war. The prince was a race of very developed beings that disappeared long ago. Oskar? I think Oskar is a knight that they left for us.
OSKARS

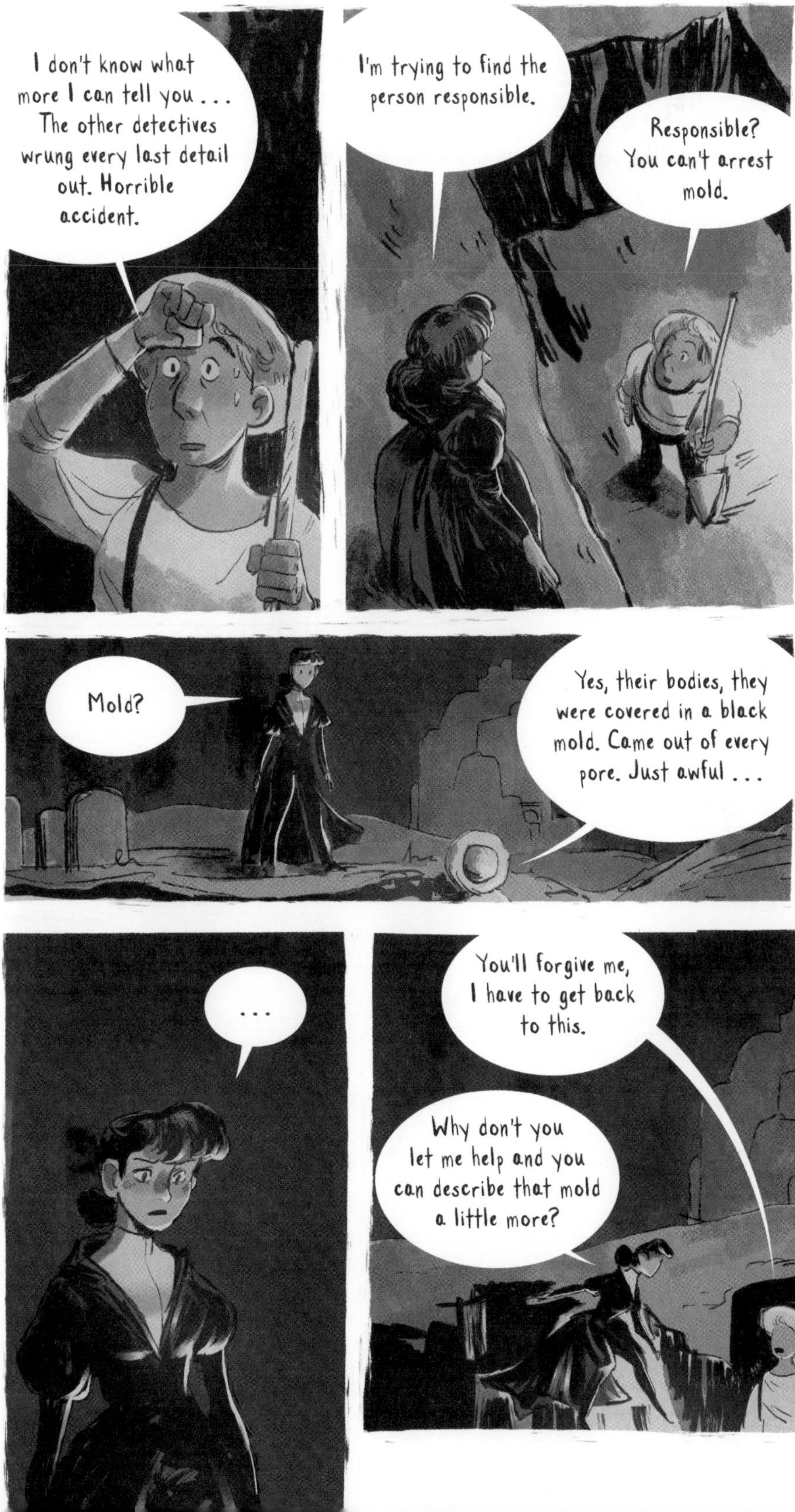
I don't know what more I can tell you . . . The other detectives wrung every last detail out. Horrible accident.
I'm trying to find the person responsible.
Responsible? You can't arrest mold.
Mold?
Yes, their bodies, they were covered in a black mold. Came out of every pore. Just awful . . .
. . .
You'll forgive me, I have to get back to this.
Why don't you let me help and you can describe that mold a little more?

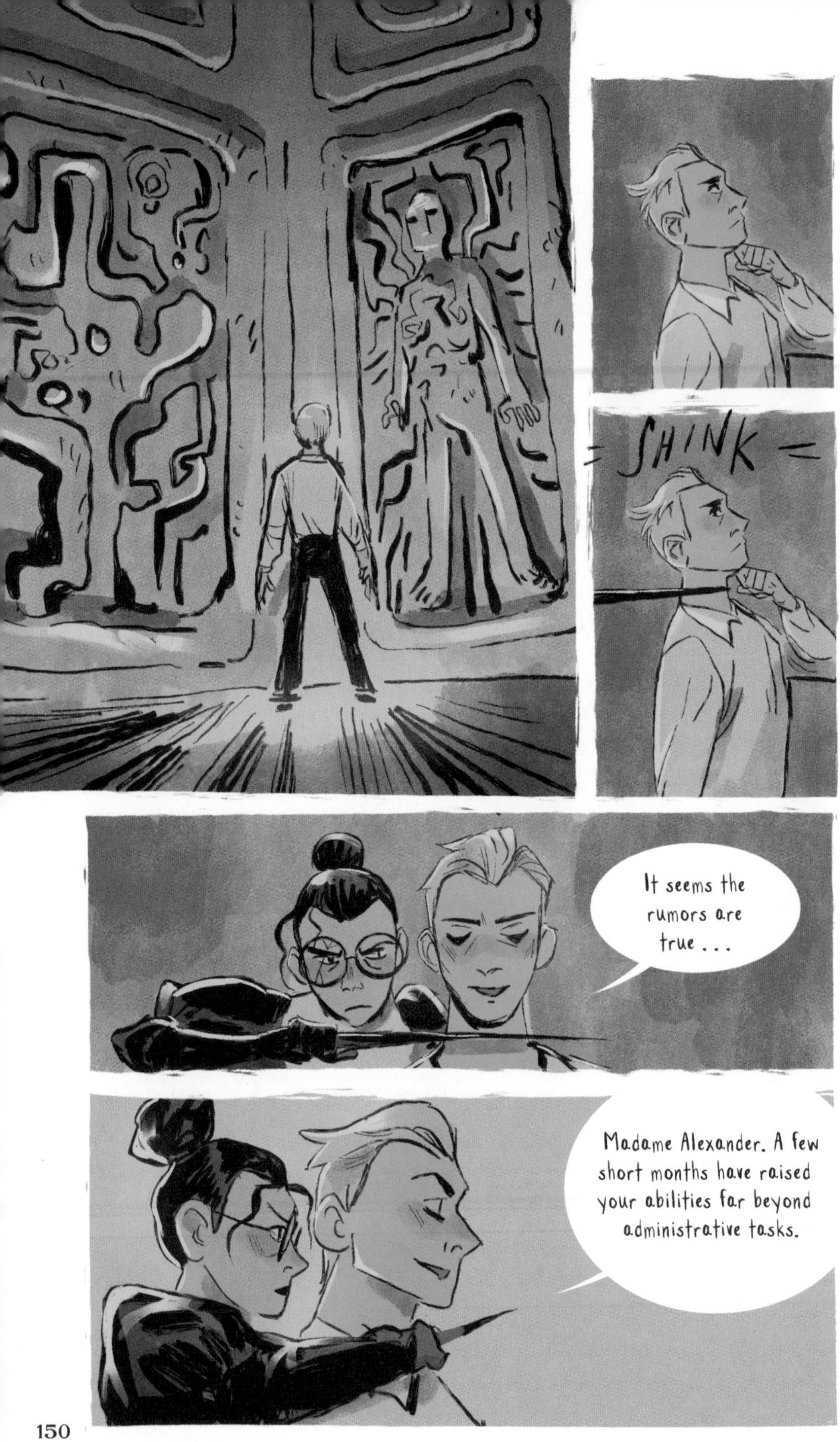
SHINK
It seems the rumors are true . . .
Madame Alexander. A few short months have raised your abilities far beyond administrative tasks.

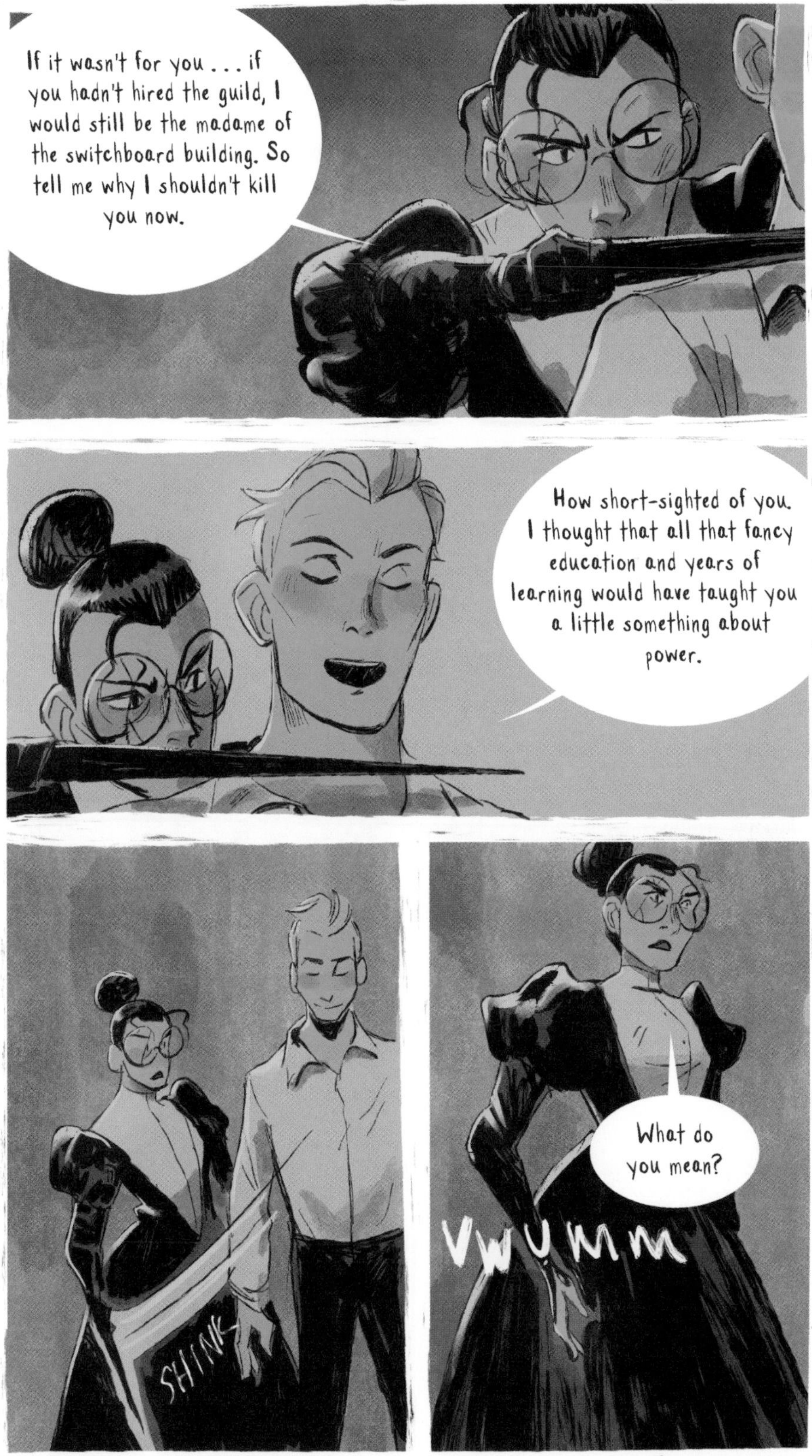
If it wasn't for you . . . if you hadn't hired the guild, I would still be the madame of the switchboard building. So tell me why I shouldn't kill you now.
How short-sighted of you. I thought that all that fancy education and years of learning would have taught you a little something about power.
SHINK
What do you mean?
VWUMM

Tell me, Madame, what makes you think you can kill that boy when a guild of highly trained assassins could not?

Those other assassins were talented, but they lacked something that I have.

And what is that?

A need for revenge. I will not fail, and not because of some silly threats from a pocket watch. Their lives are now my purpose.

Not to mention I've got a kind of ancient magic procured from the lowest levels of Oskars.

PING!

Well, Madame, the boy is your affair now. I wanted him dead so he couldn't reveal the Megantic, but we're well past that, aren't we?

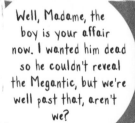

Now, wouldn't someone like yourself be interested in favor with someone like that?

What proof do you have? This sounds like more superstitious nonsense.

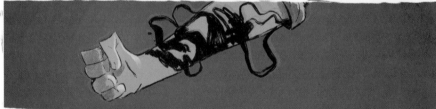

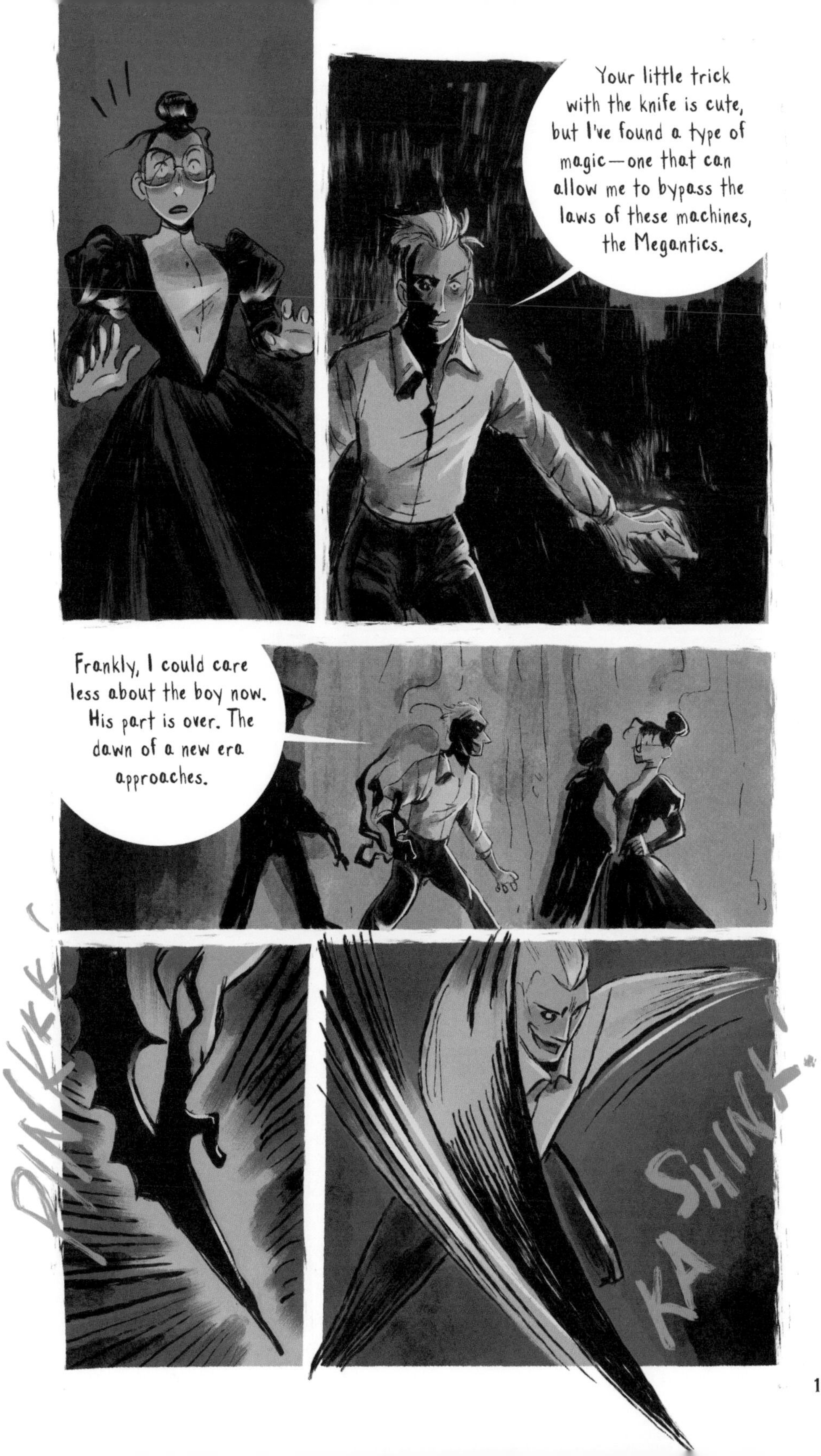

Your little trick with the knife is cute, but I've found a type of magic—one that can allow me to bypass the laws of these machines, the Megantics.
Frankly, I could care less about the boy now. His part is over. The dawn of a new era approaches.
PINKKK
SHINK
KA

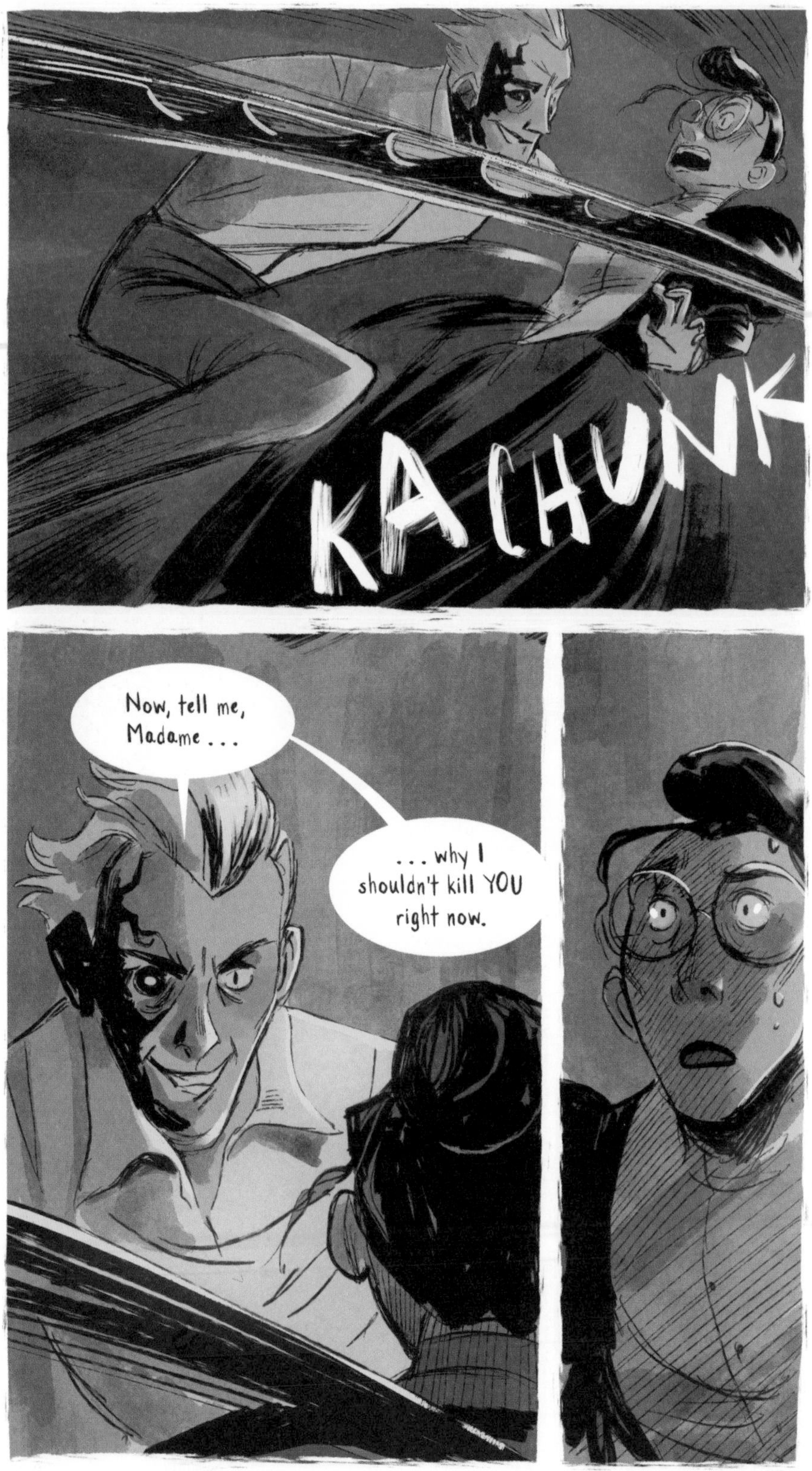
KACHUNK
Now, tell me, Madame . . .
. . . why I shouldn't kill YOU right now.

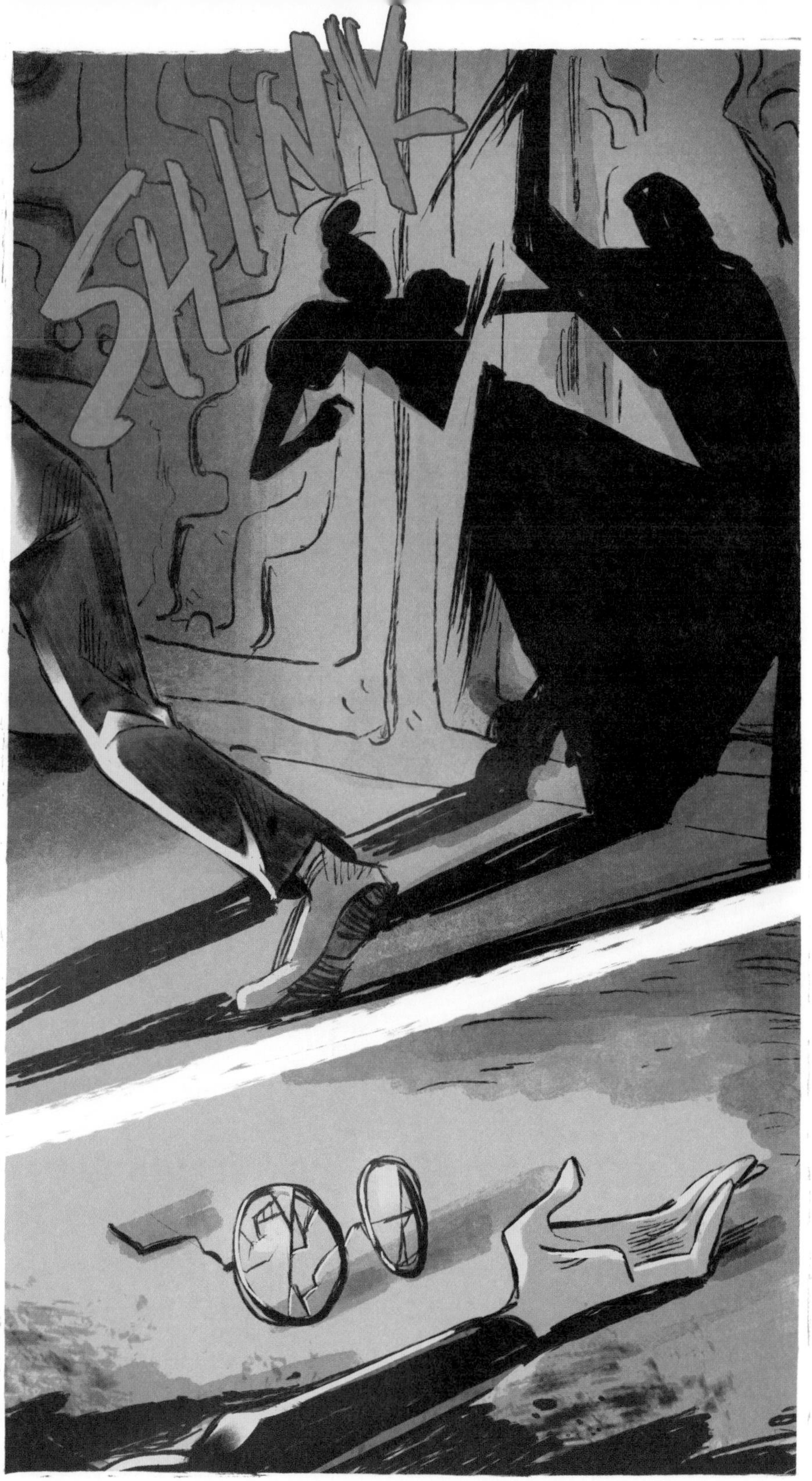
SHINK

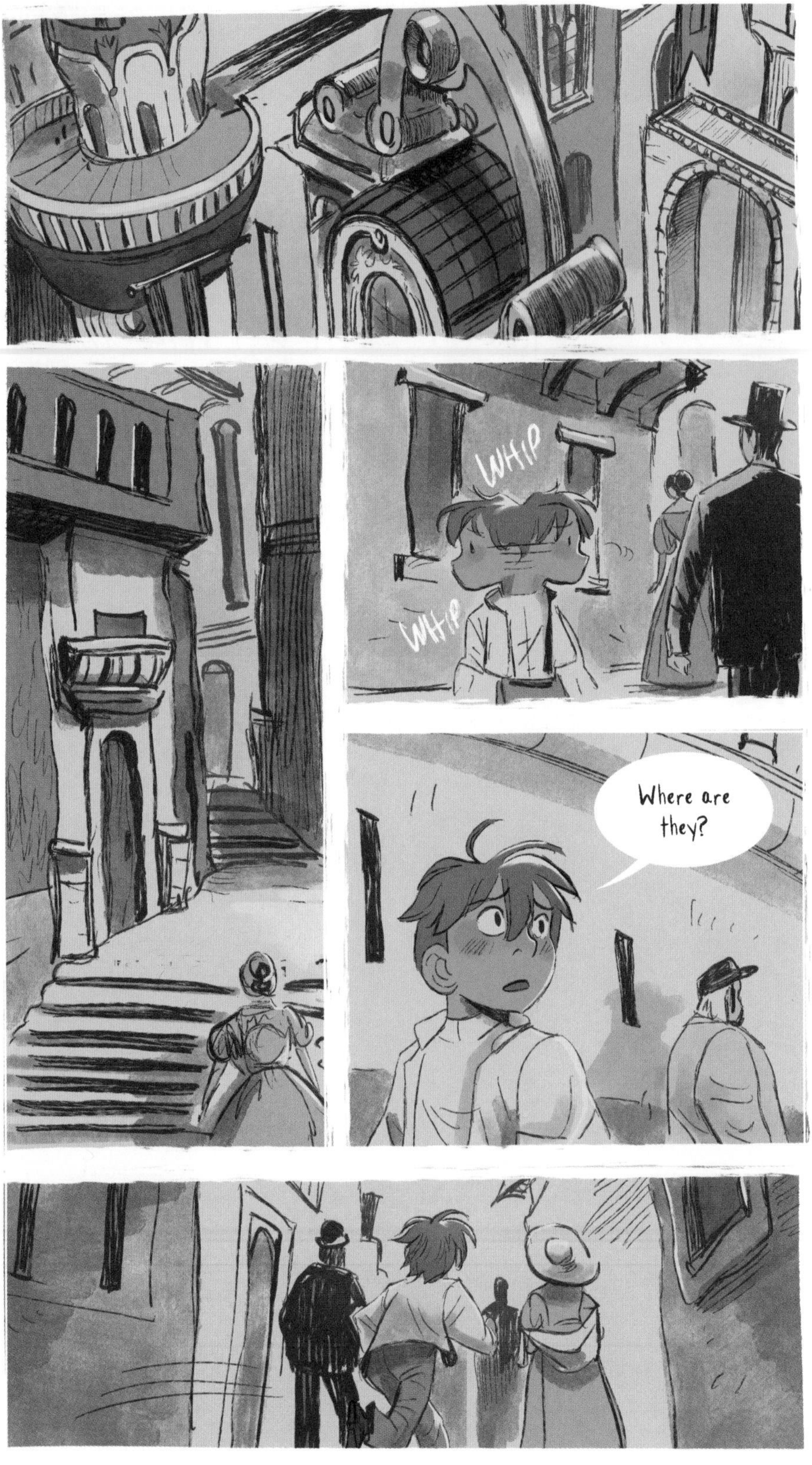
WHIP
WHIP
Where are they?

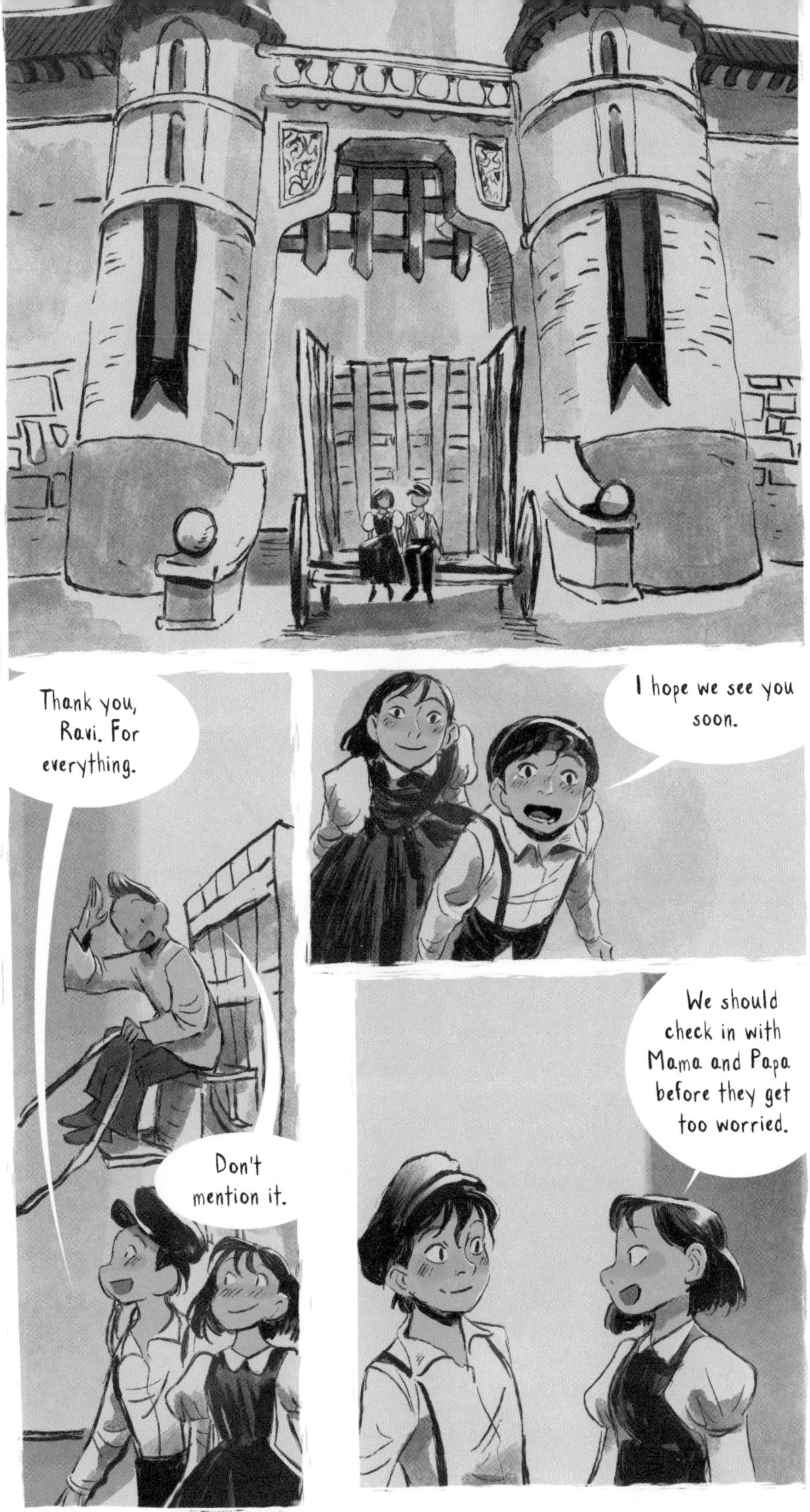
Thank you, Ravi. For everything.
I hope we see you soon.
Don't mention it.
We should check in with Mama and Papa before they get too worried.

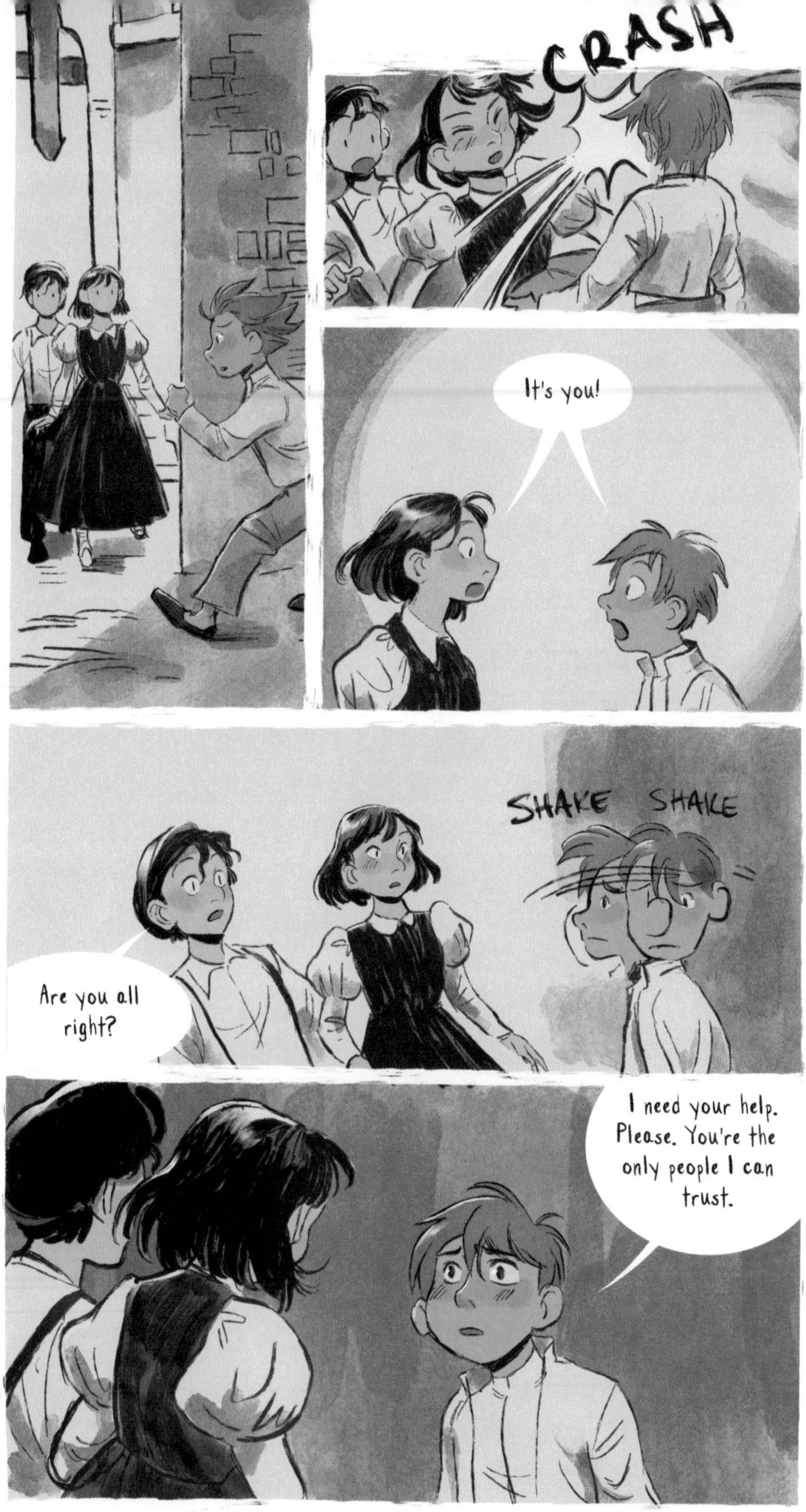
CRASH
It's you!
SHAKE SHAKE
Are you all right?
I need your help. Please. You're the only people I can trust.

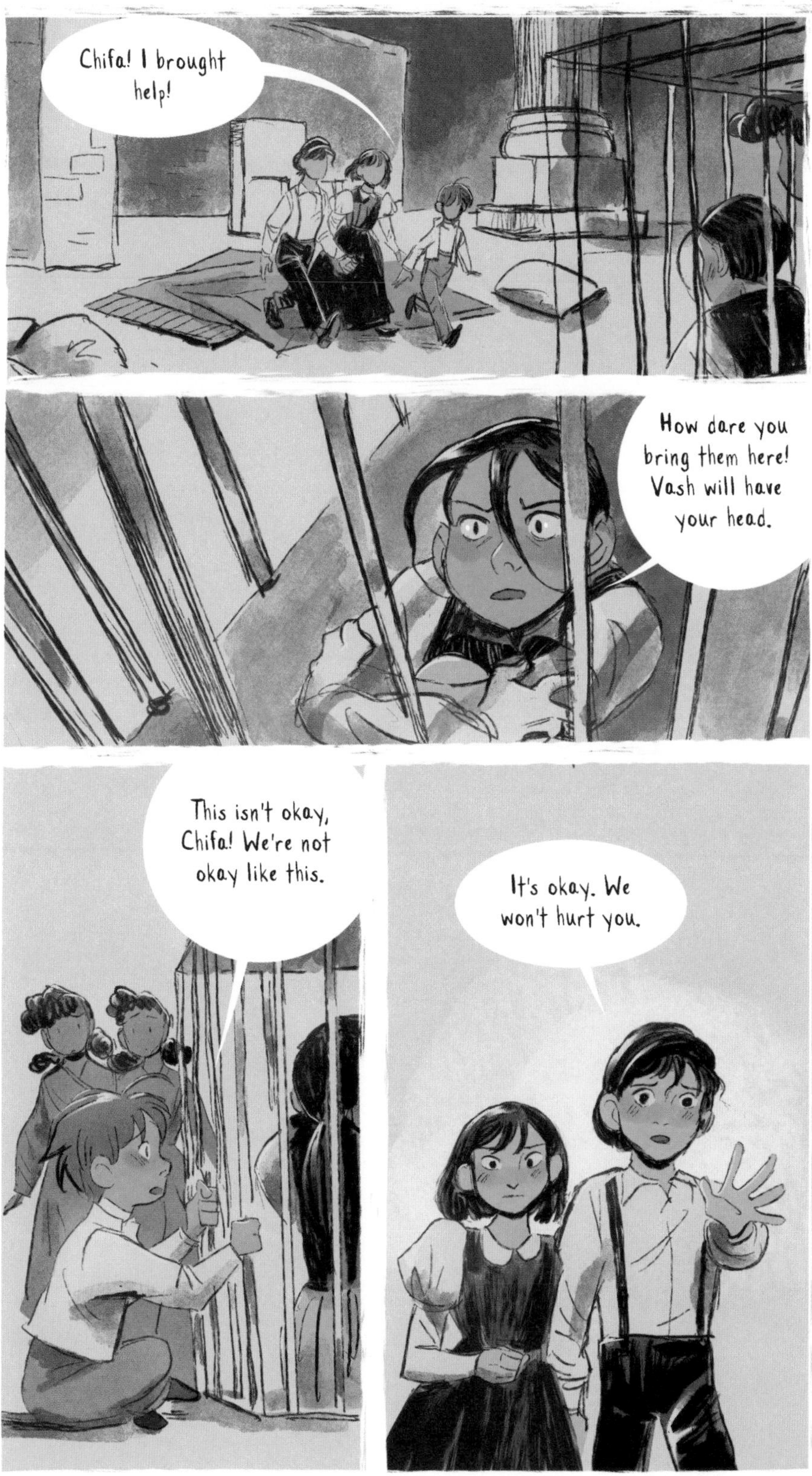
Chifa! I brought help!
How dare you bring them here! Vash will have your head.
This isn't okay, Chifa! We're not okay like this.
It's okay. We won't hurt you.

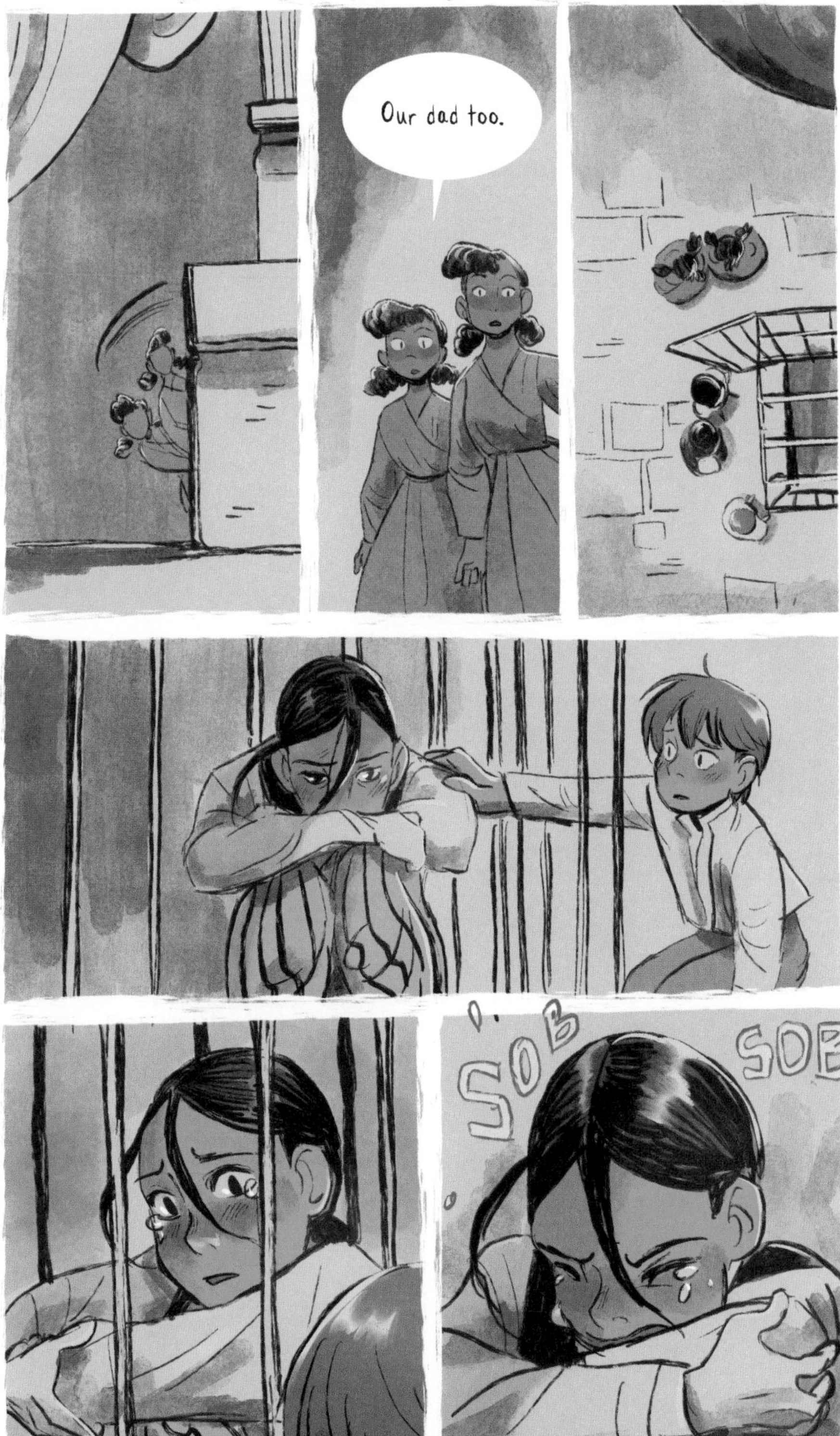
Our dad too.
SOB
SOB

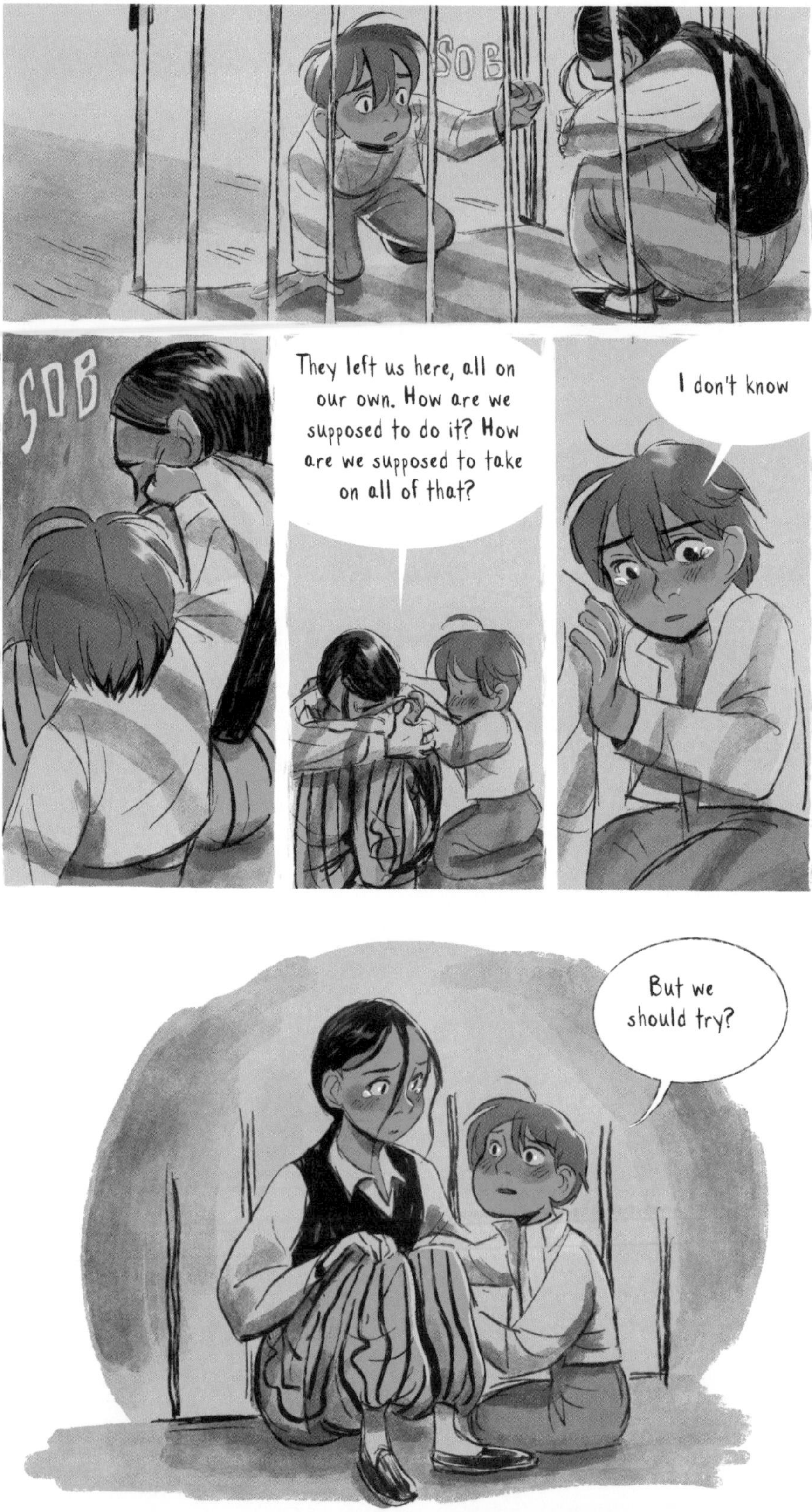
SOB
SOB
They left us here, all on our own. How are we supposed to do it? How are we supposed to take on all of that?
I don't know
But we should try?

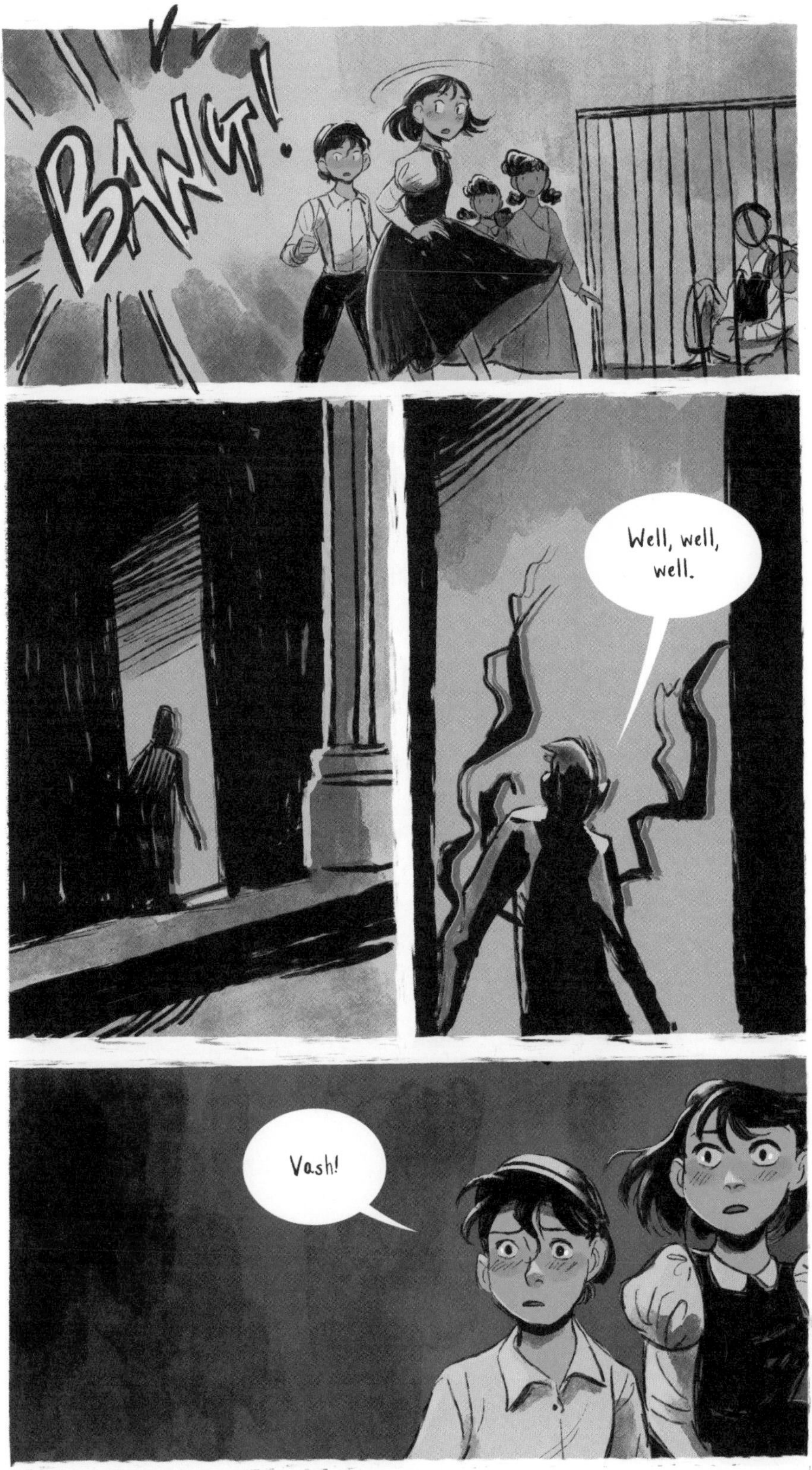
BANG!
Well, well, well.
Vash!

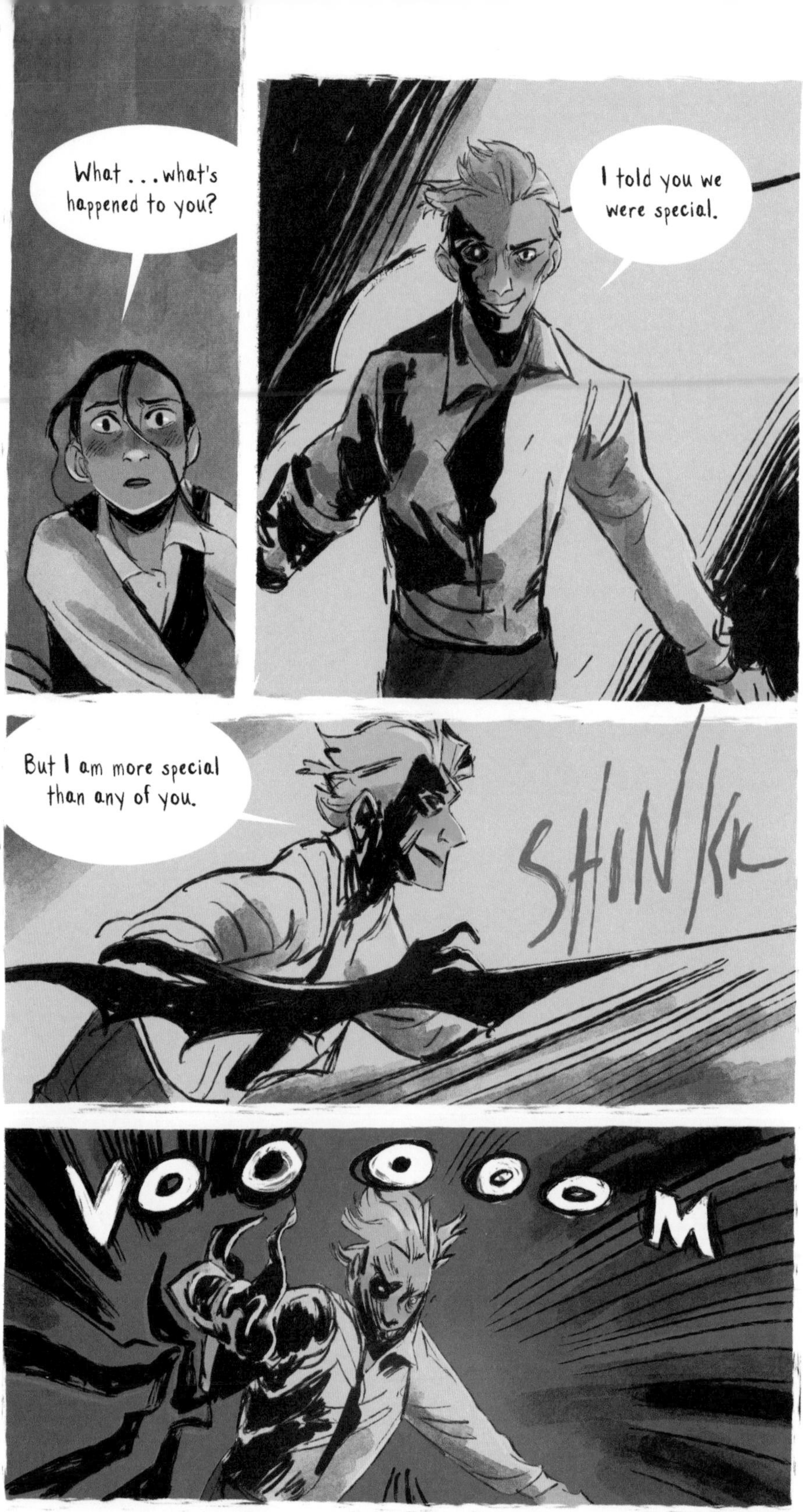

What . . . what's happened to you?
I told you we were special.
But I am more special than any of you.
SHINKK
VOOOOOOM

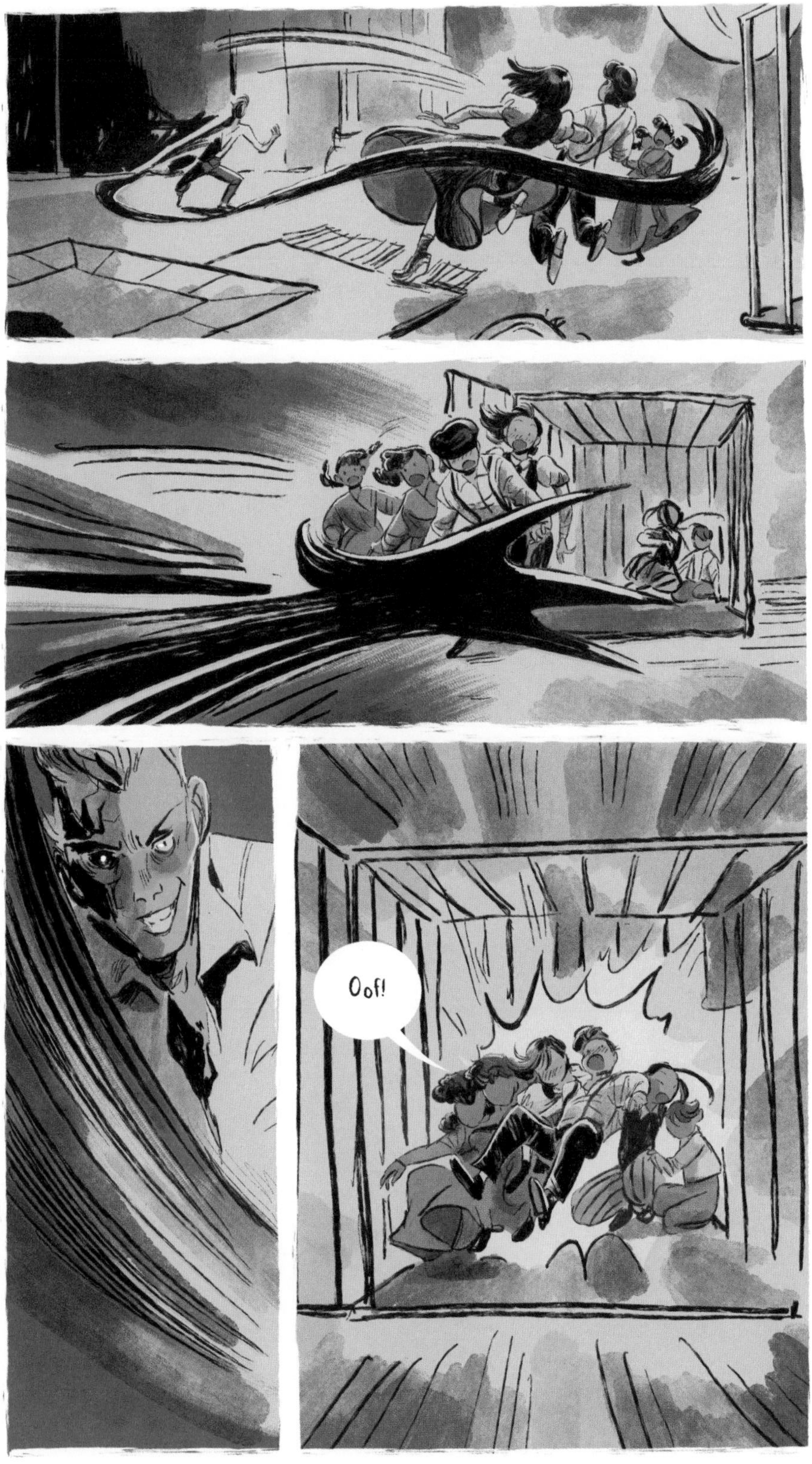
Oof!

BOOOM

But—you need four to pilot it.

The rules no longer apply to me, Chifa. You of all people should know that.

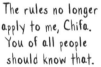

After months hiding out here in this filthy city, I've finally gained enough power to control it. I only needed you to find the Alexios Megantic. Now you are useless to me.

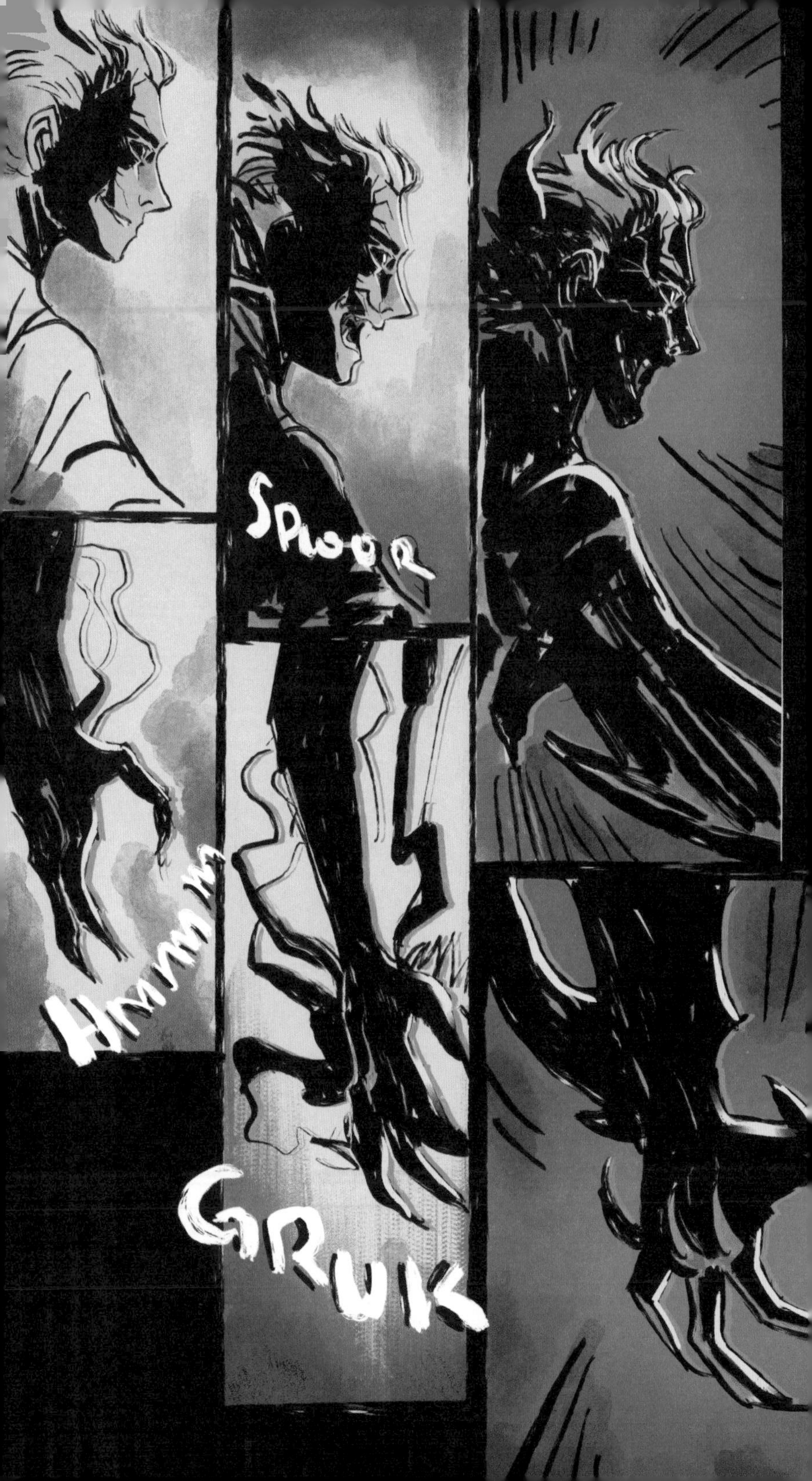
SPLOOR
HMMMM
GRUK

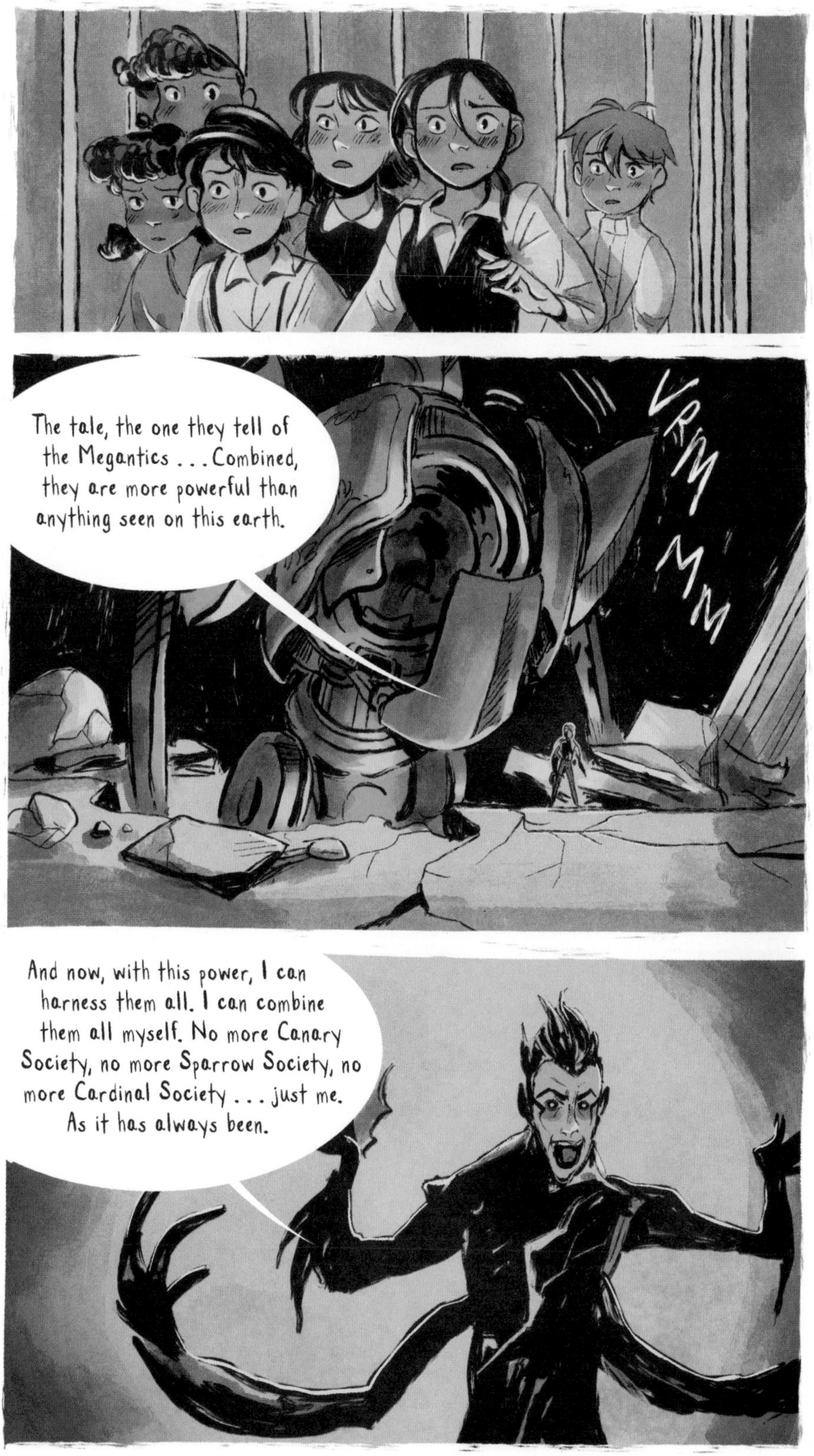
The tale, the one they tell of the Megantics . . . Combined, they are more powerful than anything seen on this earth.
VRMMMM
And now, with this power, I can harness them all. I can combine them all myself. No more Canary Society, no more Sparrow Society, no more Cardinal Society . . . just me. As it has always been.

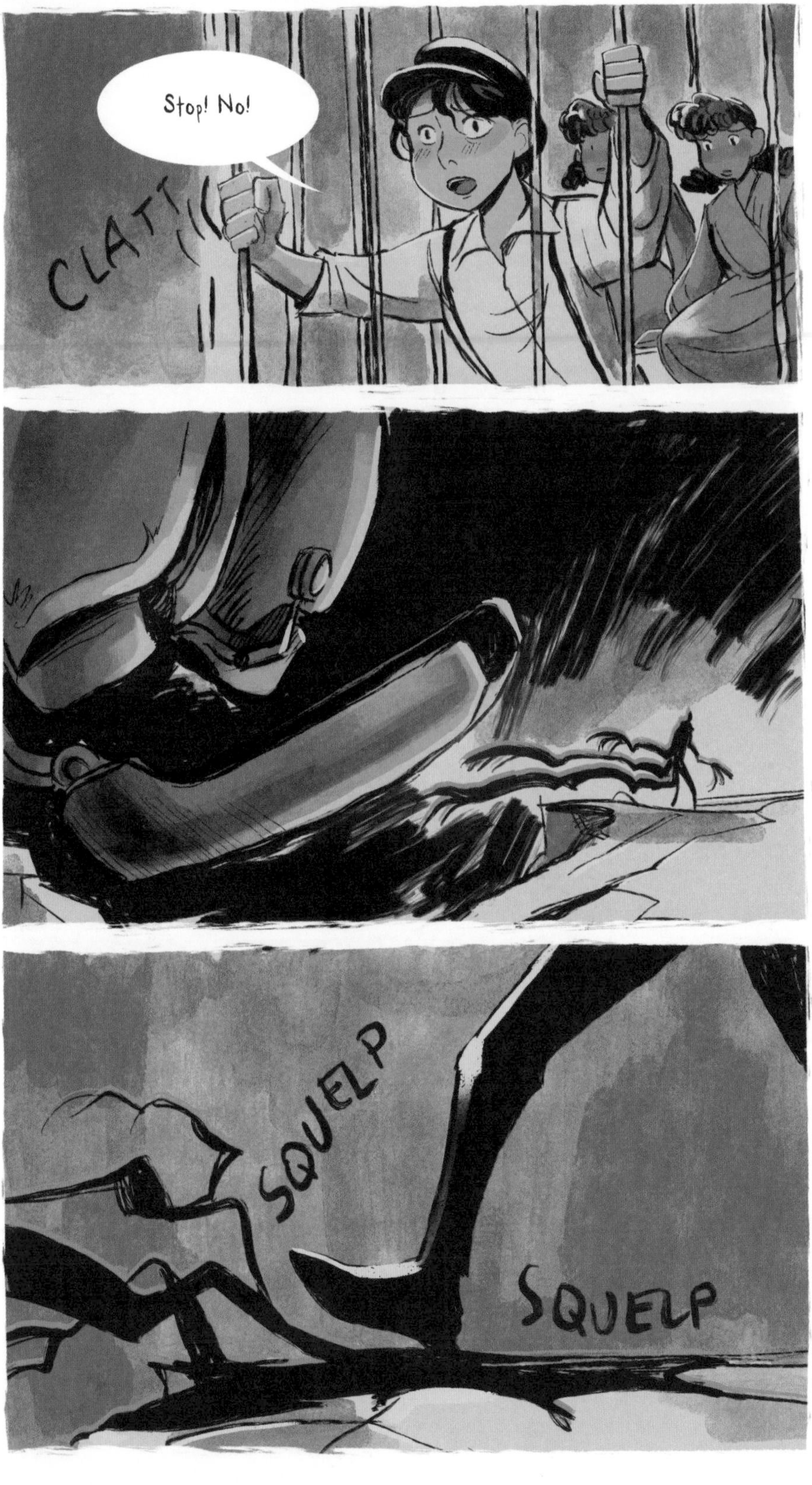
Stop! No!
CLATT
SQUELP
SQUELP

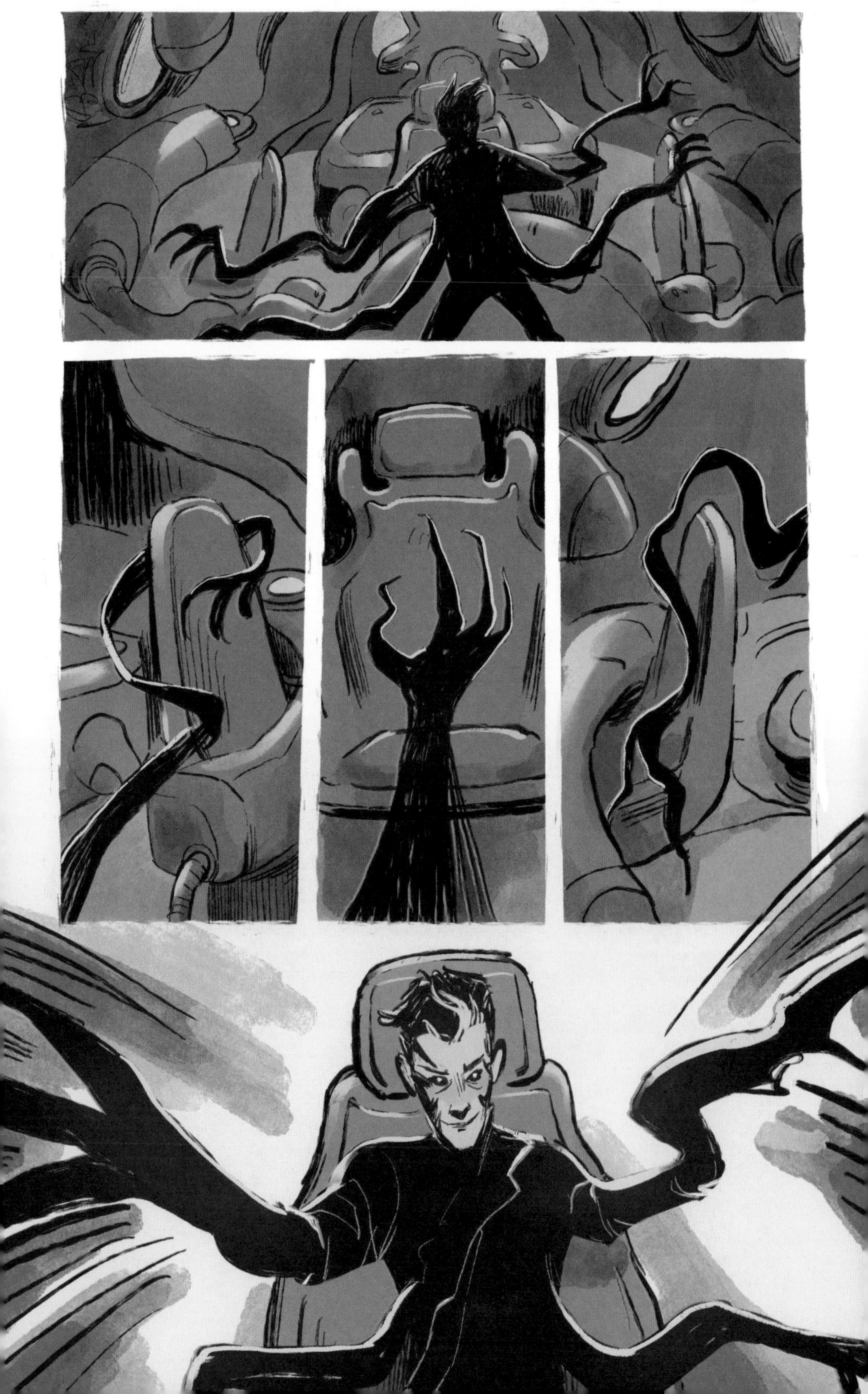

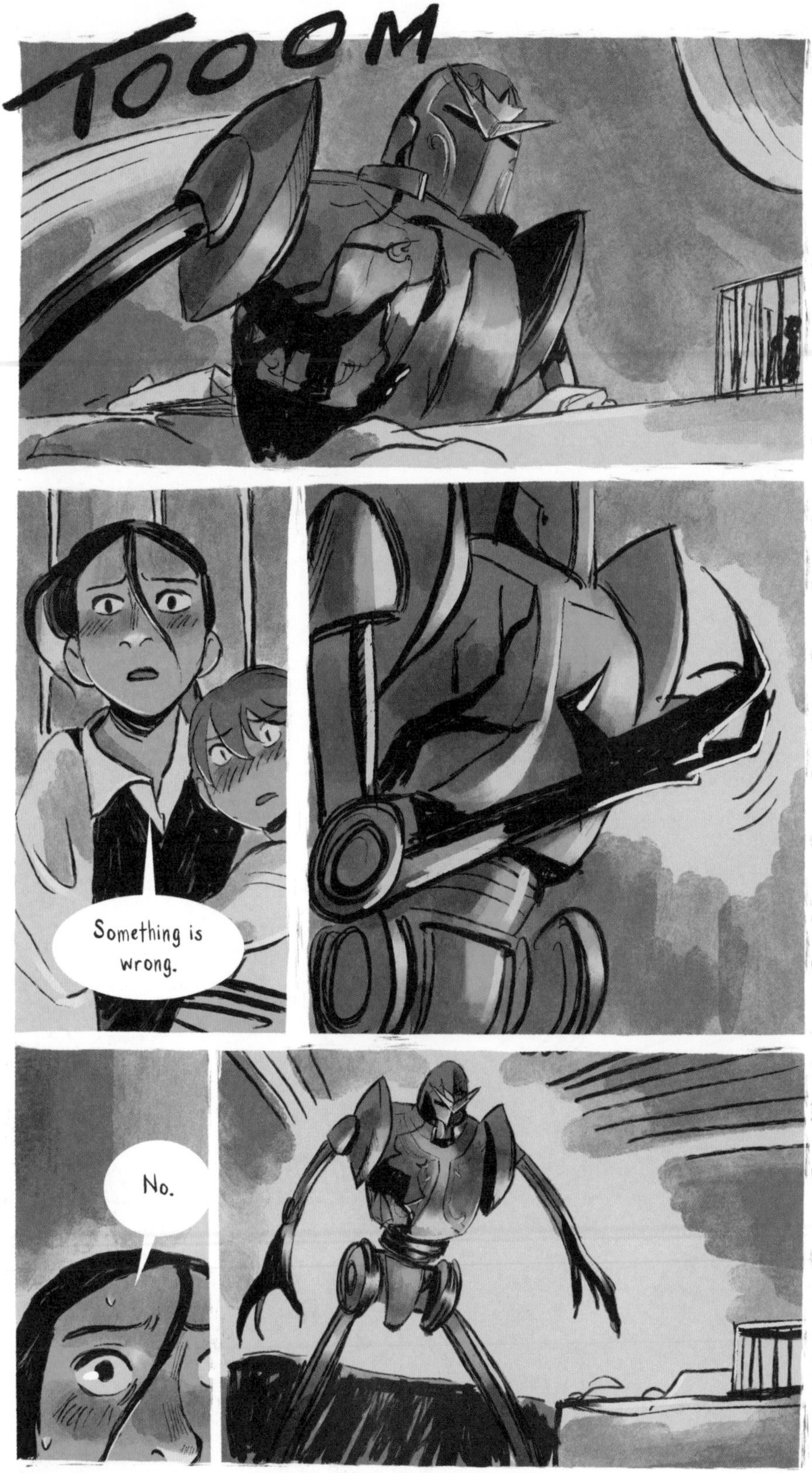
TOOOM
Something is wrong.
No.

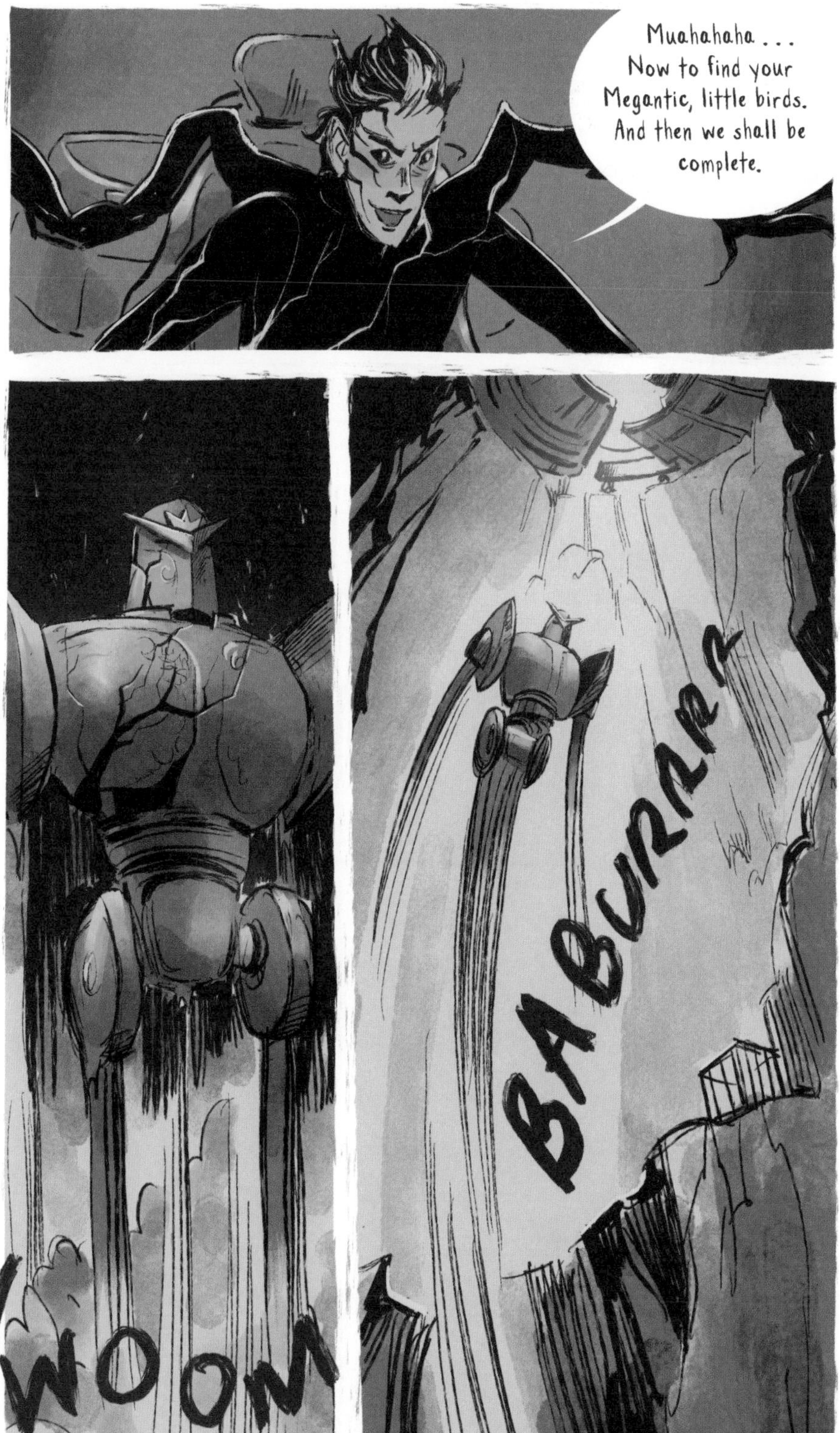
Muahahaha . . . Now to find your Megantic, little birds. And then we shall be complete.
VWOOM
BABURRRR

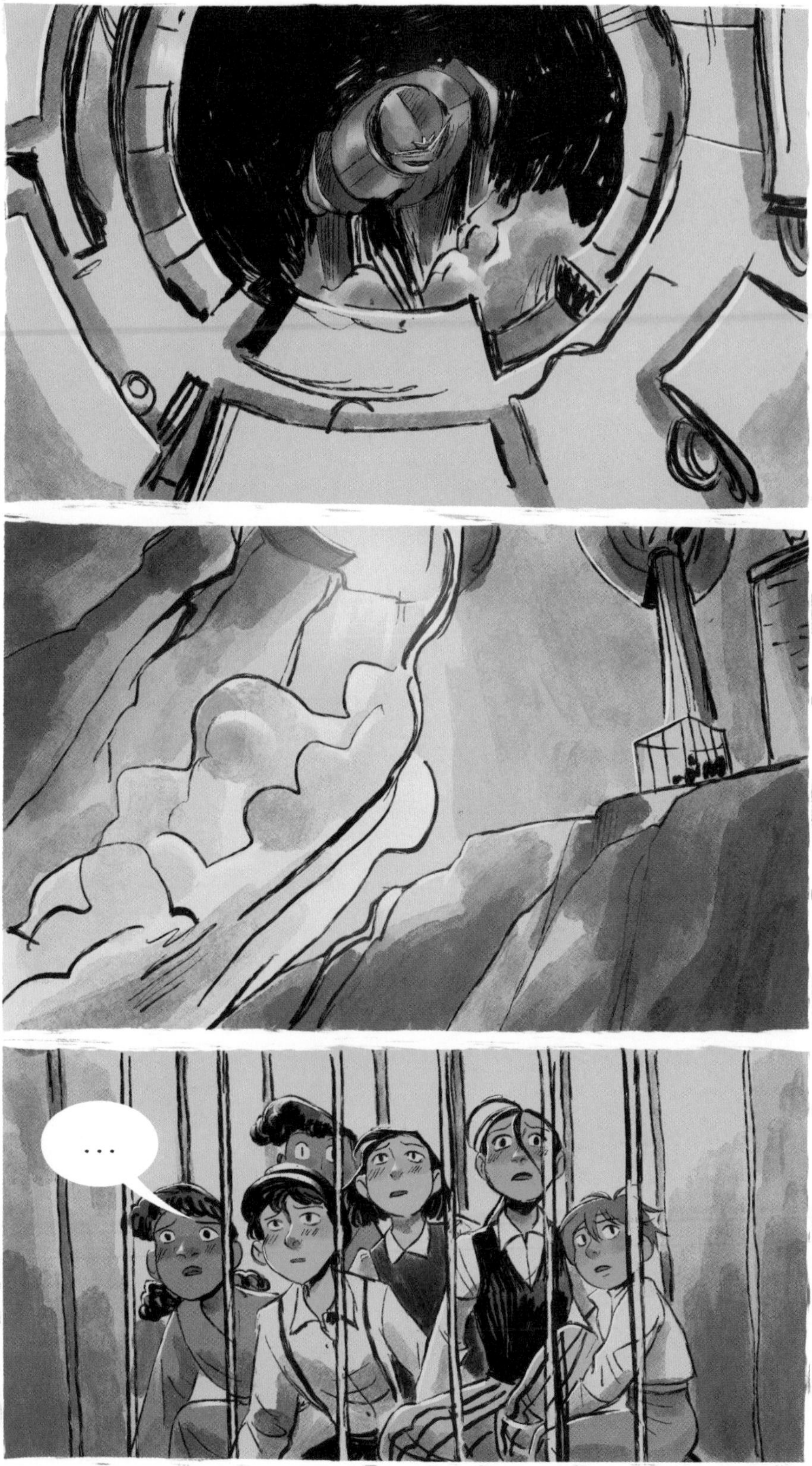
...

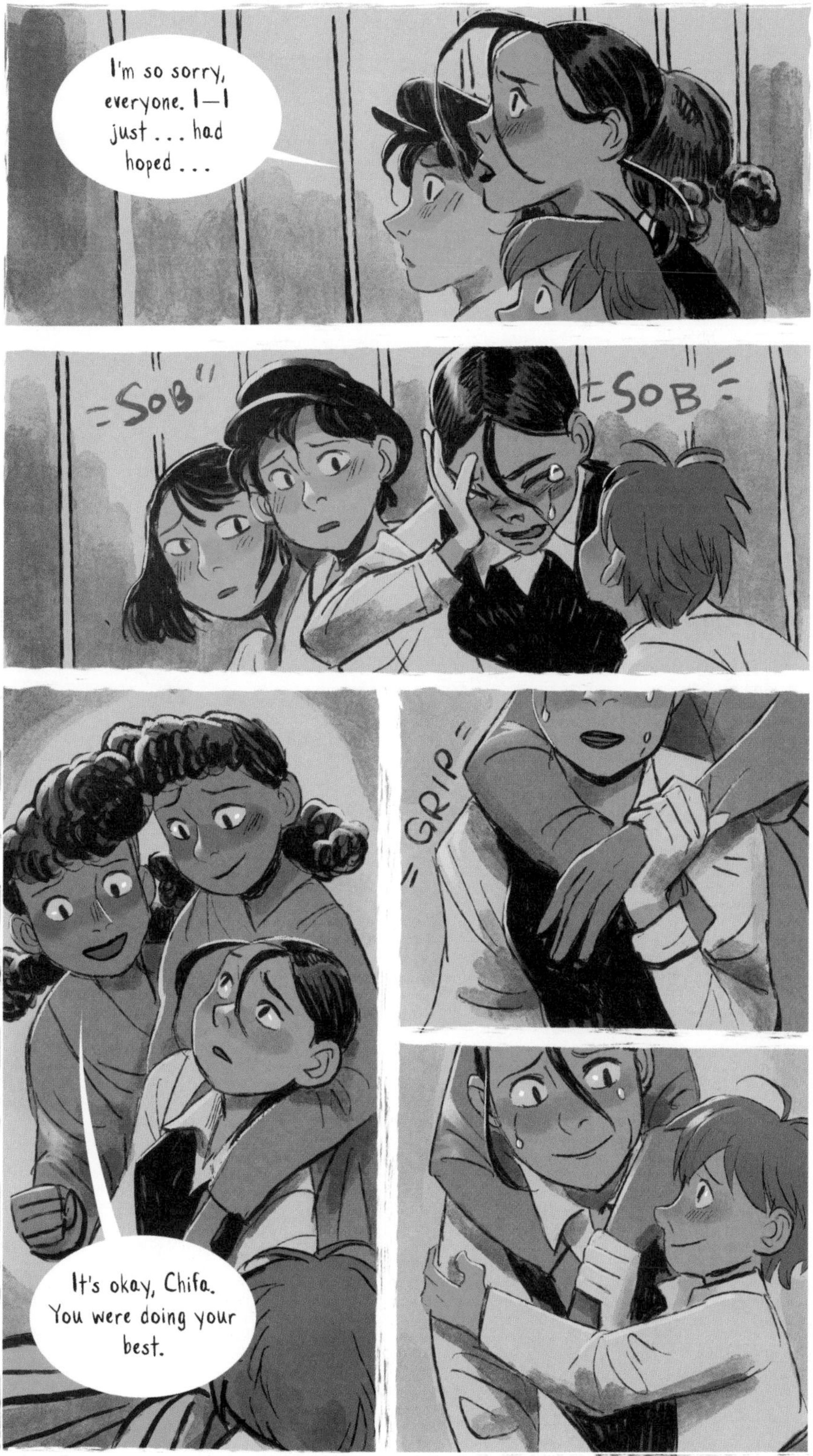
I'm so sorry, everyone. I—I just . . . had hoped . . .
SOB
SOB
GRIP
It's okay, Chifa. You were doing your best.

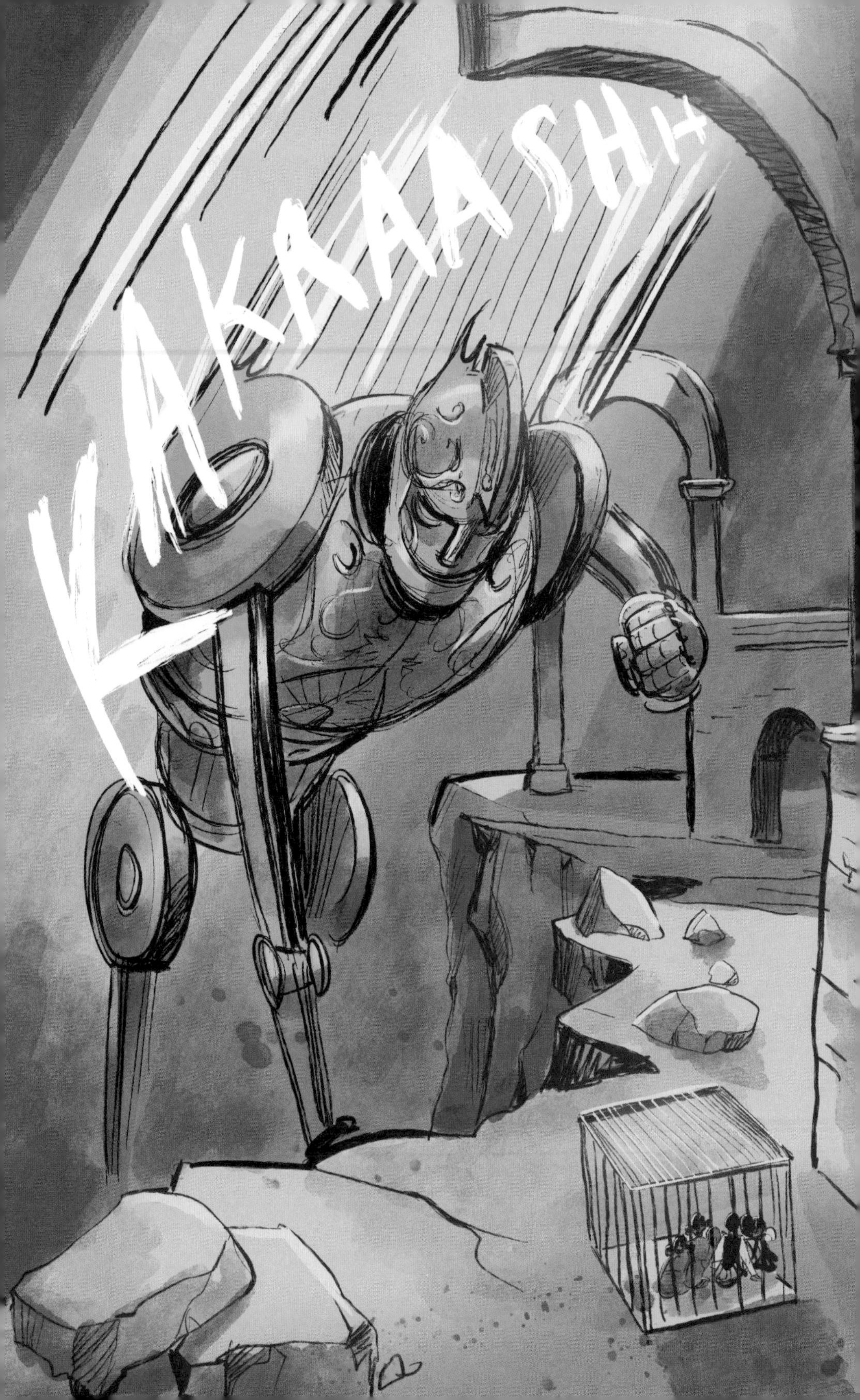
KAKRAASHH

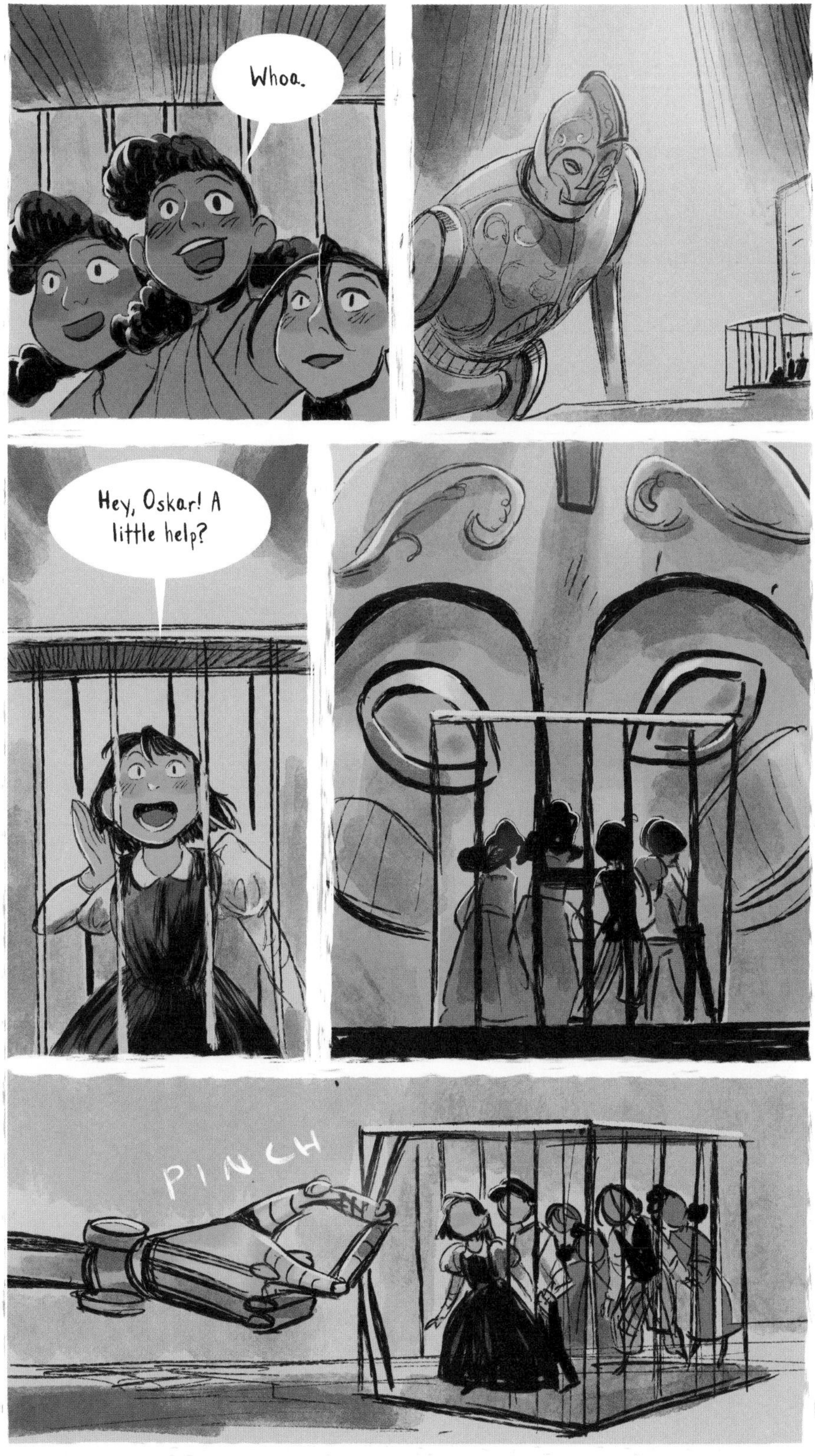
Whoa.
Hey, Oskar! A little help?
PINCH

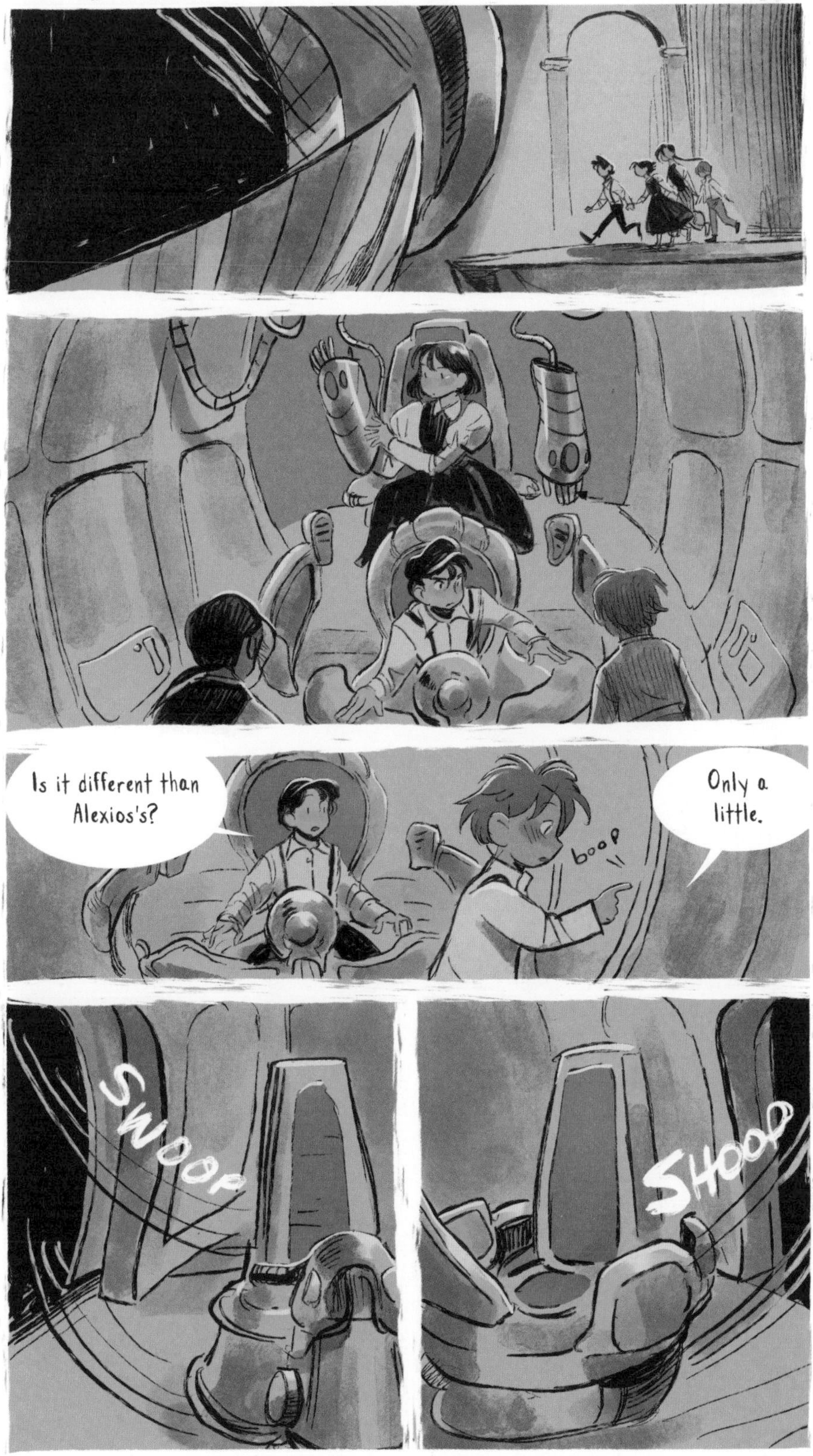
Is it different than Alexios's?
Only a little.
boop
SWOOP
SHOOP

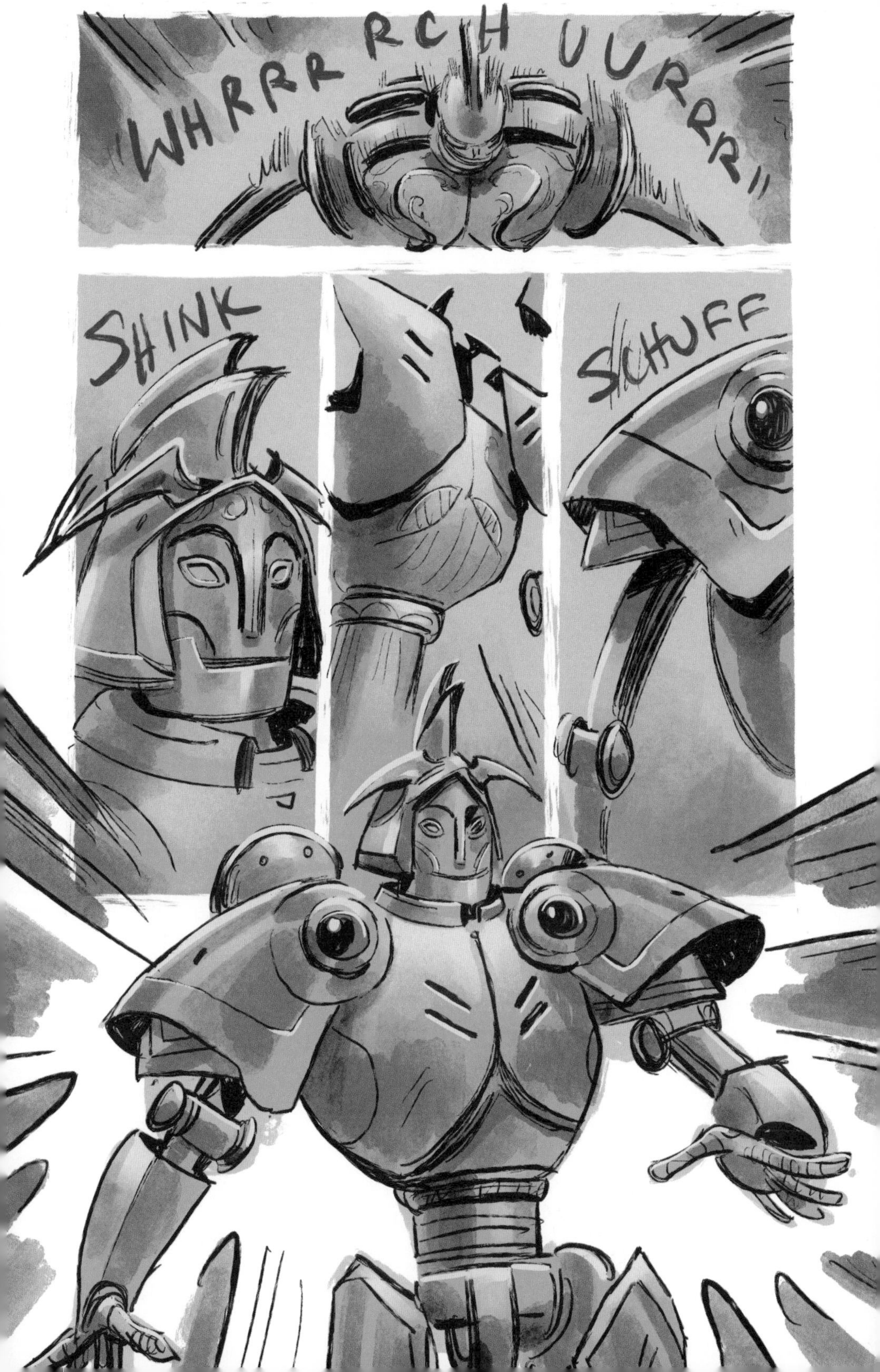

"WHRRR RCH UURRR"
SHINK
SCHUFF

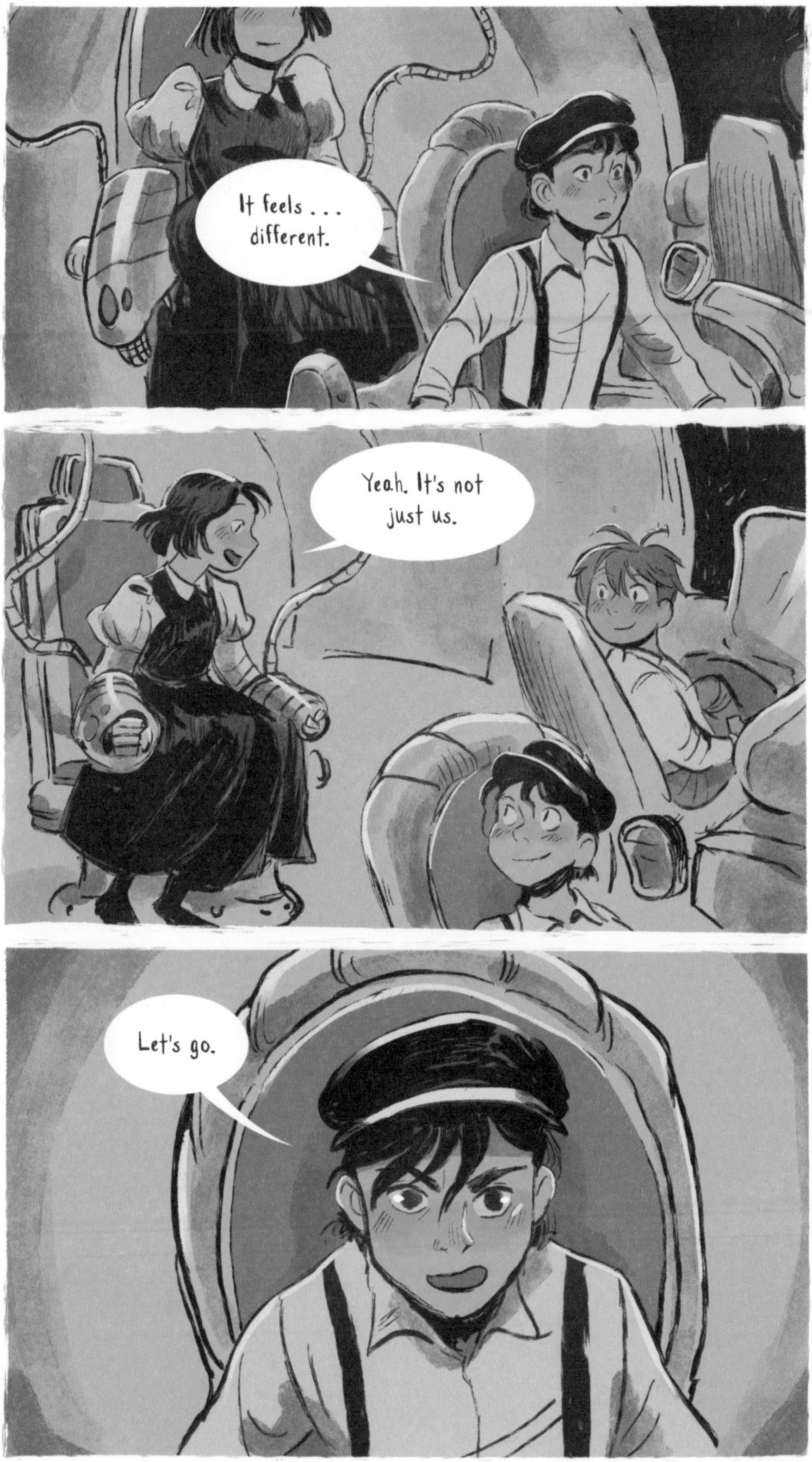
It feels . . . different.
Yeah. It's not just us.
Let's go.

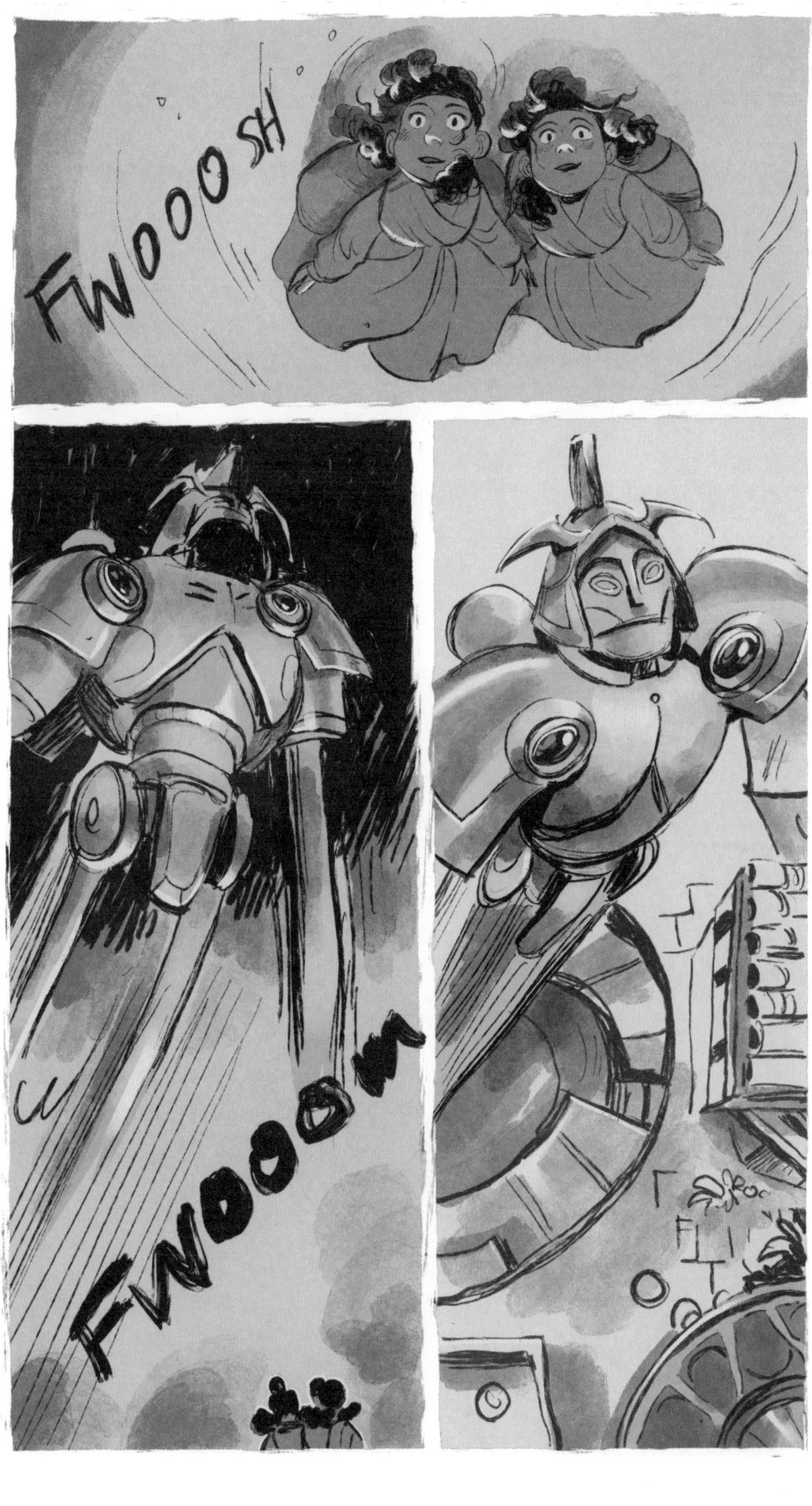
FWOOOSH
FWOOOOM

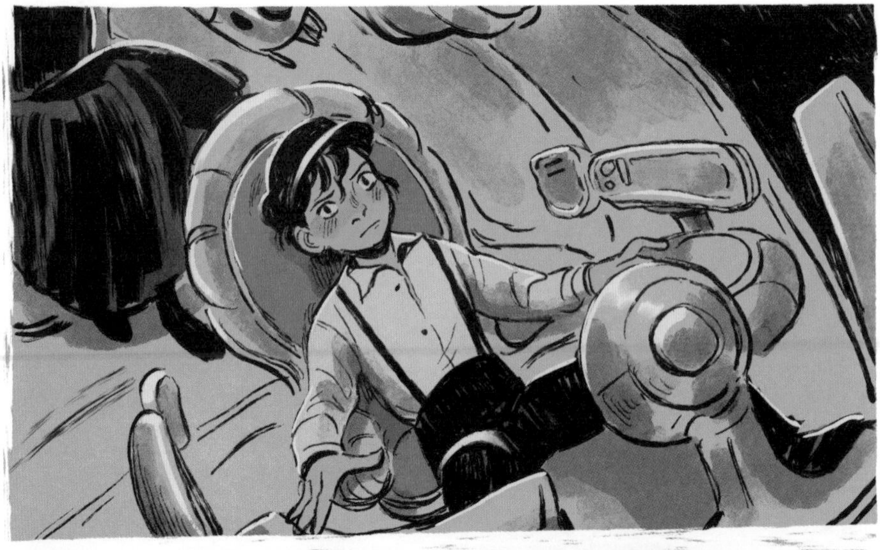

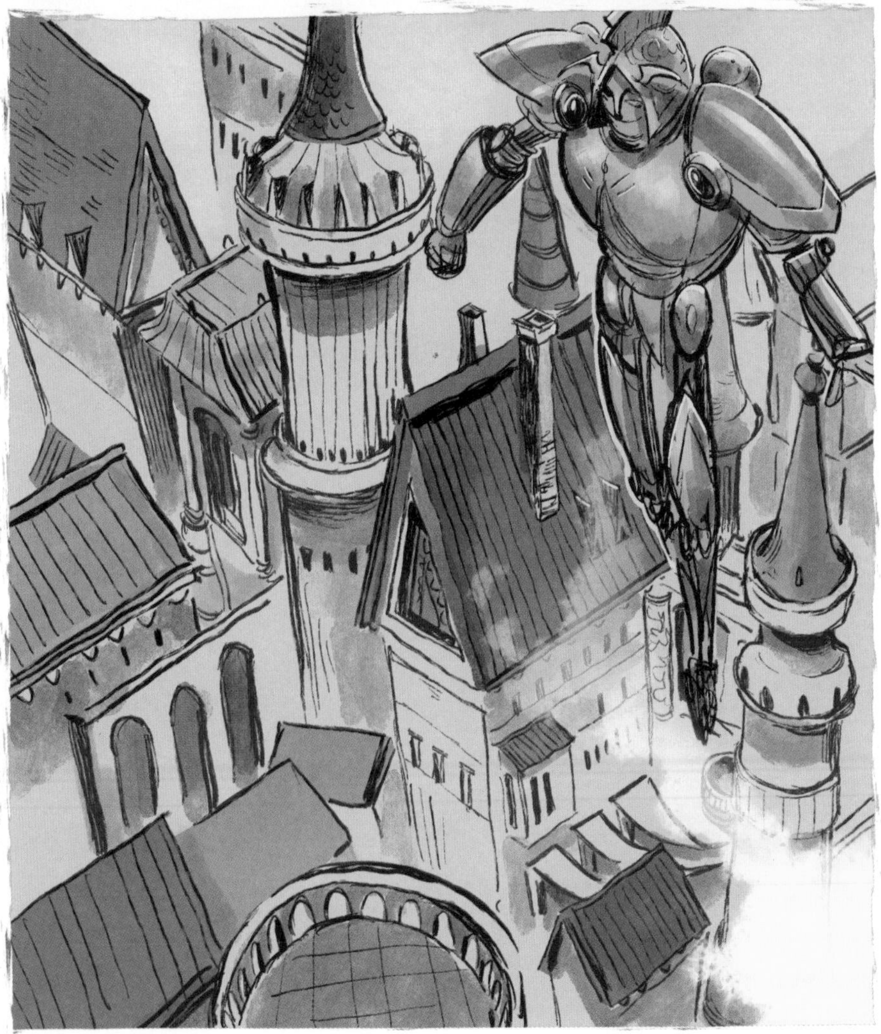

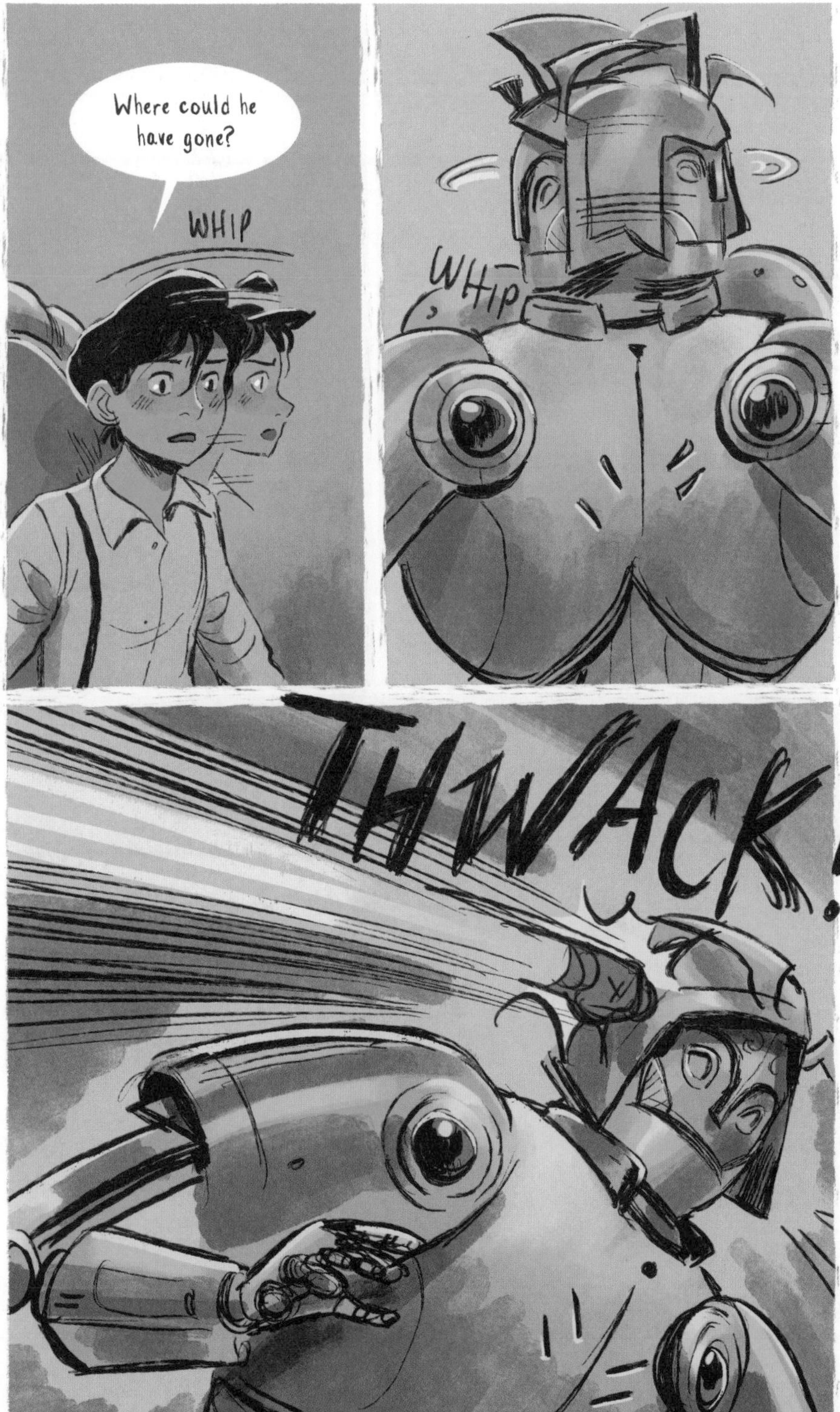

Where could he have gone?
WHIP
WHIP
THWACK!

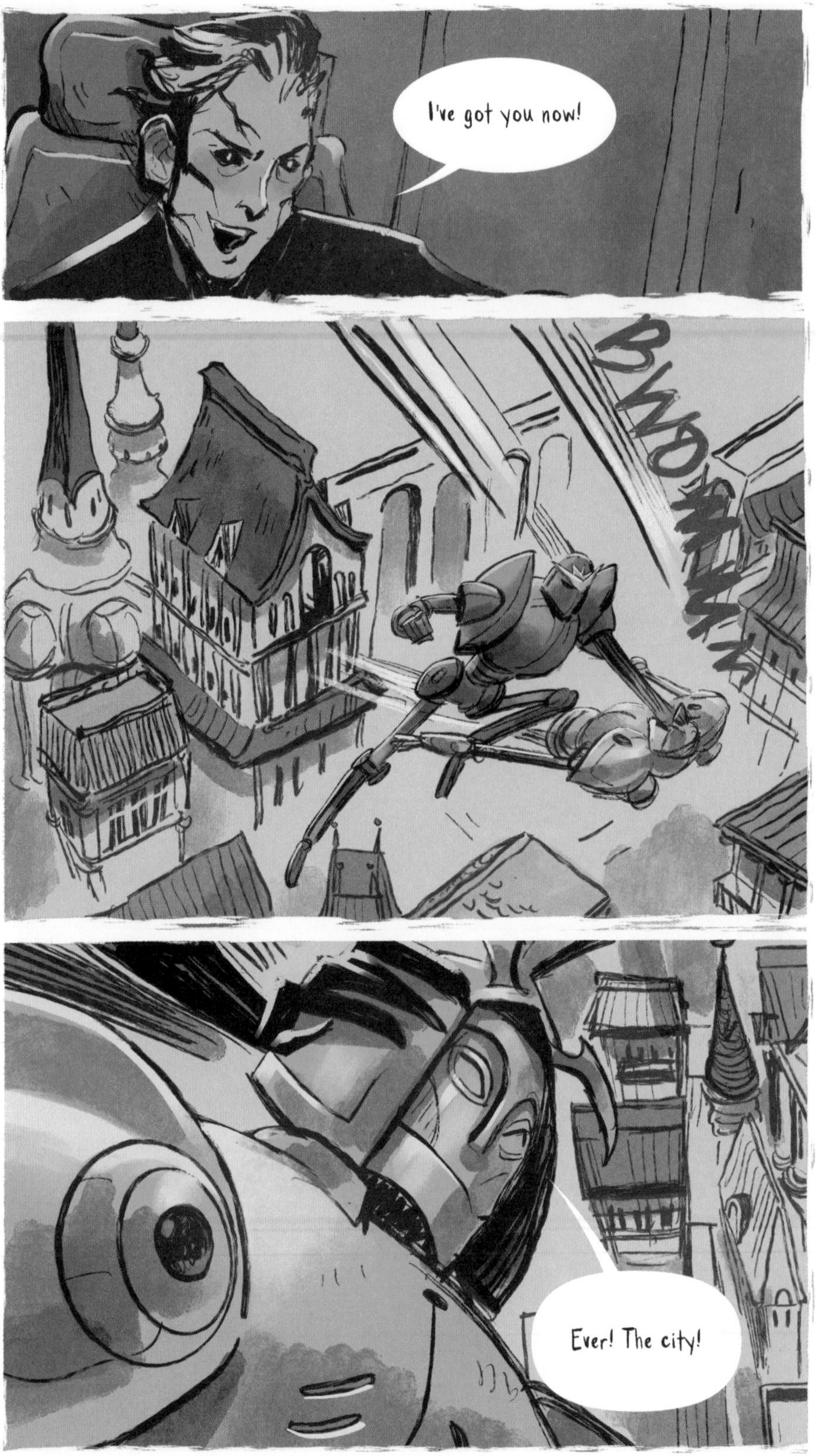
I've got you now!
BWOMMMM
Ever! The city!

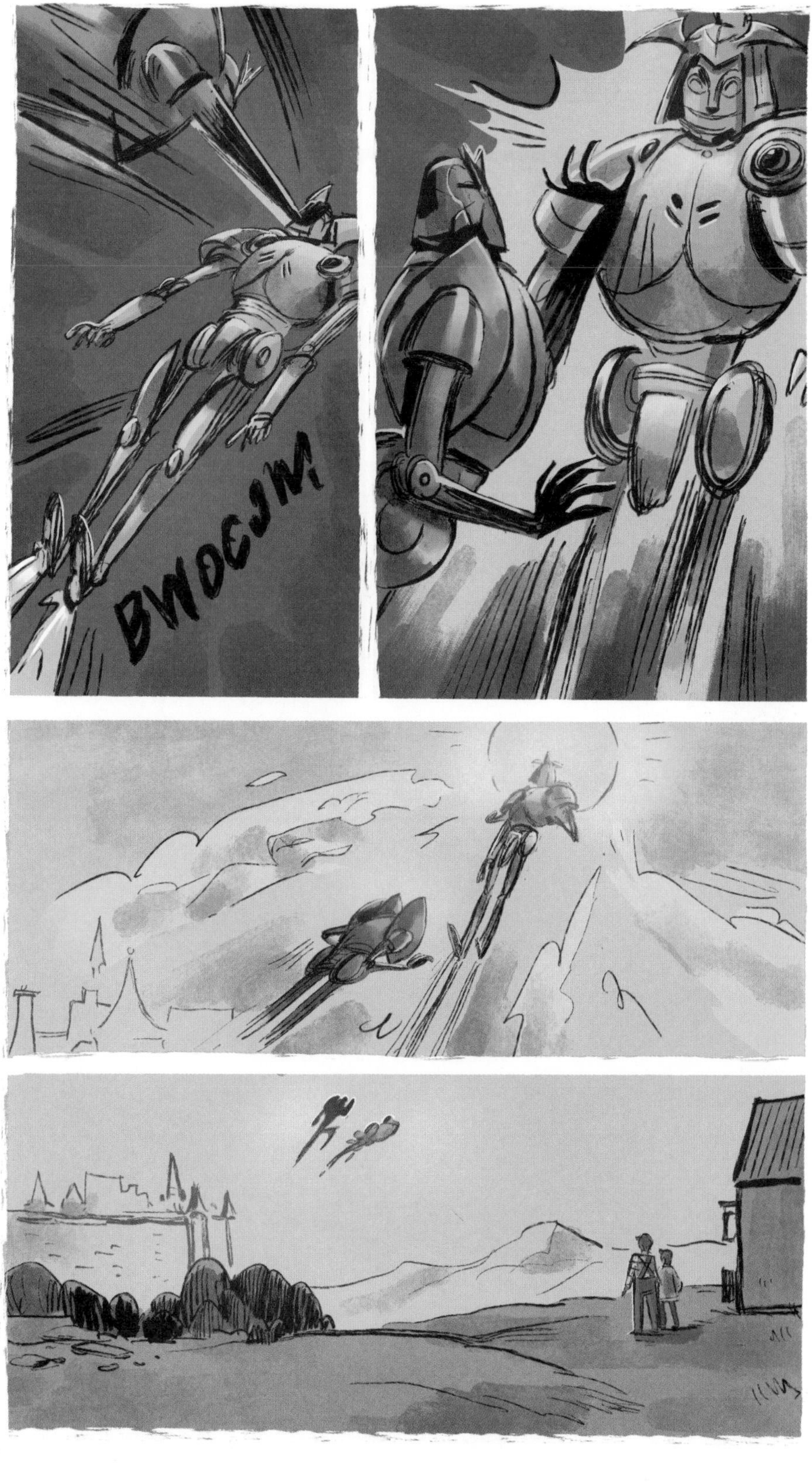
BWOOM!

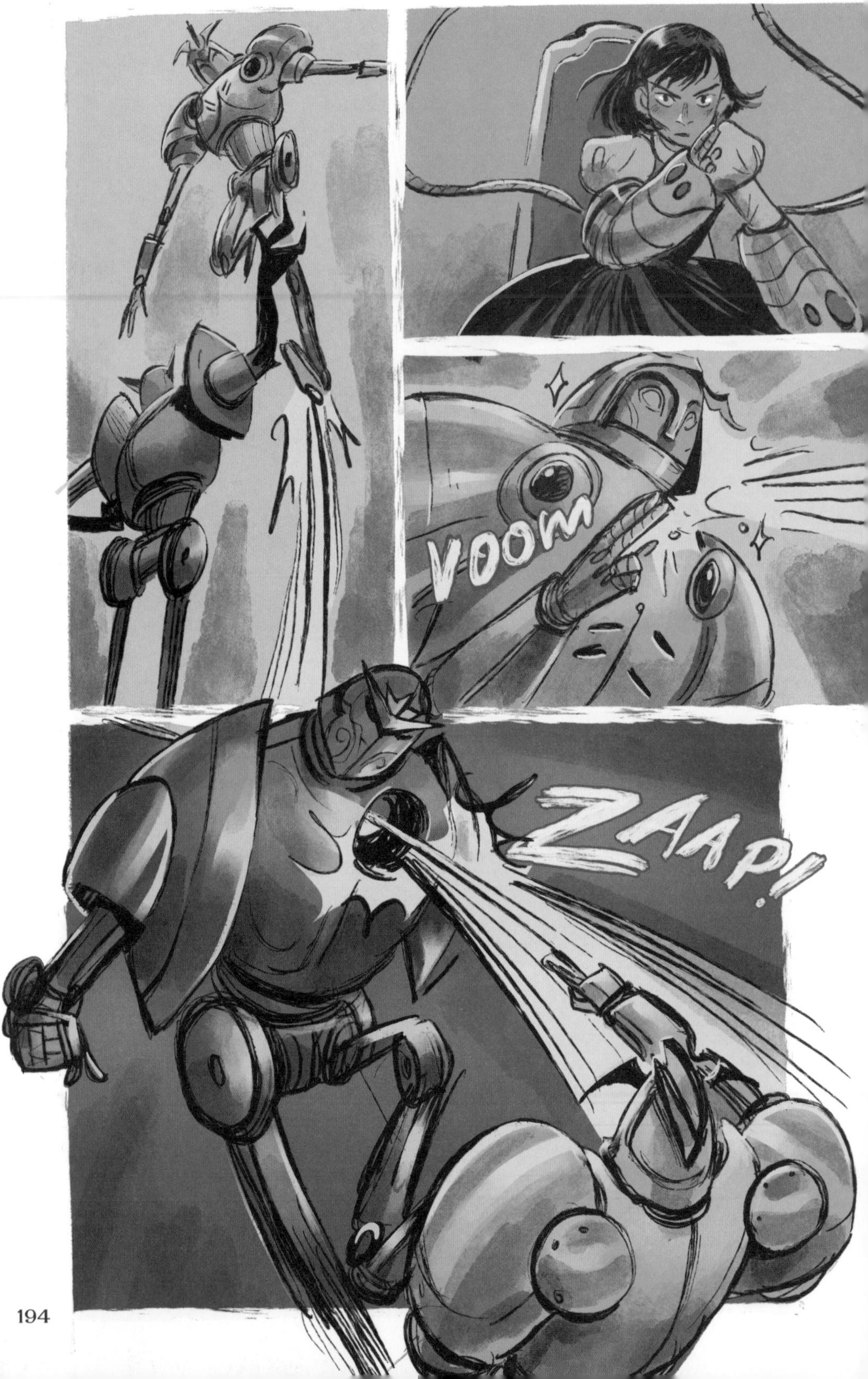
VOOM
ZAAP!

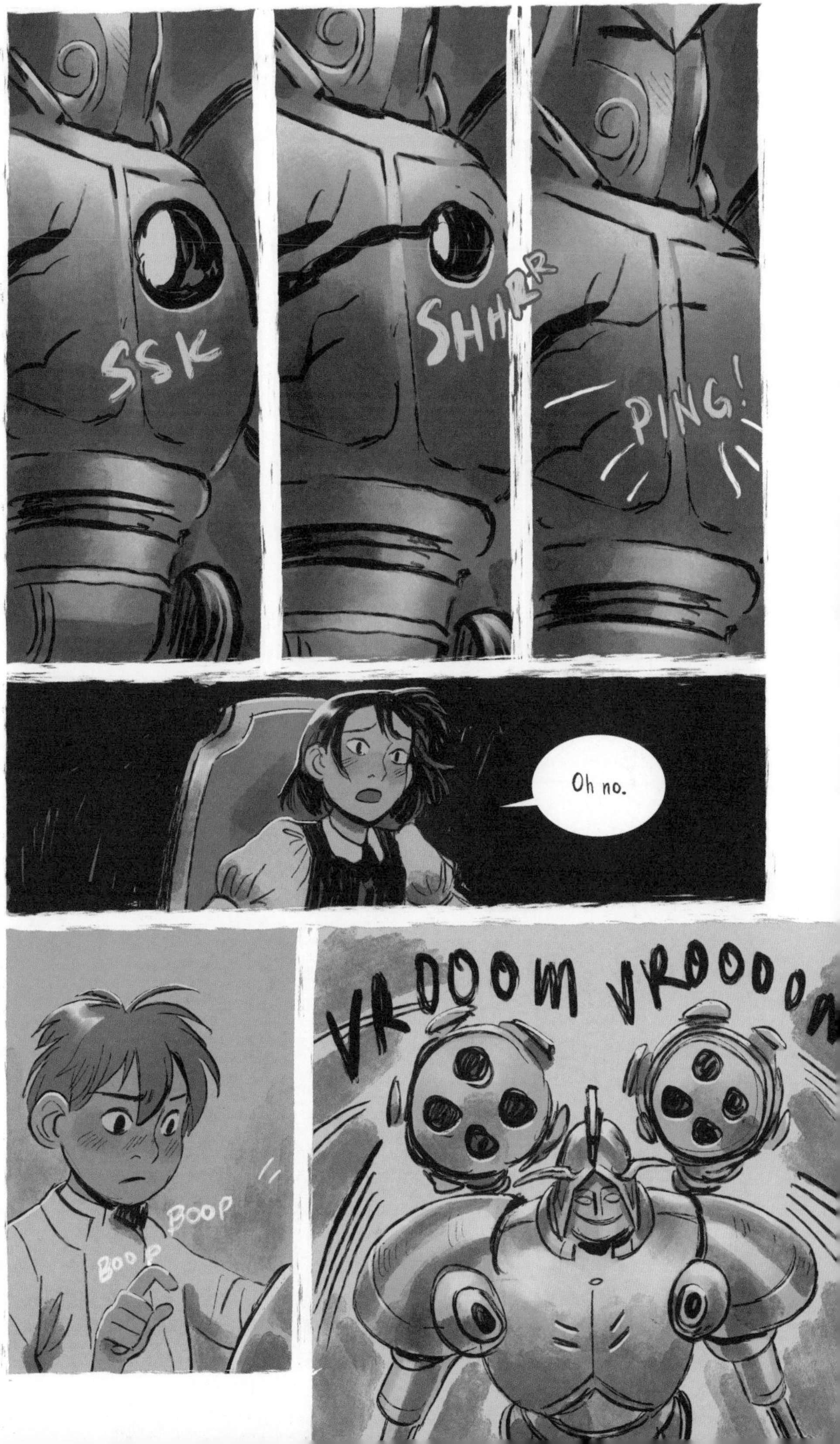
SSK
SHHRR
PING!
Oh no.
BOOP
BOOP
VROOOM VROOOOM

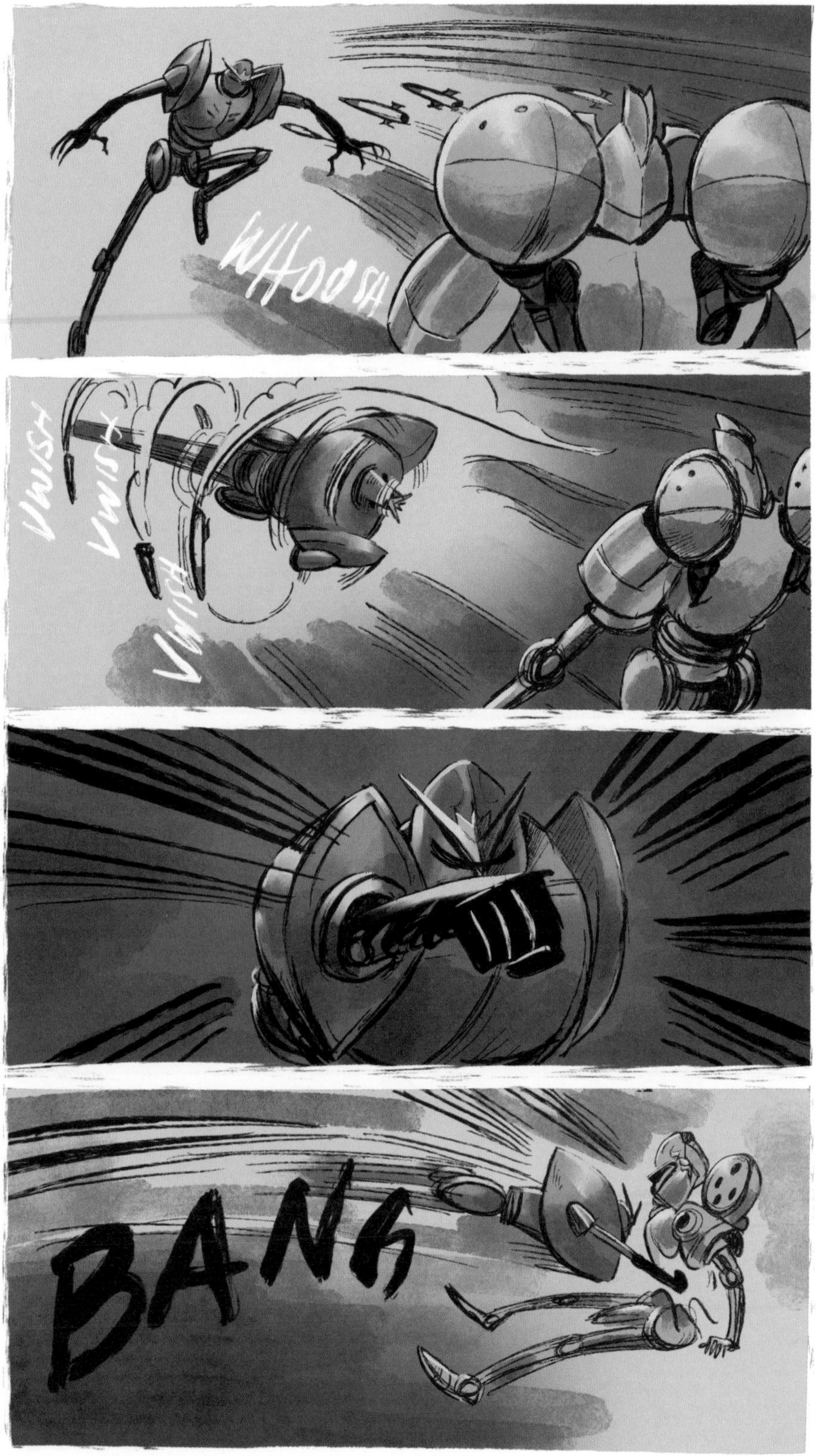
WHOOSH
VWISH
VWISH
VWISH
BANG

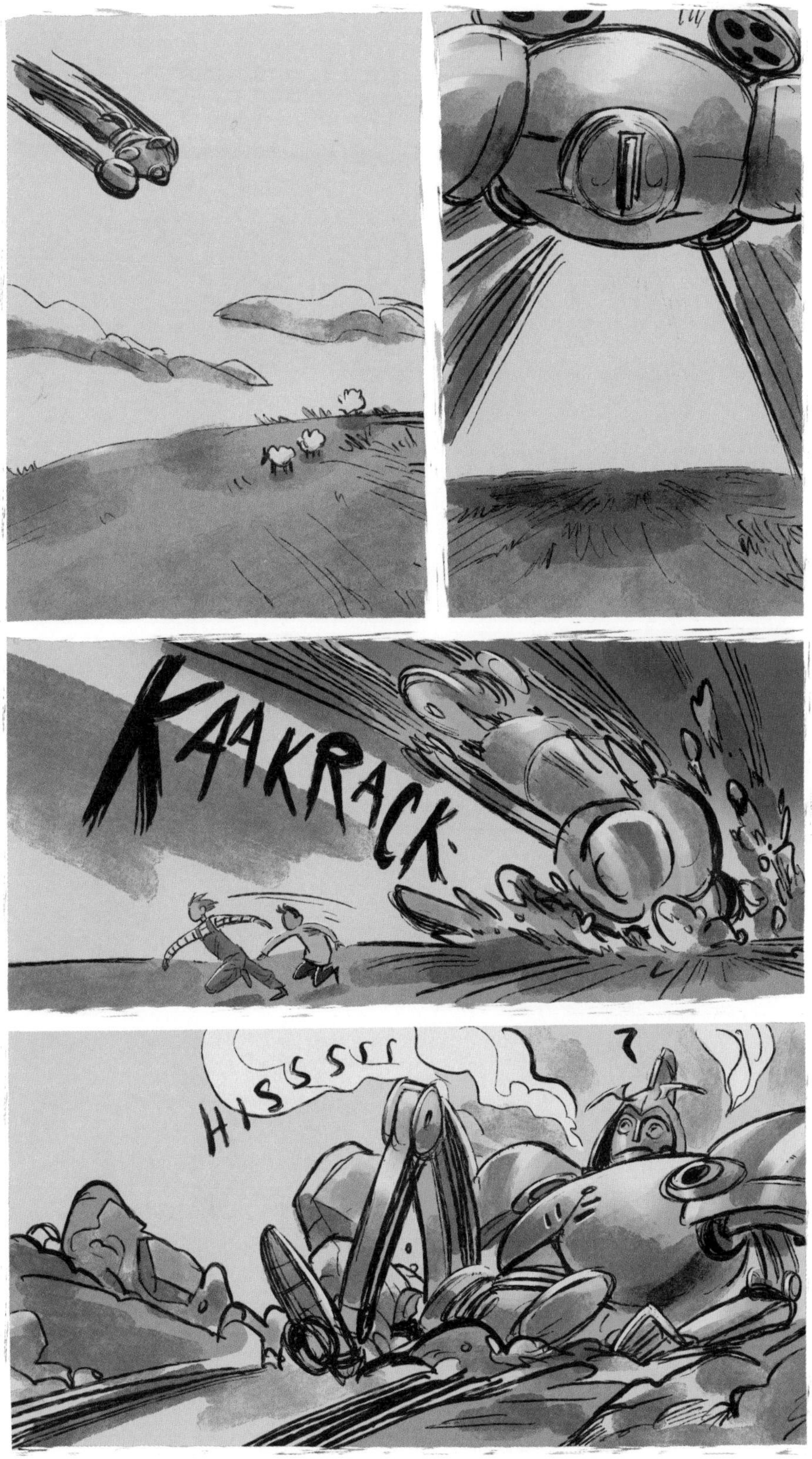
KAAKRACK
HISSSSS

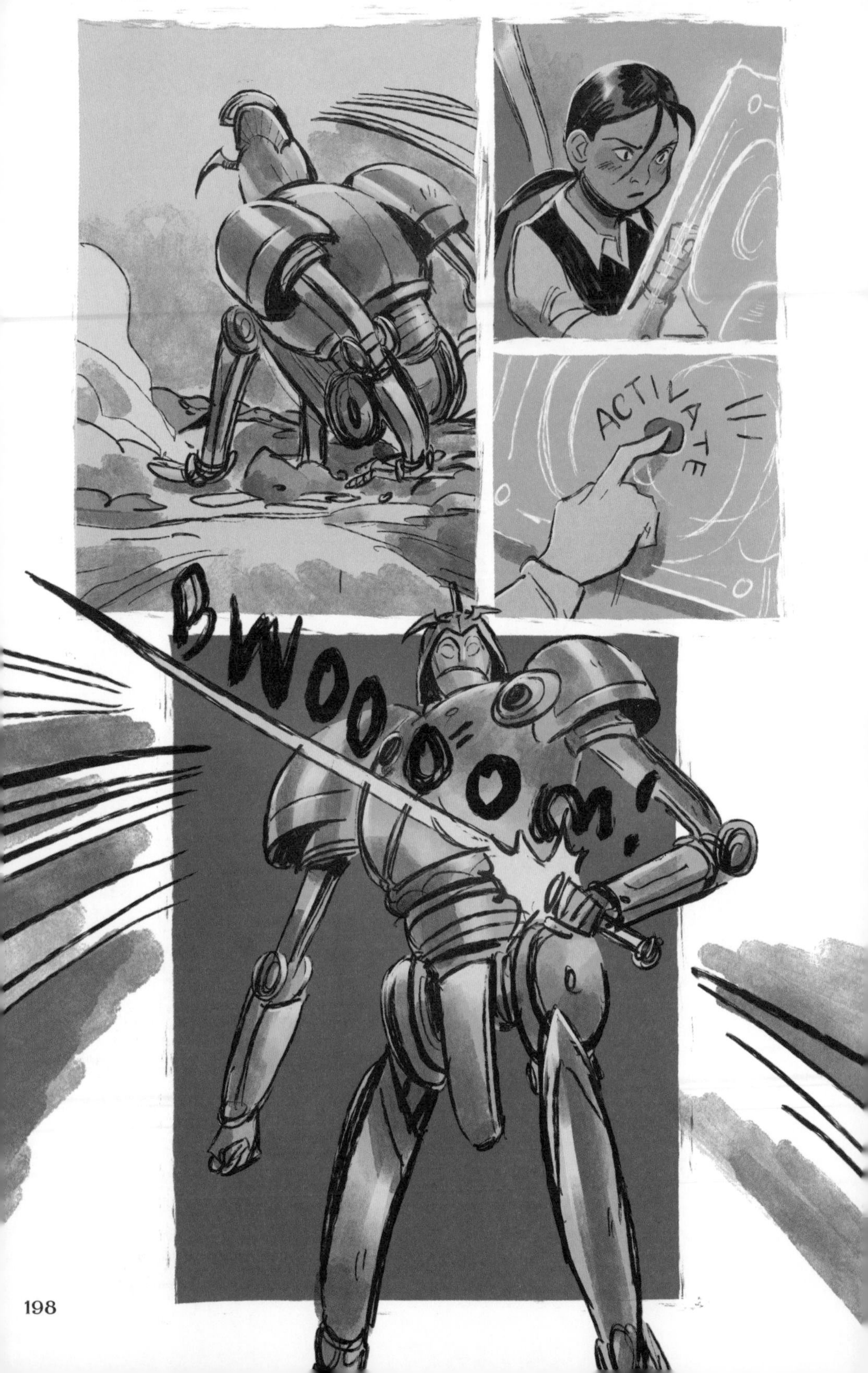
ACTIVATE
BWOOOOOM!

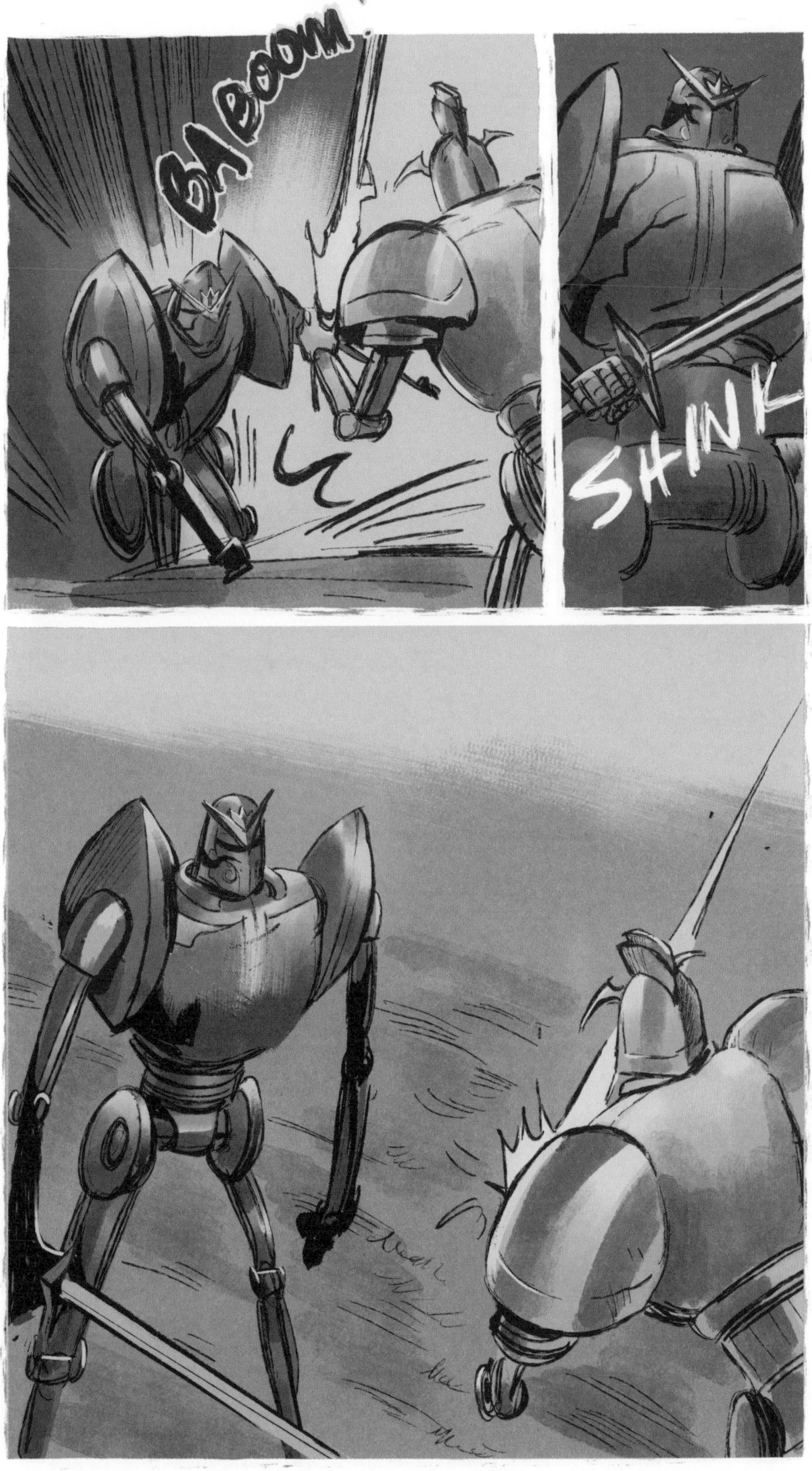
BA BOOM!
SHINK

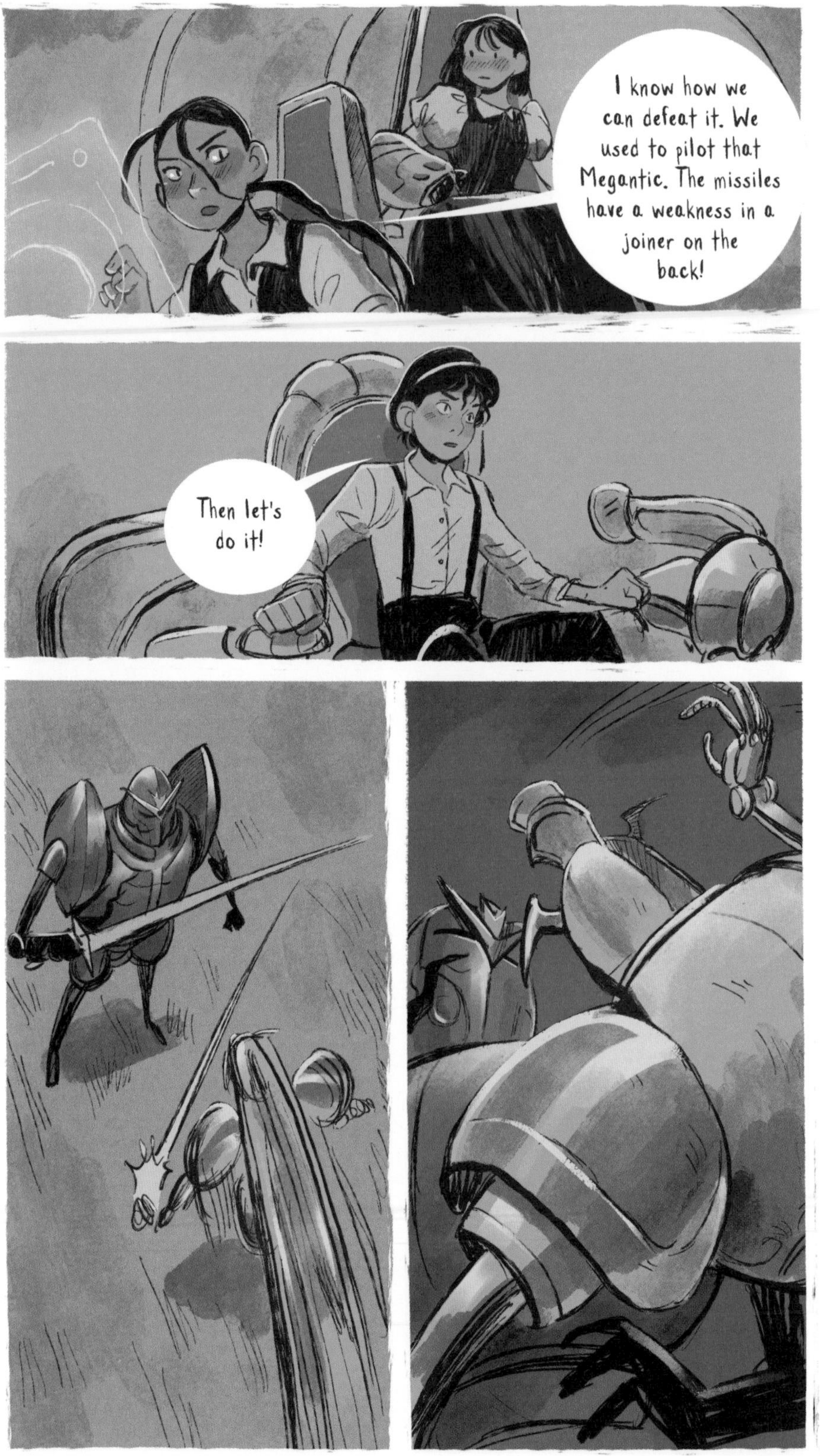
I know how we can defeat it. We used to pilot that Megantic. The missiles have a weakness in a joiner on the back!
Then let's do it!

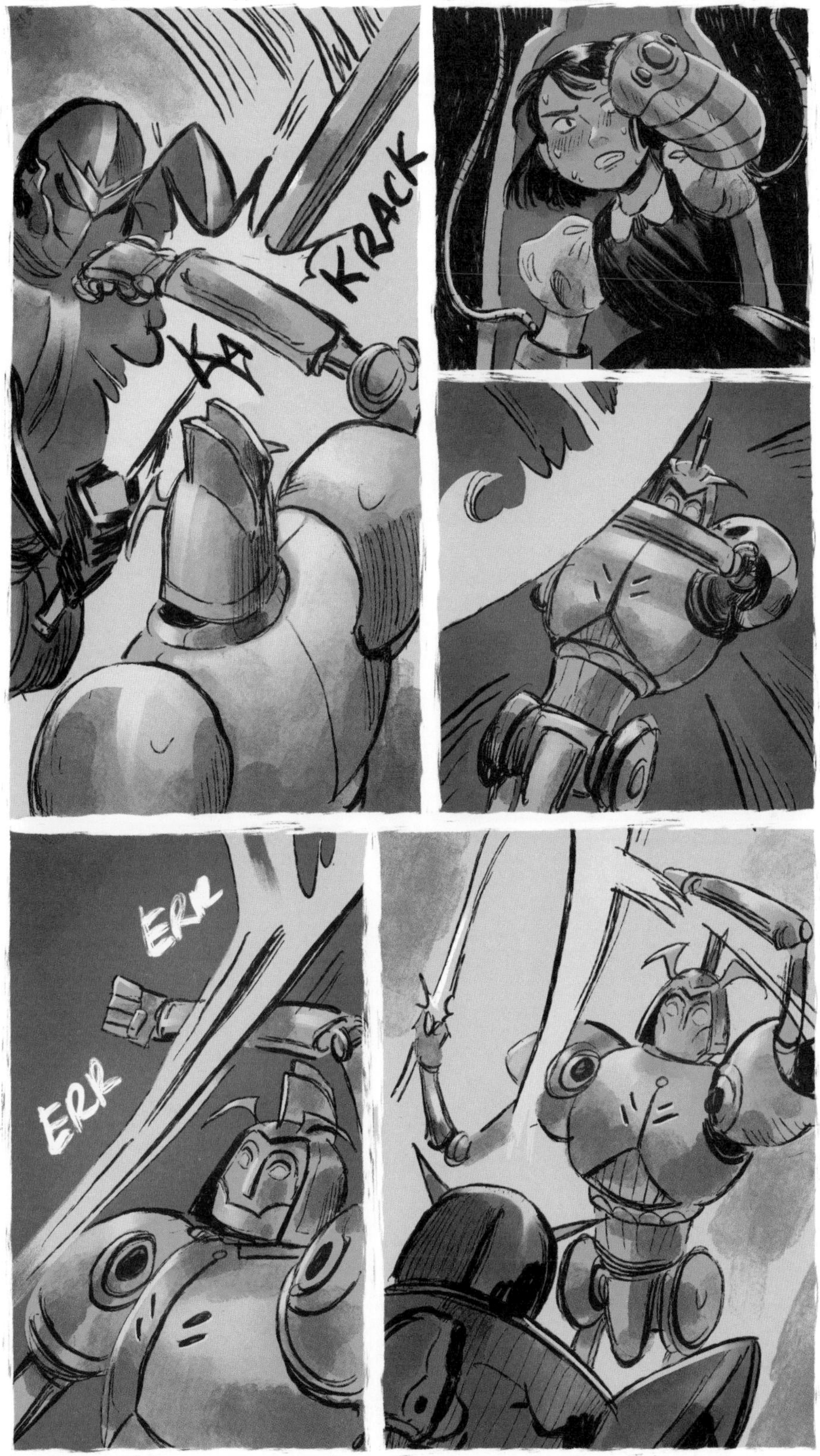
KRACK
ERR
ERR

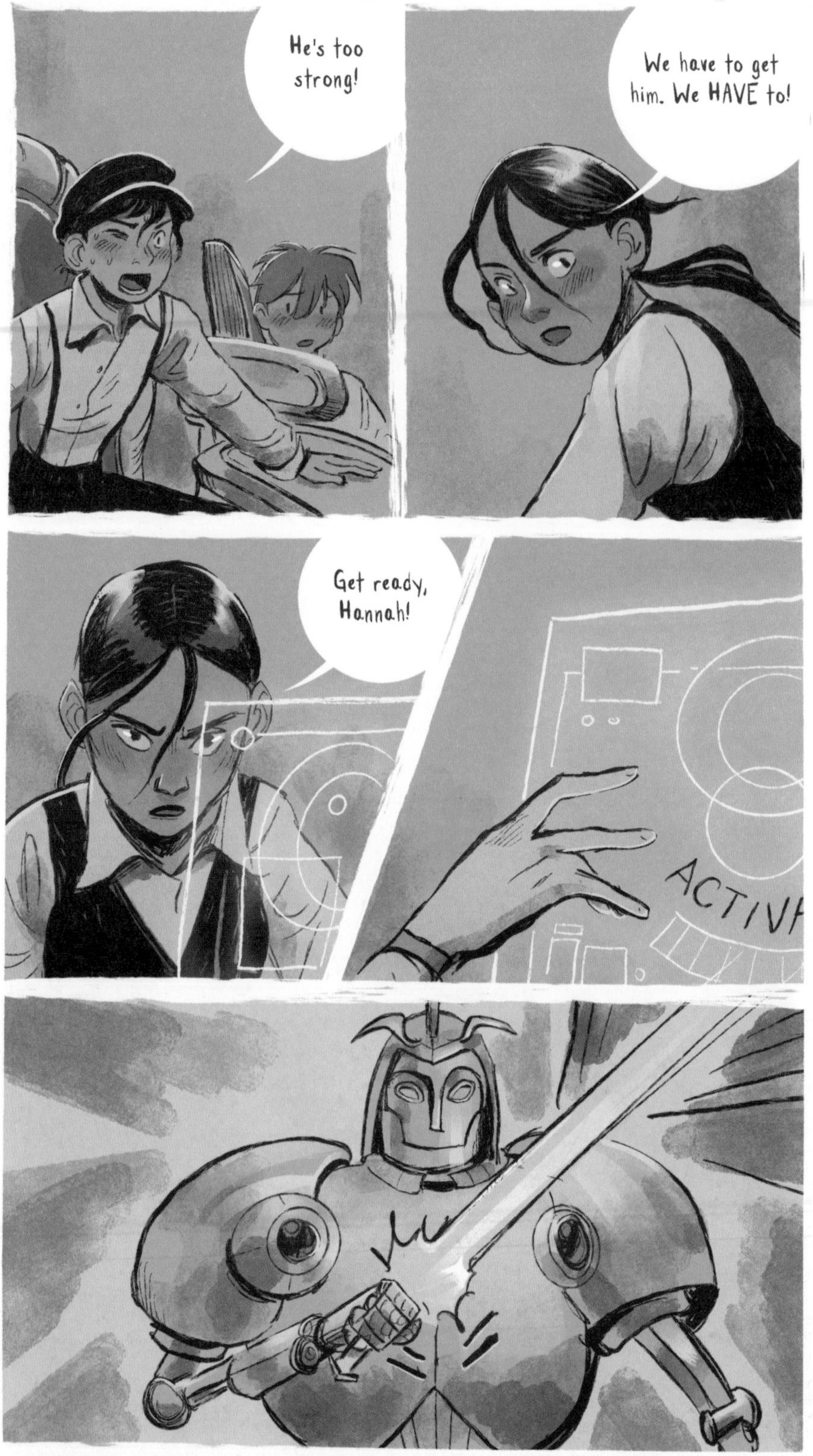
He's too strong!
We have to get him. We HAVE to!
Get ready, Hannah!
ACTIV

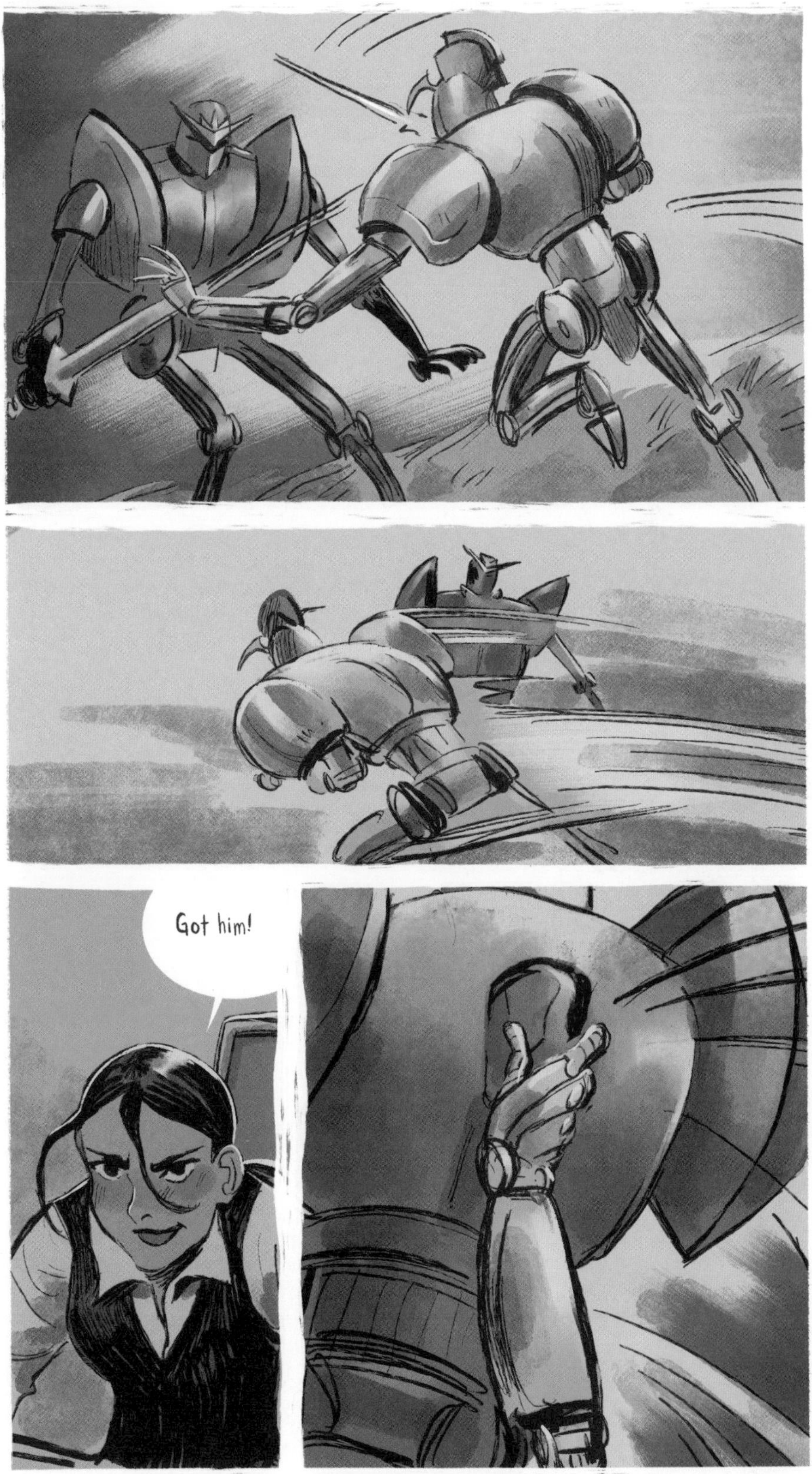
Got him!

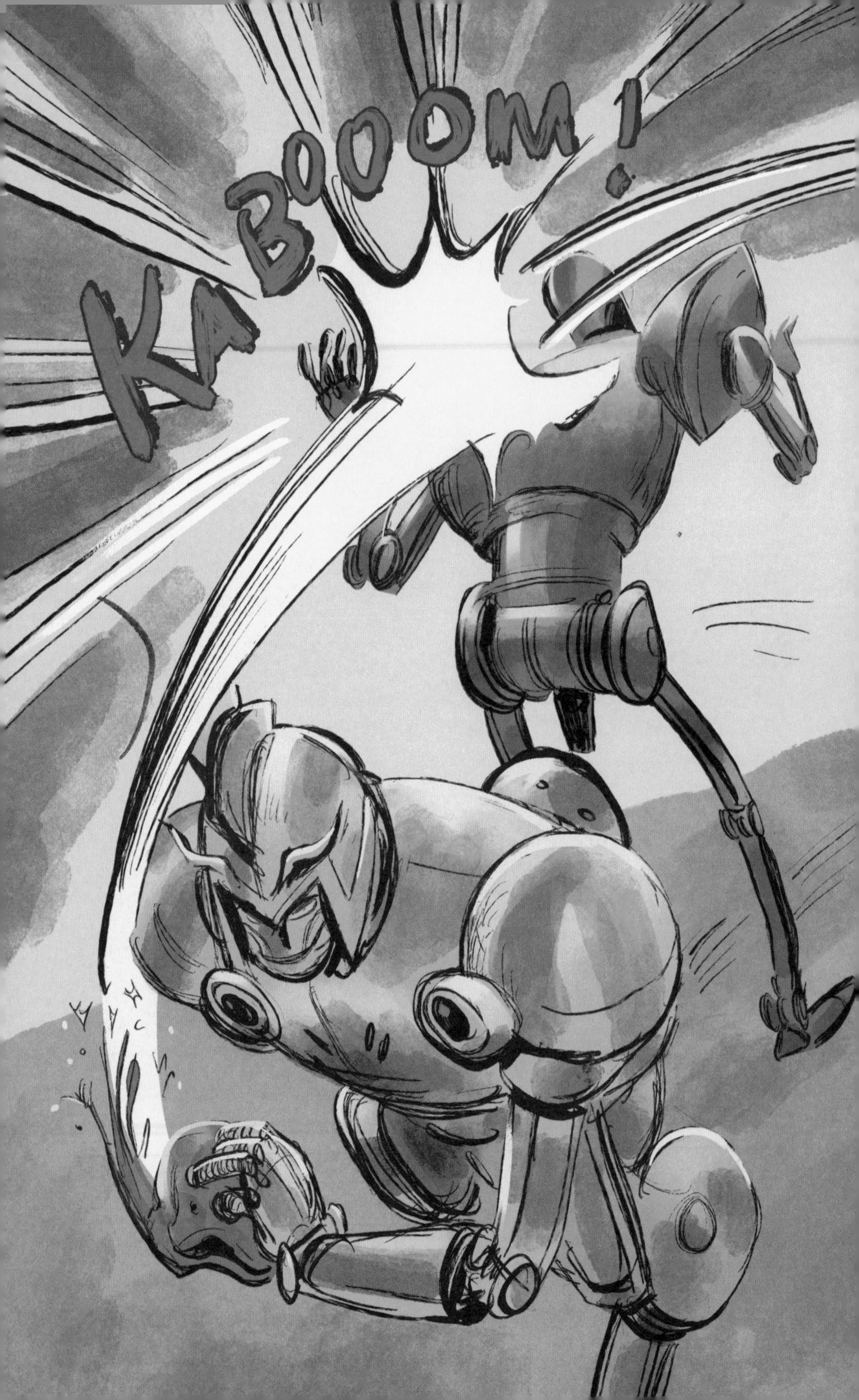
KABOOOM!

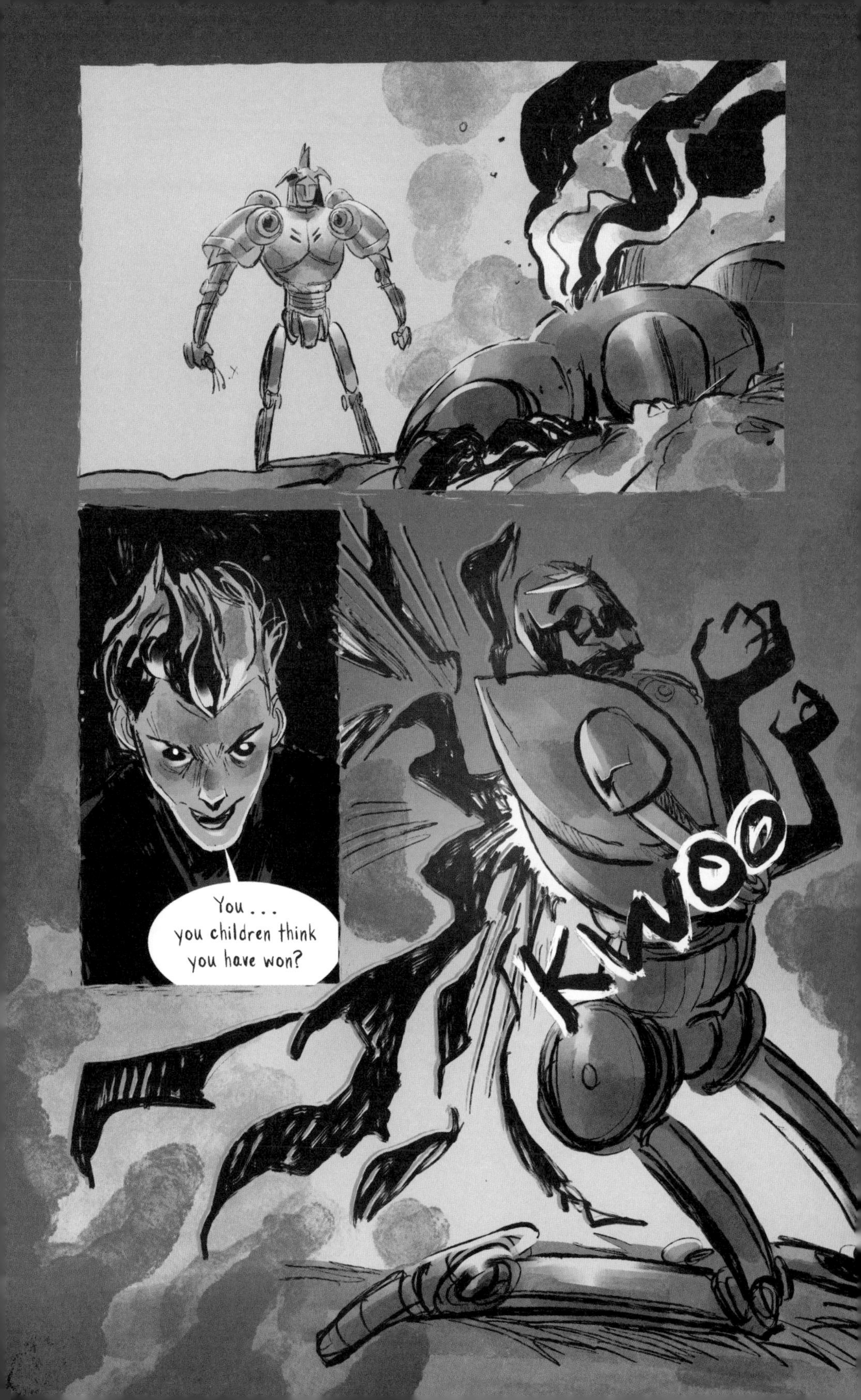
You . . .
you children think
you have won?
KWOOO

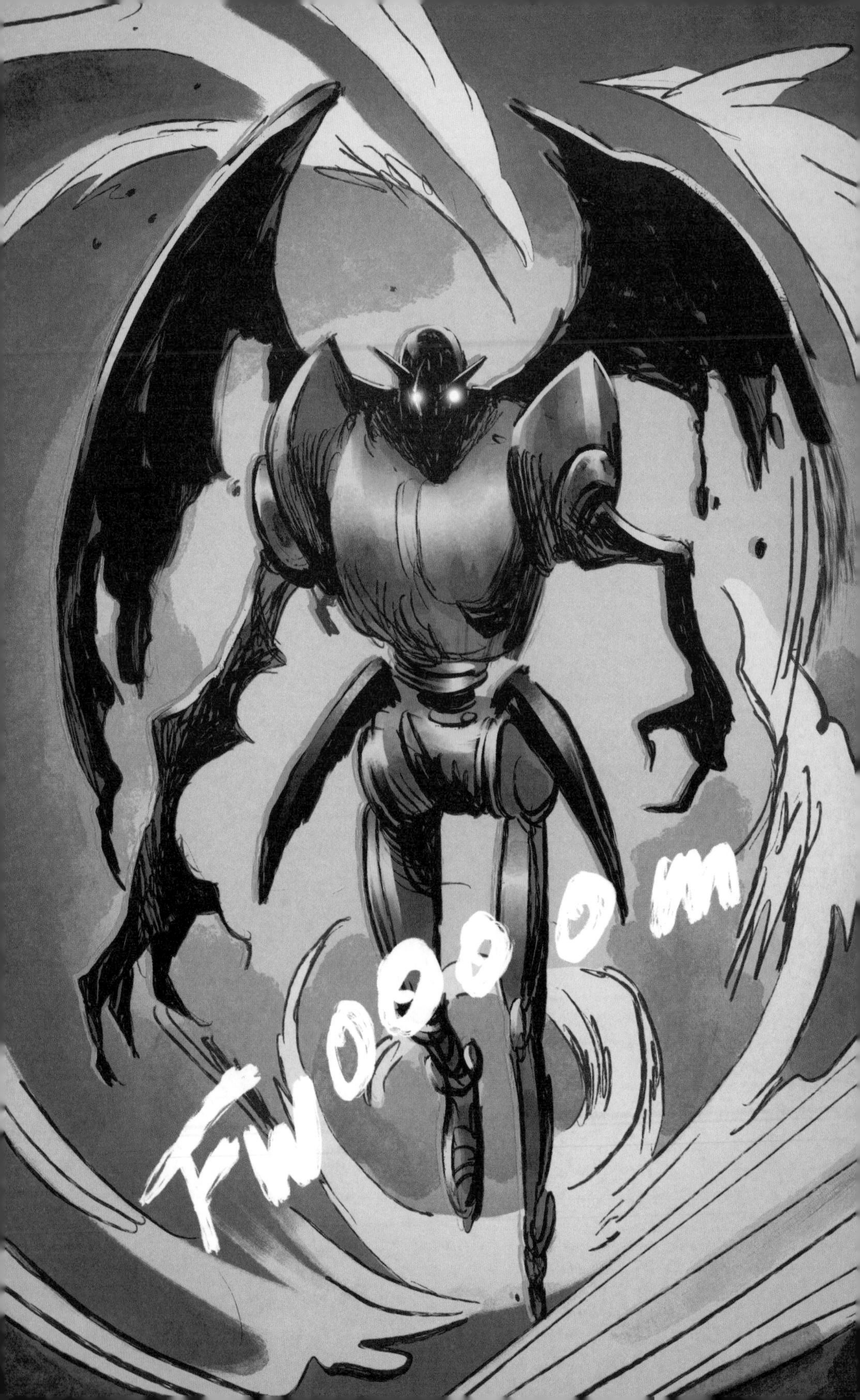
FWOOOOOM

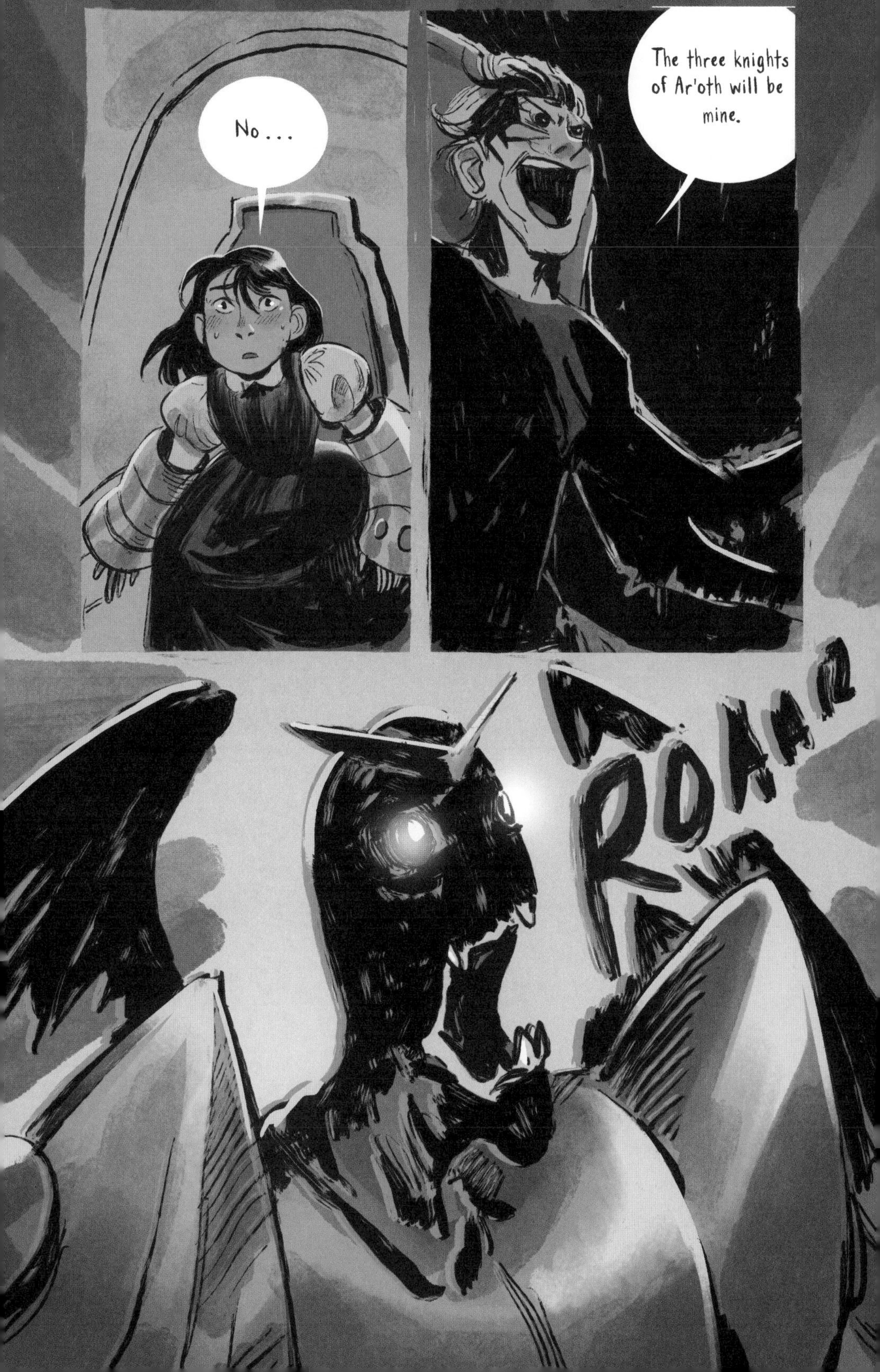
No . . .
The three knights of Ar'oth will be mine.
ROAAR

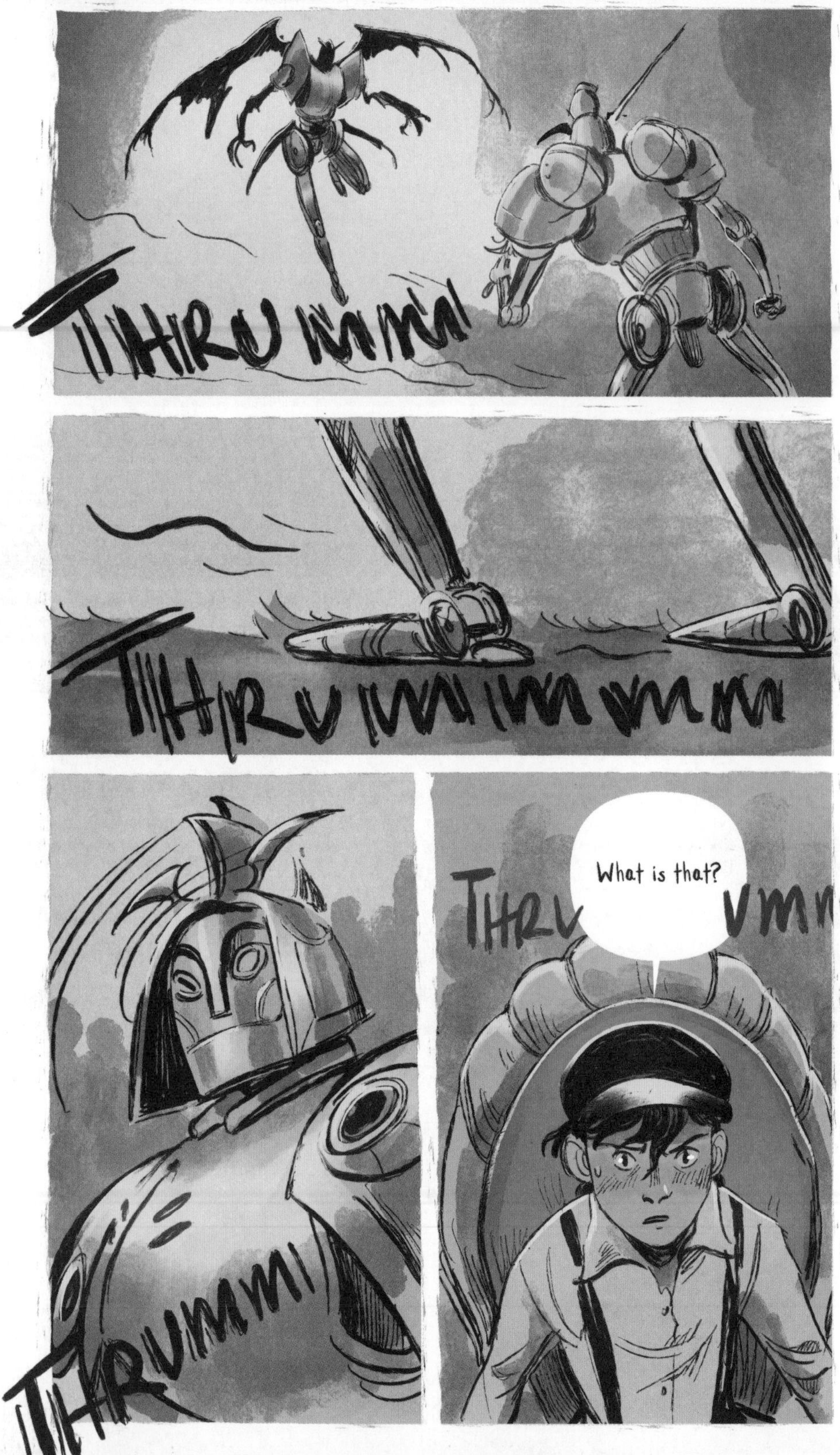
THRUMMM
THRUMMMMMMM
THRUMMM
THRU
What is that?
VMM

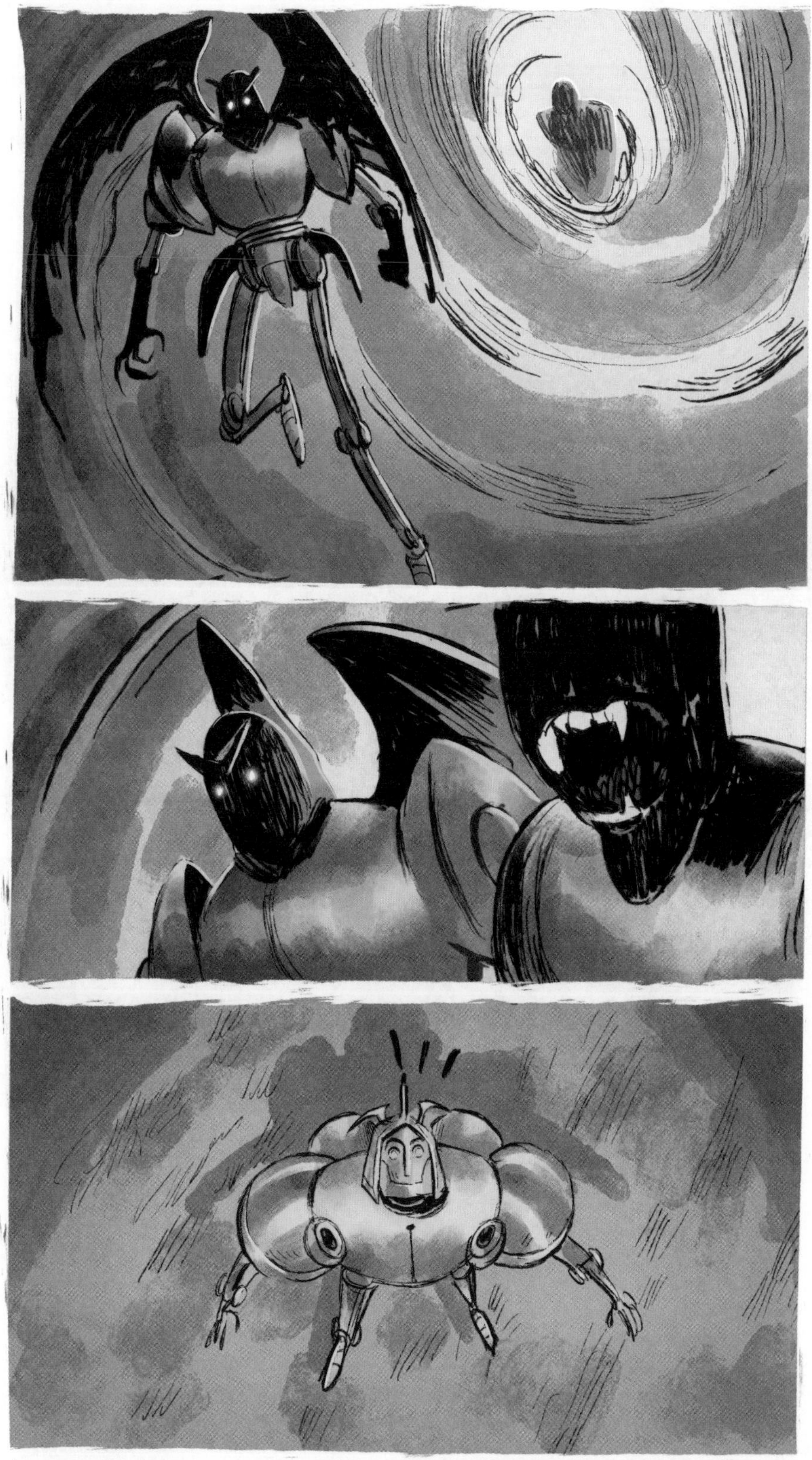

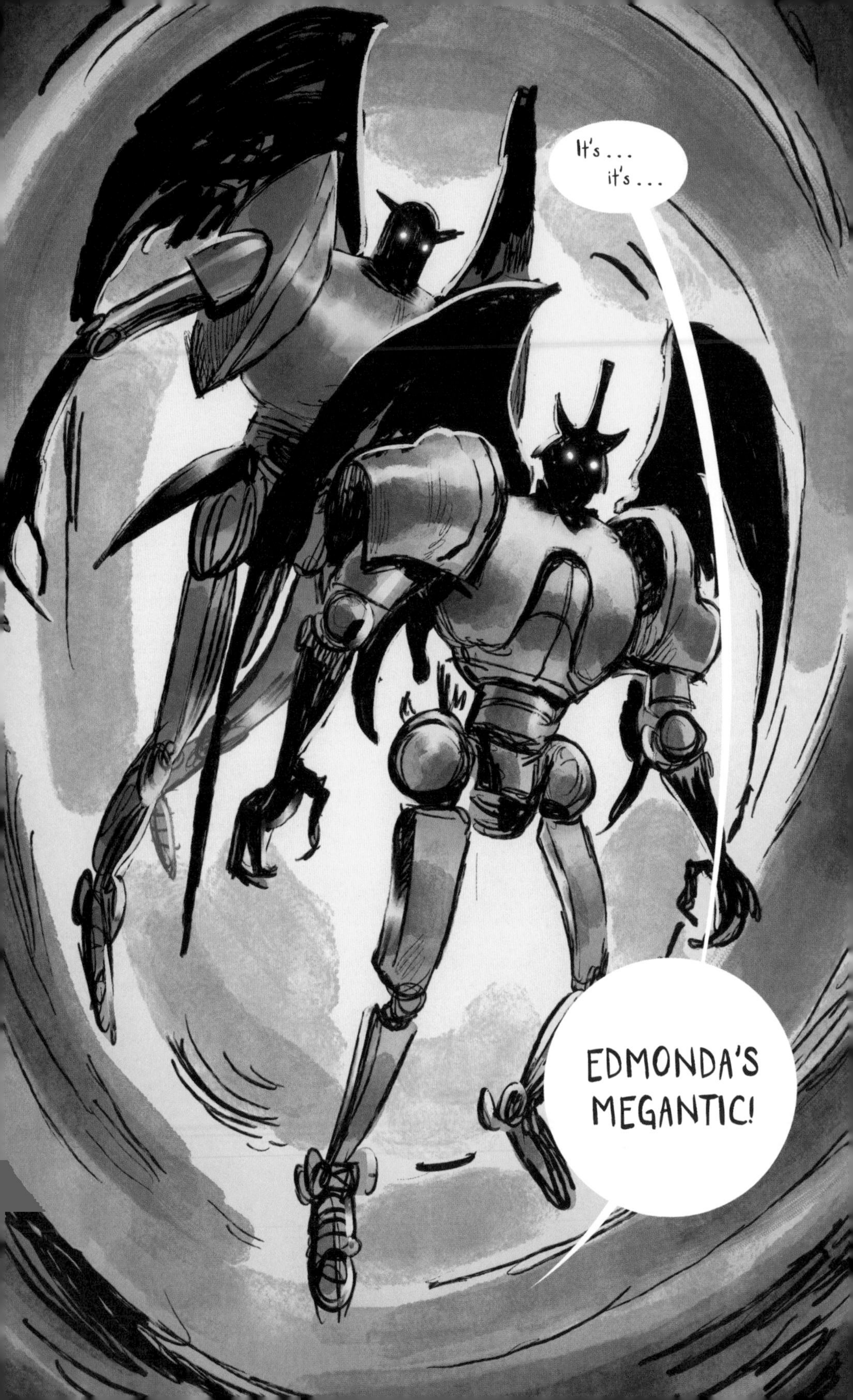
It's . . . it's . . .
EDMONDA'S MEGANTIC!

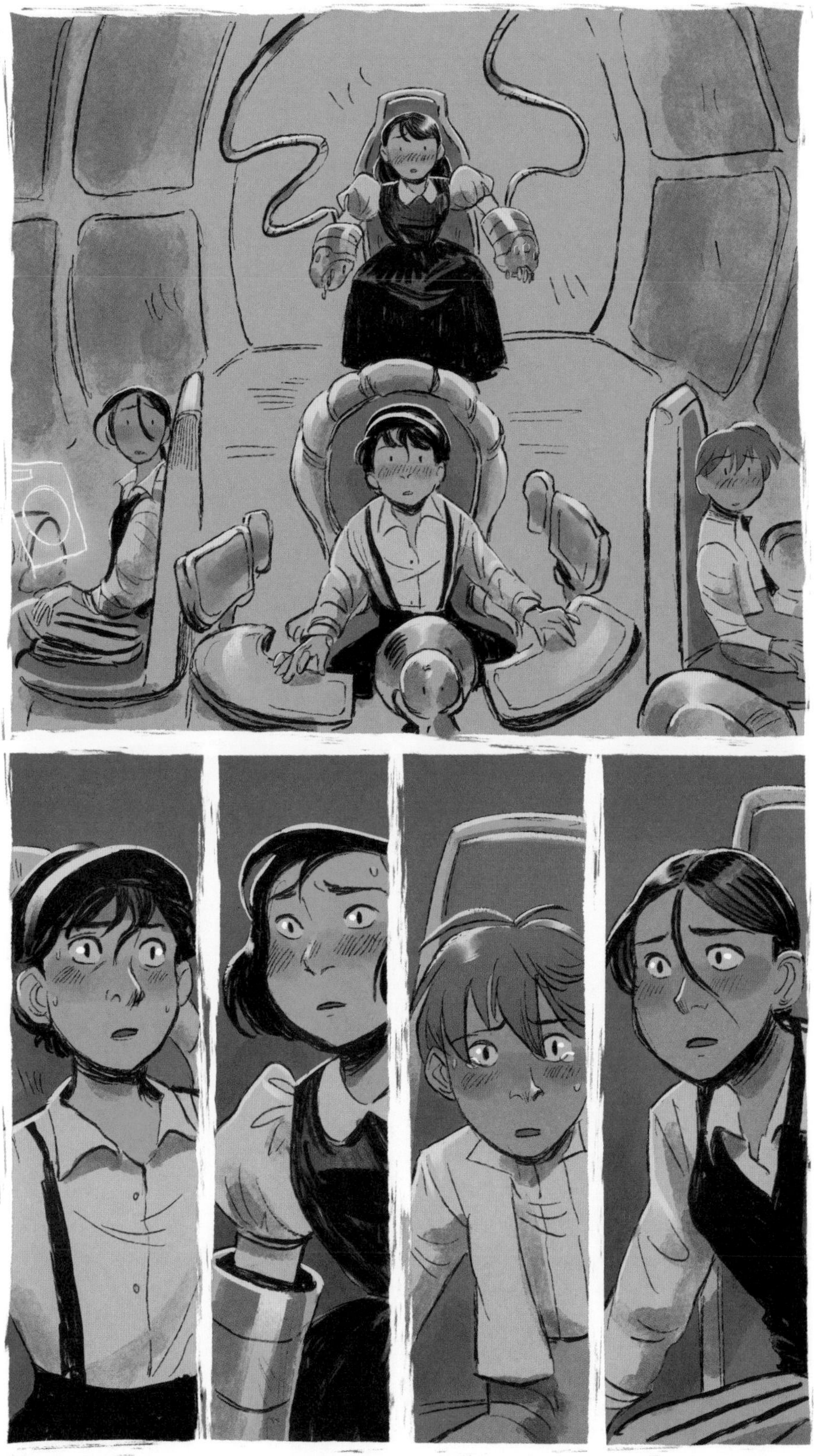

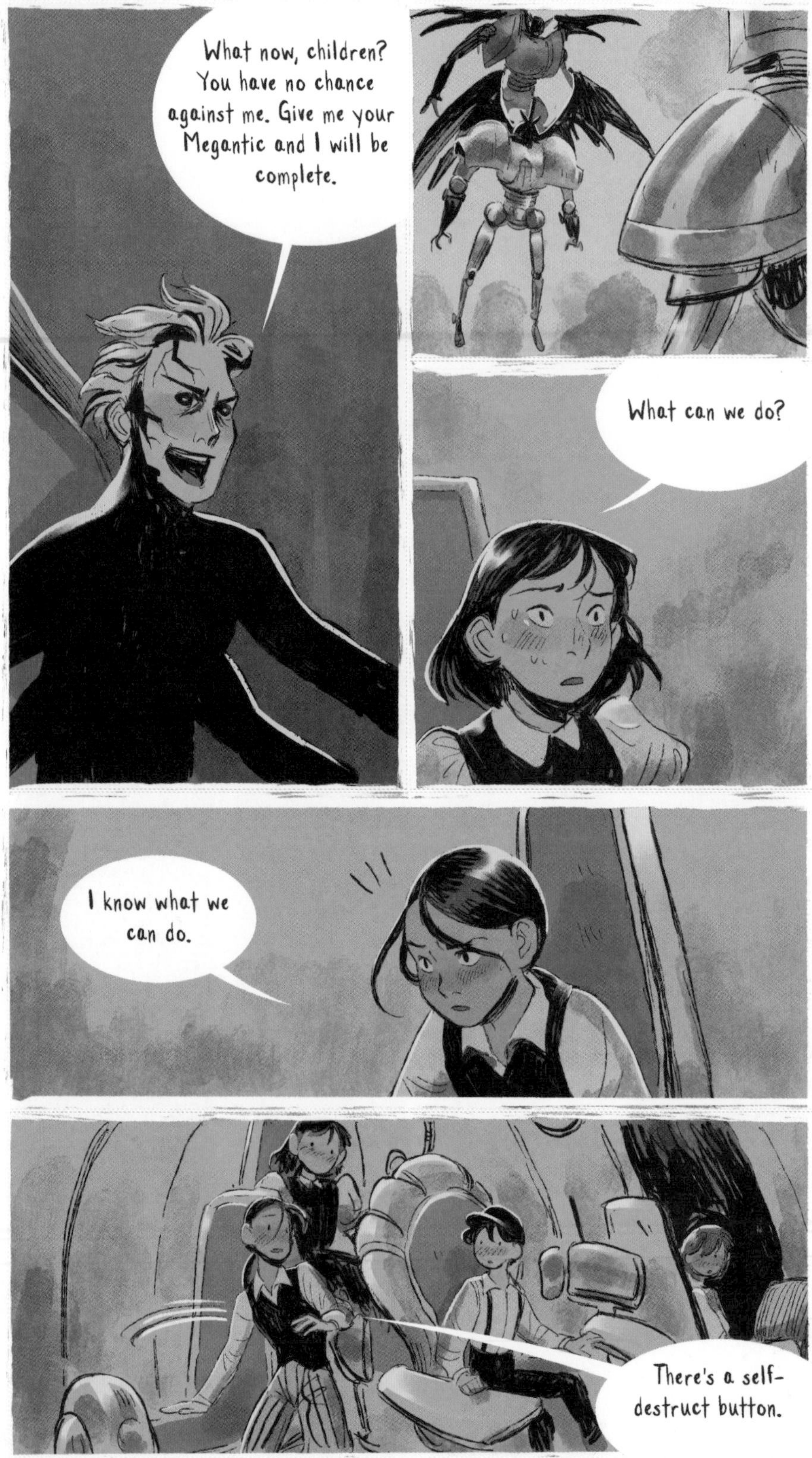
What now, children? You have no chance against me. Give me your Megantic and I will be complete.
What can we do?
I know what we can do.
There's a self-destruct button.

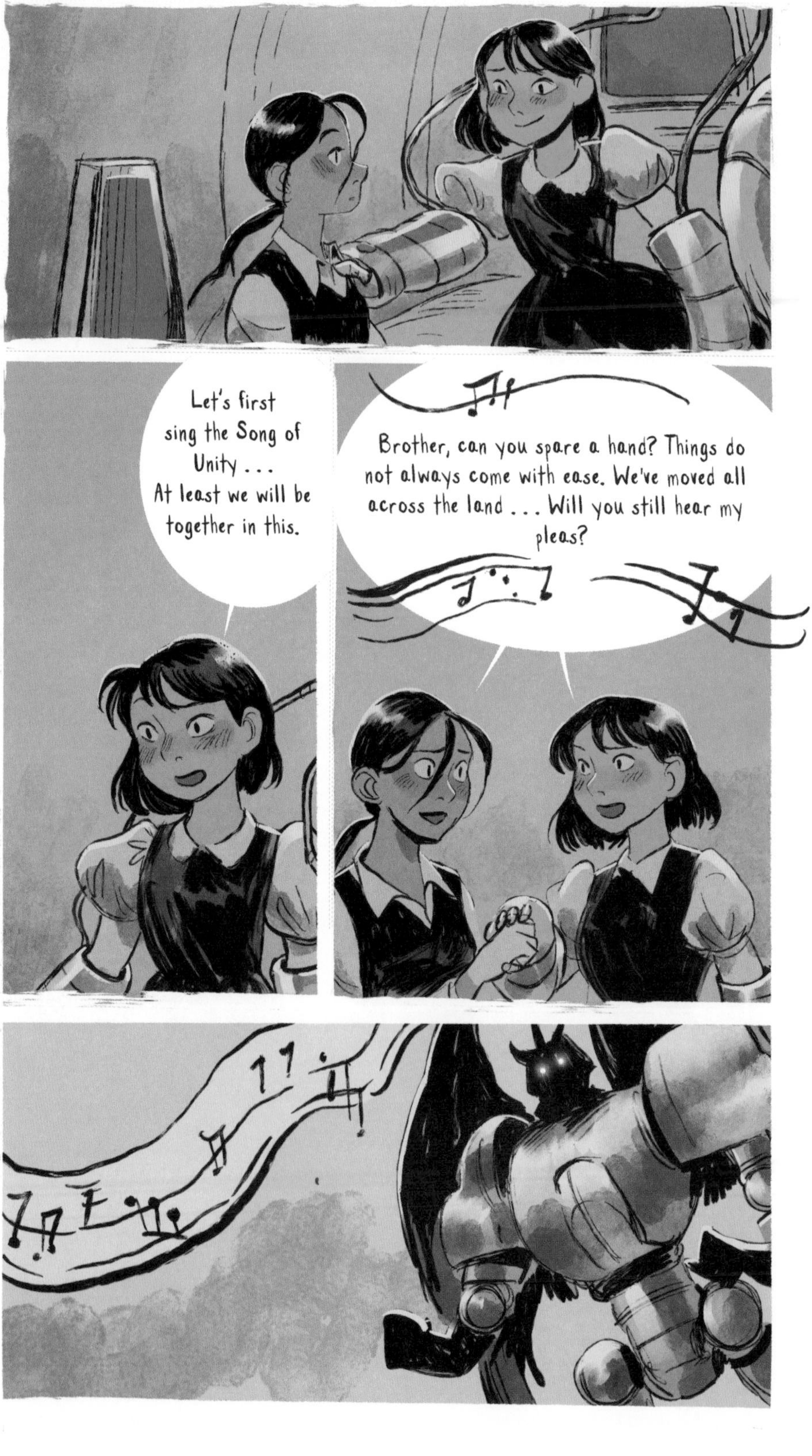
Let's first sing the Song of Unity . . . At least we will be together in this.
Brother, can you spare a hand? Things do not always come with ease. We've moved all across the land . . . Will you still hear my pleas?

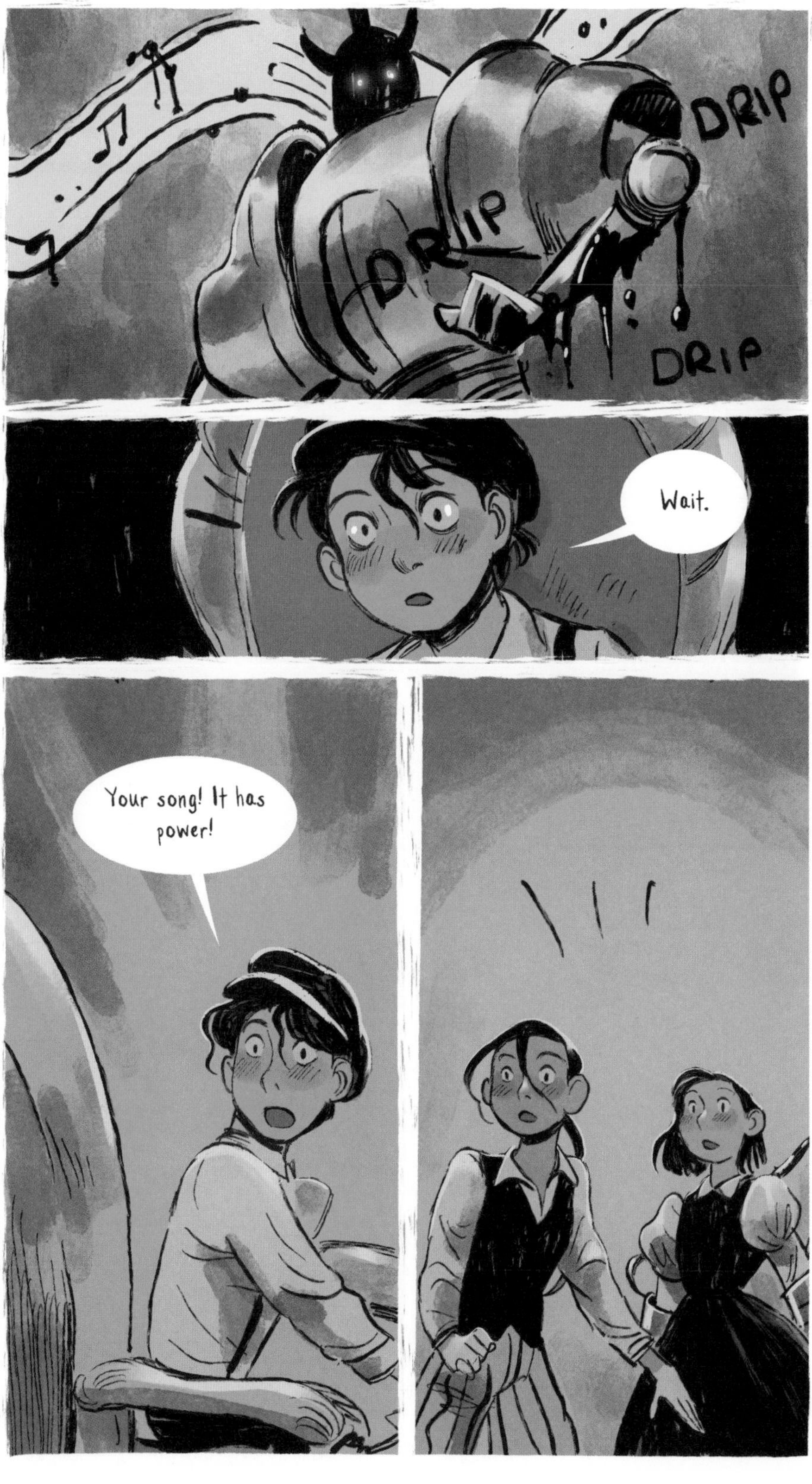
DRIP
DRIP
DRIP
Wait.
Your song! It has power!

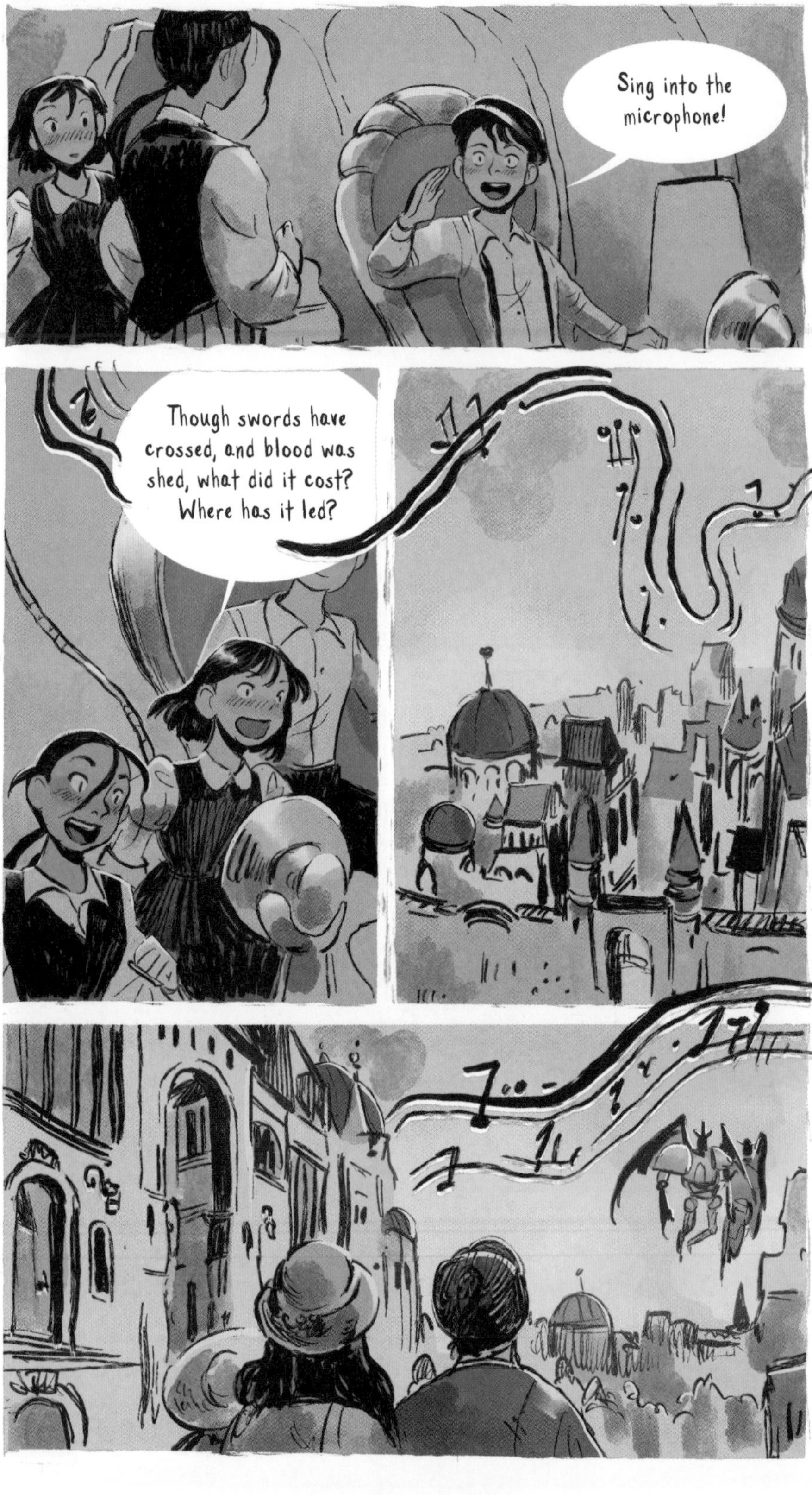
Sing into the microphone!
Though swords have crossed, and blood was shed, what did it cost? Where has it led?

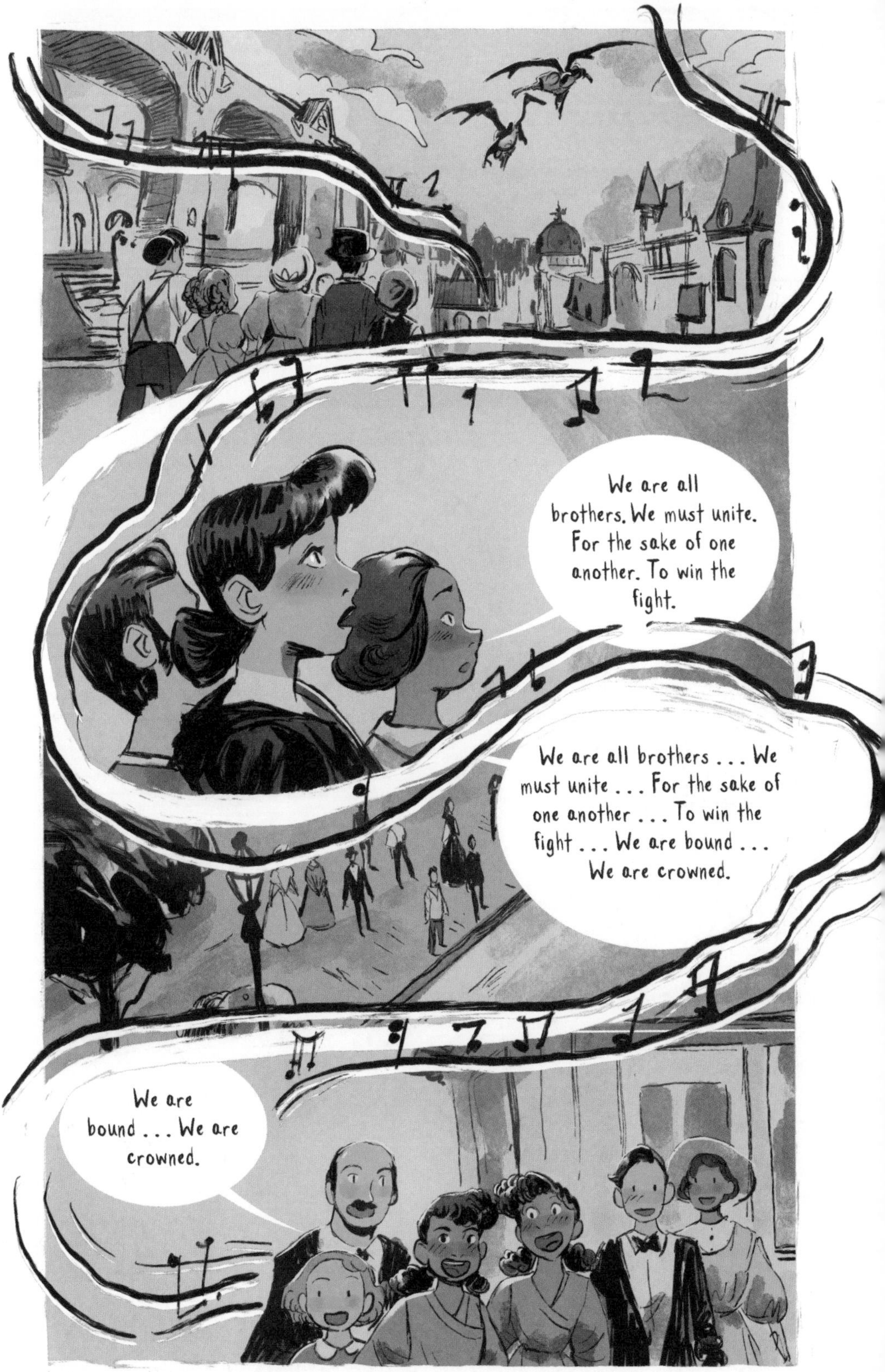

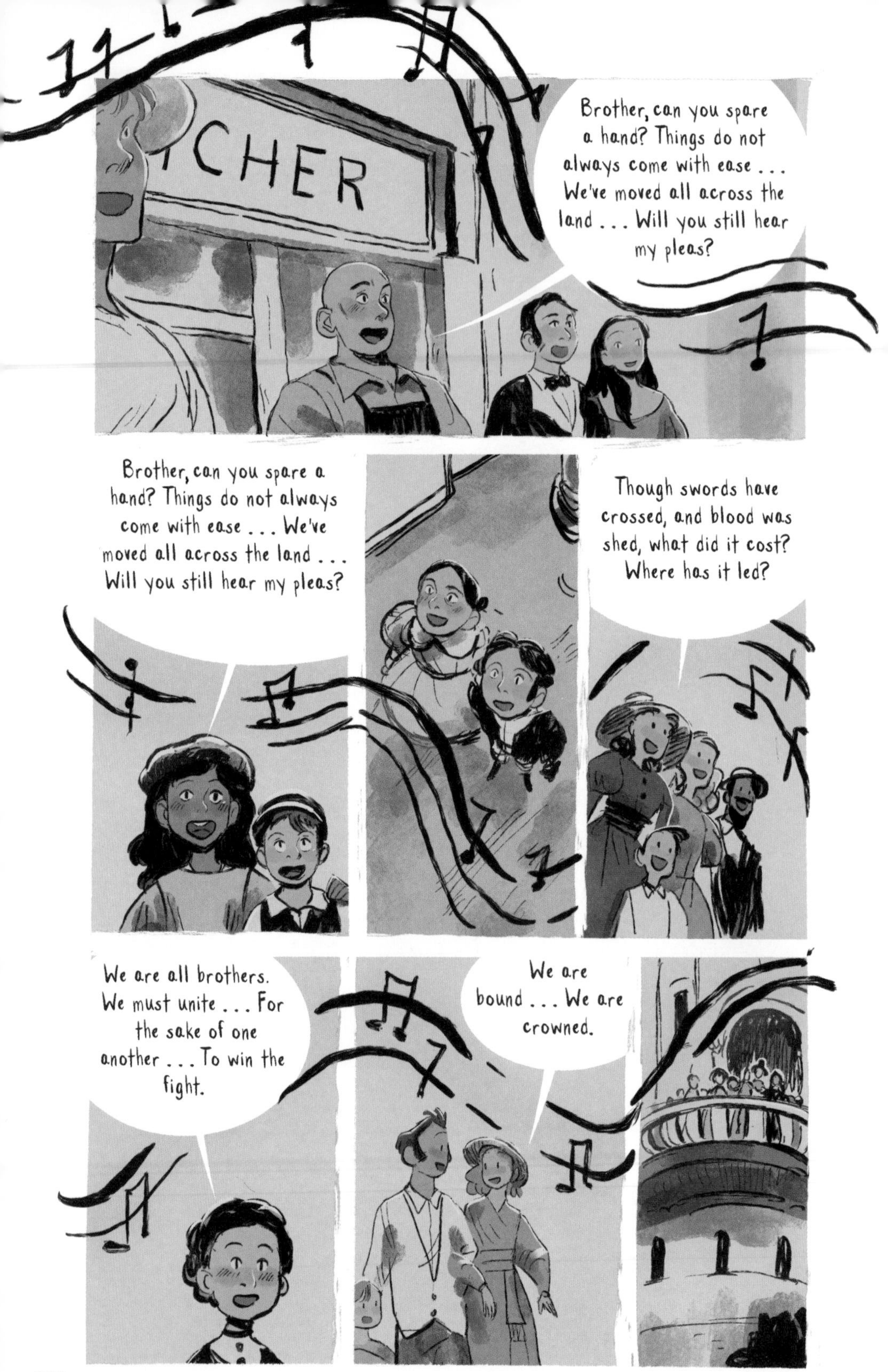

ICHER
Brother, can you spare a hand? Things do not always come with ease . . . We've moved all across the land . . . Will you still hear my pleas?
Brother, can you spare a hand? Things do not always come with ease . . . We've moved all across the land . . . Will you still hear my pleas?
Though swords have crossed, and blood was shed, what did it cost? Where has it led?
We are all brothers. We must unite . . . For the sake of one another . . . To win the fight.
We are bound . . . We are crowned.

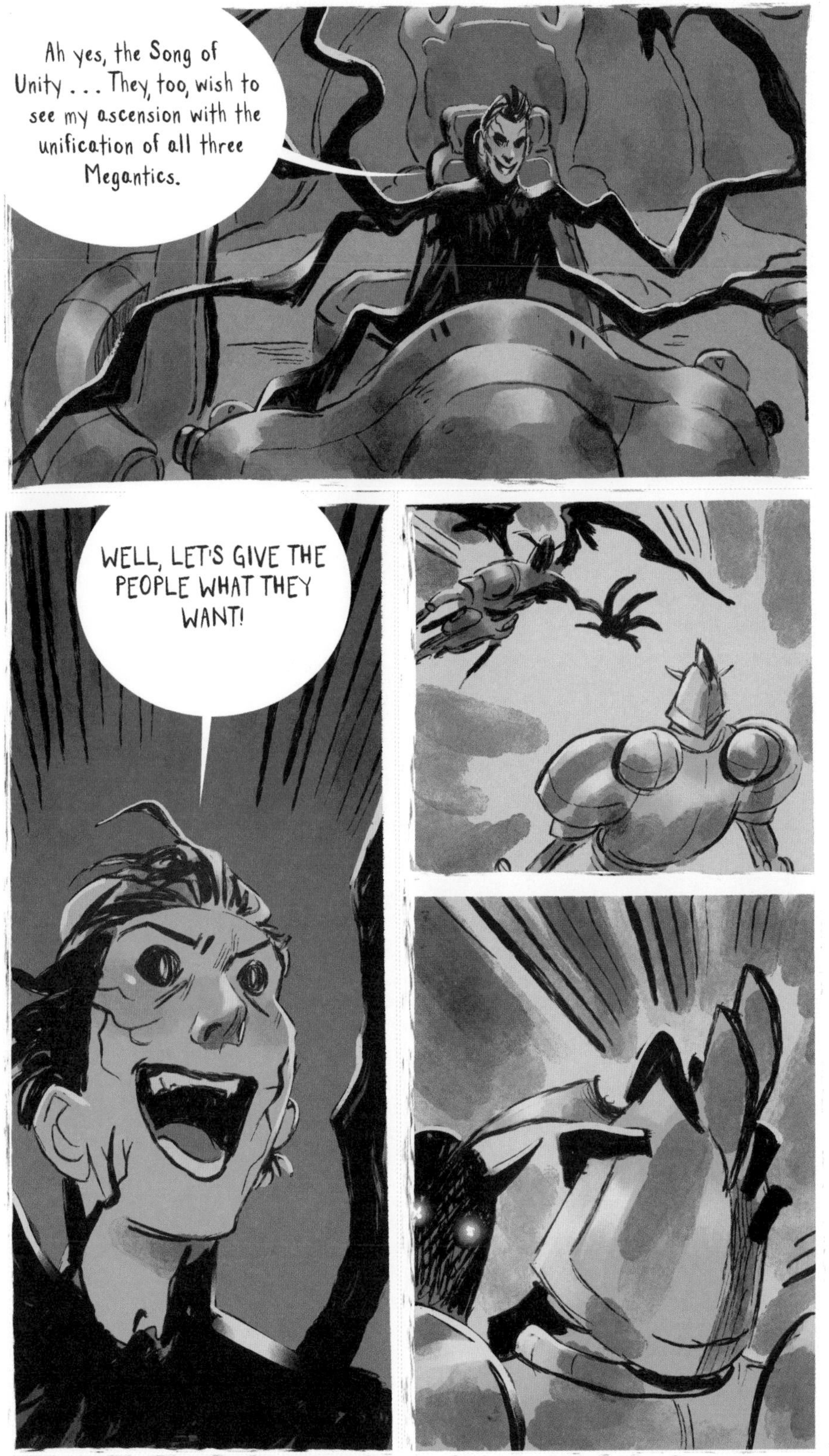
Ah yes, the Song of Unity . . . They, too, wish to see my ascension with the unification of all three Megantics.
WELL, LET'S GIVE THE PEOPLE WHAT THEY WANT!

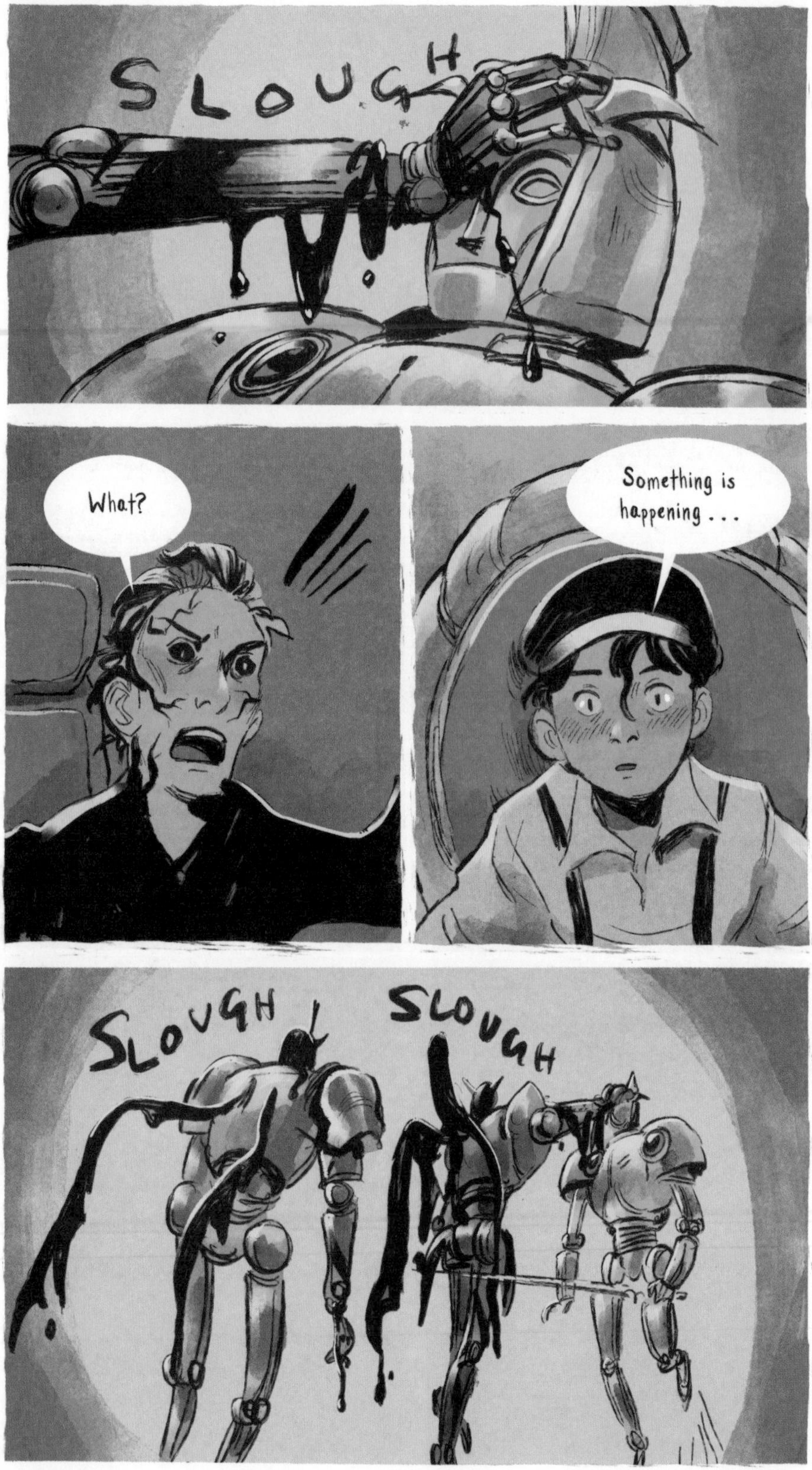
SLOUGH
What?
Something is happening . . .
SLOUGH
SLOUGH

No . . . no, what is happening?!

SLOUGH

The song . . . it must be the song! Just like your song, Hannah. It has magic! It's fighting the ancient magic!

The knights were meant to be one. But not like this. Not with just one pilot.

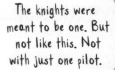

CRNHIRK

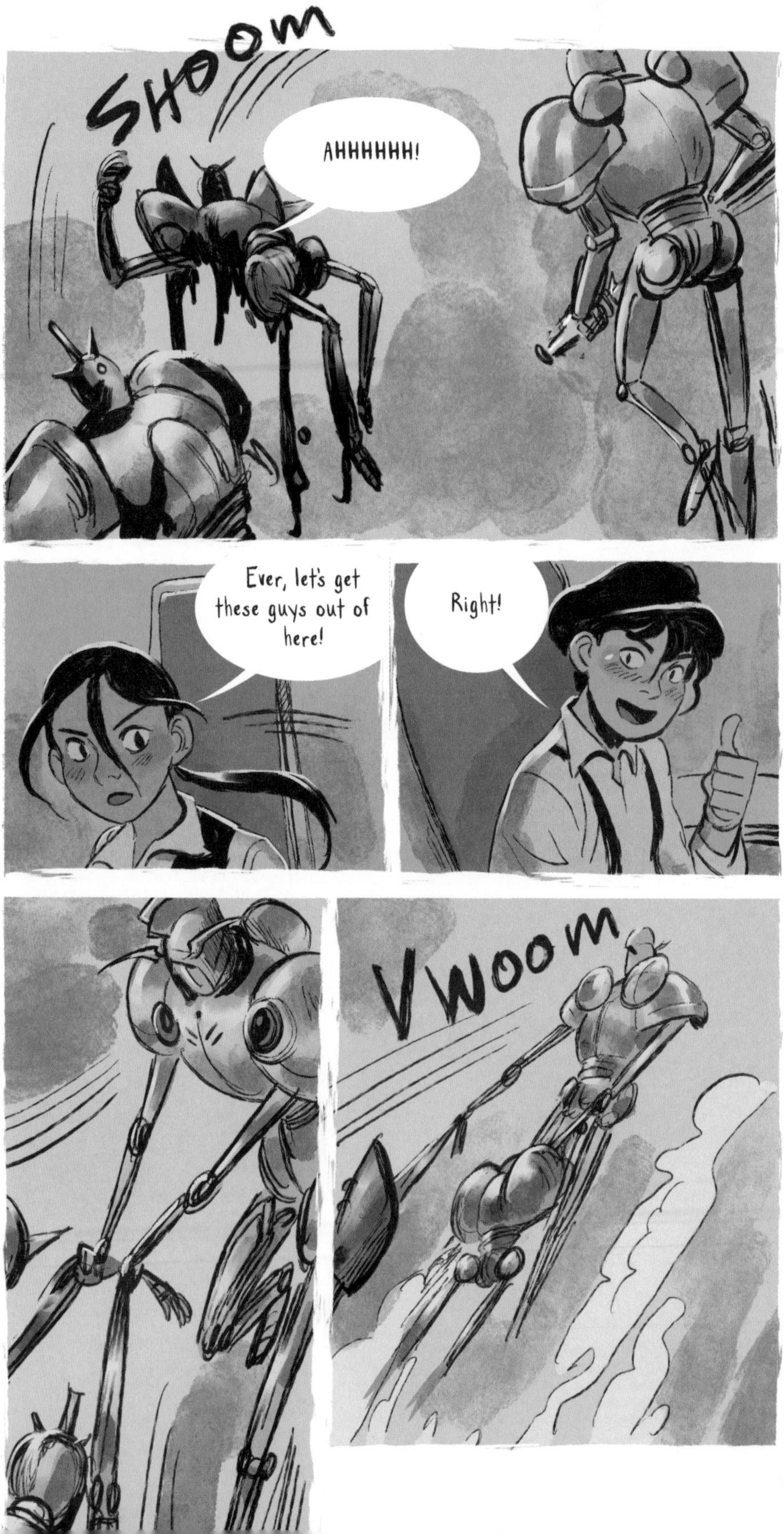
SHOOM
AHHHHHH!
Ever, let's get these guys out of here!
Right!
VWOOM

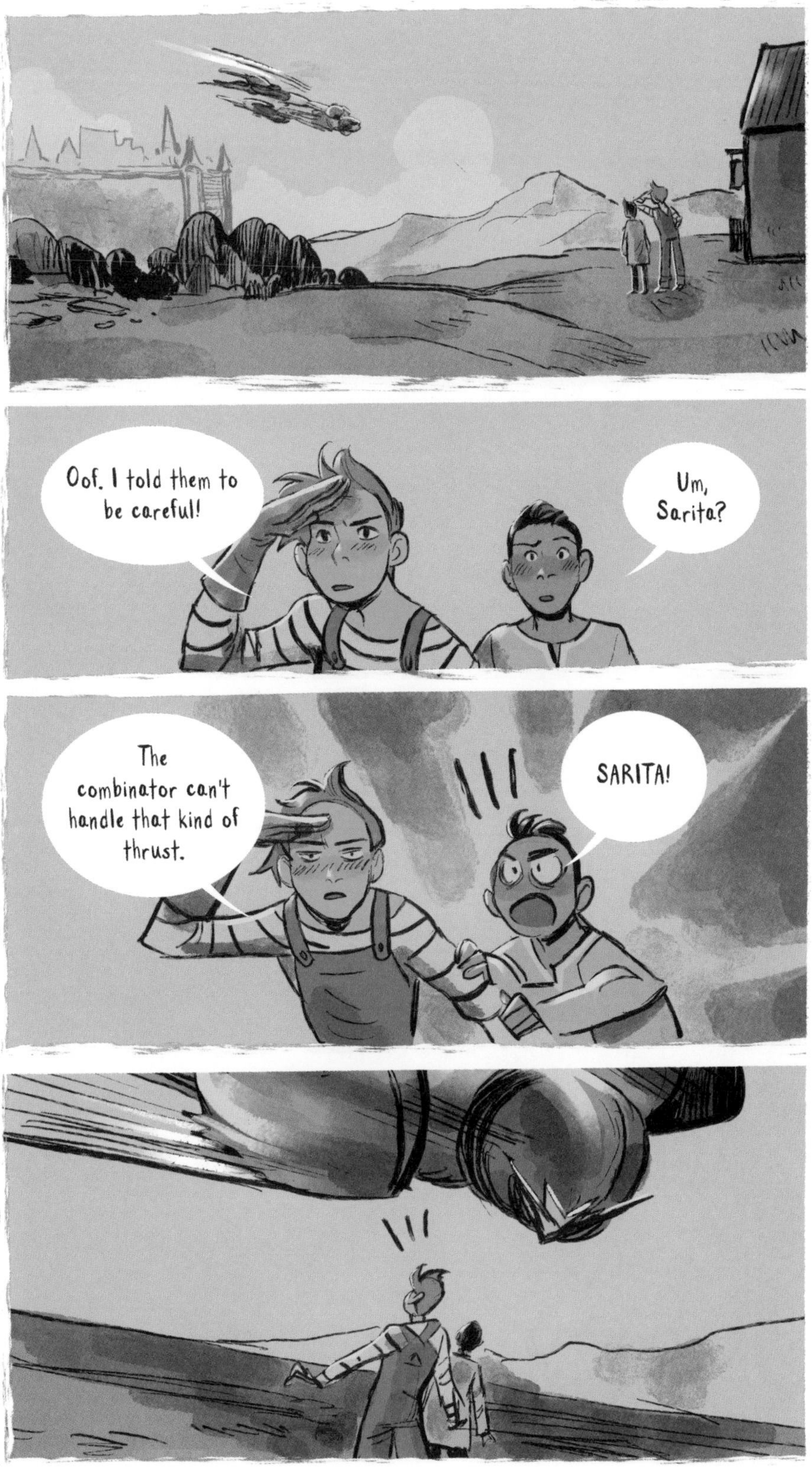
Oof. I told them to be careful!
Um, Sarita?
The combinator can't handle that kind of thrust.
SARITA!

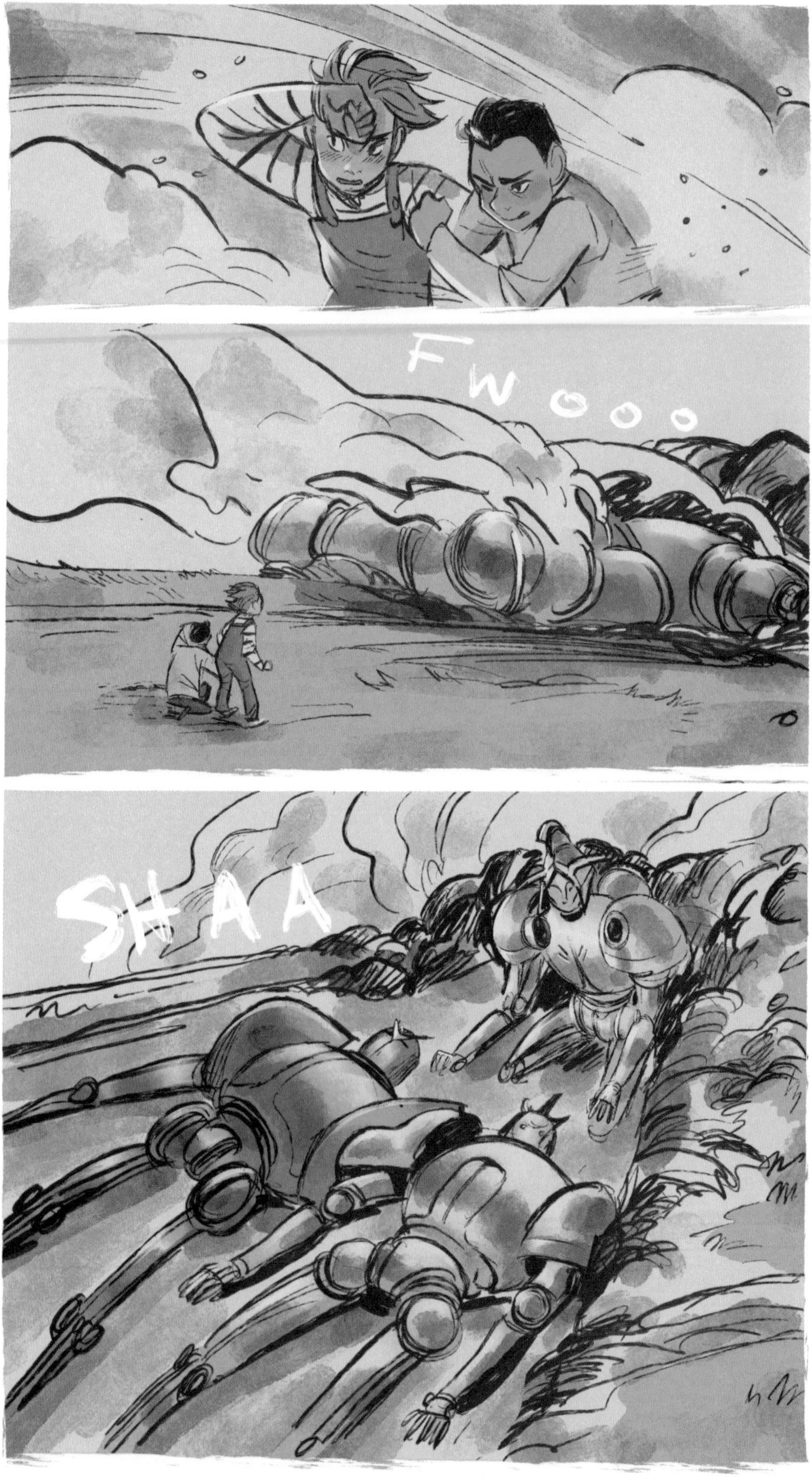
FWOOO
SHAA

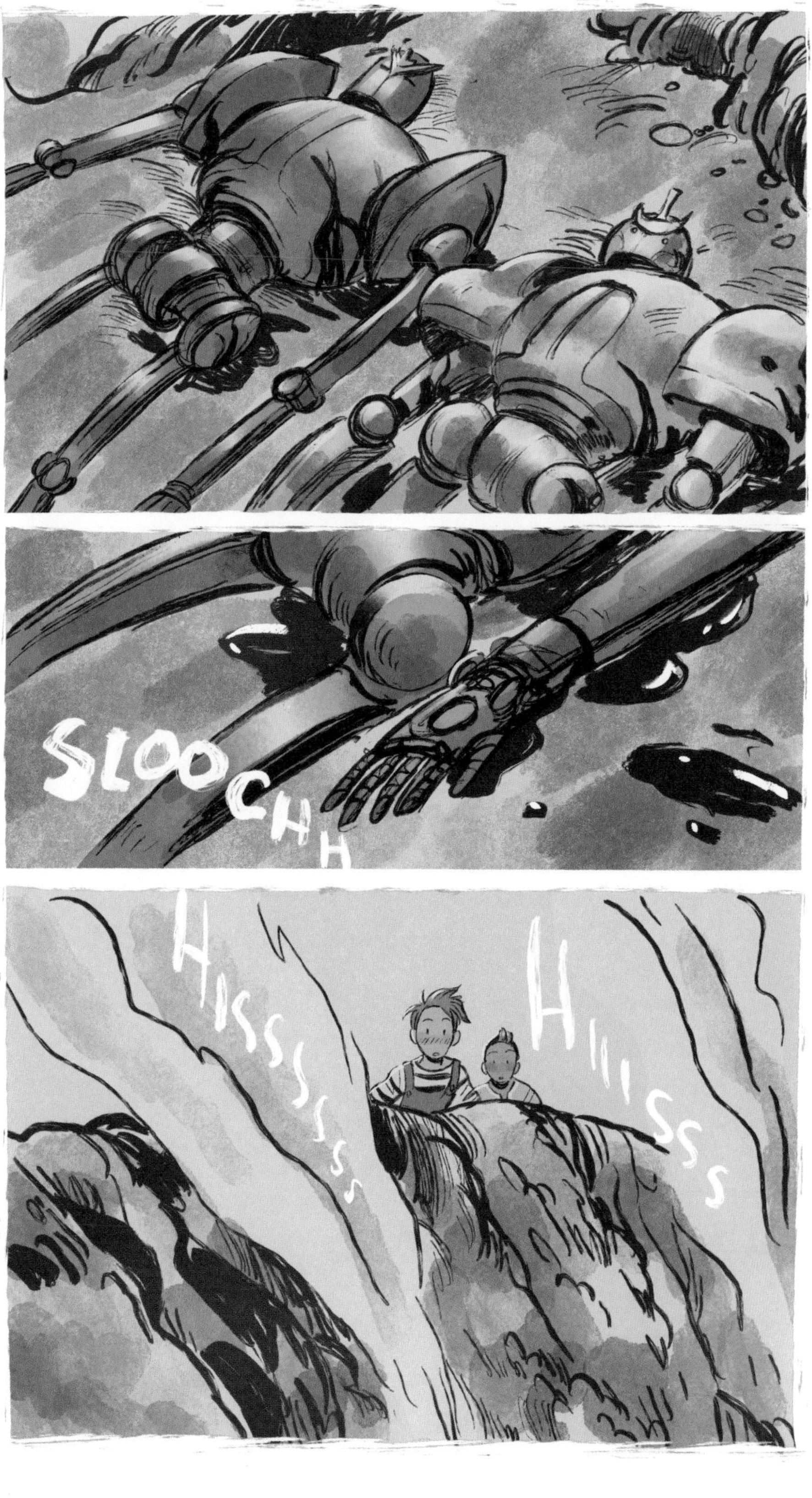
SLOOCHH
HISSSSSSS
HIISSSS

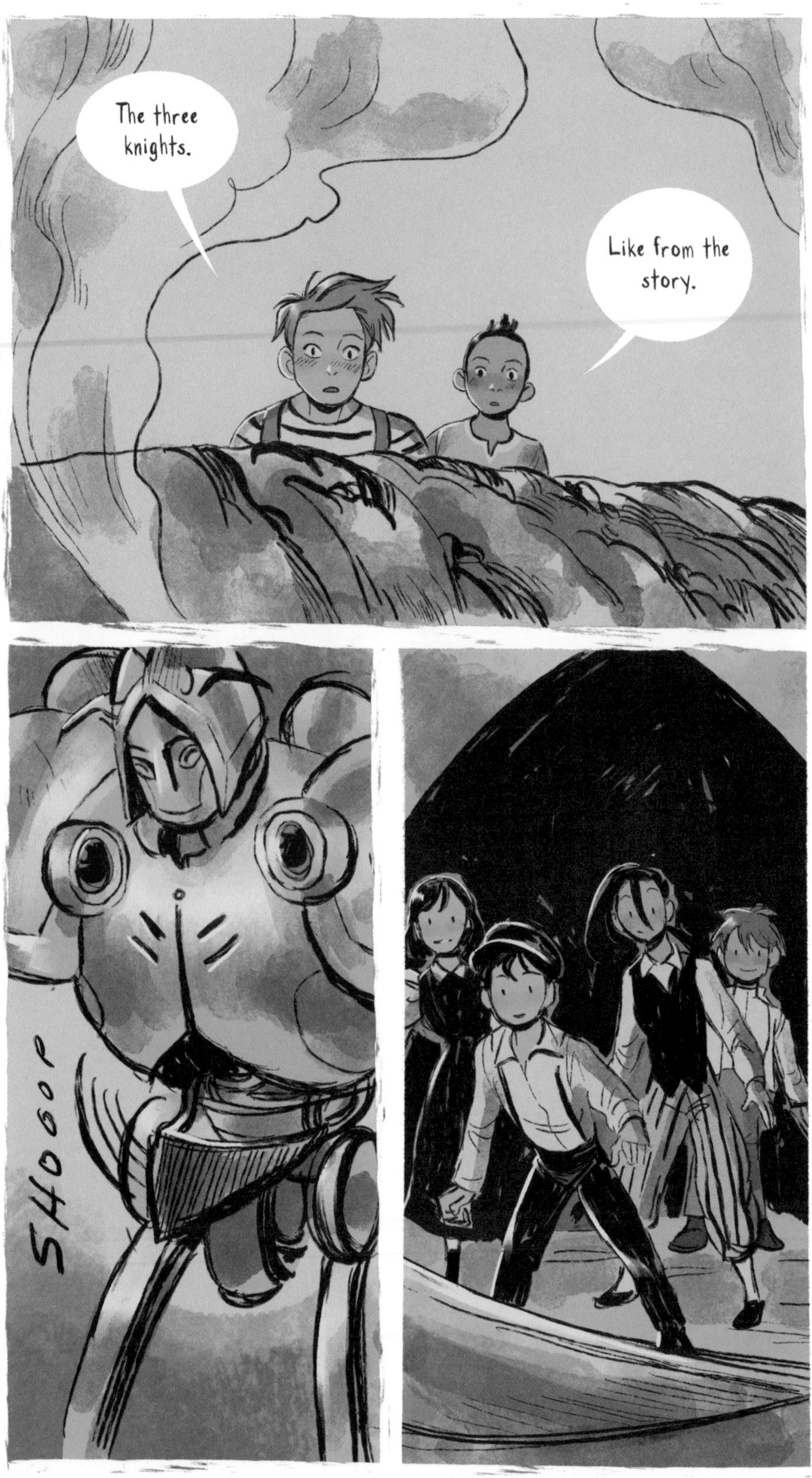
The three knights.
Like from the story.
SHOOOP

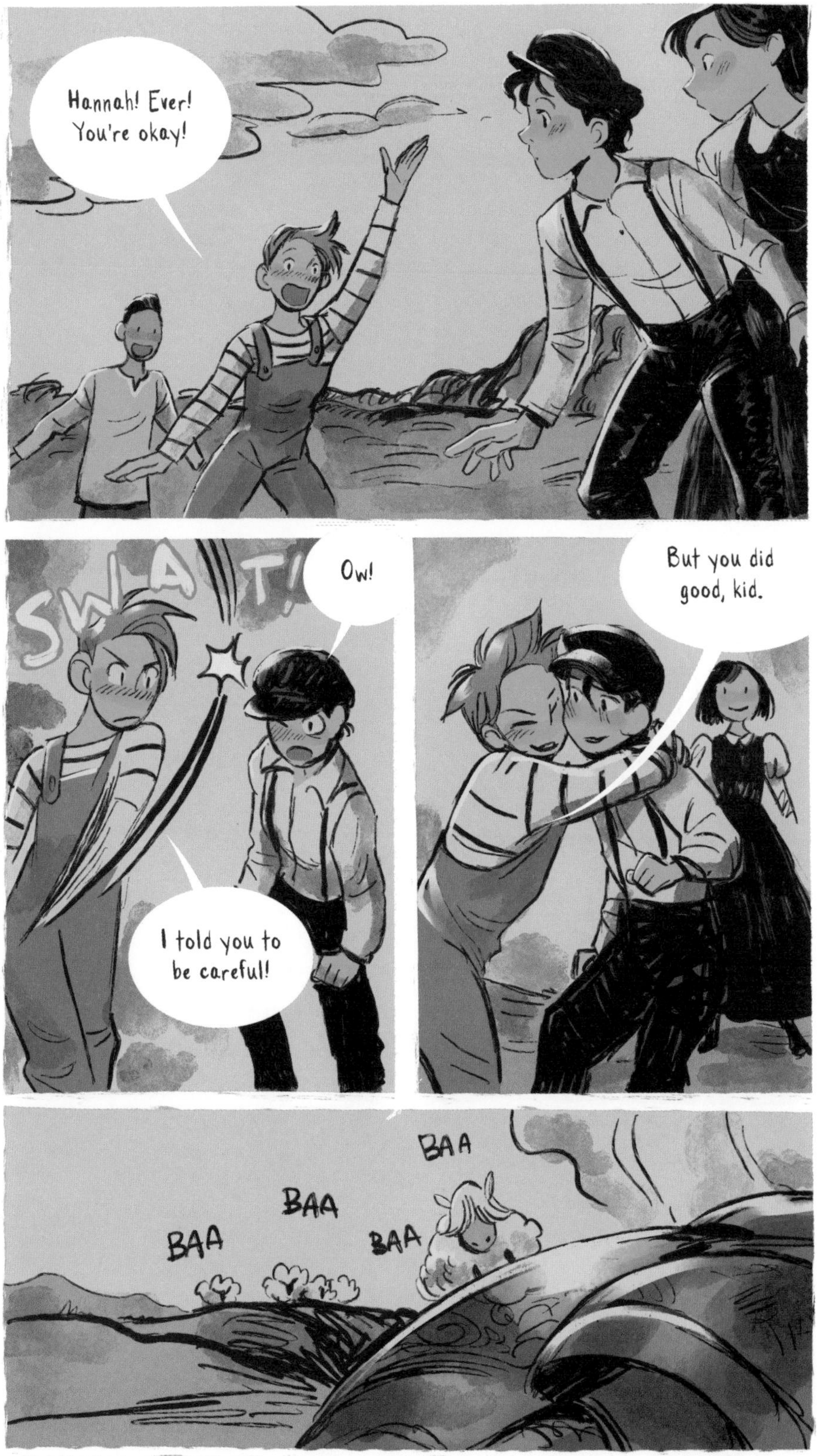
Hannah! Ever! You're okay!
SWAT!
Ow!
I told you to be careful!
But you did good, kid.
BAA
BAA
BAA
BAA

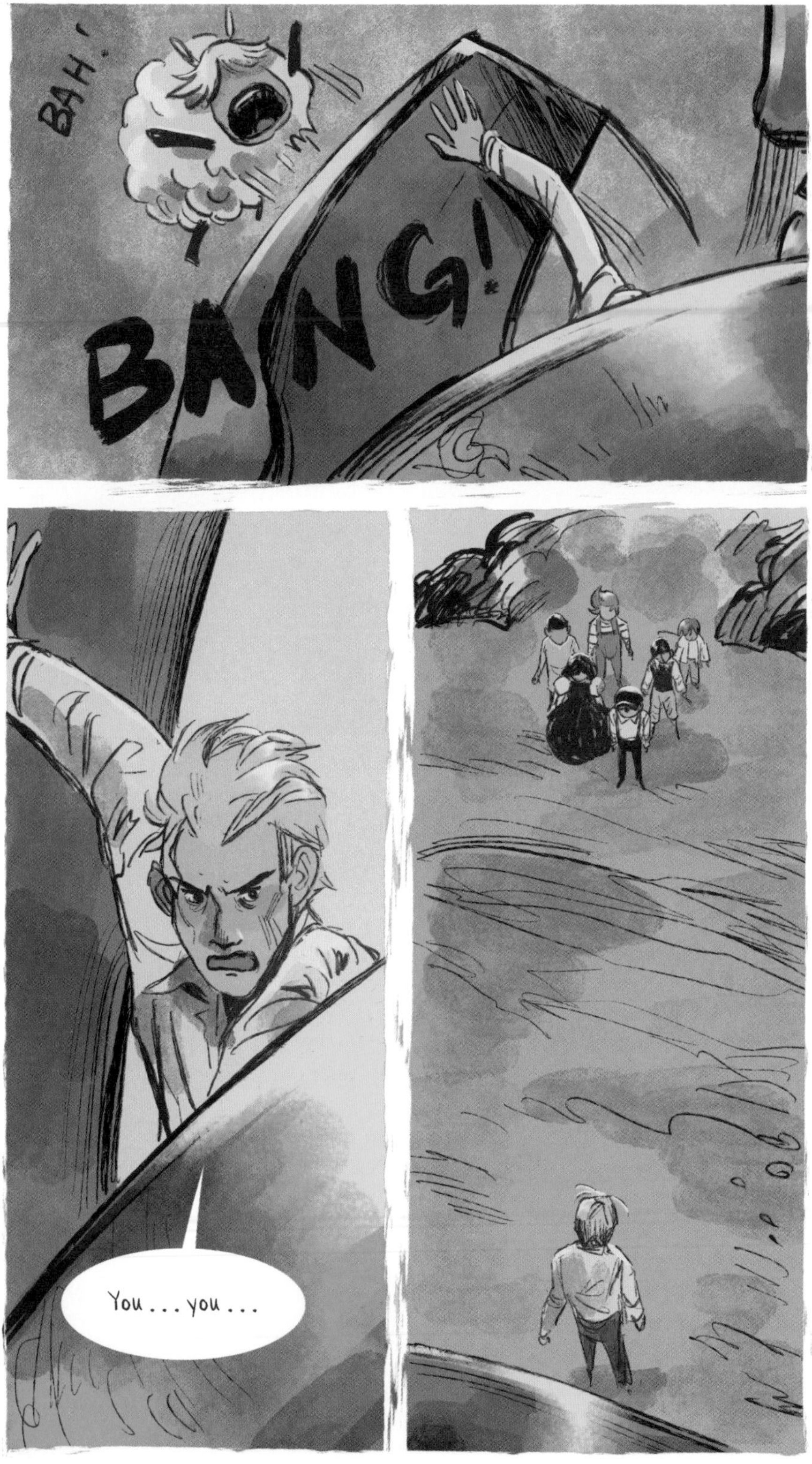
BAH!
BANG!
You . . . you . . .

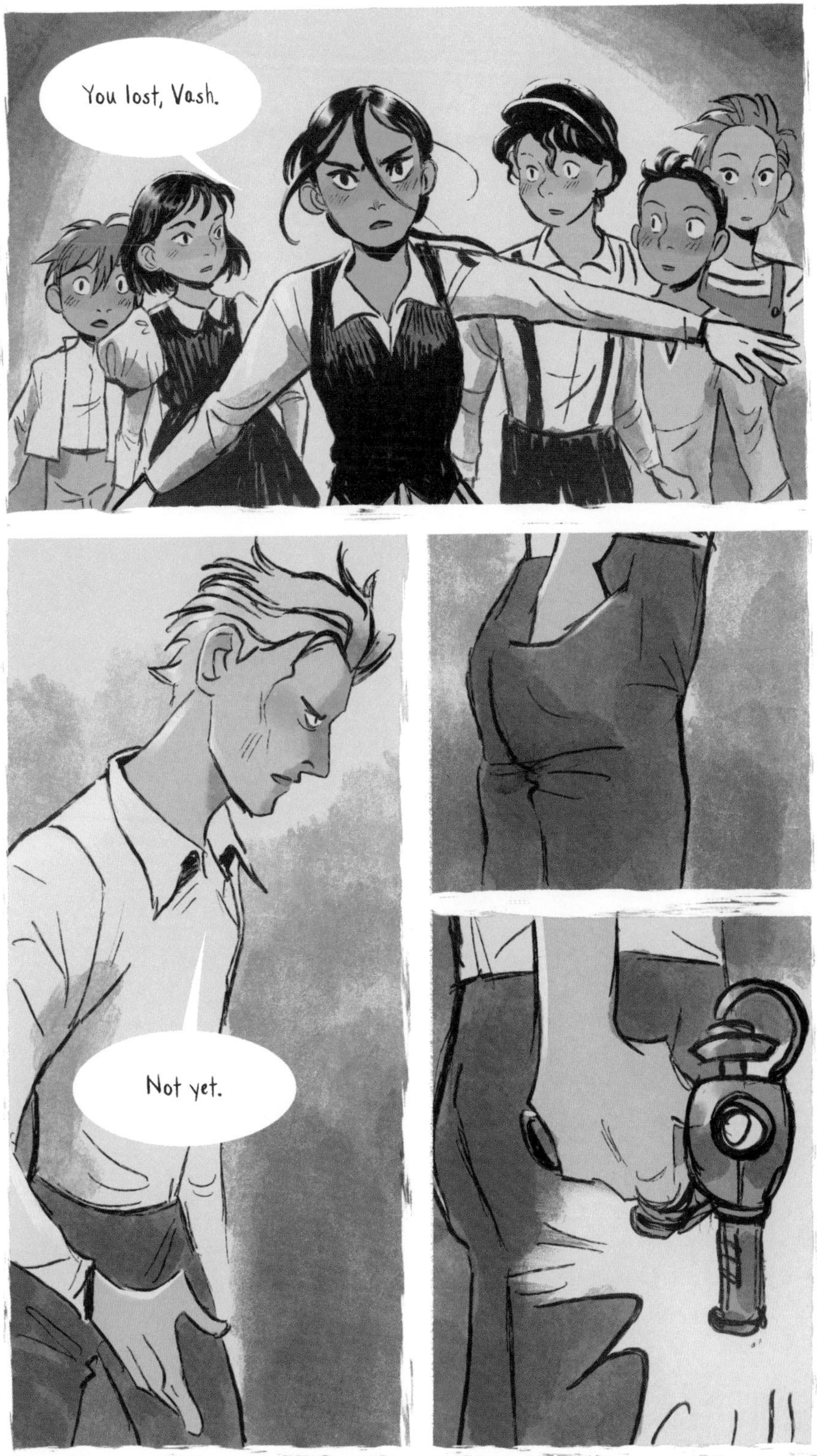
You lost, Vash.
Not yet.

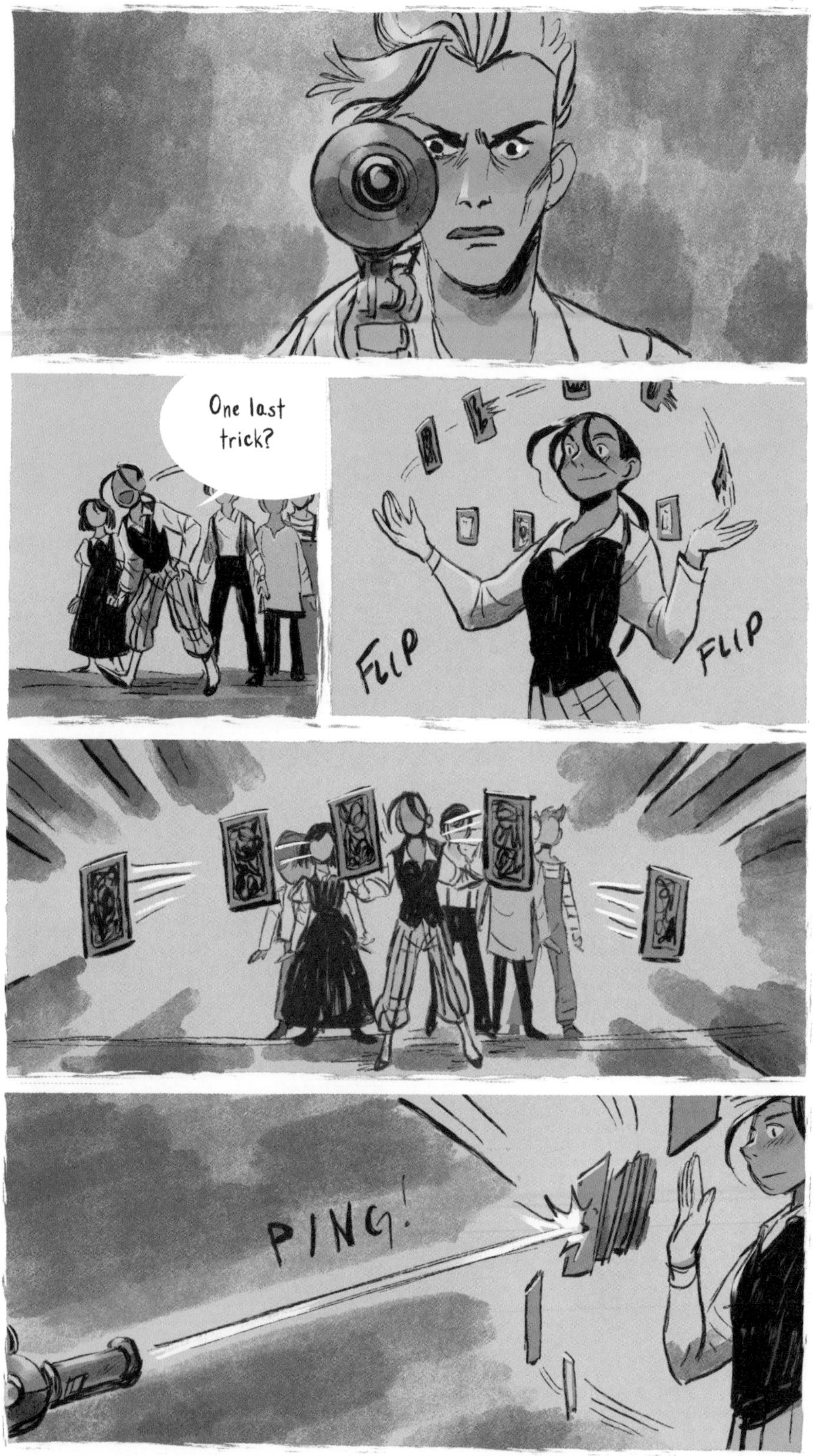
One last trick?
FLIP
FLIP
PING!

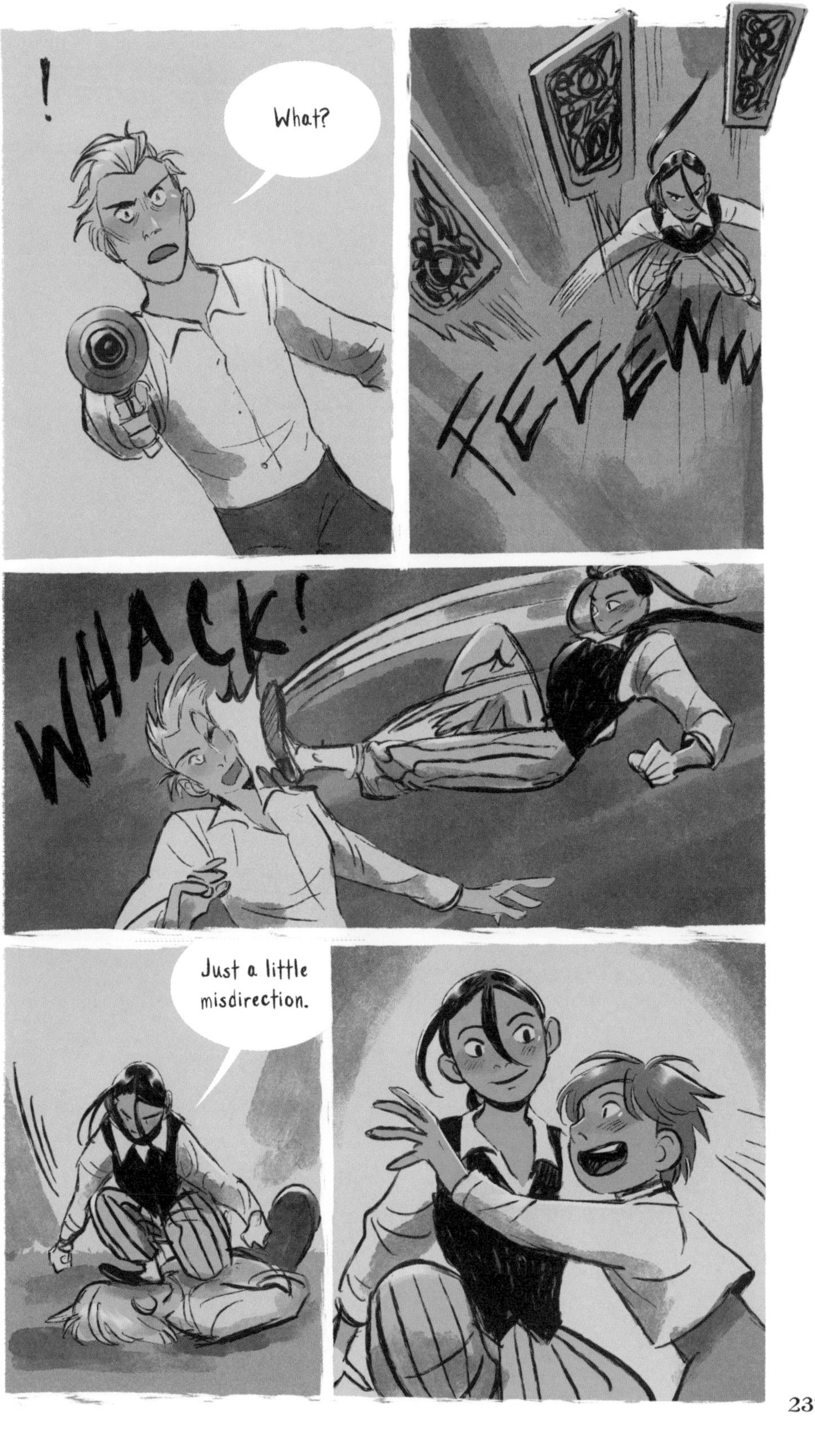
!
What?
FEEEWW
WHACK!
Just a little misdirection.

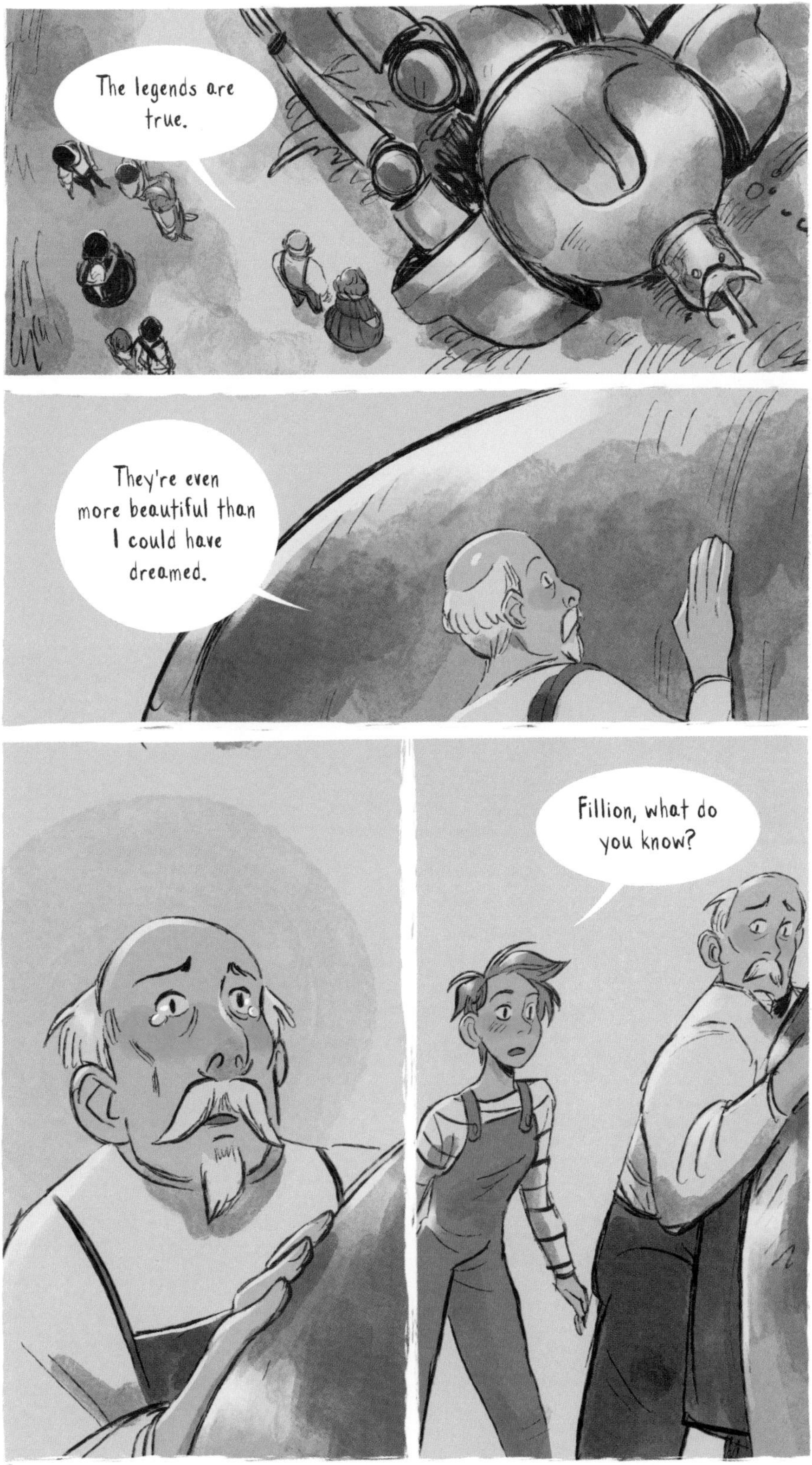
The legends are true.
They're even more beautiful than I could have dreamed.
Fillion, what do you know?

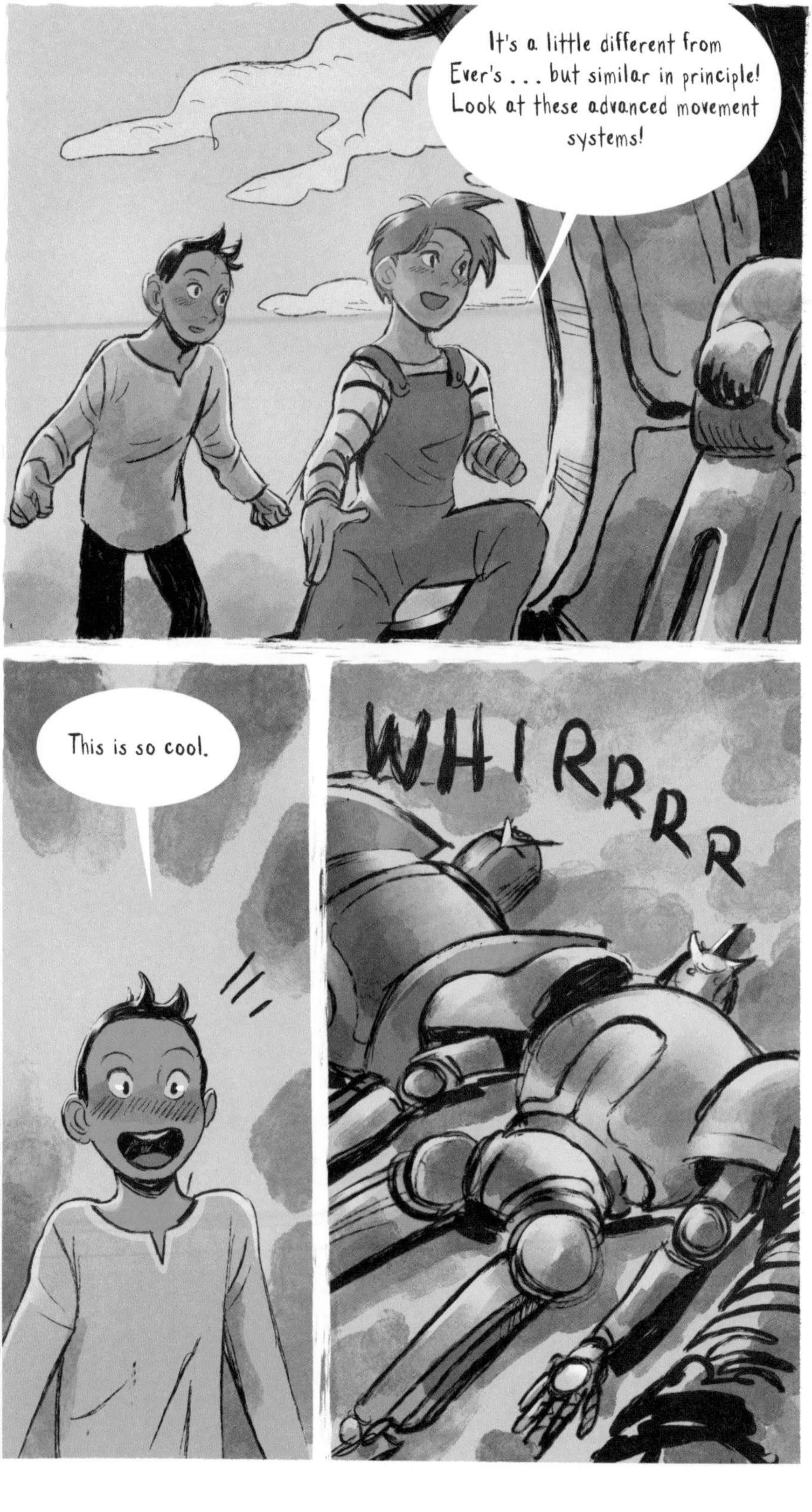
It's a little different from Ever's . . . but similar in principle! Look at these advanced movement systems!
This is so cool.
WHIRRRRR

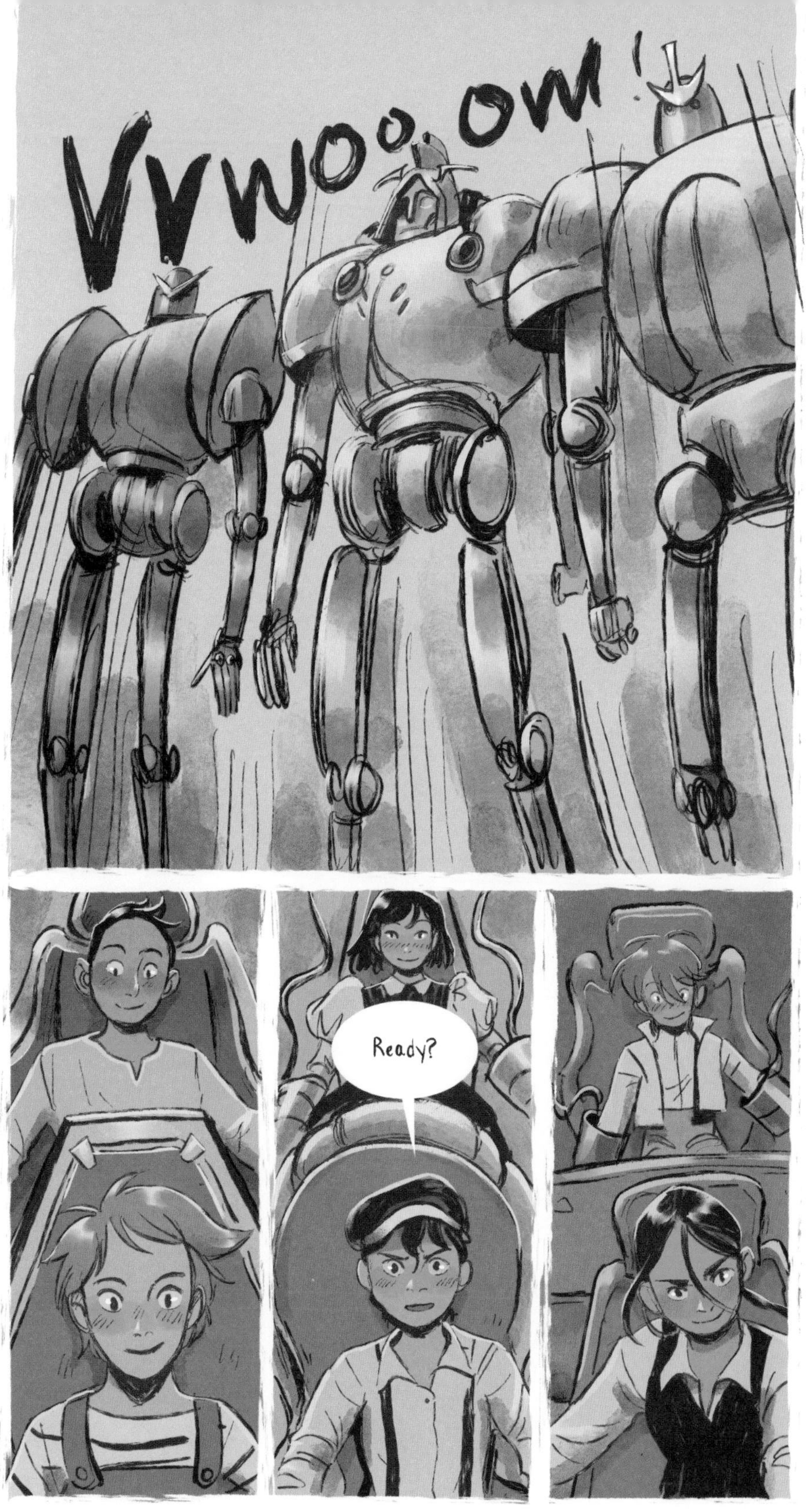
Vvwoo.om!
Ready?

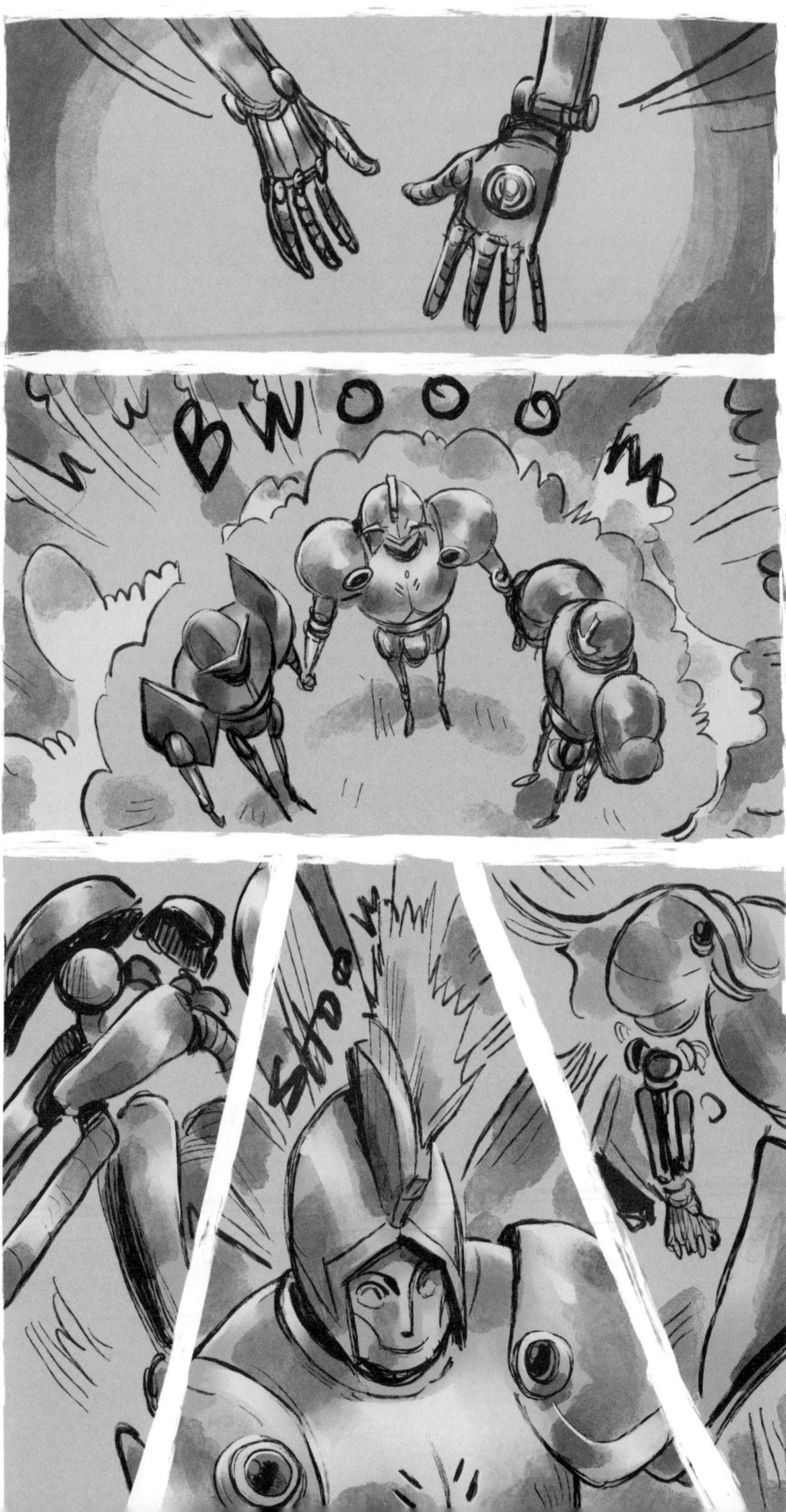
BWOOOOM
SHOOM

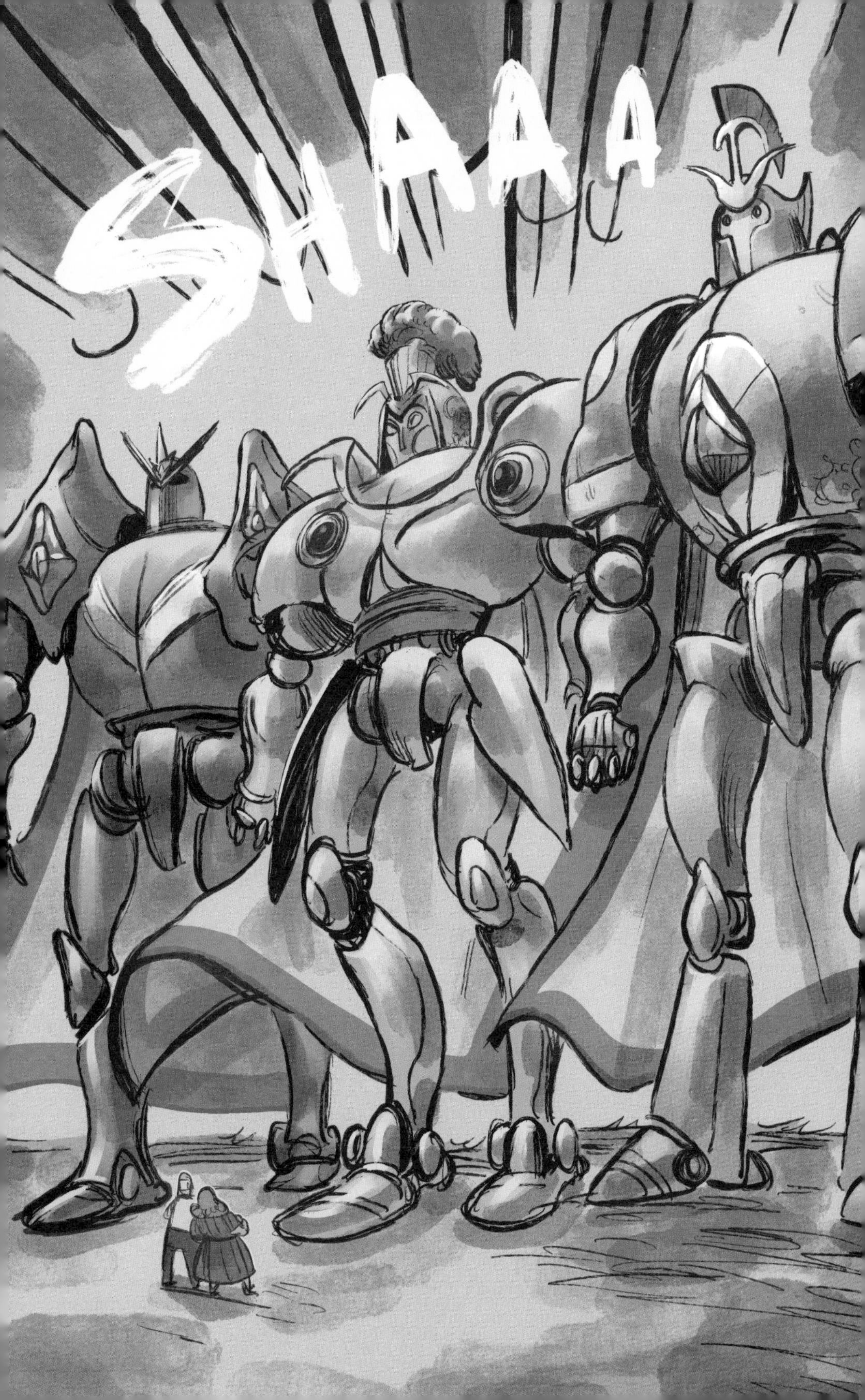
SHAAAA

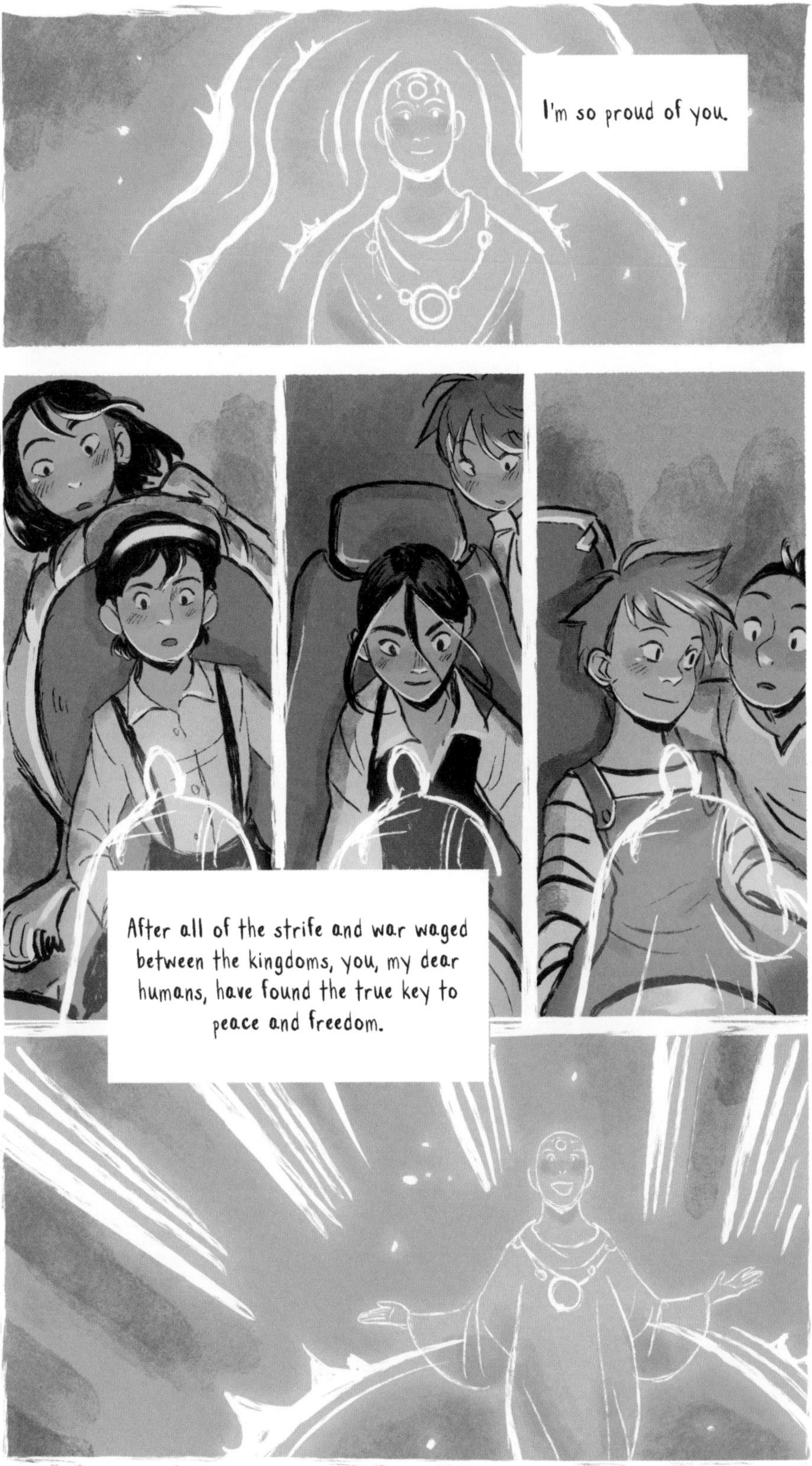
I'm so proud of you.
After all of the strife and war waged between the kingdoms, you, my dear humans, have found the true key to peace and freedom.

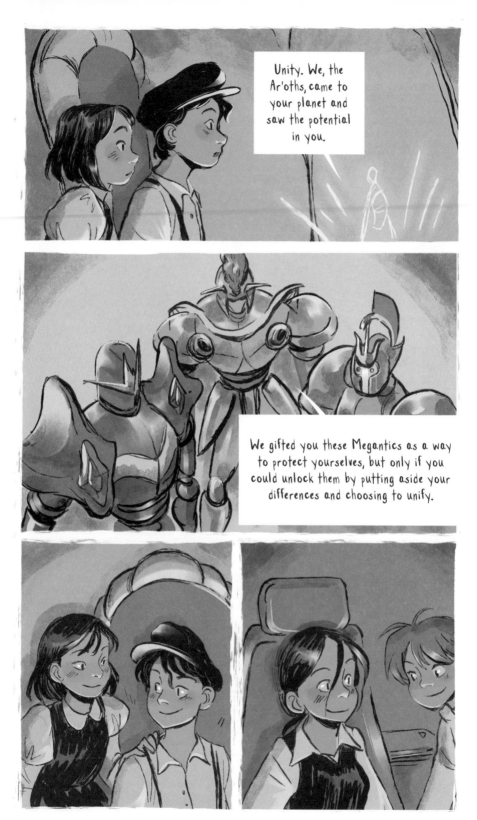

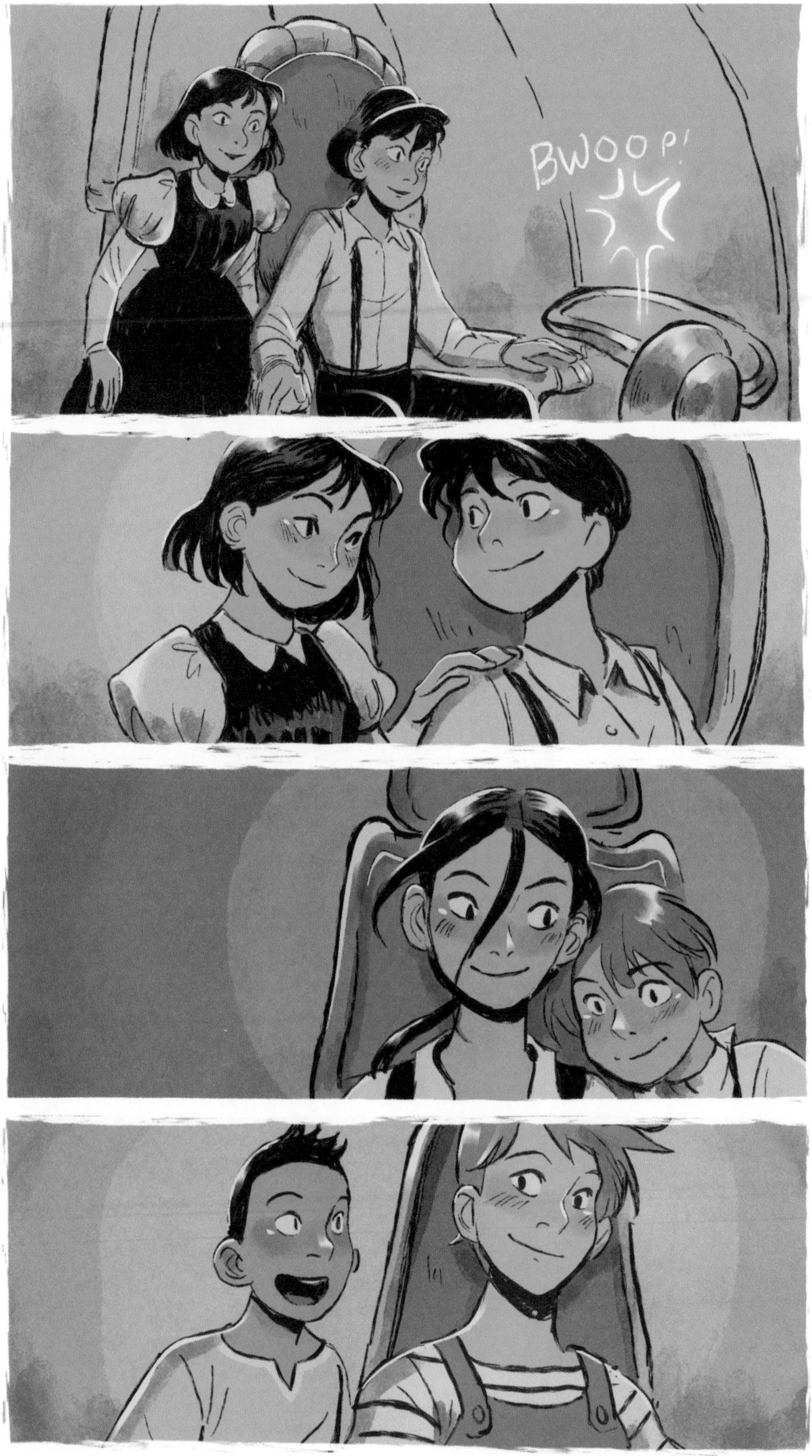
BWOOP!

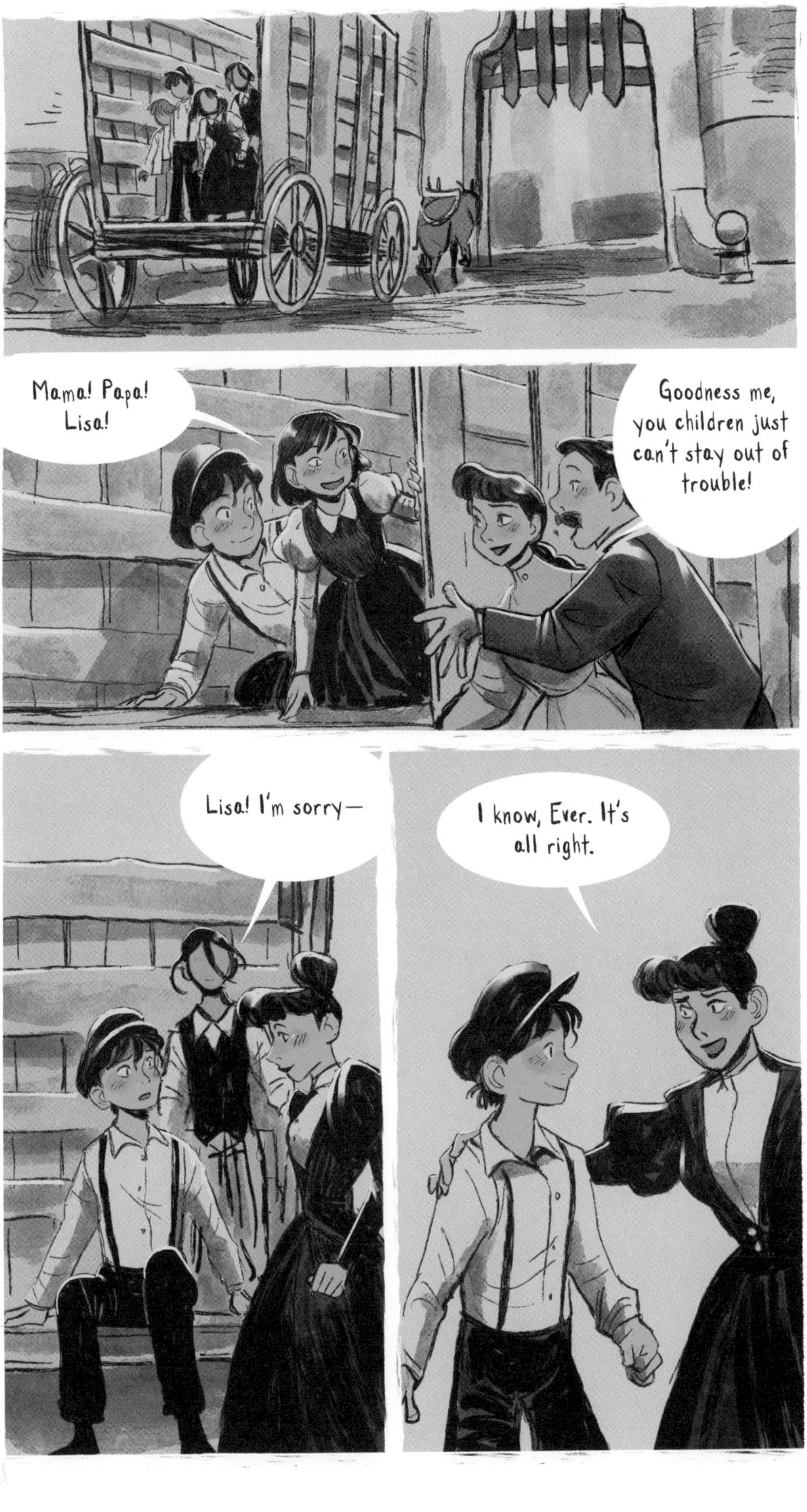
Mama! Papa! Lisa!
Goodness me, you children just can't stay out of trouble!
Lisa! I'm sorry—
I know, Ever. It's all right.

247

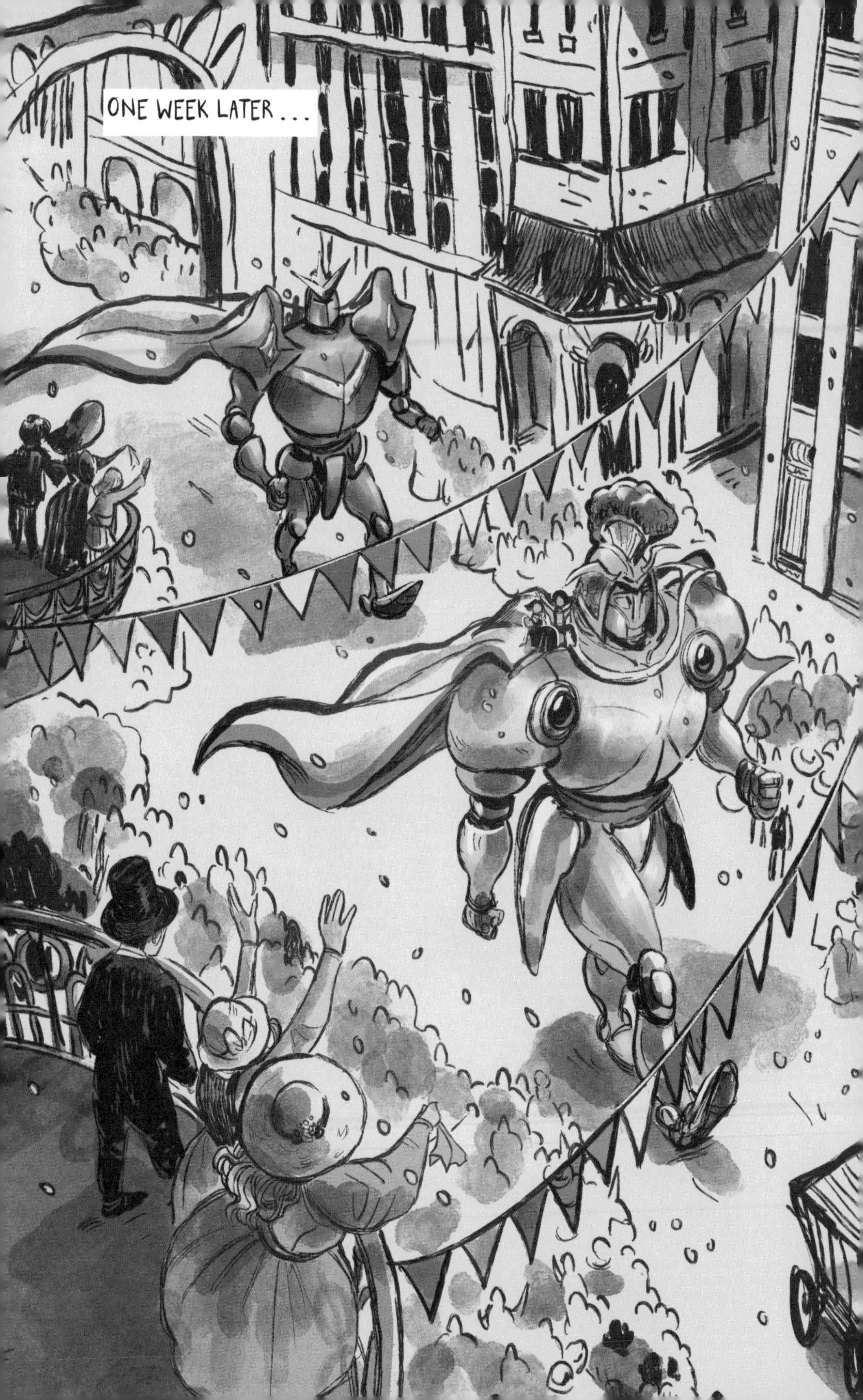
ONE WEEK LATER . . .

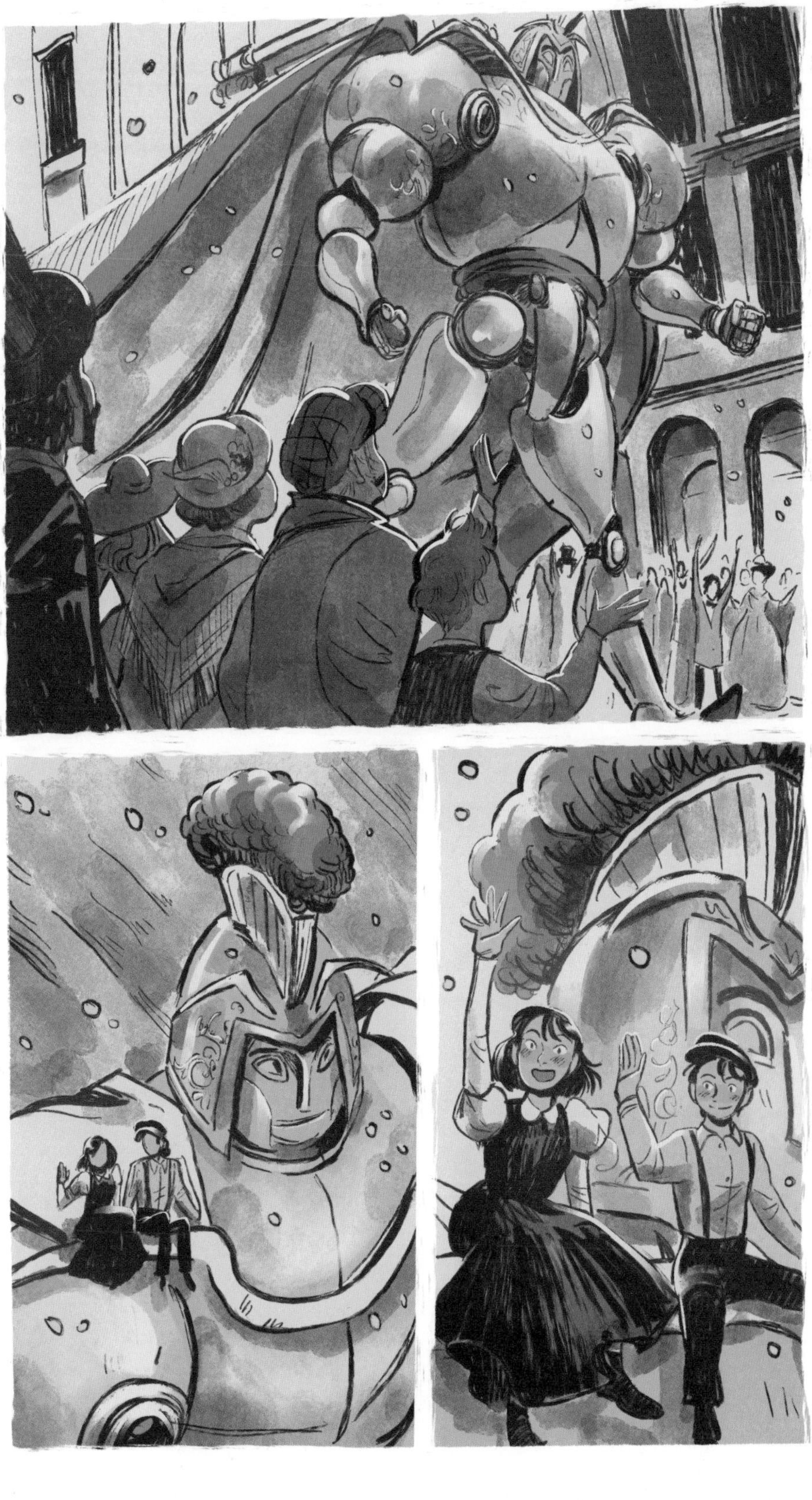

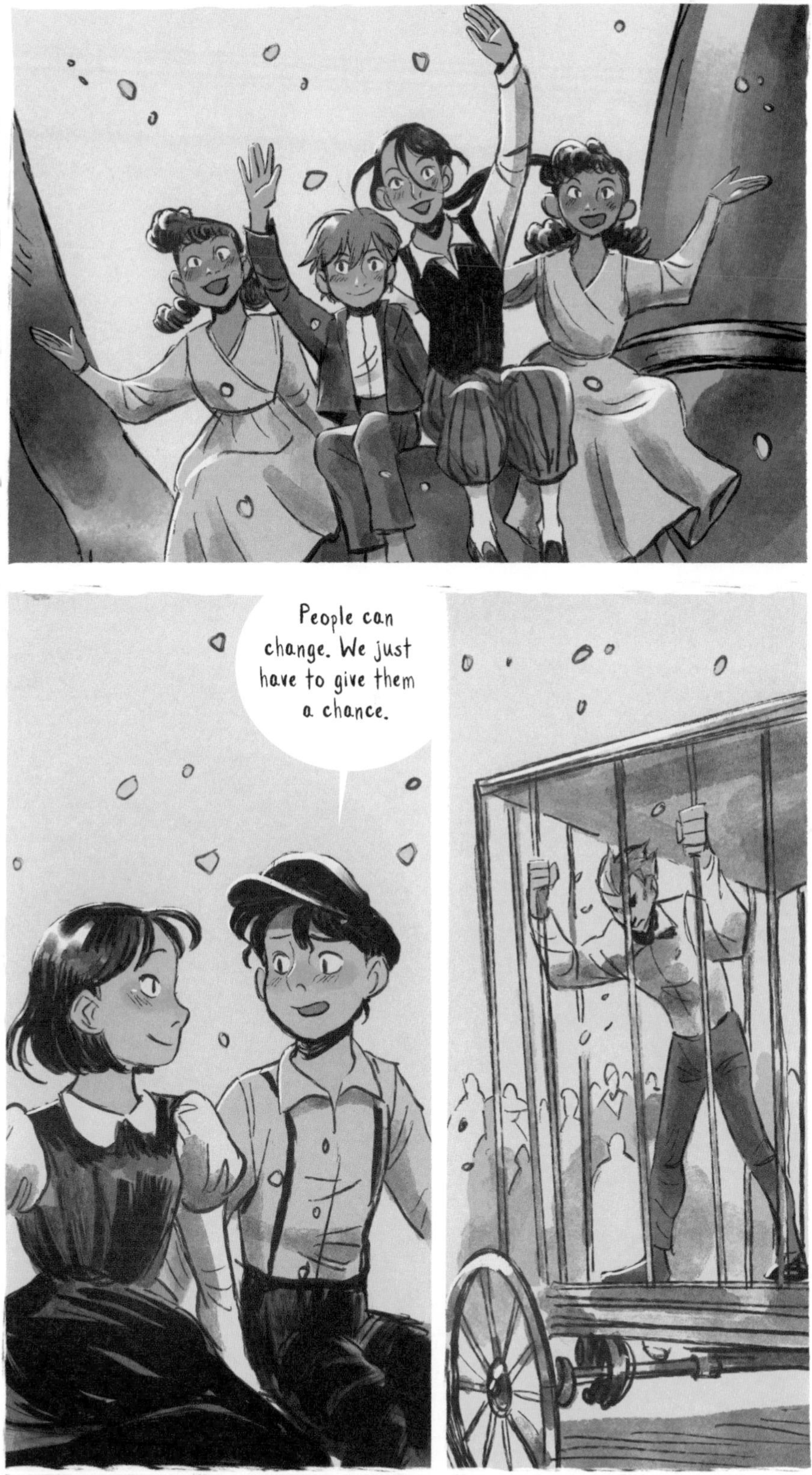
People can change. We just have to give them a chance.

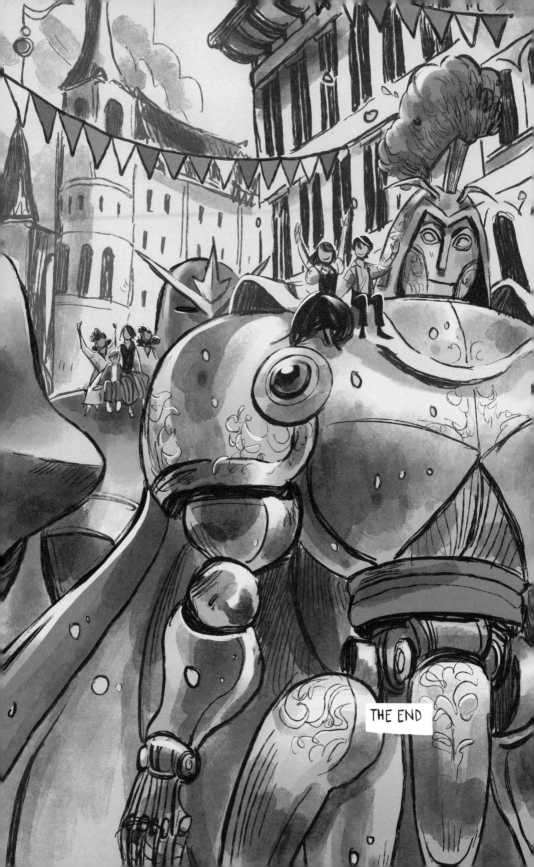

THE END